The Fall of Chron
and
Collision with Chr

CW01024743

'*Bayley has the disconcerti
novel, of removing an insp*
and making adjustments therein. . .'
Andrew Darlington
(Nebula 12)

'Bayley has taken Asimov's robotics stories one step further
. . .He brings the picaresque tradition to science-fiction
traditions.'
James Gunn

The Fall of Chronopolis is a time paradox space opera which
introduces us to the Chronotic Empire and its desperate
struggle to maintain its existence.

'*Bayley writes science fiction with the natural fluency of a man
who can't help it. He has the ineffable, unfakeable genius of a true
SF visionary. Small things do not content this man. He is tooling
along in second gear if he does not blow your mind ten times
in eighteen pages. He is at home re-inventing the nature of space-
time, stretching the limits of consciousness, reassembling reality. He
leaps past the jugular and deep into the frontal lobes. Bayley
is the Zen master of modern space opera.*'
Bruce Sterling

Barrington J. Bayley was born in Birmingham in 1937 and
began writing science fiction in his early teens. After national
service in the RAF and various jobs, he began as a general
freelance writer on features, stories, serials and picture strips,
mostly in the juvenile field. Finally returning to straight SF,
his stories appear in magazines such as *New Worlds*. His first
major novel to be published in Britain was *The Soul of the
Robot* (1976), which was followed by *Star Virus, Empire of
Two Worlds* and *Collision with Chronos*. He currently lives in
Telford, Shropshire.

Also in Pan Books by Barrington J. Bayley
Garments of Caean and Pillars of Eternity

Barrington J. Bayley

The Fall of Chronopolis
and
Collision with Chronos

Pan Books
London, Sydney and Auckland

The Fall of Chronopolis first published in Great Britain 1989 by Allison and Busby Ltd,
Collision with Chronos first published in Great Britain 1977 by Allison and Busby

This edition published 1989 by Pan Books Ltd,
Cavaye Place, London SW10 9PG

9 8 7 6 5 4 3 2 1

© Barrington Bayley 1973, 1974, 1977 and 1979

ISBN 0 330 30834 3

Typeset by Selectmove Ltd, London
Printed and bound in Great Britain by
Courier International Ltd, Tiptree, Essex

Contents

The Fall of
Chronopolis

1

With a hollow booming sound the Third Time Fleet materialized on the windswept plain. Fifty ships of the line, the pride of the empire and every one built in the huge yards at Chronopolis, were suddenly arrayed on the dank savanna as if a small city had sprung abruptly into being in the wilderness. The impression was increased by the lights that shone within the ships, outlining their ranks of square windows in the dusk. A few fat drops of rain spattered on the scene; the atmosphere was moody, clouds were gathering in the racing sky, and soon there would be a storm.

Half an hour passed before a large porchlike door swung open at the base of the flagship and three men stepped on to the turf. Two were burly men in stiff maroon uniforms, displaying badges of rank on chest, sleeves, and hat. The third was a shrivelled, defeated figure who walked with eyes downcast, occasionally flicking an uninterested glance around him.

The trio paused on a small knoll a hundred yards from the nearest timeship. Commander Haight looked about him, taking pride in the sight. The ships were suggestive of two disparate forms: basically they looked like long office blocks built on a rectilinear plan, but the crude streamlining that helped them cruise through time meant that the storeys were arranged in steps, high at the stern and low at the bows. To the commander this was reminiscent of another, more ancient type of vessel: the hulls of wind-driven galleons that once – far beyond the empire's pastward frontier – had sailed Earth's seas.

'Good to get in the open air,' he muttered. 'It gets damned claustrophobic in the strat.'

'Yes, sir.' Colonel Anamander looked uncomfortable. He always hated this part of the proceedings. Usually he had the job of seeing to the disposal of the corpse and was spared the task today only because Haight felt like taking a walk outside.

Mixing with the erratic wind came a low-pitched whine from the surrounding timeships. That was the sound of their engines holding them steady in orthogonal time. Suddenly came a louder, skirling noise. The engineers were carrying out the repairs for which the fleet had made the stop.

What a desolate spot, Anamander thought. In this region of history the timeships always chose, if possible, an uninhabited region in which to beach themselves. The mutability of time was not something to be taken lightly.

The courier lifted his dispirited eyes to the face of the commander. He spoke in a hesitant, empty voice.

'Shall I die now?'

Haight nodded, his expression contemptuous and remote. 'You have performed your duty,' he intoned formally.

The courier's self-execution was a simple affair. It relied on the vagus nerve, by means of which the brain would signal the heart to stop. This nerve, aimed at the heart like a cocked gun, was the stock explanation of death by fright, grief or depression, as well as by suggestion through a shaman or witch doctor. In his final briefing the courier had been trained to use this nerve voluntarily so as to carry out the order to kill himself once his task was done – an order that, in point of fact, could be said to be superfluous. The two officers watched now as he closed his eyes and mentally pronounced the hypnotically implanted trigger words. A spasm crossed his face. He doubled up, gasping, then collapsed limply to the ground.

Anamander moved a deferential foot or two away from the corpse. 'An unusually honoured courier, sir. Not many carry messages of such import.'

'Indeed not.'

Commander Haight continued to gaze on his fleet. 'This will be a testing time for us, Colonel. It looks like the beginning of a full-scale attack – perhaps even of an invasion. The empire will stand or fall by the efforts of men such as ourselves.'

'Strange that even his type should play a part in it,' Anamander mused, indicating the corpse. 'Somehow I can never avoid feeling sorry for them.'

'Don't waste your sympathy,' Haight told him. 'They are all criminals, condemned murderers and the like. They should be grateful for a last chance to serve the empire.'

'I wonder what they go through to make them so willing to die.'

Haight laughed humourlessly. 'As for that, it appears there's only one way to find out, and as you can see it's not a procedure to be recommended. Several times I've asked them, but they don't tell you anything that makes sense. In fact, they seem to lose the power of rational speech, more or less. You know, Colonel, I'm in a somewhat privileged position as regards these couriers. Until I speak the phrase releasing them from their hypnotic block they're unable to pronounce the key words triggering the nerve. What if I were to – I confess I've been tempted to keep one alive to see what would happen to him. He might come to his senses and be able to talk about it. Still, orders are orders.'

'There must be a reason for the procedure, apart from their being condemned anyway.'

'Quite so. Have you ever seen the strat with your naked eyes, Colonel?'

Anamander was startled. 'No, sir!'

'I did once – just a glimpse. Not enough to derange the senses – just the briefest glimpse. It was years ago. I was on the bridge when our main engine cut out for a moment after – well, never mind about all that. But there it is: I saw it, or almost saw it. Yet to this day I couldn't tell either you or myself exactly what it was I saw.'

'I've heard it leaves a mark on a man.'

'Yes, Colonel, it does. Don't ask me what sort of mark.'

Haight sniffed the air, then shivered slightly. The rain was falling faster.

'Let's get inside. We'll be drenched here.'

They crossed the turf and disappeared into the towering flagship. Half an hour later the whole fleet disappeared with a hollow *boom* that echoed around the empty plain. Shortly there came a crash of thunder and tumultuous rain soaked the savanna, pouring over the body of the courier who had died six centuries from home.

Colonel Anamander felt reassured with the thrum of the time-drive under his feet. They were building up speed, heading back into the past and traversing the planet's time-axis to bring them to the right location in both space and time: the continent of Amerik, Node 5.

As it moved, the fleet sprayed beta rays all around it into the temporal substratum – the strat, as chronmen called it. Electromagnetic energy could not travel through the strat, rendering communication difficult. The answer for short-range purposes was beta radiation, consisting of relativistic electrons moving slower than light. They did not penetrate far, but they sufficed for the timeships to keep contact with one another while in formation, as well as to maintain a limited radar watch.

Haight's orders were explicit. The hunt was on for the war craft that had violated the Imperial Millennium.

The enemy foray was well planned, as was evidenced by the failure of the Third Time Fleet to learn of it until the attackers had already passed to its rear. They had come in from the future at high speed, too fast for defensive time-blocks to be set up, and had only been detected by ground-based stations deep in historical territory. If the target was to alter past events – the usual strategy in a time-war – then the empire's chroncontinuity could be significantly interfered with.

It looked to Haight as if the assault could signal the beginning of the full-scale war with the Hegemony which the High Command believed to be inevitable. The

Hegemony, existing futureward of the Age of Desolation, had long been the chief threat to the Chronotic Empire, and it was almost certain that the raiders had been dispatched from that quarter.

If their intention was to test out the empire's ability to defend itself, then Haight promised himself forcefully that they would be disappointed in the result. Like all chronmen he was fanatical in regard to his duty; service to the empire was the chronman's creed. He felt personally affronted, not only by the intrusion into imperial territory, but also by the attempt to alter the relationship of the past to the future, a right that belonged to no one but their Chronotic Majesties the Imperial Family of the House of Ixian.

Commander Haight mulled the matter over while keeping one eye on the scan screens. The bridge, as it was called by convention, was a large, elongated hemi-ellipsoid. The controllers sat elbow to elbow along its curved walls, the pilot section being situated in the nose of the ellipsoid whereas another line of manned consoles ran along its middle axis. At the moment, the size-contraction effect caused by the flagship's velocity through the strat was not pronounced enough to be noticeably dramatic. At top speed it would become so intense at the forward end of the ship that the pilots in the nose would be reduced to a height of inches, whereas the men in the rear would retain their normal size – an effect that gave the bridge a false impression of being drastically foreshortened.

The bridge crew numbered thirty-two men in all, not counting the cowled priest who moved among them dispensing pre-battle blessings and sprinkling holy wine. Commander Haight looked over the scene from the raised desk he shared with Colonel Anamander at the rear of the bridge. It had often amused Haight to think that, with the flagship undergoing full-speed test trials, a pilot who happened to glance back saw his commander as a massive titan hovering over him like an avenging angel.

A gong sounded. A scanman called out to him.

'We have a track, sir!'

'Follow it,' rumbled Haight.

There was a slight sense of nausea as the flagship, the whole fleet following suit, shifted direction in the multi-dimensional strat. It was succeeded by a series of sensations felt only in the gut, as if one were trapped in a system of high-speed elevators. Travelling through the strat was sometimes like riding a crazy, oscillating switchback. Geodesic eddies and undulations, which time-travelling vehicles were obliged to follow, were apt to occur in it.

Haight and Anamander both watched the big monitor screen. The representation of the strat it was bringing them was roiling and curling as they rode through the disturbed region. (Haight knew that such a region often spelled danger for imperial stability: it could mean that an established sequence in orthogonal time was undergoing mutation.) Then, slowly, it smoothed out and the sick feelings no longer assailed their guts.

A blurred formation of foreign timeships hove into view.

There were three of them on the screen, held unsteadily by the scattered light of beta radiation. They were recognizably ships of the Hegemony: inelegantly tall, wedge-shaped structures travelling edge-on.

The images flickered and then yawed, swinging around and changing shape like a moving display of geometric variations. The scope was picking up four-dimensional images of the ships as they altered direction.

'Projected destination?' barked Haight.

A voice answered him. 'Prior to course change, heading toward Node Seven, bearing seven-o-three on vertical axis.'

'Fire torps.'

Down below, gunnery released a standard set of five torpedoes, and they saw them flickering away on the screen. There was little hope of any of them making a strike. Strat torpedoes were heavy, clumsy weapons whose light-duty time-drives gave them little speed and little range.

'Shall we offer battle, sir?' Anamander asked in a low voice.

Haight pondered briefly and shook his head. 'They are on a homeward flight path after having completed their work. We need to find them on the ingoing flight before they've reached their target.'

The torpedoes faded away, lost in the strat. The Hegemonic warships eventually receded from view.

Haight gave the order to proceed pastward, traversing across the vertical time-axis. A hundred and fifty years deeper into historic territory he ordered the fleet to stand by; the flagship phased briefly into orthogonal time.

They hovered over a sunlit landscape. Down below, roads and rivers made a meandering pattern among the towns and villages that were dotted here and there across the patchwork of fields. The flagship's computer library was busy comparing the scene with the official encyclopaedia, but neither Haight nor Anamander needed its report to know the worst. The geography of the place simply did not correspond to the official record. In particular, the sizeable city of Gerread was completely absent.

In orthogonal time the Hegemonic attack had already been successful.

Haight inspected the landscape carefully, looking for signs of recent devastation. There was none: it did not seem that Gerread had been removed by bomb or plague.

Instead, the Hegemonics must have used their most terrible weapon, of which the High Command had obtained some information but which they had never been absolutely sure existed: a time-distorter, capable of altering the fabric of time directly. Gerread had been simply . . . annulled. All trace of it, past and future, had vanished.

It was a sobering thought that in all probability no one except those aboard the ships manoeuvring in the strat, and those in the special Achronal Archives at Chronopolis, had even heard of Gerread any more. Once again Haight experienced the familiar burden: the terrible responsibility of being a chronman.

The priest, having finished his asperges, retired to the rear of the bridge, where he learned the dreadful facts confronting Haight and Anamander. He began to pray in a sonorous, desperate mutter. The two officers shared his feeling of horror: Gerread and all its inhabitants had been swallowed, foundering like a ship, by the infinity of non actual, merely potential time. That, at least, was how it was described technically. In church language it was the Gulf of Lost Souls.

Leaving behind it a clap of air, the flagship rephased in the substratum. Haight recalled the region of turbulence they had recently passed through. That, no doubt, had been connected with the new distortion in the orthogonal time-flow. But the battle was not yet lost. There was still strat time, and in strat time events did not vanish, once having taken place, but lingered for hours, days, sometimes months of subjective personal time. Nothing was irreversible.

They might yet snatch back those lost souls from perdition.

The fleet continued its traverse. This, Haight reminded himself, was but a preliminary exercise in how the coming time-war would be fought. Always the object would be to alter the adversary's history: reaching back and further back into the murky tale of mutated events, answering every move with a cancelling counter-move. And final victory would be achieved only when the history of one side was so completely distorted that the existential support for its fleets of timeships was removed. Even then they would continue to fight for a while, ghosts moving through the strat, never having been manufactured, manned by crews that had never been born. Then they would fade, sinking into nonactual, potential existence.

But it was some time before the warning gong sounded again and Hegemonic ships came up once more on the scope screen.

'Heading for Node Five,' the scanman informed him.

They counted the ships as they appeared blurrily on the screen. There were twelve.

'This is it,' Haight said. 'This is their incoming path. Get ready.'

Captain Mond Aton, officer commanding the *Smasher of Enemies*, had seen the Hegemonics' outgoing flight path on the scope screen of his own ship and had fully expected to enter battle. Only later, when the order to hold came from the flagship, did he realize that he had been impetuous. The homeward-bound ships would probably have refused to fight; and even if defeated, their destruction would solve nothing.

His own bridge was a miniature of Commander Haight's; it was manned by only seven men. Unlike the bigger, heavier ships that doubled as battleships and troop carriers, the *Smasher of Enemies* was a manoeuvrable, lightly manned, heavily armed destroyer. It had the speed to pursue, and elaborate chronphase equipment for accurate microsecond broadsides.

'Breaks your heart to see them go,' said the scanman, looking up from the screen, 'doesn't it, sir?'

Aton nodded. 'They haven't escaped us yet, Scanman. Those ships we see are already ghosts, though they don't know it.'

The wedge-shaped Hegemonics faded. Aton did not think too deeply about the paradoxes involved in what he had said. In the strat paradoxes were commonplace. And not only in the strat, either: since the rise of the Chronotic Empire every lowly citizen had been made aware of how contingent his existence was on the fickle mutability of time. Many were the millions who, having existed once (*once*, if that word were to be given a meaning outside time altogether), now ceased ever to have existed. Outside, that is, the roll of non-existing citizens in the Achronal Archives, which contained more history that had disappeared than it did extant history.

Unless the Hegemonic attack could be stopped, many millions more would be added to that roll.

Aton turned to Lieutenant Krish.

'Hold the bridge for me. I'm going to make a quick check.'

As he left the bridge and walked through the galleries he could feel the tension building up in the ship. This would be his third sizeable engagement and on each of the others he had liked to visit each section under his command beforehand. It gave him a feeling of integrating the vessel into a tight fighting unit. And it would be a good half-hour, he told himself, before the fleet found its quarry.

He visited the gunnery-room, where tension was, of course, at the highest pitch – and no wonder. His glance swept around the computer terminals, of which the men themselves were in a sense mere appendages. In some ships gunnery was on the bridge itself, which at first sight seemed a logical arrangement, if cumbersome. But Aton preferred it this way, although he knew some captains did not.

After a few words of encouragement to his gunners he went deeper into the ship to the drive-room.

He paused outside the door at the sound of voices, then smiled to himself. Ensign Lankar, a keen young engineer but newly inducted into the Imperial Time Service, was loudly displaying his knowledge to a drive-room assistant in his charge.

'The time-drive is really based on the good old mass-energy equation,' Lankar was saying. 'E equals MC squared. Let's take one of the factors on the right-hand side of this equation: C squared. That's where time comes in. C is the velocity of light – the distance per time of an otherwise mass-less particle. So energy is really mass multiplied by time squared. But we can also write the equation this way: M equals E over C squared. This shows us that mass is a relationship between energy and time. So now we're getting somewhere: what happens if we disturb this relationship? We do this by forcing energetic particles to travel faster than light. And now we find that the question doesn't balance any more: energy divided by the velocity of light squared no longer adds up to rest mass. But the equation *must* balance – it's a fundamental physical law. So what happens? The equation keeps the scales even by moving rest mass through time, to the same extent that the time factor is transgressed on the right-hand side.'

'But where does the strat come in, Ensign?'

'The strat is what time is made of, lad. If you move through time, that's what you have moved through.'

Ensign Lankar thumped the steel casings that bulged into the drive-room. 'And here's where it's all done. This is where we accelerate pi-mesons to anything between C and C squared. It's the most important part of the whole ship, and don't you forget it.'

Lankar's voice sounded incongruously young as he talked self-consciously down to his underling. 'M equals E over C squared,' he repeated. 'Notice that time is involved in both elements on the right-hand side. That's why pure energy can't be transmitted through the strat, only mass. So we have no radio communication with the High Command and have to use the couriers, poor devils.'

Both young men jumped up with embarrassment and saluted hastily as Aton entered. They had been seated on wooden benches well away from the main control desk, where the drive-room's senior staff were too busy for such idle talk.

'Everything in order?' Aton called gruffly, speaking over the high-pitched whine that always infected the drive-room.

The chief engineer looked up from his work. 'No problems, sir.'

Aton inspected the flickering dials briefly and went on his way. He paced the short galleries and corridors, speaking to a man here, an officer there. He was about to ascend a long ladder that would take him back to the bridge, passing by the gunnery-room, when a drone of voices caused him to pull up sharp.

It came from a nearby storeroom and had the sound of chanting. Aton felt himself stiffen. Then, dreading what he might find, he unfastened the clamps on the door and eased it quietly open.

The chanting came louder and he was able to distinguish some of the words. 'Lord of all the deep, if this be our moment for darkness . . . sear our souls with thy vengeance . . .'

He peered within. Six figures occupied the cell-like store room, having made space for themselves among the crates of chronphase spars. By the look of things this was their regular meeting place – the crates had been arranged to leave a neat cubbyhole that had a much-used appearance. All six wore normal uniforms, except that their caps had been replaced by black cloths that hung down over their ears. Five men were on their knees, heads bent and faces hidden in their arms, and they had their backs to Aton. The sixth stood before them leading the chant, a gold medallion hung about his neck, a black book in his hand. Aton recognized him as Sergeant Quelle, of gunnery. His lean sharp face bore the look of desperate rapture Aton would have expected from such a rite as this.

In the same moment that the startled Sergeant Quelle saw him, Aton pulled his pistol from his shoulder holster and flung the door wide open. He slammed a com switch on the corridor wall and bellowed for the ship guard. Then he moved into the confined space, lowering over the kneeling figures, the heavy beam pistol sweeping over them all warningly.

White faces, shocked and guilty, turned to look at him. Sergeant Quelle backed away, slamming shut his book. He bore the look of a trapped rat.

'Traumatics!'

Aton spat out the word. The outlawed sect was known to have adherents in the Time Service – chronmen were, in fact, unusually prone to be affected by its heresies, for obvious reasons – but Aton had never dreamed he would find aboard his own ship not one heretic but a whole congregation. He felt shaken.

Booted, running feet rang on the metal decks. The com speaker on the wall outside the storeroom crackled.

'Are you all right, Captain?'

'Yes, Lieutenant,' he replied, recognizing the voice from the bridge. 'Better send down Comforter Fegele.'

The guards clattered to the scene. Aton let them stare at it for a few moments. There was a strained silence.

'Better not do anything to us, Captain,' Quelle said in an impulsive, frightened voice. 'Your soul will go to the deep if you do!'

'Silence!' Aton was affronted by the continued blasphemy.

The ship's priest, Comforter Fegele, arrived, pushing his way through the guards. As he saw the evidence before him, the six men standing half-sheepishly, half-defiantly, a gasp came from deep within his cowl. He swiftly made the sign of the circle, then raised his hand palm outward.

'Depart, Prince of Abominations,' he muttered in a hurried, feverish voice. 'Depart into the deep of time, plague no more the servants of the Lord.'

The Traumatics immediately turned to him and made a curious sign with the fingers of their right hands, as though warding off a curse.

Quelle laughed fiercely. 'Don't *you* plague *us* with your exorcisms, priest!' But Comforter Fegele was already beginning an incantation of sacred names, at the same time producing a vase-like chalice from within the folds of his robe.

'Get them out of here and lock them in the cells!' ordered Aton angrily. 'Commander Haight can decide whether to charge them fleetside or back in Chronopolis.'

The guards hustled the heretics from the room, while the priest splashed consecrated wine everywhere, on the worshippers, on the crates, on the floor of the cubby-hole.

At that moment a deep-toned gong rang through the ship.

Lieutenant Hurse spoke from the bridge through the wall com. 'Message from the flagship, Captain. Enemy located on target-bound path.'

'I'll be with you presently,' Aton returned.

He made for the ladder, but suddenly Sergeant Quelle, who with the others was in the process of being hand-cuffed, burst free and lunged supplicatingly towards him.

'You need us, Captain. You need me, especially. No-body can handle a gunnery comp like I do.'

Comforter Fegele hurled a handful of wine in his face. 'You have lent yourself to foul crimes and flaunted God's commandments . . .'

Quelle appealed again to Aton. 'Let me do my duty, Captain. This is no time to cut down the ship's fighting power. Let me handle my comp.' He cringed. 'I don't want to sink into the strat . . . without . . .'

Suddenly Aton understood. The Traumatics believed that a certain ceremony could – or at least might – protect a soul if it was plunged naked into the strat, as, for instance, should the *Smasher of Enemies* be destroyed in the coming fight. That had no doubt been the purpose of the rite Aton had interrupted. It was all nonsense, of course, fanatical superstition; but Quelle, robbed of his imagined precaution, wanted to fight for his life and not sit out the battle helplessly.

And he was right about one thing. Quelle was an excellent gunner, the best the ship had. Without him the gunnery-room would be fighting below maximum efficiency.

Aton looked at the sergeant with open contempt. 'Very well. For the duration of the engagement.'

He glanced over the faces of the other prisoners and pointed to two others he recognized as also belonging to the gunnery crew. 'Release Sergeant Quelle and those two. They are to be rearrested once the invaders have been dealt with.'

Closely followed by Comforter Fegele, Aton turned from the scene and ascended the ladder to the bridge. The Hegemonic ships were already showing on the scope screen, relayed from the flagship's powerful beta scanners.

'We're closing, sir,' the scanman informed him.

It would not be long now.

But for the time being a lull fell over the proceedings, a lull during which the flagship was frantically busy assessing the situation, but in which the periphery ships, consisting in the main of destroyers like the *Smasher of Enemies*, were passive.

Aton waited for his orders, trying to fight down the feelings of shame that assaulted him. This was no time for emotion, but nevertheless that emotion was there.

Standing across the desk from him was Comforter Fegele (it was church policy for the ship's priest to be present on the bridge during an action, ever ready to give moral support). The priest looked into the brooding face of the young officer. 'You are troubled,' he murmured.

Aton had been gazing at his own reflection in the metal of his desk. His even features, with their clear grey eyes and straight, finely chiselled nose, were distorted by the metal and seemed to stare back at him across tortured aeons.

'How long has this been going on aboard my ship?' he wondered quietly. 'Had you an intimation of it?'

'No. The Traumatic sect is notoriously good at keeping its presence secret. It disturbs you, no doubt, to discover such perversions.'

'I do find it hard to understand,' Aton admitted. 'Every man on board has sworn the same oath I have sworn. And that oath is to defend not only the empire but also the true faith. How can such men turn heretic?'

'The ways of religious delusion are indeed strange.'

'I confess, Comforter, that I am questioning my own judgement in permitting Sergeant Quelle and his co-conspirators to take part in this action. How can one trust heretics and traitors?'

'The odd thing is,' said the priest slowly, 'that their perversion is probably of a spiritual character only. It has been found that heretic chronmen are nevertheless loyal to the Time Service. That part of their oath remains sacred to them.'

A signal sounded on Aton's desk. A blurry voice spoke from the annunciator.

'The following vessels will break off and engage the enemy. *Exorcist, Smasher of Enemies, Emperor's Fist, Incalculable* . . .' Aton counted twelve names in all, the same number that made up the enemy's squadron. This was necessary, probably, if the Hegemonics were to be persuaded to stand and fight rather than to flee home without accomplishing their mission.

The *Smasher of Enemies* swung away from formation. The Hegemonics disappeared from the scope screen, then came back after a brief interval, even more blurrily, as the destroyer picked them up on her own less powerful radar.

The established procedures of attack swung into action. One of the bridge controllers was getting in touch with the rest of the attack squadron. At the same time beta contact beams sped ahead of their flight path, seeking out the enemy and offering negotiation.

Comforter Fegele retreated to one side and was heard muttering prayers and blessings, dipping his hand into his chalice occasionally and sprinkling a token amount of wine on to the deck.

As soon as they became aware of their pursuers the Hegemonics put on speed and went into evasion manoeuvres. The wedge-shaped ships, five times taller than they were broad long, multiplied into a series of fading prismatic images, like a multiple exposure, as they changed direction. The pilot of the *Smasher of Enemies*, snuggled into the nose of the bridge, also put on a surge of velocity, taking them close to the maximum. Before Aton's eyes the forward end of the bridge diminished in size; the pilot became a midget, a boy-like figure, then a puppet no more than six inches high.

The flight of the Hegemonics failed to outdistance the ships of the Chronotic Empire, each of which was now picking out an adversary. The *Smasher of Enemies* vectored in on a dancing wedge. It was difficult, sometimes, to sort out the flickering images from the wavering curves of the strat as they also showed up on the scope screen, but Aton never lost sight of it entirely. He issued a clipped order to the pilot.

The destroyer plunged forward in a new burst of speed until she overtook the Hegemonics craft and swung around to place herself directly in its path. The pilot rushed the ship back and forth, veering in close to the enemy and setting up a wash of discomfiting strat waves. In answer the Hegemonic darted away and tried to weave a path past the obstacle, but the pilot stuck close.

The beta operator depressed a switch and leaned forward to speak into a microphone. 'Hello, gunnery. You have contact.'

The tense voice of Sergeant Quelle sounded on the bridge and was relayed by beta ray to his counterpart on the Hegemonic war craft.

'Stand and fight; stand and fight,' he ground out in a gravelly tone. 'Here is our proposed location.' He repeated his words in the Hegemonic language, while at the same time a string of recorded co-ordinates was beeping out on the beta beam.

After a delay of only seconds came a terse answer: 'Agreed.'

The two ships sped away on nearly parallel courses, slowly diverging until they were both faint on each other's scopes.

The front of the bridge ballooned in size as they slowed down. The pilot leaned back, his hands lifting from the controls; the steering-board was now under the control of gunnery.

A curious but necessary tradition of collaboration existed among warring timeships. The self-powered torpedoes they carried, though deployed as a matter of course, were so slow and cumbersome, so much at the mercy of strat disturbances, as to be nearly useless. To be effective a warship needed to employ its heavy-duty beamers.

But because no pure energy could travel in the strat this meant phasing into orthogonal time. A timeship that stayed in its natural medium could neither fire on, nor be fired on by, another timeship. For that reason ships willing to join battle agreed on a rendezvous where each, by leaving the strat, made itself vulnerable to the other.

The tryst (as it was dubbed) had to be both precise and momentary: a point in time without duration. How long a warship lingered beyond that instant in passing time was entirely a matter of discretion, comprising a ratio between estimated survival time and the minimum time needed to locate the enemy and focus weapons upon him. The tendency was towards microseconds, during which each combatant discharged a massive broadside. That, very often, was the end of the battle. A heavily damaged ship would be reluctant to emerge again from the protection of the strat but would try to return home.

All of which explained the crucial importance of the gunnery crew, who made these calculations.

On his desk Captain Aton watched the countdown to emergence in orthogonal time. The suspense was almost unbearable, yet in a way the battle was a non-event – one could not keep track of it in time, since it was all over in a flash. There was only the aftermath, either triumphant or dreadful.

While the minutes and seconds ticked off, the gunnery crew would be priming their comps for those vital micro-seconds. The battle bracket itself, too small for human consciousness, would be handled by the comps. Afterwards would come the frantic damage assessment by the bridge, reports, if available, on damage inflicted on the enemy, and a decision as to whether or not to offer a second tryst.

Gunnery made an announcement: 'Entering ortho five seconds from *now*.'

The whole bridge waited in tense silence.

Then the *Smasher of Enemies* shook violently, reeled, and swayed as if spinning. Even without studying the damage board closely, Aton could see that something searing had penetrated her vitals.

He glanced up at the scope screen. The Hegemonic ship had reappeared there and was executing a peculiar-looking sideways manoeuvre. Its nearer wall was stained and bubbling.

Gunnery had scored a hit.

Voices came babbling into the bridge. Then, to his surprise, Aton glimpsed a second wedge shape hovering some distance away on the edge of the screen.

Sergeant Quelle's hoarse voice came through to him on his desk com. 'They tricked us, Captain! We were fired on by two ships together – caught in between 'em!'

Aton cursed. 'Evidently a new tactic,' he said wryly to Quelle. And a treacherous one: this sort of conduct was contrary to the unstated rules of temporal war.

He turned to listen to the damage reports. An energy beam had struck the destroyer's flank, penetrated its inner armour, and burned a swathe reaching as far as the drive-room. Luckily the damage in the latter was less than total: the drive was still operating, though the orthogonal field that maintained normal time inside the ship while it travelled the strat was weakened.

Next he turned his attention to news of the rest of the battle. About half the Chronotic timeships had so far engaged the enemy. On balance, events seemed to be going their way. Two Hegemonics had already been destroyed.

His lieutenant leaned towards him. 'It would be risky going into ortho again, Captain.'

Aton nodded, feeling the weight of responsibility. This was more than a skirmish: the existence of the city of Gerread depended on it, as well as the Chronotic control of a whole segment of history.

'I'm afraid we shall have to take that risk, Lieutenant. Those ships have to be stopped.'

His voice rose. 'Scanman, there are two enemy vessels in our vicinity. Range them both for gunnery.'

He contemplated how to take on two heavily armed Hegemonics at the same time. Somehow there must be a member of his own squadron without an adversary. Or had the Hegemonics adopted some complex chess-like formation in which their ships all covered one another?

A hint of a shudder passed through his mind at the thought that he might be seeing the first stage of a large, relentlessly unfolding Hegemonic plan.

He was about to speak to Sergeant Quelle again when a sudden movement on the scope screen attracted his attention. Among the wavering lines by which the screen represented the strat an indistinct shape was expanding swiftly.

A moment later the screen itself went blank and at the same time a horrifying explosion tore through the *Smasher of Enemies*. The destroyer shuddered for a second time. The nose tipped sharply downwards and the bridge caved in.

Before he deserted his desk Captain Aton verified that all com lines to the bridge were dead. Amid a hail of collapsing metal he fled from the room with the rest of his staff, helping them through the disintegrating door and leaving himself last of all.

He knew without any doubt what had happened. The flitting shape on the scope screen had been a strat torpedo which by a hundred-to-one chance had struck home. It was the sort of bad luck no chronman liked to think about.

By the look of things the torp could have hit the destroyer close to the impact point of the earlier Hegemonic energy beam. At any rate it appeared to have exploded inside the inner armour – within the ship herself – and had caused severe structural damage.

In short, the *Smasher of Enemies* was breaking up.

A frightening, tortured creaking sound came from all directions. Aton glanced around him at the twisted, heaving corridors. He grabbed the arm of his lieutenant.

'Get to the com room. If the beta transmitters are still functioning try to raise the fleet and request help.'

The lieutenant went off at a lope. Behind him, what was left of the bridge folded up like a tin can in response to the pressures of the ship's shifting girder frame. Its erstwhile crew moved closer to Aton as if for comfort. Up the corridor came the sound of shouting and a distant, pained groan.

Another, worse danger had occurred to Aton. It was possible that the *Smasher of Enemies* was now helpless; if so, one or both of the Hegemonic destroyers could move in close enough to fire more torpedoes at point-blank range. He seized another officer.

'See if you can get to the torp section. Tell them to fire on the standard pattern, once every two minutes.'

For the moment there was no knowing, of course, if the torp section had even survived the explosion. There was no knowing if any system in the stricken ship was still operational – except that there was obviously still some power flowing: the lights still burned.

Comforter Fegele was on his knees, praying for the survival of the ship – and, Aton thought cynically, of himself. Irreligiously he yanked the priest to his feet.

'The Lord's vengeance has fallen on our vessel,' Fegele babbled. 'This is the price of heresy.'

Aton pushed him away and pointed to a white-faced young ensign. 'Vuger, you come with me. The rest of you – get some rescue work organized.' He spoke harshly, aware that morale was dropping. 'There are bound to be a number of wounded. I want the situation stabilized for when we're ready to move.' With a last glance at Fegele he added, 'The souls of the dying need your ministrations, Comforter.'

He went scrambling down the twisted ladder towards the drive-room, with Ensign Vuger stepping down hastily above his head. As they went deep into the ship the evidence of the destroyer's own destruction became even more evident: walls that had bulged, then broken open like paper bags, lines and conduits that spewed everywhere like ravelled string.

But as they reached the bottom of the ladder and picked their way through the wreckage the lights dimmed momentarily and then burned more brightly than before. At the same time a nearby com speaker crackled. Aton mentally congratulated the repair crews; they had lost no time.

He paused by a speaker and managed to get through to gunnery. The voice that answered was not Quelle's or the gunnery officer's, but that of an ordinary crewman.

'We're blind, sir. And three of our beamers gone.'

'Where's Sergeant Quelle?' Aton demanded.

There was silence. Then, in a strangled voice, the crewman said, 'Deserted his post, sir.'

Aton left the com and pressed forward, motioning Ensign Vuger to follow.

They stepped over the bodies of two dead crewmen and into a scorched area where smoke drifted and the smell of hot metal was in the air. The bulkhead separating the drive-room from the rest of the ship seemed to have melted and only now had solidified. Within the drive-room itself there was fair calm, despite the

destruction that had been wreaked. Aton saw the body
of Ensign Lankar, who a short time before had been
proudly displaying his knowledge of the time-drive, laid
out neatly alongside one wall with several others.

To the searing effects of the Hegemonic energy had
been added the punishment of the torpedo explosion. A
gyro was stuttering and giving off a deep tremoring hum
from behind the thick steel casings. Aton understood at
once that the situation was very bad.

'Are we able to move?' he asked.

A younger officer, saluting hastily, shook his head. 'No
chance, sir. It's as much as we can do to maintain ship's
field.'

'What chance of phasing into ortho?'

The other looked doubtful. 'Perhaps. Do you want us
to try?'

'No,' said Aton. It would do no good. Even if they
managed to escape from the ship, without the requisite
equipment to keep them phased most of the crew would
be thrown back into the strat after a short period of time.
And there was clearly no possibility of cruising to the
nearest node, where orthophasing could be made natural
and permanent.

So it all depended on someone coming to their rescue.

How was Lieutenant Krish getting on in the com room?

He looked around for a com, found one that worked,
and dialled. The com speaker crackled. A voice spoke
through faintly, unintelligibly.

And then the floor rose under his feet. There was
a *whoomph*, followed by a noise that vibrated on his
eardrums to such an extent that he had the momentary
impression of existing inside a deep, solid silence. Flung
against the opposite wall, dazed, he watched in fascination as the floor and ceiling strained towards each other
with a grating sound that made him think of giant bones
breaking.

The blast of the explosion seemed to continue in a
prolonged smashing and cracking. The collapse of the

already weakened ship's skeleton – and timeships always suffered a good deal of physical stress in the strat – was accelerating.

Lieutenant Krish crawled towards him and helped him to his feet. 'Another torpedo,' Aton said breathlessly. 'I'm afraid we're finished.'

The movement of the ceiling towards the deck had ceased for the moment, but he did not think the drive-room would be habitable for long. He staggered to the instrument boards. An engineer joined him and they stared together at the flickering dials.

The engineer hammered his fist on the board in frustration. 'The ship field is breaking down,' he declared woodenly.

'How long will it hold?'

'I wouldn't give it another ten minutes.'

Aton went immediately to the com set and dialled a general alert. In a loud, firm voice he announced, 'This is the captain speaking. Take to the rafts. This is the captain speaking. Take to the rafts.'

He repeated the message several times, then turned to the stricken faces of the surviving drive-room crew. 'The ranking engineer will stay to do what he can to hold the field steady,' he ordered. The engineer nodded, and Aton told him, 'I will relieve you in five to ten minutes. The rest of you, get to a raft.'

Aton already knew that his own life was lost but that hardly seemed to matter. It was his duty, now, to see that everyone still alive aboard the *Smasher of Enemies* made it to a life raft.

Before the ortho field failed. An almost impossible job.

The party advanced through the warped corridors, exploring the various departments and pulling survivors from the wreckage. The wounded they helped along or else carried on improvised stretchers. Aton knew that time was fast running out – even discounting yet a third torpedo strike, which, considering the evident helplessness of the vessel, seemed all too distinct a possibility.

When they came near to one of the ship's six life-raft stations Aton took Lieutenant Krish with him and set off towards the stern. There was no certainty that his order to abandon ship had reached all sections; he decided he would make one swift reconnaissance to ensure that the order was being carried out in a disciplined fashion, then return to the drive-room and take over there, giving the engineer a chance to reach the nearest raft.

Near Section 3 they heard a commotion that sounded even over the loud creaking of the tortured girder frame. Aton drew his beamer, signalling to Krish to do the same. They rounded a corner.

Sergeant Quelle, wearing one of the ship's only two protective suits, strode resolutely along the corridor. Behind him, like a swarm of bubbles in his wake, the heretics of the Traumatic sect ran in a chattering, terrified crowd.

Even through the suit's obscuring visor, designed to opaque itself once in the strat, Quelle's bulbous face displayed his determination to live at all costs. The gleaming brass armour totally encased his body; even if the ship field failed altogether the suit would keep him safe for a short while, maintaining a weak ortho field while its power pack lasted – long enough, in fact, to enable him to reach a life-raft.

Aton and Krish straddled the corridor, blocking the Traumatic's path. 'Where are you going, Sergeant?' Aton demanded harshly.

Quelle's answer was a muffled growl. His followers, of whom he clearly did not regard himself as any kind of leader, clustered around him, eyeing Aton speculatively.

Quelle carried a crowbar with which, Aton guessed, he intended to smash the cage where the raft was kept. Aton fired a warning shot over their heads.

'Sergeant Quelle deserted his post and has stolen a protective suit. Get out of that suit, Sergeant. You'll take your turn like all the rest.'

And then, for the third, terrible time, an explosion smashed into the destroyer, hurling them all sideways. An ear-splitting rending noise told Aton that the stern of the ship was breaking away entirely.

Quelle, with what must have been desperate strength, was the first to recover, brass suit or not. His crowbar swung down on Aton's head. Encumbered as he was, the blow was clumsy and partly absorbed by Aton's uniform hat; nevertheless Aton slumped to the floor, barely conscious. Quelle aimed another blow at Lieutenant Krish, missed, then swept hastily on, followed by the mob.

Krish draped his captain's arm around his own shoulders and hauled him to his feet. 'Get to the drive-room, Lieutenant,' Aton mumbled. 'Relieve the engineer.'

'It's too late, sir. Can't you see what's happening? The field is already breaking up.'

Aton, fighting to remain aware, saw that he was right. A fog-like flickering was in the air. An almost overpowering vertigo assailed them both, and the walls – in fact everything solid – seemed to spin on themselves endlessly. All these signs were sure indications of an ortho field going bust.

Krish half-carried Aton along the corridor. The lights went out as the power finally failed, then the emergency lighting faithfully came on to provide a dimmer, yellow glow.

And then through everything, Aton heard horrifying screams. His ship was foundering, sinking into the depths of the strat. He was hearing the screams of men who were drowning in the Gulf of Lost Souls.

Like men plunged from air into the sea, these men were being plunged from their natural, rational time and into a medium that no man could experience and stay sane.

After a few yards Aton steadied himself and, though still groggy, disengaged himself from Krish's support. He leaned weakly against the wall.

'Leave me here, Lieutenant. Continue . . . do what you can.'

Krish took his arm again, but Aton drew away.

'You *must* let me help you, sir. There may be only seconds—'

'Surely you realize that I cannot leave the ship. Save yourself . . . and whomever else you can.' Seeing Krish's indecision, his tone hardened. 'That's an order, Lieutenant.' He waved his pistol. 'I have my own protection . . . against the strat.'

'Yes, sir.' Krish stiffened. He stepped back, clearly affected then snapped off a salute that Aton returned perfunctorily.

Then he turned on his heel and strode away.

Moments after he had gone the wavering ortho field deserted the stretch of corridor where Captain Aton was standing. The pistol, with which he had been meaning to shoot himself, dropped from his fingers. In a little over a second the field swayed back again, but in that second *Aton saw it*.

The strat. The temporal substratum.

The Gulf of Potential Time.

It was only a glimpse, but even a glimpse is too much. Fortunately, or perhaps not so, the returning ortho field saved him – saved him, among other things, from remaining conscious, for exposure to the strat does not bring merciful oblivion. With the return of passing time the glimpse of eternity became a mental shock of pathological proportions. Aton instantly fell unconscious.

At almost the same time two noncom chronmen, running desperately for the life raft, saw their captain lying there in the corridor. Without even thinking about it they each seized an arm and lugged him at speed towards Station 3.

When a field of orthogonal time (that is, of time as it can be understood by the human intellect) breaks down, it does not collapse all at once. Bubbles and fragments of it cling, eddying and drifting, for anything up to ten minutes.

One such bubble had attached itself to Station 3.

The scene at Station 3 was one of turmoil. Discipline had broken down in the face of horror, and about thirty men were fighting to get aboard the raft – even though, with an orderly embarkation, room could have been found for them all. On his arrival Lieutenant Krish tried to impose a sense of command. He was cut down by Sergeant Quelle, who had found a pistol beamer and held it awkwardly in his brass suit's mechanical claw.

Quelle had good reason for shooting the lieutenant. He was anxious that no one who knew his guilty secret, apart from his fellow Traumatics, should board the raft with him. He ensured that the Traumatics went aboard first, then entered the raft himself preparatory to casting off.

But among those who boarded in the final rush were the two noncoms carrying the unconscious form of Captain Aton. They themselves were not so lucky. They dropped Aton to the floor then bravely left the raft to assist some wounded men. Quelle indignantly clanked forward to rid himself of his potential accuser, but he was too late. In that moment others in the raft decided that they had lingered long enough and activated the escape sequence. The gates closed and the hum of the raft's own emergency ortho field filled the dim interior.

The last wisps of the ship field were now dissipating, and the shattered destroyer was wholly saturated by the strat. It ceased, in one sense, to have any material existence at all: matter cannot retain its properties without the vector of time to give it substance. As such, the life raft magically passed unimpeded through several walls and floated free.

It was the only raft to leave the *Smasher of Enemies*. All the others either were too damaged or else failed to energize in time. The survivors switched on the small scope and saw, by the light of the raft's feeble beta projector, the vague image of a tall Hegemonic warship looming over them. They cowered, fearing, but eventually the ship turned and receded beyond the scope's range.

Still wearing the protective suit, Sergeant Quelle fretted. He had felt it reasonably safe to kill in the confusion at Station 3, but here there would be witnesses who could not be silenced and bodies that could not be disposed of. He sweated inside the suit, glancing at Aton and hoping he would not recover.

The raft was transmitting, as a beacon, a rotating beta beam. Otherwise there was nothing they could do. They settled down and waited, for life or a fate worse than death.

2

Node One: Chronopolis, mistress of the Chronotic Empire, seat of the Imperial Government of His Chronotic Majesty Philipium Ixian I, and the location of that repository of imperial wisdom, the *Imperator*.

Chronopolis was complex and sprawling. In the morning light (the sun had risen to that angle which most accentuated the city's panoply of splendour) her towers, arches, and minarets sparkled and flashed, casting long shadows that fell sharply across the various quarters housing her polyglot population – across the Hevenian quarter, with its characteristically arcaded architecture; across the more rigidly styled Barek quarter; and so on. For people of every nation and of every period in the mighty time-spanning empire flocked to Chronopolis.

The incredibly massive, intricate palace that occupied the centre of the eternal city was well placed, for both practical and aesthetic reasons. Like a spider at the centre of a vast web, it cast out tentacles in all directions so that it was hard to say where it left off and the rest of the city began. This enmeshment was functional as well as descriptive: the palace merged gradually into the city in the form of government departments, military offices, and church institutions – the three pillars of any state. The residence of His Eminence the Arch-Cardinal Reamoir also lay within the palace grounds, so that all strands, spiritual as well as political, were drawn into the hands of His Chronotic Majesty. And visible from the upper reaches of the palace, from where one could overlook the entire city, were the massive shipyards beyond the outskirts of Chronopolis, busy now as never before.

On this day of Imdara in the fifth month of year 204 (as measured from the pastward buffer known as the Stop Barrier – the zero point in imperial reckoning) the activities proceeding in the imperial palace were too numerous to list. The business of attending to the affairs of the thousand-year imperium went on – all under the gaze, if they so desired, of those members of the Ixian dynasty who were domiciled there – in the thousands of chambers, halls, lecture-rooms, salons, and chapels. As they did on every other day, except for the specified holy days of observance.

Of these activities, not least in importance was the education of the next generation of rulers. In one of the domestic wings Brother Mundan, one of a dozen appointed tutors, wrestled with the problem of steeping a class of young Ixians – some of them quite closely related to the emperor – in the traditions of the dynasty.

Even his brown cassock and curtailed cowl, even all the majesty of the Church that lay behind him (the Church, of course, accepting the responsibility for all serious education) was sometimes insufficient to curb the irreverence of these youngsters, who were apt to place themselves above normal values even in matters of religion. Luckily the Church placed great reliance on repetition as a method of teaching, and this generally enabled Mundan to bludgeon his charges into submission. Indeed, it would have been difficult to instil the present lesson, 'The Foundation of Empire', with its mixture of history, abstract physics and religious dogma, by any other means. Brother Mundan was repeating it to the present class for at least the twelfth time.

'And to what,' he intoned, 'do we owe the existence of the empire?'

After a pause Prince Kir, cousin to the emperor, rose. 'To the intervention of God, Brother.'

Mundan nodded. 'Correct, Your Highness. Once, time stretched unchanging from the interminable past to the interminable future, or at least it changed only slowly due to natural movements in the temporal substratum or to time-storms. There was no empire and no true religion. There was *religion*, of a sort, but it was superstition, such as some of the futureward heathens hold to. Then God acted so as to redeem mankind. At what is now called Node Six, in the city of Umbul, capital of the present province of Revere, He chose as His appointed messenger San Hevatar, a scientist working in the laboratories of the ruling Ixian family – of *your* family, Highnesses.'

Mundan's gaze settled on one who, instead of attending closely, was more interested in exchanging whispers with a neighbour.

'Princess Nulea, what are the three things that God revealed to San Hevatar?'

The girl started and jumped up. With glazed eyes she chanted the answers she had long learned by rote.

'One: the mutability of time, Brother Mundan. Two: the means of travelling through time. Three: the nature of the soul.'

'Thank you, that is correct. Through His messenger San Hevatar, God has taught us that time is mutable. He has taught us how to travel through time. And He has taught us that the nature of the soul is to persist in eternity.'

He rapped the lectern to pique their interest. 'The first of these truths shows us the possibility of the Church's mission. The second truth shows us how the mission may be accomplished. And the third truth shows us *why* it should be accomplished.'

His voice became challenging. 'And why should the Church work to accomplish its mission under the protection and banner of the Chronotic Empire?' Brother Mundan's dark eyes flashed. This point in the lesson touched the fires in his own breast.

Once again Prince · Kir proved the most apt of his pupils. 'Because time does not die, Brother Mundan. Because the soul cannot leave the body.'

'Yes, Highness, that is so,' Mundan said with a slight frown. The answer was probably lost on the densest of those present. 'The Church works to bring the true faith to all men, past, present, and future – to *establish God's Kingdom on Earth*. Even though we die we continue to exist in the past, because the past does not vanish. The Church seeks to transform our past lives and bring God into our souls.

'Let us take in turn each of the three truths revealed by Sàn Hevatar. First: that time is mutable. This means simply that even the past may be changed because in absolute terms there is no past, just as there is no unique present. Orthogonal time is but the surface of the bottomless ocean of potential time, or the temporal substratum: the hidden dimension of eternity in which all things co-exist without progression from past to future. Prior to the foundation of the empire the past could change without man's knowledge or will, due to time-storms or natural mutations, just as the wind can change direction. Now, thanks to the grace of God, the past and the future can be controlled and altered by conscious intervention.'

This intervention took the form, of course, of the Historical Office, which undertook to edit and restructure history by manipulation of key events, and of the imperial time-fleets, which in the last resort enforced the imperial writ. To Brother Mundan this seemed entirely proper and right.

He proceeded to the second God-given truth, writing some equations on the blackboard.

'These equations describe the operation of moving mass through time. You should already be familiar with them from your physics lessons, so here we will concern ourselves with the structure of orthogonal time, which is of great importance for the stability of the empire.

'Time is composed of a wave structure. The nodes of the wave travel at intervals of approximately one hundred and seventy years and are of great interest to the time-traveller since they comprise "rest points" in the tensioning of the Chronotic energy field. This is of crucial importance in the business of time-travel, because matter can be transported from one node to another and will remain in place without any further expenditure of energy. On the other hand if matter is transported to a time between nodes, or conversely is taken from between nodes and is deposited somewhere else, it will not persist in its new location without a continuous expenditure of energy, usually accomplished by means of a device called an orthophase. This is the reason why nearly all Chronotic intercourse takes place from node to node. The seven nodes covered by the span of the empire form, as it were, the seven continents or provinces of the empire, while the intervening periods comprise a series of hinterlands, benevolently governed but rarely seeing a time-ship except in time of rebellion or by order of the Historical Office.

'In ordinary life, of course, none of this is of any consequence, since the nodes are invisible to us.'

'*Why* are there nodes, Brother Mundan?' asked Prince Kir seriously.

Mundan frowned again. 'We may take it as part of God's wisdom, Highness, though technically it is, as I say, the wave structure of time. The nodes give the empire an absolute standard of time-measurement – for the movement of the nodes is absolute, not relative. We are fortunate enough to live in Node One. Today, for instance, is Imdara of the fifth month, and tomorrow will be Juno of the fifth month. When tomorrow comes it would be possible for us to travel back in a time-machine to today, Imdara – but Node One will not be here. It will have moved on, to Juno. Thus nodal time, as apart from historical time, is the time the empire uses to conduct its business. The clocks of the time-fleets measure nodal time.

'Imagine what chaos would reign if we tried to govern a time-travelling empire where time was uniform, not gathered into nodes. If it were a simple matter – say, for a man to travel into tomorrow and meet *himself* there – why, antinomies and paradoxes would abound in such confusion that no order could survive. Time itself, perhaps, would break down and the whole world would sink into the substratum. That is why God, in His great wisdom, has so arranged the universe that the natural period *between* nodes is greater than the span of a man's life, so that he will not meet himself. And it is to prevent the harmful accumulation of paradoxes that it is forbidden to travel into internodal time, except in the emperor's name.'

Princess Nulea giggled. 'Narcis doesn't think so!'

'Silence!' Brother Mundan's face became an angry red. He was well aware that certain members of the imperial household did not consider themselves bound by the laws that restrained the rest of society. But he would brook no mention of Prince Narcis's unspeakable perversion here.

Princess Nulea lowered her eyes. 'Sorry, Brother Mundan,' she murmured, smirking.

'I have a question, Brother Mundan,' another young prince interrupted. 'What happens to a timeship if it phases into orthogonal time *between* nodes, but has a malfunctioning orthophase or runs out of power?'

Mundan had been asked that question before by this very class. He was convinced the questioner was doing it because he knew it distressed him.

'In that case,' he said, fighting to keep his voice calm, 'the ship will remain in phase for a short time. Then it will outphase automatically and sink into the substratum, together with every soul on board.'

He turned, as much so as to hide his face as anything, and wrote on the blackboard the additional formulas which, together with the derivations from the mass-energy equation, described the nodal system associated with time's forward momentum.

Then, once he was sure he had recovered his composure, he faced the class again.

'Now we come to the question of the soul,' he said quietly. 'The empire itself, if bereft of religion, could subsist on the first two truths alone, though it would not be the empire we know. Knowledge of the soul is the empire's spiritual meaning, as expressed by Holy Church.'

He paused to bring home the seriousness of the third truth, almost daring them to cheek him further. But they did not. They knew that on this subject he was fanatical. Any jeering concerning the existence of the soul would be reported straight to Arch-Cardinal Reamoir.

'Prior to the revelations received by San Hevatar it was even possible for atheists to deny that the soul exists at all. Once time-travel had been demonstrated, however, the existence of the soul became indisputable.

'Why? Because time-travel proved that the past does note vanish when our awareness leaves it; the past continues to exist. And that raises the following question: what of that awareness? Must that not also continue to exist in the past even though, paradoxically, we are not "aware" of it? And what happens to that consciousness of ours at death? It cannot be extinguished – for otherwise the past would vanish.

'There is only one way to resolve the riddle, and it is this: the soul experiences itself as a moving moment of time beginning with conception and ending with death. At death the soul travels back in time to the moment of conception to live its life through again exactly as before.

This repetition continues eternally; thus is a man's past kept alive.

'From this proposition the existence of the soul is proved.

'This means that we have sat here in this room, hearing this lecture at this moment of time, countless times before, and will do so countless times again.'

With a sense of dignity Brother Mundan opened a book of Holy Scripture and began to read the words written by none other than San Hevatar.

'"There is the body and there is the soul. The body belongs to orthogonal time. But the soul, being spiritual, is eternal; yet it does not persist beyond its appointed period in time. On meeting the end of that period it travels back to the beginning, and experiences its life anew. Thus the soul has the God-given power to travel through time.

'"And why does the soul not remember the life it has already lived? It is because of death trauma, which wipes clean all the soul's memories . . ."'

It sometimes seemed to Chief Archivist Illus Ton Mayar that the Achronal Archives, which he administered, had taken on an existence all of their own and had begun to separate from the rest of the universe. Many of the staff no longer ventured into the outside world. Mayar understood their feelings: men whose working hours were spent in cataloguing time's mutations were apt to feel that the world was insubstantial. Here, in this subterranean cluster of vaults and bunkers, could be found a refuge from Chronotic instability.

The Archronal Archives were, in essence, a record of deleted time. Whenever an event was altered – whether by natural causes, or by order of the Historical Office, or by act of war – the consequences spread up and down historical time making the adjustment complete in all directions. Only the existence of the archives made such changes detectable. Protected by powerful time-buffers, the vaults were impenetrable to the powerful rectifying vibrations that echoed through the strat. Thus the records that were kept on every facet of the empire remained intact and could be compared with time as it currently stood.

It was a record of ghosts. Millions of men, women, and children, entire cities, nations, and cultures, that now had never existed, were stored in the archival computers. Research into these vanished communities could be a fascination experience, but to undertake it one had to be a staff member. Not even the universities were allowed such information – there was a theory that it would weaken the fabric of time, and besides, it might reflect on the permanence of the empire.

And there were times when Archivist Mayar himself wished that he did not have to know.

In the sepulchral dimness of Vault 5 the humming note of the computer was almost menacing. The bank of winking indicator lights seemed to be spelling out a mocking message of doom.

The operator's voice was sombre as he handed Mayar a thick print-out sheaf. 'The results have been double-checked, sir. There isn't any doubt about it – we knew almost straight away.'

The section had been carrying out what was known as an Anomalous Population Check. The Archives' Current State Bank was continuously matched, as a matter of course, with a similar information bank – unprotected by time-buffers – on the surface. When they failed to match, an Anomalous Population check was immediately undertaken so as to map out any unauthorized changes in time.

Mayar barely glanced at the print-out before handing it back. 'I shall have to inform the emperor,' he said heavily. That meant a visit to the palace – never a prospect he relished.

As if to accentuate the blow, Mayar had that morning received indirect confirmation from another source. Units of the Third Time Fleet had arrived in the capital, badly damaged from an engagement with the enemy. Mayar had heard that the Third Time Fleet had been beaten and forced to withdraw, and he was willing to bet that the consequence of that battle was staring at him now. Gerread, a city of some importance in Node Five (it had been a fair-sized town even in Node Four), had been elided from history, and the souls of its inhabitants (as theory would have it) dispersed into the formless dimensions of the strat like drops of rain in the ocean.

At least they had not suffered the fate of chronmen who, when their ships were destroyed, sank as conscious entities down into the gulf.

Without another word he left the operator and went through a double door leading to a long, low corridor. From all around him as he walked up the corridor came the muted sound of work going on in the surrounding chambers. Once, he pased another archivist, garbed in a white smock like himself, and muttered a perfunctory greeting. He avoided meeting the fellow's eyes, for the stricken look he knew he was apt to find there was becoming more pronounced among his staff lately. He was becoming concerned to know which way the growing cult of despairing isolationism in the archives would turn.

Once in his own quarters, he discarded his white gown and took the hundred-foot elevator to the surface.

As he passed through the shaded frontage of the surface building the bright sunlight hit him like a staggering blow, making him slightly dizzy. He entered the emblazoned coach that was waiting and instructed the chauffeur to take him to the palace.

The sights and sounds of Chronopolis washed over him as they drove through the streets. It all seemed slightly unreal. Did any of this really exist? Could anything that was liable to vanish from time be said to have substance? The familiar dreamlike sensation all achronal archivists were prone to came over him and he found himself wishing he were back in his quiet, cool vaults.

Once, to get some fresh air, he opened one of the coach windows, but instantly he was invaded by a low-key roaring that hung over this part of the city. Glancing overhead, he saw a drifting pall of smoke. Both the noise and the smoke came from the shipyards some miles away, where the tremendous armada that was to conquer the Hegemony was now nearing completion.

With a frown of distaste he closed the window again.

The coach travelled through the great arcaded entrance of the towering palace. Mayar was met in the reception chambers by Commander Trevurm, one of the emperor's select team of aides and advisers.

Calmly he gave him the news. Trevurm listened with head bent, then nodded.

'We already know of it. Commander Haight is here. He came in with ships of the Third Fleet this morning. They fought the Hegemonic raiders who did this.' He paused. 'How far does the mutation extend? Have you carried out a mapping?'

'We have, Commander. The elision covers everything related to the founding and sustaining of the city that was known as Gerread. There is no replacement.'

'No alternative city?'

'None.'

Trevurm sighed. 'This kind of thing is hard to grasp. You come and tell me there was a city called Gerread, which I have never heard of, and I have to believe you.'

'Before it was eliminated you had heard of it,' Mayar said, feeling how inadequate words were to express time's mysterious movements. 'Only last month you and I were speaking to its governor . . . or rather . . . I was speaking . . .'

'I cannot recall it.'

'Naturally not. It never happened. The meeting vanished along with the city, along with its governor.' And yet I am here and *I* met Governor Kerrebad and *I* remember it, Mayar thought wildly.

He turned his mind to more practical considerations. 'Has the emperor been told?' he asked.

Trevurm shook his head. 'Not yet. But it cannot be delayed further.'

He rose to his feet. 'I would prefer it if the news came from you,' he said. 'Commander Haight's interview with His Majesty will no doubt be uncomfortable enough without his having to bear the tidings as well.'

Mayar acquiesced and followed the commander deeper into the gorgeous palace. They passed through executive sections, through social sections where nobles and their guests relaxed with their various expensive entertainments. Finally they were in the inner sanctum. Mayar was obliged to wait while Commander Trevurm disappeared for a few minutes, after which they were admitted into the presence.

In a modest-sized room whose walls were of dark, panelled oak carved into curious patterns, His Majesty the Emperor Philipium I sat at one end of a long gleaming table of polished mahogany.

He was not an imposing figure: merely a tired old man sitting hunched and shrivelled at the corner of a table. His eyes had a deadness to them such as is brought on by continual fatigue or by a too-prolonged effort. The only touch of distinction to his grey face was a short pointed beard that was much faded. His costume, too, was modest and unregal; a tunic and breeches that were colourless and shiny with much use.

The two who entered bowed low. They could not help but notice that the emperor's right arm shook visibly. He suffered from the trembling palsy, which Mayar knew to be due to degenerative changes in the ganglia at the base of the cerebrum. The disease was incurable and grew chronic with advanced age.

They then turned to bow, less deferentially, to the second occupant of the room, who hovered like a shadow in the corner. In contrast to His Majesty, Arch-Cardinal Reamoir wore the most sumptuous of ecclesiastical garments. His floor-length cope was trimmed with purple fur and boasted orphreys richly patterned in gold and variously dyed tussore silk. Spun gold figured, too, in the coif which covered his head and which was decorated with the symbols of the Church.

The aloof prelate accepted their bow with a casual blessing.

'And what is this bad news I have been warned to expect?' The emperor inquired in a dry voice.

Briefly and concisely, Mayar gave him the facts. The old man's face sagged. At the same time, a look of puzzlement crossed his features.

Mayar knew that look. It happened every time someone was told of events or things that had been removed from the stream of time. Automatically one tried to remember what had gone, however much one knew that it was impossible.

With the emperor, puzzlement was soon replaced by muted rage at the realization that an ungodly enemy had succeeded in altering even his memories. 'This is bad,' he said shakily. 'This is very bad.'

Arch-Cardinal Reamoir moved forward silently. A hand stole from beneath his cope and squeezed the emperor's shoulder comfortingly. Philipium reached up and patted the hand.

'Your Majesty will recall,' Mayar continued, 'that this is the second such attack. The first was not entirely successful, for it only modified the history of the coastal port of Marsel, and that not seriously. This, however, is an unmitigated disaster. We must presume that the enemy has now perfected his new weapon.'

'Yes! The time-distorter!' The emperor's face clearly showed his distress. 'Why does the Hegemony have such a device and we do *not* have it?' His right arm trembled more markedly, as it usually did under stress. And indeed, the enemy's possession of the time-distorter was frightening. When the Historical Office decided to change some aspect of history, months or years of preparation were needed to select some key event or combination of events whose alteration would produce the desired result. A big operation was usually required, entailing a staff of thousands to carry it out.

Yet apparently the distorter could mutate history simply by focusing some sort of energy that acted on the underlying temporal substratum. The threat to the empire was real and disturbing.

'God is testing us,' murmured Arch-Cardinal Reamoir smoothly.

'As always, you know best, old friend.' The emperor seemed to draw courage from anything Reamoir said. God forgive him for the thought, but Mayar simply could not see the arch-cardinal's influence as a healthy one.

'These indignities will cease once my invincible armada sets forth,' the emperor said, glancing up at Reamoir. 'The Hegemony will be part of the empire. The distorter will be ours.'

'Your Majesty,' Mayar said diffidently, 'a weapon as effective as the time-distorter must seriously be taken into account. There is very little defence against it, once its carrier ship has broken through into historical territory. I would go so far as to say that it is capable of destroying the empire itself.'

'*Archivist Mayar!*' Reamoir thundered, his face suddenly blazing. 'Take a care what you say!'

'I said only that it is *capable* of destroying the empire,' Mayar replied defensively. 'I did not say that such an event could come about.' And if he did openly say it, he would be in serious trouble. The Two Things That God Will Not Do were as important a part of religious dogma as the Three Revelations of San Hevatar. The Two Things That God Will Not Do were that, once having given it, He would not take away the secret of time-travel from mankind; and that He would not allow the Chronotic Empire ever to perish.

It was dangerous to argue with the head of the Church. But Mayar, fearful of the calamity he saw hovering over them all, pressed on.

'What I say, Your Majesty, Your Eminence, is this: God has promised that the empire will not fall or be removed, but He has not promised that it will not meet with misfortune or be defeated in war. As Your Eminence will tell us –' he bowed his head again towards the arch-cardinal – 'the doctrine of free will means that even the mission of the Church may fail. God has left such matters in our hands, and we are fallible.'

He licked his lips and continued hurriedly. 'As chief archivist I am familiar with the changes of time. I know that their consequences can be dismaying and unexpected, and that precautions taken against them can prove to be futile. I do not think I am exaggerating when I say that the archives perform a function fundamental to the integrity of the empire. And I fear the distorter. I ask myself what degree of change the archives can accommodate. I believe they will break down altogether under the impact of the weapon.'

'And what do you propose we should do?' Philipium's eyes had lost their deadness now. They were glittering.

'It occurs to me that the Hegemony is carrying out these attacks because it feels itself threatened by us, Your Majesty. In my opinion we should seek a truce and abandon our plans for conquest – at least until we know more about the time-distorter.'

The emperor turned beady eyes on Commander Trevurm. 'And what is your opinion?'

Trevurm stroked his chin and sighed. 'There is much sense in what our friend says,' he admitted. 'The time-distorter brings an unknown factor into the equation.'

'So you both advise caution?'

'Yes, Your Majesty.'

'Have you both forgotten the mission of Holy Church?' said the arch-cardinal to Trevurm and Mayar, affecting a shocked tone. 'Your Majesty, we are doing God's bidding. The armada must do its work. The heathen must be converted by its power.'

'But at the risk of wreaking havoc with the structure of time?' Mayar protested.

Reamoir turned and spoke for the benefit of Philipium alone. 'What else should we do? Have we not tried to convert the Hegemony by peaceful persuasion? Our missionaries have gone forward in time, not only to the Hegemony but even beyond, to little avail. Many have been spurned and ejected back to their own time. Some have even been martyred. The pride and stubbornness of the future people is displeasing to God; only force remains. God will go with our armada; He is on our side. All will be well.'

'All will be well,' echoed Philipium. 'The armada must proceed. The only question to be answered is when. And that is a matter for the Military Council, not for amateurs.' He gestured irritably.

'I understand, Your Majesty,' Mayar said, feeling defeated.

The emperor rose from his chair and clutched at Reamoir, holding up his trembling right arm. 'My arm, see how it shakes,' he said, his voice hollow-sounding. 'Listen, my friend – I have had a vision in a dream. God has told me that if the Hegemony is subdued my affliction will vanish.'

'That indeed will be a miracle, sir.'

'Yes. God's message is clear. All will be well.' He turned to Mayar. 'And yet your forebodings are not without substance, Archivist. We are merely human and we can err. Even I am merely emperor, not *Imperator*. Come, we will consult a wiser being.'

Philipium tottered towards the door. Outside, attendants were waiting and accompanied them through the cloistered passages of the inner sanctum. From ahead came cheerful noises of talk and laughter, growing steadily louder until eventually a pair of large doors, quilted and padded with stuffed satin, drew open to admit them.

They entered the main inner chamber of the court.

Strictly speaking it was more than a chamber, being the size of a ballroom. Tastefully arranged here and there were couches, tables, and chairs. The arched recesses that skirted its circumference formed a motif that was repeated in the ribbed and curved formation of the ceiling. All in all, the effect was most pleasing and restful to the eye.

A favourite meeting place, the court chamber had a relaxed air and nobles and privileged persons from all parts and nodes of the empire came and went through its several entrances. The Ixian family predominated, of course, its members hailing from all periods of history – though in their case the term 'history' was practically redundant. The Ixian dynasty was fully mobile through time, being the only family permitted to intermarry with its descendants and ancestors.

One end of the court chamber was kept clear. Emperor Philipium I made towards it with tottering step, followed by the arch-cardinal, Mayar, and Commander Trevurm. A hush fell over the scene as his presence was noted, but then the chatter started up again.

One of his young daughters, Princess Mayora, approached him with a smile, but he brushed her aside and stood before the great panel, featureless and of a dull gold colour, that occupied that entire end of the chamber.

'*Imperator*,' he called in a weak husky voice, 'grant us an audience!'

After a pause the gold panel rumbled up to reveal a square-cut cavity. There was the whine of motors.

The machine they knew as the *Imperator* slid out on giant castors and stood in the vacant space as though surveying the chamber. A deep hum issued from within its body.

Even though he had seen it several times before, Mayar still could not prevent a sensation of awe as he beheld the huge machine. It towered over them like a miniature castle, with its odd crenellated towers, one at each corner, and its walls plated with matt greyish-black metal. It had a distinctly regal appearance entirely in keeping with its function. For though the *Imperator* was a machine – admittedly much more advanced and mysterious than a common computer – it was also, in some indefinable way, *alive*.

More than that, it was in principle the true titular head of the empire. Emperor Philipium I – like any emperor before or after him – held his position by proxy, as it were. The rationale behind this system was quite clear: the *Imperator* contained the distillation of the minds of all the Chronotic emperors, of whom there had been five before Philipium, as well as of many other members of the imperial dynasty whose wisdom seemed to merit it, this distillation being accomplished by a transfusion from the memory centres of their brains after death.

Not that the *Imperator* was merely a receptacle of their dead intelligences; it was much more. No one quite knew what went on inside the *Imperator*, or what it did with these borrowed personalities. They never emerged, that was certain; the *Imperator* had a nature of its own.

The origin of the machine was equally obscure to the outside world, being a state secret. San Hevatar was reputed, by legend, to have had a hand in its manufacture. Mayar, however – he was not privy to this state secret either – had received a very good indication from a member of the Ixian family itself, that there *was* no secret, that no one, not even the emperor, knew where the *Imperator* came from or how long it had been there.

The hum from within the machine grew deeper and the *Imperator* spoke in a full-bodied baritone that thrilled the hearer with its presence.

'You have summoned me?'

Philipium nodded, leaning on an attendant. 'Advise us on the matter we have been discussing.'

There was no need to explain further. Every room in the palace, as well as every department of government, was wired for sound for the *Imperator*'s benefit. No one felt embarrassed by this state of affairs, since the machine had never been known to repeat anything it had heard.

The humming faded almost to inaudibility before the *Imperator* spoke again.

'What has been will be.'

The machine rolled back on its castors, disappearing into its private chamber. The gold panel slid down into place.

Mayar had expected nothing better from the interview. The *Imperator* undertook no executive function. While it was consulted occasionally, the cryptic nature of its pronouncements rendered it more in the style of an oracle. More than one emperor had spent days trying to puzzle out the meaning of its statements, only to have to ignore them in the end.

'*What has been will be,*' Philipium muttered feverishly. 'How do you interpret those words, Reamoir?'

'The *Imperator* understands the mysteries of time,' the arch-cardinal replied smoothly. 'It intimates that the victory of our invincible armada is foreordained.'

The emperor gave a grunt of satisfaction. 'The enterprise against the Hegemony must go ahead . . . all must be prepared to the utmost.' He lifted a shaking hand to his attendant. 'To my quarters. I must rest. Later I will receive Commander Haight.'

He moved off. Commander Trevurm bade Mayar good day and went about his business. The arch-cardinal, disdaining civilities, also drifted off.

Mayar allowed his gaze to wander over the court chamber. He was feeling dismal. He was about to make his way back to the archives when Princess Mayora rushed up to him.

'Chief Archivist, it is *so* long since we saw you here.'

Mayar smiled politely. 'Regretfully my stay must be short, Your Highness. I must return to the vaults.'

'Oh, nonsense. You can easily spare an hour or so. Come over here.' She seized him by the arm and led him towards a couch.

Disarmed by the young woman's charm, Mayar obeyed. Once seated, she turned and faced him directly.

'So what have you been talking to Father about?' she said breezily.

Mayar was embarrassed. 'With all respect, Your Highness—'

'Oh, yes, I know,' she interrupted with an impatient wave of her hand. 'State confidence. Still, I know what it was all about. Daddy's enterprise against the heathen.' She leaned closer, her eyes sparkling with excitement. 'Will there be great battles in the substratum? Awful mutations in time?'

'I fear there will, Your Highness,' Mayar said heavily.

She drew back in an expostulation of surprise. 'Well, don't sound so gloomy about it. Look over there – there's Captain Vrin.' She pointed out a tall chron officer in full dress uniform – resplendent tunic, plumed hat, and waist-high boots belled at the top – who was talking animatedly, surrounded by spell-bound young women. 'He's in the Third Fleet. He's just come back from a battle at Node Five. Isn't it exciting?'

Mayar turned his head away, feeling that if he tried to speak his voice would choke him.

Noticing his reaction, Princess Mayora pouted in disappointment. 'Well, if you're going to be so serious about it you might as well go and talk to my brother Philipium,' she said. 'There he is over there.'

Mayar followed her gaze and located Philipium, the eldest of the emperor's sizeable brood. Aged about forty, he had already begun to resemble his father and sported the same type of beard. He was destined to become Emperor Philipium II, although the date of his coronation was not permitted to be made known to anyone in Node I, particularly to the present emperor. Gazing upon him, Mayar allowed his thoughts to dwell for a few moments on the perplexing intricacies of time such a situation presented. Futurewards of Node One – in the internodal hinterland – was a Philipium the Younger who was not emperor but who remained until his dying day merely the son of the emperor. Yet eventually Node One would travel onwards, past the death of Philipium I, and Philipium II would become emperor. The soul of Philipium the Elder would travel back in time to be reborn; but in *that* cycle of his eternally recurring life, the cycle succeeding the current one, he would not be emperor but merely the father of Emperor Philipium II.

Likewise Mayar, in the next cycle of his recurrent life, would find himself living in the internodal hinterland that Node One had left behind. He would be removed from the centre of the empire and so, he hoped, would find life a good deal more peaceful.

The eternally repeated rebirth of the soul into the same life was one of the few dogmas of the Church that had been scientifically proved. That, together with the nodal structure of time, provided the empire with a form of passing time that, so to speak, transcended ordinary sequential time. At the same time the system of nodes was extremely convenient for the average mind, such as that of Princess Mayora, who sat with him now. She was happily able to ignore the enigmas and paradoxes that time-travel entailed, leaving such troublesome matters to the theoreticians of the Historical Office, of the Church's Order of Chronotic Casuistry, and of Mayar's own Achronal Archives.

Did these people surrounding Mayar have any idea what the mutability of time meant? It was quite obvious that Princess Mayora did not. Like nearly everyone else, she regarded the gorgeous palace in which she lived as permanent, secure, and unalterable. The Chronotic wars were centuries away. Mayar glanced despairingly at the ingeniously vaulted and domed ceiling. If only they could realize, he thought, that all this could be magicked away, could *never have been*.

Princess Mayora giggled. 'Oh, look! Here's Narcis!'

Into the chamber strolled two identical youths, their arms fondly about each other's necks. Looking closely at them, one could see them for Ixians. One could see in them, perhaps, what their father the emperor might have been in his youth: the oval face, the straight poetical nose. Here, however, their lithe upright bearing, their unblemished skin, turned Philipium's tottering figure into a travesty.

On looking even closer, one might discern that one of these apparently identical twins was in fact a few years older than the other. Their story needed no explication to Mayar. Narcis, youngest son of the emperor, a strange, wayward homosexual, had in defiance of all the laws of the empire travelled a few years into the future where he had met and fallen in love with *himself*. He had, moreover, persuaded his future self to return to Node One with him. The two now spent their time mooning about the palace together, flaunting their forbidden love for all to see.

Arch-Cardinal Reamoir, whenever he chanced to come upon them, would give them the sign of the curse, whereupon the two young Narcises would laugh with glee. But in the atmosphere of the Ixian dynasty their love affair was not nearly as shocking as it would have sounded outside. Ixians married only Ixians, to keep the imperial line pure. At first this had meant marriages that spanned centuries, a man marrying, perhaps, his great-great-great-grandniece. But gradually all distinctions became blurred. Marriages between brother and sister, parent and child, were no longer frowned on. The blood was what mattered.

And as for the crime of 'going double' – of consorting with one's future self – in a world where it was forbidden even to tell a man what lay in his future, well, young Ixians did not feel that Chronotic laws were made to be obeyed.

Princess Mayora waved to her double-brother. The Princes Narcis came towards them.

'Good day, Chief Archivist.' Narcis$_1$ greeted him with a smile.

'Good day to you, Your Highness.' As they came close Mayar could hear the faint whine of the orthophase that Narcis$_2$ wore on a belt at his waist to enable him to live outside his own time.

'Come and talk to the archivist,' Princess Mayora demanded. 'He appears to need cheering up.'

Narcis gazed at Mayar with dreamy eyes while fondling the back of his double's neck. 'He is too old,' he said bluntly. 'Old people talk only of dreary things, of war and politics and religion. We live for love, do we not, Narcis?'

'Yes, Narcis.'

Smiling together, the two wandered away.

Meantime in another part of the palace's inner sanctum Narcis's other brother, Prince Vro Ixian, was busy receiving the report of Perlo Rolce, owner of the Rolce Detective Agency.

Prince Vro's apartments were gloomily lit and carelessly furnished. The cleaning staff was rarely allowed in and dust lay everywhere. To remind him of his great sorrow, one wall of the main room was taken up with a tridimensional hologram screen that gave a direct view into a mausoleum about a mile distant so that it seemed an extension of Vro's dwelling. The sarcophagus occupying the centre of the burial chamber gaped open, empty.

The burly detective sat stiffly in a straight-backed chair facing the prince, who stood in a curious stance at the other end of the room, head cocked and one hand resting negligently on a table. Three or four years older than Narcis, he had the same cast of face, but his eyes were more penetrating.

Rolce was used to Ixian peculiarities. This was not the first time he had been engaged by a member of the imperial household. He spoke directly, without prevarication.

'Your Highness, since our last meeting I have followed up the evidence suggesting that the Traumatic sect might have been involved in the affair. I can now confirm it categorically: it *was* the Traumatic sect who stole the body of Princess Veaa from its resting place.'

Vro looked pleadingly at the empty sarcophagus. 'But for what purpose?'

Rolce coughed before continuing. 'The motives for the crime are far from pleasant, Your Highness. The Traumatic sect, as you must know, is prone to bizarre practices. Rejecting the teachings of the Church, its members worship a god they call Hulmu and whom they deem to dwell in the uttermost depths of the strat. Hulmu, by their doctrines, feeds on the trauma that the soul experiences on separating from the body at death, but is usually robbed of his pleasure because the soul passes back in time and finds refuge in its body again. Therefore the sect practises certain rites, ending in human sacrifice, that they claim give the victim's soul to Hulmu.'

'What has this to do with my beloved Veaa?' said Vro harshly. 'She is dead already.'

'Your sister died of a brain haemorrhage, and later was embalmed by the Murkesen process, which leaves all the vital tissues intact,' the detective explained. 'Someone in the Traumatic sect apparently believes that these two factors together have left her soul in a state of suspension, and that it has not departed into the past.'

'You mean she is still *alive*?' Prince Vro asked in a shocked tone.

'No, Your Highness,' Rolce replied hurriedly. 'One should not pay heed to heretical theories.' Then, seeing Prince Vro's lips curl, he added, 'Even according to the Traumatics your sister is deceased. It is merely that her soul *is believed* to be still accessible to Hulmu. They hoped, by means of rites or medical experiments, to release her soul from its latent state and offer it to Hulmu. A personage of such exalted rank was, of course, a great prize to them.'

A low moan escaped Prince Vro's lips and his face expressed ashen horror. Then he turned away and began to give vent to strangled sobs, while Rolce sat impassively and stared at the nearby wall.

The private detective had come across many weird situations in the course of his work and the predicament of Prince Vro aroused no comment in his mind.

He knew that the prince had been desperately enamoured of his sister Princess Veaa. The emperor had even indicated that he would consent to a marriage between them. And then had come her sudden death. In an orgy of mourning Prince Vro had designed her mausoleum personally, placed her embalmed body in the sarcophagus with his own hands, and installed the direct-wire hologram to his private apartment so that he would never forget her.

Sadly, his misfortunes had increased still further. The embalmed body had been stolen from the mausoleum, for no explicable reason. Exhaustive police investigations had proved fruitless. Eventually Vro had called upon Rolce's services.

Rolce had wondered why the prince had not followed the example of his brother Narcis and travelled back in time to when Veaa was still alive (though that might, he reflected, entail complications of a personal nature). But the speculation was sterile. Vro seemed as deeply in love with the corpse as he had been with the living woman.

With difficulty the prince recovered his composure. 'And what has become of her now?'

Rolce frowned. 'At this point the affair becomes perplexing. I gained most of my information so far by infiltrating one of my men into a secret Traumatic cell. Unfortunately his guise was eventually penetrated and the fellow was murdered. I then used more direct methods to track down the cor – to track down the princess, and ascertained that she had been removed from Node One on an internodal liner. However –'

'They can do that?'

The detective nodded. 'The sect is very resourceful. It has good contacts in the internodal travel services.'

'I see,' muttered Vro. 'And how soon before my beloved Veaa is found?'

The other gave a worried sigh. 'The trail has petered out, Your Highness. Quite frankly I do not understand it. I have never come up against such a blank wall before. Even if the body had been disposed of in some way – and I seriously doubt that it has – the methods I have used should have given me some information about it. Everything that happens leaves a trace that the trained investigator can pick up.'

'What are you babbling about, Rolce?' Vro swung around and confronted the older man, hands on his hips. 'You are not doing your job! Is your fee not inducement enough?'

'It is not that, Your Highness!' the investigator protested. 'My entire agency – which is an organization to be reckoned with – is engaged solely upon this one assignment. We have never failed yet. But something odd seems to have happened.'

For the first time Perlo Rolce displayed a degree of discomfiture. He shifted uneasily in his chair.

'At my headquarters we have the man who shipped out the body of Princess Veaa,' he said. 'We are certain we have not mistaken his identity. Earlier we picked up his thoughts on the subject with a field-effect device.'

'And?'

'He does not know anything about it any longer. He does not remember leaving Chronopolis on the requisite date.'

'His mind has been tampered with.'

'That might be the explanation if we relied on physical persuasion alone. He knows nothing of Princess Veaa, except vaguely as a one-time member of the imperial family. Yet we know for a fact that he had custody of the body for a considerable period of time.'

'Just what are you suggesting?'

The investigator looked, briefly, straight into Vro's eyes, something he had never done before. 'I do not know,

Your Highness. I am a detective, not a Chronotician. But I am beginning to get the feeling that something outside my control has closed off the investigation.'

He hesitated before going on. 'The phenomenon is not unknown to me. Of late, there have been a number of such cases. Odd details that do not mesh together – a cause not producing the usual effect, or an effect not preceded by the usual cause. Only someone like myself, trained to notice details, would pick them up. In my belief the war with the Hegemony is beginning to touch us, even here at Node One. Time is under strain.'

The prince brooded on his words. 'It almost sounds as though you were looking for excuses,' he said in a surly tone.

'Your Highness, I assure you of my sincerity.'

'Well, are you implying you wish to leave off the assignment?'

'The Rolce Agency does not abandon assignments,' Rolce told him. 'There is one move still left to us. We have procured an orthophase and I am negotiating for the clandestine use of a time-travel unit.'

'I could have arranged that for you,' Vro interrupted in a mutter.

Rolce shrugged. 'On of my agents will phase himself into the past and carry out a surveillance of our prisoner at the time he hid and transported the body of Princess Veaa. If we find that he did not commit these acts – *as we know he did* – then it will demonstrate that time has mutated in some peculiar way, leaving loose ends.'

'In a very peculiar way,' Prince Vro agreed huffily. 'Are you not aware that a time-mutation leaves no loose ends and is generally undetectable after the event?'

'I am aware of it, Your Highness, but I must deal in facts.' He rose and handed the prince an envelope. 'Here is my written report of all information to date.'

'Thank you, my good fellow. Come and see me again soon.'

After the detective had gone the young prince stood

for a long time with the envelope unopened in his hand, staring into space.

Defeat is never a pleasant thing to have to recount to one's master. Commander Haight's large, rugged face was stonily impassive as he answered the emperor's probing questions concerning the attempt to save Gerread.

At length Philipium I uttered a deep trembling sigh. 'No blame,' he said, to Haight's relief. 'The action was gallantly fought. Tonight the Military Council meets. We shall be discussing what action to take between now and the launching of the armada. There will be some, no doubt, who wish to abandon the enterprise and make peace overtures with the Hegemony.' He looked closely at the commander. 'How do you read the situation?'

'The armada must be launched as soon as possible, Your Majesty – much sooner than was originally planned. The time-distorter is a terrible weapon. I cannot guarantee the ability of the defensive forces to ward off every attack that might be made.'

'Can we not set up time-blocks?'

'Time-blocks cannot be kept in continuous operation without years of preparation, Your Majesty. And I am advised that the rearward Stop Barrier already consumes one-third of the imperial budget. Our only safeguard is to overwhelm the Hegemony without delay. Otherwise I can foresee disaster.'

The emperor grunted contemptuously. 'Don't tell me you're another who thinks the empire can fall.'

'Naturally not, Your Majesty,' replied Haight, taken aback by the suggestion. 'But serious damage can be wrought from which it would take centuries to recover. More to the point, the Hegemonics must know of the armada we have in preparation. It will form a prime target for their attentions. They will certainly try to destroy it before it is completed.'

This time it was the emperor's turn to be startled. 'They could penetrate even this far – to Node One?'

'Even that cannot be discounted, though it's unlikely in my view. They will try to attack it indirectly by wreaking such changes in our future that the effects will reach far back in time, delaying or preventing the construction of the armada in the first place. It could be done if their knowledge of Chronotic history is detailed enough.'

'And it probably is,' Philipium confirmed in a worried tone. 'I have heard there has been some intercourse between agents of the Hegemony and a dissident religious sect known as the Traumatics.' He shook his head in exasperation. His right hand began to tremble more noticeably.

'The assembling of the armada simply cannot be hastened,' he informed Haight. 'The project is already at full stretch; there are no more resources that can be put into it.'

'Your Majesty, if we leave matters as they stand at the moment, there is no saying how things will end.'

'You speak as though you were one of my ministers, instead of merely a commander in the Time Service,' Philipium said with a warning note of reproof.

'I beg Your Majesty's pardon. It is my concern over the situation that prompts me to speak so.'

'Everyone, it seems, has decided to be impudent today. Still, you have seen action at first hand. You know how things look at the frontier. What suggestions have you for strengthening the forward watch? We could,' he added as an afterthought, 'release some ships completed for the armada for that purpose.'

'That would help, Your Majesty, but the first priority must be to gain parity with the enemy over the matter of his new weapon. To that end I advocate a raid into Hegemonic territory with a force strong enough to overcome any local resistance, in an effort to capture a sample distorter.'

'Do you think that is a feasible operation?'

'Yes, if we have agents who can find out where a distorter is kept, so as to give us a target point. The

Hegemony consists of one node only, which makes the matter simpler.'

The emperor opened a lacquered box and sniffed at a pinch of the reddish powder it contained. He was thoughtful. 'We do have agents in the Hegemony. Mostly among those whom our early missionaries converted to the true faith. Needless to say they are already at work on the business of the distorter, but messages are slow to reach us due to the inability to transmit through time.'

He inhaled more snuff. 'You will attend the meeting of the Military Council tonight. We will discuss this.'

'With great pleasure, Your Majesty.'

In the event Illus Ton Mayar delayed his departure from the palace for an hour or two. Princess Mayora was an insistent host, and despite his gloomy manner, she continued to inveigle him into conversation with the socialites who flitted in and out of the court chamber. He even spoke with Captain Vrin and heard from him a first-hand account of his part in the recent battle for Gerread – an account, he suspected, already polished with much retelling, even though the battle-damaged timeships had arrived only a little before dawn.

But his nagging desire to return to his underground vaults eventually overcame the pleasure of social life. He was about to tender his farewells to the princess when a liveried servant approached him.

'His Highness the Prince Vro would speak with you, Archivist, if it is convenient,' the servant informed him.

Although couched in the politest terms, coming from a prince the message was an order. Puzzled, Mayar followed the servant and shortly came to Vro's morbid quarters.

The prince leaped up with alacrity when he entered. 'Ah,' he greeted, 'I tried to contact you at the archives, but they said you were here at the palace.'

Mayar glanced surreptitiously around the place, trying not to seem inquisitive. 'An audience with His Majesty your father,' he explained diffidently.

'More mutation, eh?' Vro gave him a querying, penetrating look.

'I'm afraid so.'

He relaxed a little. Prince Vro had always struck him as being the most intelligent of the imperial family. The business with the body of Princess Veaa was known to Mayar, of course . . . but that was entirely a personal affair.

He tried to keep his eyes away from the wall-wide holocast of the vacant mausoleum. 'How may I serve Your Highness?' he asked.

'Ah, you come straight to the point. A man after my own heart.'

Holding nothing back, Prince Vro told him how he had hired the Rolce Detective Agency to hunt down Princess Veaa's body. He recounted, as well as he could, the conversation he had held with Rolce an hour before. When he came to speak of the peculiar difficulties and anomalies Rolce had been encountering, Mayar grew more and more agitated.

'Could time become dislocated in the way Rolce suspects?' he asked Mayar.

'From natural mutations – no,' Mayar told him. 'The natural movements of the substratum always smooth out cause-and-effect relationships in both directions. But in principle there's nothing to prevent dislocated phenomena arising through some sort of artificially applied distortion. Excuse me, sir, but may I be permitted to sit?'

Prince Vro nodded sympathetically. Mayar edged himself to the straight-backed chair Perlo Rolce had recently occupied. He felt weak and dizzy.

'A detective agency – of course!' he exclaimed, his voice hoarse with sudden understanding. 'It's logical. Only a detective would notice details on so small a scale. Even the Achronal Archives cannot keep track of everyday events.'

'But what does it all mean?'

'It means what Rolce says it means. That the war with the Hegemony is going badly. It's that damned distorter of theirs. Cracks are appearing in the order of things – little cracks, at first. Eventually they'll get bigger.'

'What an amusing prospect.'

Mayar looked at him sharply.

'Well, you might as well get used to the idea, Archivist. It's got to happen. Nothing can stop the war now. You have observed, of course, that my father the emperor is a religious maniac. Aided and abetted by that incredible bigot Reamoir, he is determined to hurl his armada at our descendants in the far future. I am even expected to command one of its squadrons myself!' Vro's lips twisted cynically. He moved away to gaze into the mausoleum. 'No doubt all will shortly come crashing about our ears. But all of this means nothing to me. I care only for saving my beloved Veaa.'

Mayar scarcely heard his last words. He passed a hand wearily across his brow. 'We are living in a dream,' he said in an exhausted voice. 'This world – it is all an illusion. Only the strat is real . . .'

'An interesting point of view.' Prince Vro turned to face him again.

'In my archives are records of nations, cultures, whole civilizations that have been removed from time,' Mayar said. 'Millions of people – mere figments, of whom we have a record only by a technical trick. How can something that vanishes and changes be real? That is why I say only the strat is real – and even then, what is the strat? We do not know. This time-travel: it is merely a way of moving from one part of a dream to another.'

'Your view of life comes close to my own,' Prince Vro told him softly. 'Nothing is real; no matter is of more significance than any other. That is what I tell myself whenever my intellect chides me for my obsession with my beloved Veaa.'

The prince handed Mayar a thick envelope. 'Since you are able to take Rolce's suspicions seriously, I want you to do some work for me. This is his report. I'll send him to you tomorrow to explain it personally.'

'Work, Your Highness?' Mayar accepted the envelope gingerly.

Vro nodded. 'With his investigations and the contents of your files, it should be possible to carry out a – what do you call it – a mapping, should it not? I want you to help Rolce locate the princess. If detective work in orthogonal time is not enough, then perhaps you can turn something up in strat time.'

When Mayar left Prince Vro and made to leave the palace, clutching the private investigator's report, his mind feverish, he chanced to pass by the audience chamber where he had earlier spoken with the emperor.

The huge frame of Commander Haight emerged from the chamber. Grim-faced, he swept by Mayar without a word.

After him came the emperor, leaning on the arm of an attendant. He stopped when he caught sight of Mayar, who bowed low.

'Still here, Archivist?'

'Your Majesty, there is a recommendation I would make.'

The notion had been in his mind for some months, but in the last half-hour it had jelled into a firm desire. Philipium frowned, not liking to be accosted so, but he signalled Mayar to continue.

'I am becoming increasingly concerned for the safety of the archives, Your Majesty. I have come to the conclusion that the present arrangements are unsatisfactory.'

Now Philipium became displeased. 'The time-buffers surrounding your vaults were installed at colossal expense,' he admonished. 'You approved them at the time. Now you tell me they are no good.'

'I feel that the situation is changing rapidly, Your Majesty. My new proposal will entail less expense. The buffers are satisfactory up to a point – but if the enemy should succeed in getting behind us, as it were, and attacking the year in which the buffers were erected, then they could be obviated and the archives would be rendered useless for their purpose.'

Philipium's grey face lost its anger as, with eyes downcast, he considered the point. 'So?'

'The only really foolproof way of making the archives safe from orthogonal mutations is to locate them in the strat. This could not be done before, due to the communications problem – it's necessary to have continuous computer contact with the records of the Imperial Register, so as to detect anomalies, and there was no way to do this. The technical problem has now been solved. We can float at anchor in the strat while connected by cable to the offices of the registrar.'

'By *cable*?'

'The technique is a new one known as graduated phasing, Your Majesty. The Achronal Archives should then be proof against any orthogonal changes.'

'Very well, I approve. I will issue an authorization.'

The secretary in the emperor's retinue immediately made a note of the proceedings. Mayar bowed low and left.

Philipium retired to his private quarters, dismissed the retinue except for one personal servant, and sent for his favourite comforter. With a hoarse, deep-seated sigh he sank into a comfortable couch and accepted a dose of the medicine that quieted his shaking a little.

The comforter arrived. This was Philipium's favourite relaxation. An atmosphere of peace and silence, the lights shaded to rest his aching eyes.

The comforter sat to one side of the emperor so as to be out of his line of vision. He opened the book he carried and in a gentle, soothing voice began to read.

'There is the body, and there is the soul. The body belongs to orthogonal time. But the soul, being spiritual, is eternal; yet it does not persist beyond its appointed period in time . . .'

Elsewhere Narcis$_1$ and Narcis$_2$ disported on a couch that was more luxurious than their father's and surrounded by orchids, while the atmosphere of the boudoir was pervaded by sweet perfumes.

They looked into each other's eyes, smiling and sated. 'One day soon something strange will happen,' Narcis$_2$ said in a sad, dreamy voice. 'Something very, very melancholy.'

'What is that, dearest?' Narcis$_1$ murmured.

'*He* will come and steal you from me. Like a thief in the night. The third one.'

Briefly there dawned in Narcis$_1$'s eyes the realization of what the other was talking about – the day, barely a year ahead, when by natural ageing they would reach the date when he had secretly appeared in his future self's bedroom and seduced him. It was a paradox he had never really bothered to work out for himself.

'Yes, I shall have a visitor,' he said wonderingly. 'He will enchant me and entice me away. Away into the past!'

'Don't talk like that! I shall be left all alone!' Narcis$_2$ covered his face with his hands. 'Oh, I hate him! I hate him!'

Narcis$_1$ gazed at him with teasing, imagining eyes.

3

The Seekers, the Pointers, the Pursuers, all were present. The Choosing could go ahead.

The ceremony was in the apartment of a rich member of the sect. One of the elegant rooms had been converted into a temple. The altar, containing a representation of the Impossible Shape (an abstract of warped planes, said to echo the form of Hulmu), was lit by shaded cressets.

All knelt, the ceremonial black cloths draped over their heads, save the vicar, who stood facing the assembly, wearing the Medallion of Projection, which showed a gold miniature of a holocast projector. On his head was a low flat-topped hat. Upon this hat he placed the black Book of Hulmu to allow the vibrations of its words to flow down into him.

The orisons began. 'Lord of all the deep, perceive us and know that we thy servants act out our parts . . .'

The chanting grew louder. The vicar feverishly muttered an incantation, known only to sect members of his own rank, which acted on a hypnotically planted subconscious command. Almost immediately he went into a trance.

He spoke with the voice of Hulmu.

It was a harsh, twanging voice, quite unlike his own or that of any other human being.

'Are my Seekers present?'

'We are present, Lord!' cried one section of the congregation.

'Are my Pointers present?'

'We are present, Lord!' chanted another group.

'Are my Pursuers present?'

The remainder of the gathering spoke up. 'We are present, Lord!'

'Then let my Pointers choose.'

Abruptly the glazed, empty look went out of the vicar's eyes. He removed the black book from his head.

'All right, let's get on with it,' he said conversationally in his normal tone.

The tension went out of the meeting. They removed their black headcloths. The gathering was suddenly informal.

The Pointers huddled together. One of them pulled a cord. A curtain swished aside, revealing a complete set of Chronopolis's massive street directory.

A sect member with a self-absorbed face thoughtfully selected a volume.

Another snatched it from him, bent back the covers, and flung the book to the floor so that it splayed its leaves on the tiles.

Yet another picked it up and smoothed out the pages that fortune, through this procedure, had selected. He stared at the ceiling while allowing his fingers to roam at random over the paper.

Everyone watched in silence as his fingers slowed to a stop.

'Eighty-nine Kell Street,' he read out. 'Precinct E-Fourteen. Inpriss Sorce, female.'

'Inpriss Sorce,' someone said, savouring the name. They all started wondering what she was like: young or old, pretty or plain; what her fear index was.

'The Pursuer team will begin operations tomorrow at nine,' the vicar intoned.

'Inpriss Sorce.' All the Pursuers began murmuring the name to themselves with a growing sense of pleasure.

They were glad the victim was a woman.

Inpriss Sorce was thirty years old. She had a neat, slightly melancholy face with light-brown eyes, and an average figure. She lived in a two-room apartment and worked as a clerk for Noble Cryonics, a firm that did a great deal of work for the government.

Once she had held a better-paid job with the Historical Office, but had lost it when a jealous comforter cast aspersions on her piety. The post she held now, though it reduced her station in life, did not require vetting by the Church. It did, however, entail living in a poorer part of the city. Also, most of her friends from the Historical Office now wanted little to do with her, so she was, for the time being, lonely.

She had come home from work and was wondering what to do with the evening when the Pursuers paid their call.

The casers had already been at work some hours before. One of them met Rol Stryne and Fee Velen as they arrived at the entrance to the apartment block. Briefly he explained the layout of Inpriss Sorce's small dwelling. The window in the living-room gave access to a fire escape.

'Very good,' said Stryne. 'Give us half an hour.'

Velen carried a large tool-box which he lugged awkwardly as they mounted the stairs. On the third floor Stryne found the right door and knocked on it. When it opened, they both pushed their way inside.

Inpriss Sorce was carried back by their onrush. 'What – what do you want?' she demanded shrilly.

Their eyes flicked around the small apartment. Stryne looked at Inpriss, studying her face, his gaze roving up and down her body. He liked what he saw and was feeling a warm glow of anticipation.

Hulmu had chosen well. It was going to be good; Hulmu would be entertained.

The girl retreated to the far wall and put her hand to her throat. 'What do you want?' she repeated in a whisper. She had seen the expression in their eyes. 'Just tell me what you want.'

'This is the most important day of your life, lady,' Stryne told her. 'You're going to experience . . . what you never experienced before.'

They both took the black cloths from their pockets and draped them over their skulls.

Inpriss shrank back in horror. 'Oh, God! No! No!' She let out a weak scream, but before she could finish it they had seized her and Velen had clapped a hand over her mouth. She was trembling and almost unresisting as they carried her to a table from which Stryne swept cups and books. They placed her on it. Stryne took stout cord which he looped around the legs of the table and, using specially prescribed knots, caught her wrists and ankles.

When Velen took his hand from her mouth she no longer screamed. They rarely did; the appearance of the infamous Traumatic sect was calculated to inspire helpless terror. Instead she began to pray in a trembling, sobbing voice.

'It's no good praying to your God like that,' Stryne said conversationally. 'He doesn't exist, it's all a con. Before we've finished here you'll be praying to Hulmu, the authentic god who created us by projecting us on to the screen of reality.' He liked to engage the sacrificial victims in a dialogue, to establish a rapport with them.

Humming meditatively – a nervous habit that came over him at moments like this – he noted her carrying satchel lying on a chair. Caressingly he opened it and inspected the contents. Small personal effects, identification papers, a voucher for a bank account, money, and a few letters.

He placed the satchel on a ledge near the window.

They opened the tool-box and began taking out their equipment.

The girl ceased praying and lay gasping with fright. Stryne waved a meter near her head. Her fear index was high – nearly eighty. That was good.

'How are you going to do it?' she asked them. *'Please tell me how you're going to do it!'*

'Mmmmmm . . . There are so many ways. The knife, inserted slowly? The Terrible Vibrator? The Exit by Burning?' He showed her the various instruments one by one.

Her head had raised itself off the tabletop, straining, to look. Now it sank back again. Her face collapsed into despair.

Velen set up a hologram screen and a laser projector. The screen hovered slantwise over the girl like a descending wing. Velen flicked a switch; the screen came to life. The Impossible Shape of Hulmu gyrated and twisted hypnotically against a background of shifting moiré patterns. Stryne and Velen knelt on either side of the girl, watching her face, their backs to the screen.

'Hearken to Hulmu!' declared Stryne.

And the first of the ceremonies began.

Inpriss went into a slight trance brought on by the holo projection. In this state the words and responses from

Stryne and Velen penetrated deep into her consciousness.

'You are to be sacrificed to Hulmu,' Stryne told her. 'Your soul will not return through time to your body; you will never live again, as others do. You will belong to Hulmu. He will take you with him deep into the strat.'

'Hulmu will take you with him,' reiterated Velen in a sing-song voice.

'You must pray to Hulmu,' Stryne whispered in her ear. 'You belong to him now.'

While they intoned the rituals Velen switched on more of their apparatus. Devices gave out strange buzzes and clicks that grated on the nerves; alien whines filled the air. Stryne applied a prong to the girl's body and began delivering pain in intermittent, increasing amounts. Everything was designed so as to enhance the trauma, and Inpriss Sorce was now catalytic with terror.

She came out of the trance with a start and he let her see the Exit by Burning device ready for use in his hands. Her eyes widened and her face sagged. Her mouth opened but her voice was too paralysed to scream.

There came a knock on the outer door.

Stryne and Velen looked at each other. 'We'd better see what it is,' Stryne said.

They left the room, closing the door behind them, and paused. Stryne opened the door to the corridor.

The caser was there. 'You timed it nicely,' Stryne said to him.

They stood there, not speaking. Stryne bent his ear to the inner door. There was a scuffling from inside. Then he heard the window open.

A minute later they entered the room. Inpriss Sorce was gone. She had slipped the special knots Stryne had tied and escaped by the fire escape. With satisfaction he saw that she had shown the presence of mind to snatch up her satchel so that she would not be without resources.

'We made a good start,' he breathed.

The pursuit was in progress.

4

For some weeks Captain Aton had been forced to wear military prison garb. Now, on the day that his court-martial was due, the guards brought him his full duty uniform. He dressed slowly and carefully, but had no mirror in which to check his appearance.

The walls of his cell were made of grey metal, which reminded him of the starkly functional interior of the destroyer class of timeship in which he had served prior to his arrest. He missed the deep vibration of the time-drive, and even more so the sense of discipline and purpose that went with active service. Instead, his solitude was broken only by the shouts and clangings that made up the daily life of the prison. It depressed him to know that he was in company with deserters and various other malefactors. Occupying cells in his block were some religious offenders – members of the Traumatic sect – and Aton would hear their calls to Hulmu echoing through the night.

The Traumatic sect. That struck a chord in Aton's mind. A puzzled frown crossed his face as he tried to recollect why, but the answer eluded him.

He heard footsteps. The door of the cell grated open to reveal two burly guards and his defence counsel, a nervous young lieutenant.

Aton was already on his feet. At a signal from one of the guards he stepped into the passage.

'The court is convened, Captain,' the lieutenant said with a diffident cough. 'Shall we?'

They walked towards the court block ahead of the guards. Despite his predicament, Aton found time to feel some sympathy for his counsel, who was embarrassed at being in the company of a doomed man.

'We might have a chance,' the lieutenant said. 'The field-effect reading is in our favour. I shall argue incapacity.'

Aton nodded, but he knew that the hearing would go the same way that the earlier investigation had.

Gates swung and clanged as they were let out of the penitentiary area of the prison. An elevator took them further up the building and without further preamble they were admitted into the courtroom.

Aton was to be judged by a tribunal of three retired commanders. One glance at their seamed faces told him that they felt about the matter much as he would in their place: that there was no excuse for cowardice.

The prosecutor, an older and more practised man than Aton's counsel, turned suavely to regard the accused before reading out the charge.

'Captain Mond Aton, serving in His Chronotic Majesty's Third Time Fleet under Commander Veel Ark Haight, it is laid against you that on the eleventh day of cycle four-eight-five, fleet-time, you were guilty of cowardice and gross dereliction of duty in that, the vessel under your command being crippled by enemy action, you abandoned your ship the *Smasher of Enemies* ahead of your men; and further that you fought with the men under your command so as to board a life raft, thus saving yourself at their expense. How do you plead?'

The young lieutenant stepped forward. 'Sirs, I wish to tender that Captain Aton is unfit to plead, being the victim of amnesia.'

'I plead not guilty,' Aton contradicted firmly. 'I do not believe I am capable of the acts described.'

A faint sneer came to the prosecutor's lips. 'He does not believe he is capable!'

With a despairing shrug the counsel for the defence stepped back to his place.

Inexorably the prosecution proceeded to call witnesses. And so Aton was forced to experience what he had already experienced at the preliminary hearings. First to be called was Sergeant Quelle, his chief gunnery noncom. With blank bemusement he heard him recount how he, Aton, a beamer in each hand, had killed all who stood in his way in his haste to leave the foundering *Smasher of Enemies*. Occasionally Quelle glanced his way with what seemed to him a spiteful, fearful look. At those moments a double image flashed into Aton's mind: he seemed to see Quelle's face distended and made bulbous as if seen through a magnifying glass or through the visor of a strat suit. But the picture faded as soon as it was born, and he put it down to imagination.

Seven other witnesses, all crewmen from the *Smasher of Enemies*, followed Quelle. All repeated his tale, pausing sometimes to glare accusingly at their captain. They named the men and officers they had seen Aton gun down, and told how they had succeeded in disarming him only once the life raft was floating free in the strat and the *Smasher of Enemies* had broken up. Then, after an agonizing delay, they had eventually been located and picked up by the flagship. Aton had been arrested and sent to Chronopolis.

Of all this Aton remembered practically nothing. He could recall some details of the battle with the Hegemonics, in a confused kind of way, but it all had the aspects of a dream. As for the events Quelle and the others spoke of, it was just a blank to him. The only thing he could remember was coming to and finding that life raft 3 was being hauled inboard the *Lamp of Faith*, Commander Haight's flagship.

Could he really have murdered, among others, Lieutenant Krish? Could he have fallen prey to such animal panic, in the grip of some mental derangement, perhaps? If so, the derangement was still affecting him, for everything seemed still possessed of a dreamlike quality. He simply could not reconcile what was happening with his own image of himself, with his love of the Time Service, and with his loyalty to the empire.

The prosecutor conceded the floor to the defence. The young lieutenant called his one and only witness.

'Major Batol,' he said to the slim officer who entered, 'what is your function in the Time Service?'

'I am a doctor and surgeon.'

'Do you recognize the accused?'

The major eyed Aton briefly and nodded.

'Will you please tell us the result of your examination of Captain Aton earlier.'

Major Batol turned to the tribunal. 'I examined the captain with a field-effect device. This is a device that responds to the "field effect", that is to say the electrostatic nimbus that surrounds the human body and brain. By its means it is possible to ascertain a person's mental state and even what he is thinking, since thoughts and emotions leak into the field. The technique may be likened to eavesdropping on the operation of a computer by picking up its incidental electromagnetic transmissions—'

'Yes, you may spare us the explanations,' the head of the tribunal said sourly. 'Come to the point.'

'Captain Aton has total amnesia of the period under question,' Major Batol informed them.

'And what would be a likely cause of such amnesia?' asked the defence counsel.

'It is almost certainly traumatic in origin,' the major said. 'Remember that the destroyer was foundering into the strat. Anyone who happened, for only a moment, to see the strat with his bare eyes would undergo trauma sufficient to account for amnesia of this type.'

'Thank you, Major.'

The prosecutor was quick to come forward. 'Major Batol, would you say that a man suffering from the trauma you describe would be capable of purposeful action, such as fighting his way aboard a life raft?'

'It is highly unlikely that he would be capable of any action whatsoever, certainly not of an integrated kind.'

'And is there any evidence to say *at what point* in the proceedings this experience of Captain Aton's took place? Ten minutes before he entered the life raft? Five minutes before? *Or only a moment before?*'

'None. Traumatic amnesia can obliterate the events leading up to the trauma as well as those following it.'

'Thank you very much, Major.'

When the time came for him to sum up his case, Aton's counsel did the best he could. He began by speaking of Aton's excellent service record and of his three previous engagements, for one of which he had received a commendation. He stressed the fact of Aton's amnesia, trying to suggest that this threw something of a mystery over the whole affair.

'It is odd,' he said, 'that Captain Aton should be unable to make any reply to the accusations that are made against him. Finally—' he confronted the tribunal, his face white – 'I request that the witnesses for the prosecution should themselves undergo a field-effect test!'

The prosecutor jumped to his feet. 'The prosecution objects to that remark! The defence is imputing perjury in my witnesses!'

The tribunal chief shifted in his seat and looked grim. 'Use of the field-effect device is not recognized in civil law, and this tribunal takes its cue from the civil establishment where the laws of evidence are concerned,' he said to the defending lieutenant. 'Although we were prepared to listen to the opinion of Major Batol, in law the amnesia of your client has not itself been established. Your request is denied.'

That, Aton knew, had been the counsel's last desperate fling. The tribunal spent little time deliberating its decision. When the commanders returned from the inner chamber, the tribunal head looked at Aton with no hint of compassion.

'Captain Mond Aton, we find you guilty. The evidence of eight independent witnesses can hardly be gainsaid. As for the effort by the defence to suggest your actions were the result of a personality change, and thereby to mitigate your guilt, that argument cannot be accepted. Even if true, it remains that an officer named Captain Aton committed the offences, and an officer named Captain Aton stands before us now. Personality changes are not admitted in an officer of the Time Service.'

He paused before coming to his grave conclusion. 'Your sentence is the only one that can be expected. From here you will be taken to the laboratories of the Courier Department, where you will perform your last service to the empire. And may God restore your soul.'

As he was led away, Aton passed by Sergeant Quelle who was sitting in the anteroom alongside the others who had given evidence against him. They all – Quelle especially – looked at him with glittering eyes. They could not hide their triumph.

'Most unusual,' murmured the technician.

He was sitting casually across from Aton in the briefing-room. 'I think this is the first time I've had to deal with someone of your calibre,' he said. 'Mostly we get common murderers, thieves, petty traitors – scum like that.'

He eyed Aton with unveiled curiosity. His manner was relaxed and he seemed to think of his job as a mildly interesting technical exercise instead of as the bizarre method of execution which it was to be for Aton.

'I'm supposed to teach you as much as you need to know to perform your task properly,' the technician resumed, 'but as a chronman yourself you hardly need to be told very much, of course.'

'All chronmen fear the strat,' Aton said emptily. 'It surrounds us. We never forget that.'

'Are you afraid?'

'Yes.'

The other nodded. 'You're right to be. It is fearful. This business is worse for you than it is for some criminal of low intelligence, I can see that. Still, we all have our job to do.'

He doesn't pity me, Aton thought. He has no sympathy for me at all. He's probably processed hundreds of men – it doesn't mean anything to him any more.

The technician came around the table and placed a head-set over Aton's cranium. He felt electrodes prodding his scalp. The other retreated back to his chair and glanced at tracer dials, making entries on a sheet of paper.

'Good,' he announced. 'Your cephalic responses are adequate – we'd expect them to be, wouldn't we? Some of the dimmer types get out of this business by not having the alertness to be able to target themselves once we put them through. So it's the gas chamber for them.'

'How soon?' grated Aton.

'Hm?'

'*When do I go through?*'

'Oh—' the technician glanced at his watch – 'in about an hour.'

Aton steeled his nerves to face the coming ordeal. He had been languishing for nearly a week since his trial, waiting for his name to be called. Despite that the department dispatched a daily stream of messages to the distant time-fleets it never seemed to run short of couriers.

He reminded himself that he had been in the strat before – millions of times, in fact. Everybody had. Only nobody remembered it. When the body died, the soul, robbed of the body's existential support, found itself in the strat. That was what caused death trauma – the bedazzlement of the soul when faced by potential time. But because it had nowhere to exist apart from the body, and even though shock reduced it to a state midway between unconsciousness and a dream-like trance, it hurried back along its time-track, experiencing its life in reverse at a tremendously speeded-up rate like a video-tape on rewind, until it reached the moment of conception. At which point it began to live again.

Thus Aton's imminent punishment would be something like the experience of death, except that not simply his soul but his body too was to be catapulted into the strat, and except that he would be pumped full of drugs to keep him conscious even under the impact of unspeakable trauma. An unconscious courier would be no good; he would not be able to guide himself towards his destination.

While the technician continued marking his papers, Aton began to speak in a low, haunted voice.

'Scientists have debated whether the strat really exists as an independent continuum,' he murmured, 'or whether it is only an apparency our own machines have created; merely the result of that crucial act of accelerating pi-mesons faster than light. In the Time Service we are accustomed to thinking of the strat as an ocean, with orthogonal time as its surface . . . but perhaps the strat is only the world itself, scrambled and twisted because one no longer obeys its laws.'

The other man looked up, fascinated to hear this talk from one of the couriers. It was an unusual reaction; commonly three men or more were needed to hold them down.

'The Church has an answer to that, at any rate,' he pointed out to Aton. 'The strat is real, but not as real as the world of actual time.'

'Yes . . . the Church has an answer for everything,' Aton replied, only slightly cynically. 'The strat is the Holy Ghost, connecting God with the world. In the Time Service one inclines to take a more pragmatic view. Now that I am to be exposed unprotected to what chronmen fear most, it's not surprising if my mind dwells on what its true nature might be.'

'Your collected state of mind is, if I may say so, admirable,' the technician admitted. 'In your place, however, I would not be disposed to take the teachings of the Church so lightly. A comforter will be at hand at your dispatch to offer final consolation. Need I point out that the view you have just put forward – that the strat does not exist apart from the visible world – denies the Holy Ghost and is tantamount to materialistic atheism?'

A mocking smile played around the technician's mouth and Aton realized the man was toying with him. He remained silent.

'In any case,' the technician continued after a pause, 'the strat would appear to be what you called it just now:

an ocean of potential time. For one thing, it has depth. It's some years since the Church forbade any further deep-diving expeditions, but no doubt you know what happened to the earlier ones. The pressure of potential time gets stronger the deeper you go. Some of the ships had their ortho fields crushed.'

Aton shuddered slightly.

'Do you resent what's happening to you?' the technician asked.

Aton shook his head, shrugging. 'They say that I am a coward and a murderer. I don't know if it's true or not. But if it is, then this is just . . . for an officer.' If he truly thought that he had committed those crimes, then he would almost have welcomed the punishment as a chance to redeem himself.

The technician rose. 'Over here, please.'

A high-backed chair with dangling straps stood on the other side of the room. The two guards pinned Aton's arms to his sides and forced him into it. The straps passed across his chest and over his thighs and forearms.

'When your mission is accomplished you are instructed to die,' the technician said softly. 'The method will be the simple and direct one of vagal inhibition. To that end we will now implant a trigger word with which, at the appropriate time, you can excite your own vagus nerve and stop your heart.'

A needle pricked Aton's arm. A coloured disc began to rotate in front of his eyes, attracting his gaze and holding it even against his will. A voice murmured soothingly in his ear.

Presently Aton fell asleep.

VOM.

When he awoke the word lay somewhere in his mind like a dead weight. He was vaguely aware of it, but he was unable to speak it, either aloud or mentally. That would not be possible until a certain phrase, spoken by a voice he would recognize when he heard it, released the word from its confinement.

The coloured disc wheeled away. In its place was put a more elaborate piece of apparatus that included, on the end of a flexible cable, what looked like the helmet of a diving-suit without a face-plate.

The technician glanced at his watch again and became more animated. 'Time presses on. The dispatches you are to carry have already arrived. Now then. There are two reasons why we have to use live couriers to communicate with the time-fleets, and why those couriers have to be expendable. In the early days we tried other means – fast launches and one-man boats. But the time-drive is too bulky and expensive for such an application, especially if it is to have sufficient speed. So we evolved the method that will propel you. A massive generator will build up tremendous potential; that energy will be used to catapult you through the strat at high speed – much faster even than a battleship can move – and will give you sufficient momentum to reach your destination.

'At first this method was tried out on unmanned missiles and even men in strat suits, but they would not do. The missiles got lost without a hand to guide them through the strat's turbulence. A strat suit falls down on several counts: it's bulky and so raises the energy requirement, its batteries would be able to maintain an ortho field only over short journeys anyway, and in any case using a strat suit defeats the whole object of the exercise because a courier needs to see the strat with his own eyes. It might work if we could include a scan screen such as a timeship has, but the weight of that would be prohibitive.

'You will have *some* equipment with you, which will help you steer yourself towards your target. But what all this means is that for a while you're going not just to *see* but to *live* in nonsequential strat time: in four-dimensional and five-dimensional time. No one can tell you what that will be like. Nevertheless we have to train you as well as we can so you'll be able to carry out your task.'

The diving-helmet was lifted over Aton's head to rest on his shoulders on a harness of foam rubber. He was in darkness. The technician's voice came to him again, tinnily through the tiny earphones.

'The purpose of this apparatus is to familiarize you, however inadequately, with what you will see immediately on entering the strat. It's a mock-up, of course, since we cannot reproduce the real thing. The important thing for you to learn is how to keep your direction. Remember that reaching your destination is the only way you can ever leave the strat, and therefore *the only way you can ever die.* This, I assure you, will become your most vital concern.'

Suddenly Aton was assailed by an explosion of sense impressions. So meaningless were they that they seemed to be pulling each of his eyes in separate directions. He closed his eyes for a few moments, but when he opened them again the barrage had increased in intensity. A steady bleeping sound was in his ears.

He felt as though he was swaying back and forth.

Eventually he began to glimpse recognizable shapes that emerged out of the welter of images and just as quickly vanished again. At this point the technician's voice entered again and in persuasive tones provided a running commentary.

The ordeal continued for about half an hour. The technician taught him how to know when he had changed direction from his appointed course and how to correct it with the equipment he would be given. At last the helmet was lifted from his head and the restricting straps unfastened. Somewhat disoriented, Aton rose.

'Well, you seem to have got the hang of it,' the technician announced.

'Half an hour's training? You really think that is enough?' Aton asked in a blurred voice.

'Perfectly. Your mission is not too difficult. Merely harrowing.'

Aton was trying to form an idea that had just occurred to him. 'Why . . . do we have to die?'

The other looked at him, puzzled. 'You are condemned men.'

'I know that. But why such an elaborate method? Oh, I know the practical reason for the hypnotic conditioning: men of the Time Service should not have to dirty their hands by executing condemned criminals. So the criminals have to do it themselves. But why are you so careful to ensure that the couriers should die *after only one trip*? Why not use them again? It seems to me that their usefulness is not finished.'

The technician looked thoughtful and withdrawn. 'There is no doubt, a reason,' he murmured. 'Frankly, I do not know what it is. But everything has a reason. I never heard of anyone going into the strat twice.'

'The fleet commanders have strict orders not to allow a courier to live after arrival, not even for a few hours. Why? What would be the harm?'

'An act of mercy, perhaps.' The technician glanced up at a winking light on the wall. 'It's time to fit you out.'

A section of wall slid aside. Aton, the two guards at his back, followed the technician into a narrow circular tunnel that sloped sharply downward. They emerged after a few minutes into a place totally unlike the clinical briefing-room Aton had just left. It was a large area with walls of flat, grey metal. A heavy droning hum came from an incredible array of equipment that took up the further end of the space.

The power of the droning sound struck right into Aton's bones. He gazed briefly at a large circular metal hatch that was clamped to the far wall with bolts and fitted with view windows. Then he was being tugged to one side where white-coated men eyed him speculatively.

A hoarse shout made him look to the other end of the room. A bizarrely accoutred figure was being dragged struggling towards the metal hatch. The man wore what appeared to be a tray, or small control board, extending outwards from his waist. His face was obscured by a rubber breathing-mask, and his body was criss-crossed with straps. Alongside the trio of prisoner and guards, contrasting with their exertions, paced the calm figure of a comforter, sprinkling holy wine from an aspersorium.

The muffled shouts grew more desperate as the disc of steel swung open. With practised skill the courier was eased inside and the hatch bolts screwed tight.

'That's more commonly the manner of their exit,' the technician remarked to Aton. 'I may say I find it a pleasure to be dealing with someone who has more nerve.'

Aton ignored the praise. The humming sound swelled, grew to climactic proportions, then ended in a noise like a prolonged lightning strike, accompanied by a vivid flash from within the dispatch chamber.

A singing silence followed. For some moments the air was charged with energy.

The technicians began to equip Aton for his journey. First the dispatch case was strapped to his chest. Then came the tray-like control panel, fastened around his waist so as to bring its knobs within easy reach of his hands.

During the session under the simulator Aton had been told that he would be aware of his proper course by reason of something mysteriously described as 'like a wind blowing in your face'. This wind represented his initial momentum. The control tray was a device acting like a rudder; it would enable him to guide himself along his course like a speedboat.

He felt the prick of hypodermic needles as stimulative drugs were pumped into his veins. An oxygen mask and earphones were added.

The comforter appeared by his side and began to murmur words he could scarcely hear. He felt the cold touch of drops of wine. He was ready.

The steel hatch swung open.

As he was propelled unresistingly towards the hatch and glimpsed the narrow rivet-studded chamber it guarded, a fog seemed to dissipate from his mind. Suddenly, and for the first time, he understood clearly and vividly just what was happening to him.

And he understood why!

His amnesia lifted like a curtain. He recalled the terrible events on board the *Smasher of Enemies*: his discovery of heresy within his command, the repeated savage hammer blows sustained by the ship, and Sergeant Quelle in a strat suit striding along surrounded by fellow heretics.

The rest was plain. Who had put him aboard the life raft he did not know – his memory ended some time before that – but evidently the heretics had reached the raft too. They must have suffered agony to realize that once they were rescued Aton could denounce them, and his subsssequent amnesia must have seemed almost miraculous to them. They had taken full advantage of it, bringing their false charges against him so as to rid themselves of a potential accuser. A desperate, daring manoeuvre.

And what had caused Aton's loss of memory? *A glimpse of the strat.*

Would he recognize it a second time?

He turned, about to say something even as he realized that it was too late now to offer the truth. But he was given no time to speak. They bundled him through the circular hatch and swiftly screwed it up behind him.

He stood in a replica of the standard octagonal execution chamber. Death seemed to seep visibly into the cramped space from the leaden walls, which gave the appearance of being several feet thick. There was a peculiar tension in the air he had experienced only once before: when he had helped to remove the protective shields from an operating time-drive to effect emergency repairs.

A face peered in at him through the view window, distorted and blurred by the immensely thick plate. As the powerful generators swung into action a drumming noise assailed Aton, making the walls vibrate. The noise built up, deafening him. Despite the oxygen mask a feeling of suffocation seized him. He felt as though he had been seized by a giant hand that squeezed, squeezed, squeezed—

And then a numbing blow hit him on all sides at once and the chamber vanished. He had the impression of being shot forward at tremendous speed as though out of the mouth of a cannon.

Utter darkness. Blinding light. Which was it?

It was neither. It was whirlpools of the inconceivable. It was visions which the eye accepted but which the brain found unrecognizable: reality without the sanity that made reality real. The brain reacted to these visions with terror and dwindled in on itself to seek refuge in death or unconsciousness. Such sanctuary was denied Aton, however. The drugs that coursed in his blood pre-empted the closing down of the mind and condemned it to full alertness.

Yet alongside this jarring shock was a start of recognition. He *remembered* it now. This was what he had seen for a bare instant aboard the *Smasher of Enemies*.

Aton went reeling and spinning on a five-dimensional geodesic. There was no point of comparison to the space or time that he knew. The wind of the strat blew against his face like a cloying mist composed of ghostly pseudo-events, and whenever it ceased or lessened, his hands went instinctively to the control knobs at his waist.

But this phase, in which his mind still clung to its allegiance to passing time, lasted only seconds. Then the continuum of the strat seeped into his every cell and time ceased.

Eternity began, and Aton's sanity disintegrated.

Luckily one did not need to be sane to accomplish one's mission. One needed to know that there was an escape, that one could die. One needed to know that failure would mean to sink endlessly into the strat.

Therein lay the cunning of the courier system. Neither the senses nor the intellect could understand the environment in which they found themselves, but some primeval instinct enabled the mind to find a direction. The courier strove with all his being to reach the distant receiving station where he would be permitted to stop his heart.

Until that goal was attained, Aton lived in a world that was timeless. He could not measure the duration of his journey either in seconds or in centuries, because there *was* no duration. There could be no such thing as duration without a before and an after, and in this state nothing preceded and nothing followed. He skirled and spun. He went through titanic processes where five-dimensional objects menaced him as though they were living beings, but nothing began and nothing ended.

After a while his brain seemed to revive and to attempt to recover its old mode of perception. It was, he realized, beginning to come to terms with the five-dimensional strat and to abstract three-dimensional worlds from it.

Captain Mond Aton lived his life over again, beginning with conception and ending with his being sealed into the dispatch chamber at Chronopolis. After that, everything was just a vague shadow.

The illusion – could it be called an illusion? – was absolutely real. Every incident, every pleasure, every pain and every effort exercised his soul anew. And not merely once. His life became like a film strip and was run through hundreds, thousands, millions of times over. The continued, reiterated experience became unbearable.

Interspersed with this continual re-enactment were other experiences that were more or less intelligible. At first he thought he had somehow been dumped back into orthogonal time in a different body and a different life. But soon he realized that the dreamlike episodes that so much resembled events in the real world were phantoms: mock-ups located in the strat. The strat was eternity. And eternity, as he had learned at training college, was the storehouse of potentialities. Somewhere in this vast insubstantial ocean were mock-ups of everything existing in orthogonal time, as well as of every fictitious variation of what existed. And also there were mock-ups of that which did not exist but which could be thrown up into the world like flotsam on a beach by some convulsion of the strat.

After enduring all this for millenniums, or microseconds, an odd feeling of strength came over Aton. The strat was no longer so strange to him. It was as if *he himself* was transforming into a five-dimensional being. He was able to look down on his life as an entirety and give his attention to any part of it.

Sequential time would seem, after this, flat and narrow. But his fingers still moved over the steering controls. His mind still strove to release itself in the only way possible.

His target, a fleet of timeships, loomed ahead of him. Protected by their own orthogonal time-fields they stood out clearly as glowing solid bodies surrounded by the swirling strat. Aton's earphones were beeping as he came within range of the homing signal.

Then he whirled around as something darted in suddenly from one side. It was the image of a man, which he saw sometimes as a three-dimensional figure and sometimes as a four-dimensional extension. The man was burly, bedecked like a stage magician in a flowing cloak and coloured hose. In place of eyes his sockets were filled with glittering, flashing jewels. He grinned wolfishly at Aton, at the same time directing a bazooka-like tube from which issued a billowing exudation.

The purple mist struck Aton like a physical force. He felt his whole body vibrate; he veered aside to avoid the attack.

The intruder lunged at him again. Hissing, the bazooka tube went into action for a second time, and Aton saw that what it actually did was to distort the substance of the strat. With alarm he felt himself being sucked into the turbulence; he worked his rudder controls frantically.

Then both the apparition and the strat fled. He stood limply in a steel-clad chamber identical to the one he had

left an eternity ago, and a loud humming noise filled his
ears.

Just before the grinning jewel-eyed man had pounced
Aton had recognized the galleon-like battle wagon that
was to receive him. As irony would have it, the ship was
Commander Haight's *Lamp of Faith*.

5

Exhausted with fear and fatigue, Inpriss Sorce collapsed
with a sigh on to a rickety couch. She pushed straggled
hair out of her eyes and looked around the cheap, dismal
room she had just rented.

The two weeks since she had escaped from Chronopolis
had nearly driven her insane.

It was lucky she had the satchel containing money and
bank cards from her apartment in Kell Street, otherwise she would have been completely helpless. Her one
thought had been to flee as far away as possible. Everyone
knew that once the Traumatic sect had chosen someone
for sacrifice they would do everything possible to track
the victim down and complete the rite.

Briefly it had occurred to her to go to the police with
her story, but she had heard of people who had done that
. . . only to be sacrificed by Traumatics inside the police
force once they were taken into protective custody. The
vision of some stone cell from which she could not escape
filled her with claustrophobic panic.

No. The only answer was flight. To hide, to become
too small to be noticed.

Only it was so difficult! This was already her third
hiding place since quitting the eternal city, and the third
time she had changed her name. The first move had been
to a town barely fifty miles from Chronopolis, and for a
few hours her eagerness to be safe had fooled her into

thinking that she *was* safe. Then, coming home to her new apartment, she had spotted the two men who had tortured her, walking down the street and glancing up at the houses one by one.

And so she had had to leave, after only one day. But that had not been the end of it. She had left Amerik and gone to Affra, but they had followed. By good chance she had caught glimpses of them several times and so had been warned – in the jetliner passenger lounge and hanging around the transit and accommodation centres. And so finally, not caring about the expense, she had taken several jetliner trips in quick succession, zigzagging about the globe to shake off pursuit before retreating here to an old, out-of-the-way city in the middle of Worldmass.

Besides the two men she knew – Stryne and Velen, they had called each other – how many others she would not recognize had kept watch for her and hunted her down using all the methods that could be used to find a person? By now she had become afraid of everyone and everything.

She wondered if it was possible to live with terror indefinitely.

Idly her thoughts turned to the Church. Could a comforter help her? But churches would be dangerous places to approach. The sect could be watching. As it was, for the first time she felt some relief. Virov was well off the main routes and this tiny room, in a back street away from the main thoroughfares, had a closed-in, cupboard-like feeling. The narrow window admitted no direct sunlight at any time of the day and that, too, gave her a perverse feeling of safety, as if it was a room the world could not see.

She would get a job, would survive somehow. She would make no friends for years to come.

She opened the window and relaxed with the sound of the breeze and with Virov's quaint, well-melded odours.

Then she heard a nervous, tuneless humming from the other side of the door.

Mmmmmmmmm . . .

With a fear-stricken cry she flung herself against the door, trying with her body to hold it closed. Her slight frame was far from sufficient to resist the force that pushed it open from the other side.

The feral-faced Stryne moved into the room, followed by Velen.

'Nice to see you, Inpriss. Let's carry on where we left off, shall we?'

For an hour they enjoyed themselves with her, going through the ceremonies slowly. The hologram screen pounded out a sensuous, sinister mood, showing Hulmu in a playful aspect and filling the room with weird light. They went through the litanies that reminded Inpriss Sorce of what awaited her soul in the depths of the strat, where Hulmu would use her for his own purposes, and they urged her to forsake and vilify the false god of the Church.

After the Sporting of Shocks, where mild electric currents were applied to various parts of the body at random, they decided to carry out the Ritual of Mounting. First Stryne had intercourse with her and then Velen, while they both chanted the Offering of Orgasm.

Panting and sighing with satisfaction, they paused for a while, looking down at the glazy-eyed woman.

'That's enough for here,' Stryne said. 'They want to finish the rituals in the local temple.'

'We have to move her?'

Stryne nodded.

Velen frowned petulantly. 'Why didn't you tell me before? I thought this was going to be our show.'

Stryne shrugged. 'They have some special equipment they want to use. It will be spicy. Come on, help me get her ready.'

'Now listen, lady,' Stryne said when they had dressed her and put her on her feet, 'we're going to take a short walk. Act normal and don't try to scream for help, because we'll only use a narco-spray on you and get you there anyway.' He shoved her satchel into her hand. 'Right, let's move.'

Velen had finished packing their equipment into his tool-box. They went down the wooden stairs and out on to the street, which was overhung with tall silent houses and wound down a steep incline.

Inpriss walked as if in a dream. The air was heavy. Virov was a city totally unlike Chronopolis. Thick scents cloyed along its antique streets and alleys: the smell of coffee, of spices, of exotic blossoms. In other circumstances she would have liked it here.

Perhaps she could commit suicide, she thought wildly. Killing herself would be one way of saving herself from whatever horrible thing it was the Traumatics would do to her soul at death. Would she have the opportunity? But then she remembered that if she succeeded in dying free from their attentions, her soul would travel back in time and she would live her life again.

Would it end with this same nightmare? A curious thought occurred to her. If the Traumatics gave her soul to Hulmu she would not repeat. Inpriss Sorce would vanish from ordinary time. Did that mean that the Traumatics had never before, in her previous repetitions, threatened her? She tried to imagine what kind of life stretched ahead of her without their intervention.

Or had they always chosen her for a victim? And had she always cheated them by committing suicide? The eternal recurrence of this nightmare was, in itself, a horrible thing to contemplate.

They emerged on to one of the town's main concourses, close to the bazaar, and walked past open-fronted shops, many of them selling handmade wares. The street was quite crowded. Stryne and Velen stuck close to her, one on each side. Stryne nudged her warningly whenever she faltered.

Suddenly a commotion erupted from a side street. A gang of brawling youths swayed and spilled on to the sidewalk. Inpriss felt herself jostled and pushed roughly aside. A bottle narrowly missed her face and thudded on the head of a ginger-haired young man who was punching someone else in the stomach.

Stryne clutched at her with a snarl, and then, with a feeling of wonderment, Inpriss realized that she had been separated from her captors. Bewildered, unable to make sense out of noise and confusion, she struggled through a tangle of violent bodies. Something struck her a blow on the face.

Uncertainly she stood for a moment on the edge of the crowd. She caught a glimpse of Velen trying to ward off blows from an acned thug.

Then she ran and, unable to believe her freedom but exulting in it, ran and ran without pause.

The Internodal travel official was a pinch-faced man wearing a shot peaked cap. He was circumspect when Inpriss tendered her application and read it slowly while rapping his fingers on the desk.

'The travel quotas have been cut down, citizeness,' he told her coldly, 'due to the hostilities.' He peered closer at the form. '"Reason for journey: migration." You intend to live in Revere?'

'Yes.'

'Why?'

'I just—' Inpriss wrung her hands. She hadn't known these it would be like this.

She had got out of Virov in disguise, buying a ticket on a charabanc, and had tried to settle in a smaller town a few hundred miles away. But the Traumatic sect had caught up with her *again*!

For the third time she had escaped, again by a lucky accident. Her tormentors hadn't known there was a back way out of the house, through a door hidden by a curtain. A few minutes after their arrival they had left her alone for a moment to carry in a box. She had slipped away.

To escape three times! It seemed miraculous to Inpriss.

Perhaps God was helping her, she thought, but she couldn't depend on miracles. It had become plain that the Traumatics could find her in any part of world. Only one other recourse was open: to flee into the future and hope that the Traumatics could not, or would not, pursue her down the centuries. She had returned to Chronopolis with the intention of boarding a chronliner.

But it was dangerous and more difficult than she had anticipated. To obtain a permit to leave Node I she had to use her real name. And the official was proving obstructive.

'I *have* to leave,' she pleaded desperately. 'There are some people I have to get away from!'

The official looked at her expectantly.

She fumbled in her satchel. 'Look, this is all I have, except for the fare. Five hundred notes. I'll land in Revere with nothing.'

She laid the money on his desk. The official coughed, then began shuffling his papers, tidying up the desk. When he had finished, the money had magically vanished.

'It's not really in order . . . but I think I can stretch a point for a charmer like you.' He winked at her, his manner suddenly cheery and patronizing in a way that filled her with disgust.

He filled out her travel permit and she hurried to the offices of Buick Chronways, one of the three commercial enterprises that had imperial charters for internodal services. There was a chronliner due to leave in a few hours, and she spent the remaining time walking the streets, keeping always to busy places.

It was dark by the time she went to the big terminus. As she passed through the barriers and set off down the long boarding ramp she could see the chronliner towering up out of its well. It had none of the grey-clad grimness of the military vessels of even greater size. Though of the same general design, it was covered with brightwork and along the flank of its upper storey the name *Buick* stood out in flowing graceful letters.

With a rush of hope, feeling the press of the crowd around her, she moved towards the humming timeship.

6

The crew of the receiving chamber took Aton out of it quickly, silently and efficiently.   .

They entered wearing strat suits, because the chamber was always partially energized in readiness for any couriers that might be *en route*. Once through the hatch Aton was relieved of his equipment: the tray-like rudder control, the oxygen mask, and the earphones. The dispatch case they left strapped to him. No one could handle that but the commander whose duty it was to accept all messages from a courier personally.

Aton, meantime, stood staring blankly with arms akimbo, not speaking, not moving.

Two ensigns came up to either side of him and took a light grip of his upper arms. A door slid open. They urged him forward. They were used to this detail. For a while newly arrived couriers were quite helpless, were scarcely able to keep their balance, bumped into walls, could not find their way through doors.

Dimly Aton sensed all around him the regular activity of the gigantic flagship, which was much bigger than the destroyers he was familiar with.

Steadily they mounted through the pile of decks and storeys, riding on elevators and moving corridors. The chronmen they passed flicked one glance at Aton, then looked away. Everyone was embarrassed to stare at a man who had just died, and was about to die again.

Aton's consciousness seemed to have retreated a long way from his perceptions, as though in using his senses he was looking the wrong way through a telescope. At the same time everything had a curiously flat, two-dimensional appearance to him. In the strat his mind had begun to accustom itself to four-dimensional, even five-dimensional figures. By comparison the three-dimensional world was weirdly listless, a series of simplified cartoons drawn on paper. No depth. Sounds, too, were flat and empty, without resonance.

He was feeling an urge to leave this paper world. To complete the process that had begun with his being discharged from the dispatch chamber.

To die.

They came to the officers' quarters in the upper reaches of the timeship. Aton recognized hints of comfort that would have been out of place aboard his own *Smasher of Enemies* or even aboard most battleships. Then they went through some double doors into an area displaying real, though modest, luxury, such as would not be found anywhere in the Time Service except in one of the great flagships.

It was Commander Haight's private suite. They halted before a walnut door carved with simple designs. The ensigns knocked, entered, saluted, and departed. Aton faced his former commanding officer.

Haight, sitting at a mahogany table, looked at him gloomily, broodingly. From a replayer in a corner came quiet, moody music, viols and trombones convoluting a web of melancholy calm.

Standing near Haight was a man Aton knew as Colonel Anamander. Like Haight he had the granite impassivity common to many senior officers in the Time Service, but his features were more amenable, slightly less uncompromising.

Haight lifted a hand in a half-hearted gesture. 'Later, Colonel.'

'Yes, sir.' Anamander skirted around Aton and exited.

The commander rose and approached Aton, who stared straight ahead, the muscles of his face slack. As if he were an inanimate object Haight unstrapped the dispatch case from his chest and carried it to the table.

Before opening it he glanced up at Aton again and suddenly his eyes narrowed in recognition.

'Captain Aton, is it not?'

After a long pause Aton forced his larynx into action. 'Sir,' he croaked feebly.

'Captain Aton,' Haight repeated sourly to himself. 'An extraordinary case. One that surprised and distressed me a good deal. I have wondered if you would end up here.'

Aton found his voice. 'Am I to terminate my life now, sir?' He waited expectantly for Haight to pronounce the releasing words.

'Wait until I am ready,' snapped the commander. He eyed Aton calculatingly, then sat down and broke the seals on the dispatch case.

For what seemed like a long time he studied the papers he found within, and outwardly became oblivious of Aton's presence. The viols and trombones pursued each other unendingly through winding, cloying themes, and listening to the music, Aton found himself drifting back to a seemingly strat-like state. There was no before or after. The intricate melody hung on the air like a perfume and Aton stood stock-still in an eternal moment, unable to locate the transition between one note and another.

Commander Haight jutted out his lower lip as he finished studying the papers. He laid them aside, frowning. Then he leaned back in his chair. His grey eyes settled on Aton's face, concentrating there with an almost obsessive interest.

'The dispatches originate from the emperor himself,' he announced gruffly. 'The raid into Hegemonic territory is to take place. And the *Lamp of Faith*, no less, is to conduct the mission. That, surely, is a measure of its importance.'

Aton said nothing and Haight continued, his eyes never leaving the other's face. 'Do you realize how successful the Hegemonics' attacks have been over the past week or two? Cities and regions eliminated or mutated. At

Node Five the entire continent of Australos was altered. It is now peopled by tribes of Stone Age aborigines. Even worse, there are numerous cases of causal discontinuity. You know what that can do to the fabric of time. The work of the Historical Office is being set at naught. And all due to the Hegemonics' new weapon, the time-distorter. Once our scientists had called such a device impossible. Now—' He spread his hands.

His gaze became heavy, penetrating. 'Speak, Captain Aton,' he said in a deep voice. 'Tell me what it is like in the strat.'

Aton blinked and stuttered. 'It is – it is—'

He fell silent.

Haight nodded. 'I know that it is beyond description. And yet something could be described. Words are never entirely useless. Try to collect your thoughts. To remember. Take possession of yourself once again. Speak, Captain.'

Aton struggled, then said, 'Sir, should I terminate my existence now?'

'Ah, you wish to obey your orders and escape this realm. And it is my beholden duty to see that you do. Yet I could not tell you how many times I have been tempted to forget my duty at these moments. There is a comforter at the Imperial Palace – Brother Mundan is his name – whose father fell into the strat some years ago, following a collision between timeships. Mundan cannot forget the strat since then. He dreams of it, has nightmares about it, tries to imagine what the Gulf of Lost Souls is like. After a lifetime in the service I am filled with a similar curiosity.'

The drift of Haight's speech came through only faintly to Aton.

'Most of the couriers who stand before me are, of course, low types,' the commander continued. 'Mentally degenerate, hopeless cases. But you, I tell myself, are of different mettle. Despite your astonishing dereliction, you are presumably a disciplined officer. Given time, you might recover your senses. You might be able to answer my questions.'

He lumbered to his feet, walked around the polished table, and stood close to Aton, peering straight into his eyes. 'On this occasion I think I will commit a dereliction of my own. At such a time – for in my opinion the raid had little chance of succeeding, it is suicide – a small peccancy will go unnoticed. No, Captain Aton, you are not to die now. You are to live, to recover, and perhaps to tell me what you have experienced.' He turned and pressed a button.

'This is Captain Aton,' he said to the two batmen who entered at his summons. 'See that he is made comfortable in the guest bedrooms. But do not allow him to leave this suite.'

Blood was pounding in Aton's veins as he was led away. This turn of events went entirely against his indoctrination. He felt his nerves falling apart as the death wish, thwarted of its expectation, began to burn up his brain.

Planning the raid occupied Commander Haight and his staff for a whole day.

The information contained in Aton's dispatch was less precise than might have been hoped for. The base from which the Hegemonics carried out their attacks when using the distorter was named, but there was very little guidance as to where on the base it was kept or on what would be found there.

To raid an operational military base was a requirement of no mean order, which was the reason why the *Lamp of Faith* had been selected even at the risk of losing the flagship. It had the speed, the firepower, and could carry a sufficient number of fighting men to hold the base for a short while.

For there was even more at stake than the increasingly unstable situation within the empire. The Historical

Office was determined to acquire a sample of the time-distorter before the Hegemonics, overwhelmed by the might of the armada, decided to destroy it. Possession of the distorter, or rather of the principle by which it worked, opened up limitless possibilities for the easy restructuring of history.

Aton, meanwhile, spent the time lying on his bed and staring at the ceiling. Gradually his mind began to clear. Little by little he felt as though he was being reinserted into the world of orthogonal time. But he still behaved like a robot or a zombie. The batmen brought him meals; he ate nothing. They asked if he wanted anything; he made no answer.

He felt as though his body was made of dead flesh, his mind of dead thoughts.

Eventually Commander Haight walked into his room unannounced. 'Well, how are you feeling?' he demanded gruffly.

Aton was silent.

Haight walked over to him and peered down. He poked Aton in the chest, as though making sure he was still alive. He grunted.

'I'm no psychologist. God knows what those hypnotic commands will do to you while I'm fouling up the programme. Still, even that should be interesting to watch.' Haight sighed. 'You know, I'm curious to know why couriers *have* to die. Something of a mystery surrounds it. The instructions are very strict – I'll be in serious trouble if this business gets back to Chronopolis – but nobody will tell you the reason. As far as I'm able to ascertain, it's a Church secret.'

He paused thoughtfully. 'I'm tired of seeing you in that convict's garb. Let's go the whole hog.' Turning his head he let out a bellow.

'Sturp!'

Instantly one of the batmen appeared. 'Sir?'

'Go and fetch a captain's uniform somewhere, to fit Aton here.' He threw himself into a deep chair. 'Maybe it will help you get your bearings,' he remarked, 'if the cloth of the service doesn't unnerve you. Tell me, do you feel any disgrace over what you did?'

'Did?'

'Shooting down your own men! Deserting your ship!' Haight was in an aggressive mood. His face went slightly purple as he roared the accusations at Aton.

'No, sir.' He strove to recall the events he should feel ashamed of, but for the moment could not.

Haight leaned forward earnestly. 'The strat,' he urged. 'Try to describe it now.'

Aton looked up at the ceiling. His mouth opened and closed. He licked his lips.

'One sees one's life, not as a process, but as an object,' he said. 'Something that can be picked up, handled, remoulded like a piece of clay.'

Haight laughed shortly.

'Would you like to die?' he asked after a moment.

'Yes.'

'*Why?*'

'When you have lived through your life millions, billions of times in every detail, the purpose of living is exhausted. There is nothing left that's new. One wants only to forget, to find oblivion; that way, if one must live again, one will not realize it's for the billionth time. It will seem new.'

'Death is the only positive experience remaining?'

'One has been cheated. Death is an event; once begun it should be completed. Mine was only partial death. It yearns to be complete. I must die naturally, so as to forget.'

Haight mulled over his words. 'Mm. It seems that our couriers are more fortunate, after all, than the poor chronmen who drown in eternity when their ships go down.' He shot Aton a look of contempt. 'What is the strat? How would you describe it?'

'It is a place of terror.'

With a slightly bleary look Haight climbed to his

feet. 'Don't be too sure you've seen the last of it. We move out in an hour. I'm going to get some rest till then.'

The big man padded away. Aton had remained motionless throughout the exchange. He continued to stare at the ceiling, where by some projective trick of the imagination various incidents of his life were being played out before his eyes.

Big as a city block, the step-storeyed *Lamp of Faith* moved through the eternal geodesics of the strat like a glimmering shadow. Riding in support were three escort ships of the destroyer class, designated as expendable in Commander Haight's despairingly realistic battle plan.

Beyond Node 7 the formation hurtled into the no-man's-land separating the empire from the Hegemony: a great uninhabited wilderness of over a hundred years' duration. Once the squadron was futureward of the imperial forward alert posts, the destroyers shot ahead of the larger flagship. It was here, where the entire Earth was a radioactive desert, that the Hegemony's beta-radar stations would probably pick them up.

Given sufficient warning the Hegemonics might try to set up time-blocks. These installations, though costly and requiring effort and skill, could bring a timeship travelling in excess of a certain velocity to a savage halt, precipitating it into orthogonal time where it was vulnerable. For this reason a timeship usually moved cautiously if it was suspected that a block was being attempted. Yet the *Lamp of Faith* needed to move fast to arrive at its target with any chance of success.

On the bridge, Commander Haight did not allow himself the luxury of personal feelings. His fatalistic gloom was relegated to the closed corners of his mind as he brought the full force of his attention to bear on the operation in hand.

He had already received the precombat blessings of the Church. The comforter still moved about the bridge asperging each man in turn. As he traversed the room from end to end his cowled figure changed size dramatically due to velocity contraction. In the nose of the ellipsoid he was barely a foot tall.

A gong sounded. The scanman spoke.

'Enemy approaching. Two items.'

Presently the louvred wedge shapes of the Hegemonic ships appeared on the swirling strat screen. They hovered and turned close by the flagship looking like prismatically cascading towers, showering images of themselves as they kept pace.

'Release torpedoes,' ordered Haight automatically.

The torpedoes trundled away without hitting their targets.

'They are offering tryst, sir,' the beta operator informed him.

'Ignore.'

The second beta operator spoke up urgently. 'Sir, I think *Incalculable* has gone ortho!'

'Full speed astern!' roared Haight.

Their stomachs lurched as the *Lamp of Faith* decelerated fiercely. The nose of the bridge ballooned in size; the pilot was near normal height.

The three destroyers had been strung out ahead of the flagship in a staggered echelon. *Incalculable*, the leading vessel, had clearly run into a time-block.

Although the destroyer had probably been annihilated by now, in an instantly withering barrage of fire, the success of his ploy occasioned Commander Haight a grim satisfaction. The two remaining destroyers – *Song of Might* and *Infuriator* – had, like the *Lamp of Faith*, managed to check their speed in time. Slowly the depleted formation cruised through the block region. Instruments on the bridge flicked and pinged as they registered the blocking field, which was designed to retard the c-plus velocity of pi-mesons in a moving ship's time-drive, thus preventing the passage through time.

The steady thrum of the time-drive changed to a lower pitch. Even at their present speed, too slow for its relativistic field to be efficacious, the block had a damping effect.

Then they were suddenly through it and were picking up speed again.

And now they had passed beyond the Century of Waste and were into the territory of the Hegemony. Their journey now would be short. The Hegemony, unlike the empire, comprised only one node – did not extend over the entire Earth's surface, in fact. Indeed, as far as was known, only the empire imposed its authority on other centuries. No similar grand design had been detected anywhere in the future.

In terms of history, the Hegemony began at the fringes of the Century of Waste and continued for about a hundred years up to its domestic node, and for a similar period after that. By the time of the succeeding node (Node 10 by imperial reckoning) it appeared to have changed its political character and no longer called itself the Hegemony. What it would call itself after receiving the empire's attentions was, at this point, a matter of speculation.

'Several enemy vessels converging,' said the scanman.

'Ignore.'

They would be subject to a considerable number of interception attempts from now on. The pilot was busy tracking the *Lamp of Faith* through the multidimensional continuum in a preplanned zigzag. The manoeuvre had two purposes: to render more difficult any further stopping exercises by means of time-block and to disguise the ultimate target.

The screen operator tried to get them a glimpse of what chronmen called 'the surface' – the orthogonal time-scape they were invisibly skimming through. This was occasionally possible by adroit handling of the scanning equipment. But on this occasion the strat defeated him. The roiling, multidimensional geodesics, the rapid course changes, turned the surface of reality, even though he managed to focus the instruments in that direction, into a senseless collage without one recognizable shard.

More important was the abstract metering that told them where they were. In the bowels of the ship was a device of extraordinary subtlety: an inertial navigator capable of noting and computing shifts of position on a six-dimensional scale. Without this gadget to make a timeship free of reliance on surface-based reference points, the operation of warships would have been quite impracticable.

As the minutes ticked by tension in the bridge became almost unbearable. Haight accepted readiness reports from all sections. Gunnery, commando, technical teams, were all pent up and waiting to go.

Wedge ships flew around them thick and fast. By now the Hegemonics knew that something was up. The Time Service had already carried out a few retaliatory raids on their bases and cities, but generally had been too busy trying to defend imperial history. The appearance of the mighty battle-wagon flagship on their territory probably came as an unpleasant surprise.

And, the nature of the strat being what it was, they had little chance to prepare. Warnings could not go ahead of them any faster than the *Lamp of Faith* itself travelled; even if the Hegemony used the courier system, which was doubtful, they would not have installed the expensive catapult apparatus midway between nodes. And they could not attack the intruders until they emerged into ortho.

A thought occurred to Haight. From the defenders' point of view he was now travelling on the incoming, attacking flight path. If the raid was to be successful and the *Lamp of Faith* to return home again, then somewhere in the strat must already be the outgoing homeward flight path with the flagship hurtling along it. That was one of the paradoxes of this business: that the strat contained every chronman's future, even though he himself could not determine what that future would be. Only in orthogonal time, and at the very nodes themselves, was time regarded as determinate.

'Base Ogop in scanner range!' announced the scanman excitedly.

Haight sounded the alerting klaxons. The elements of the operation were now coming to a climax. One of the beta operators, in touch, but barely, with the destroyer vanguard, was babbling reports and figures.

'*Song of Might* and *Infuriator* due for ortho in one minute five seconds. Our approach due in three minutes—'

Another operator broke into Haight's attention. 'Twelve Hegemonic ships harassing formation.'

Haight licked his lips. Down below the commandos and technical teams were pouring into their exit bays. The word for them to go would have to come from him. But first the approaching enemy ships, as well as Base Ogop's defensive armament, needed to be dealt with.

'How much weight have they got?'

The operator was studying his blips with a frown, glancing occasionally at the big strat screen. 'Three at least are of the Hegemonic Tower class. Most of the others look like the Ranger class.'

'Going ortho!' yelled the destroyers' linkman. The vicarious excitement of their exploit was upon him.

A sudden silence fell upon the bridge.

These were probably the most crucial few seconds of the whole enterprise. The destroyers *Song of Might* and *Infuriator* did have one advantage: they were not engaging in a tryst. They were emerging from the strat without warning and it would take the pursuing Hegemonic ships seconds or minutes to realize what had happened and follow suit. In that time the destroyers had to silence Base Ogop's guns, prevent any ships there from phasing into the strat, or at least do as much of all that as possible to soften up the approach for the *Lamp of Faith*.

'Report?' demanded Haight impatiently.

The linkman was intent upon his earphones. '*Infuriator*'s drive crippled, severely holed, but armament intact. *Song of Might* undamaged.' He strained to hear what was being said. 'Base defences inoperable . . . five warships grounded . . . two got away.'

It was much better than he had feared. He nodded brusquely. 'Right. We're going in.'

A minute later the great ship phased into materialization on the main yard of Base Ogop.

Every window on the exterior of the huge battle wagon tuned to transparency. The crew could see the shattered base all around them.

Haight surveyed the scene on the bridge's main monitor screen. They were parked on a yard perhaps half a mile in extent. Ringing it were buildings in a foreign, exotic style, some of them burning, others dashed to the ground. Nearer at hand were the wrecks of column-like timeships, either tumbled across the concrete or sagging and smoking.

Towering above it all was the mighty *Lamp of Faith*, vaster and more powerful than any timeship the Hegemony had built. It had crushed smaller vessels, trucks, and machinery beneath it as it settled its full weight on to the yard. With its rows and tiers of windows it would have looked in place lining the street of any major city, except for its beam projectors and torpedo tubes.

Scanning the environs, Haight spotted the *Infuriator* lying propped athwart a blockhouse, exactly like one building thrown on top of another. Further off, beyond the other side of the base, the *Song of Might* hovered in the air in a stand-off position so as to provide the flagship with covering fire.

Haight picked up a microphone and sent his voice haranguing throughout the ship. At ground level, the port porches opened. Combat chronmen and technicians surged through to take possession of Base Ogop, hurrying away from the timeship before the anticipated assault from the strat met it.

Less than half a minute later Hegemonic craft began to flick into existence. Within microseconds heavy-duty energy beams had been focused on them and they either exploded into flame or fled back into the strat to lick their wounds.

Colonel Anamander looked at the commander, his lips curling. A timeship standing in orthogonal time had every advantage over one trying to attack it from the strat. It was not a tryst situation where each party was prevented by the rules of war from phasing out of the strat earlier than his antagonist and so pre-empting the appointed moment. This was like shooting ducks out of the air. They had simply to sit still and watch for ships to appear, focusing and firing before the enemy had a chance to do likewise.

Very soon the Hegemonics gave up the unequal fight. They were leaving it now for Base Ogop to be relieved by slower air and land forces.

Haight imagined those forces would start arriving in ten to twenty minutes. He reckoned on being able to hold the base for up to an hour. In that time the sample distorter would have to be found.

Reports began coming in. Fighting with the base staff. The technical teams going over the damaged ships, examining the workshops, questioning prisoners for some knowledge of the coveted weapon.

He controlled his impatience and sat stolidly, as if made of stone.

Fifteen minutes later radar reported strike aircraft converging from three directions. The *Lamp of Faith* lifted off the shipyard and hovered at two thousand feet. As the aircraft approached at supersonic speed their courses were tracked and plotted. At almost the same instant that the timeship released missiles to down them, the strike planes fired their own missiles. Those hurtling towards the *Lamp of Faith* were licked out of the sky by energy beams. The flagship's own projectiles found their targets. Somewhere beyond the horizon the attacking planes rained down in fragments.

There was a lull. Occasionally surveillance craft screamed overhead at a height of miles. Haight let them go. The timeship could stave off any amount of missile attack. The real fight would begin when the enemy brought in their own energy beamers.

So far the technical teams had discovered nothing. Haight was becoming worried. Half an hour after their landing, huge vehicles appeared over the horizon, moving swiftly forward on what was probably an air-cushion principle. Large-aperture beamer orifices were plainly visible. Behind them came troop-carriers carrying, he estimated, thousands of men with full equipment.

He put the *Lamp of Faith* down on the ground again to lower its profile.

The blue flashes of high-energy beams began to criss-cross one another like swords. Molten metal ran down the sides of the *Lamp of Faith* as the beams slowly ate into the structure of the ship.

Then the exchange died down as the flagship's weapons put the Hegemonic beams out of action. But the respite could only be temporary. More and more projectors would be brought up until the ship's resources – and those of the two destroyers – were beaten down.

As it was, the *Infuriator* had been silenced and the *Song of Might* had only one projector operating. Haight gave orders for any survivors on the grounded ship to come aboard the flagship. *Song of Might* he sent back into the strat for its own protection.

'If we stay any longer, sir,' Colonel Anamander reminded him, 'we may not get away.'

He was referring to the possibility that the Hegemonics might be able to erect a time-block to prevent their escape pastward.

'My orders are perfectly explicit, Colonel,' Haight told him. 'We are to stay *until the distorter is found*, whatever that might mean.'

'Even if it means losing the *Lamp of Faith*?' Anamander seemed to find the notion incredible.

But Haight merely shrugged sardonically. 'Yes . . . so what if we do? We are all expendable.' His gaze flicked around him, as though he were able to look through walls and see his command in all its entirety. 'What of the *Lamp of Faith*? Do you imagine the empire cannot manage without it? The Invincible Armada will include a thousand ships as good as this one.'

The ship lifted off again and drifted beyond Base Ogop's boundary to attack a concentration of projectors that was building up there. But it was forced to retreat. So many of its own beams were out of action that it was being out-gunned, and while it left its central position, Hegemonic troops poured into the base to fight it out with the chron commandos.

The officer in charge of the technical teams spoke to Haight over a vidcom. His face was haggard with desperation.

'There's no distorter on the base, sir. We've been through everything.'

Haight cursed. 'There *has* to be one!' he snarled.

'Sir—'

The *Lamp of Faith* lurched. One corner of the ship hit the concrete with a huge crunching sound. Moments later the whole mass slammed down as the lifting engines cut out and the great vessel rocked from side to side.

'Should we phase out, sir?' questioned Colonel Anamander in a low voice.

'What did I just tell you, Colonel?' Haight growled. 'We don't leave until we are successful, and that comes from the emperor himself.'

Captain Mond Aton had been largely unaware of events taking place outside the small bedroom where he lay. But he felt the sudden lurch followed by the impact, and knew that the ship was losing power.

The knowledge provoked only slight interest in him. The batman had brought him a passably fitting uniform. He had donned it and inspected himself in a full length mirror.

For a moment it had made him think he was back aboard the *Smasher of Enemies*. Things had started clicking into place in his mind.

The room shifted in perspective and suddenly acquired depth. It glowed with new colour. He was no longer in an insubstantial two-dimensional world. He could understand his surroundings again.

Now he lay quietly, considering the remarkable situation he was in.

After a while other distant noises began to intrude into his consciousness. The hissing of energy beams biting deeper into the ship. The spit of beam pistols closer by.

He rose and went into the main lounge. As he did so, Commander Haight burst in and slammed the door behind him, a gun in his hand.

'What's happened?' Aton asked calmly.

Servants hurried into the room. Haight waved them away. He stepped to the large mahogany table and opened a panel in its top, turning a dial-like device this way and that.

Then he sat down at the table, his pistol pointing at the door, his free hand near the device, toying with a switch.

'We couldn't find a distorter,' he rumbled. 'Now the Hegemonics are all around us. The power has failed and our beams are gone. There's fighting inside the ship.'

'Is that a destruct device?' Aton asked, eyeing the switch.

Haight nodded. 'The one on the bridge doesn't work. A long time ago I had an additional one installed here.'

'Then what are you waiting for?' Aton inquired pointedly.

The commander grunted. 'The Hegemonics have offered a truce! It seems they want to talk to us, so I've agreed. Might as well hear what they have to say.'

'They are coming here?'

'Where else?'

Aton took a seat at the other end of the room. For some minutes they waited in silence.

At length there was the sound of footsteps and the door opened. Colonel Anamander entered. He surveyed the room and raised his eyebrows at Haight, who nodded.

Into the room came two tall slim men. They wore brocaded garments of yellow cloth that accentuated their slimness and gave them a formal elegance. The most striking feature of their apparel was their headgear: cylindrical hats over a foot high, surmounted by curved lips that projected forward for several inches.

Commander Haight kept his gun trained on them. 'Forgive me if I do not rise to make a proper greeting,' he said in a gravelly tone. 'Announce yourselves.'

One of the two stepped forward. He looked at Haight with none of the rancour that was evident in Haight's own expression.

'I am Minister Ortok Cray, and I am a member of the Ruling Council of Saleem, which is, as you know, the faction which has hegemony in the federation you know as the Hegemony. And this—' he gestured to his companion – 'is Minister Wirith Freeling, of the same council.'

Haight did not show his considerable surprise. 'I am privileged indeed,' he murmured. 'I am Commander Haight, a loyal servant of His Chronotic Majesty Philipium the First.'

Minister Ortok Cray glanced at Aton as if expecting to be introduced to him also. 'I can assure you that there is no need to threaten us with your weapons,' he told Haight. 'It is not our intention to trick you or even to capture your ship. It is our wish that, after making the necessary repairs for which we shall offer every assistance, you should return to Chronopolis and convey our sentiments to your master.'

The Hegemonic spoke with a drawling accent. Haight, however, used to the variegated dialects and languages of the empire, scarcely noticed its strangeness.

'Sentiments?'

Minister Wirith Freeling made an expansive gesture. 'I don't know if you are aware of how difficult communication between our two civilizations is made by religious differences. To a large extent our cultures are ignorant of each other – by far the greater ignorance, however, is on *your* side.'

Commander Haight was proud of, rather than insulted by, this ignorance. 'It is no part of our habits to pander to heathens.'

Ortok Cray sighed. 'But in the present circumstances, surely some intercourse would be advisable? As it is, the empire appears not even to know the elementary facts of the Hegemony's history.'

Commander Haight's opinion was that, once the Invincible Armada was launched, any conversation between the two would be extremely one-sided. It was true, of course, that no real study of Hegemonic culture had been undertaken, and such cultural contact as there had been had consisted of proselytizing Church missionaries. He could not see that it was in the least important. But he laid down his gun.

'Come to the point.'

'We wish to end the war and come to an understanding based on co-existence.'

'Hah! You fear the armada.'

'Indeed. But do you not also have much to fear?' The mildness disappeared from Ortok Cray's face and Haight found himself confronting two men of steely determination.

'We have shown that we are ready to risk all to defend ourselves,' the Hegemonic leader continued. 'You know what the time-distorter can do. It is a weapon so terrible that, if it is employed without restraint, then the user stands in as much danger as the victim. That, no doubt, is why you have not made use of it against us. But our situation is so desperate that we will stop at nothing.'

Aton spoke up from the other side of the room. 'You had expected *us* to use the distorter?'

Haight glared at him in displeasure for the interruption. Ortok Cray turned to regard the young captain.

'It is, after all, an invention of the Chronotic Empire,' he said. 'Our acquisition of it is quite recent.'

'And just how *did* you acquire the distorter?' Haight grated. He and Anamander exchanged puzzled glances.

'That, naturally, I cannot tell you. The important thing is that we have it and will continue to use it. Furthermore, so far we have used it only at low power and with small aperture. If driven to it we will pull out all the stops. In no circumstances will we surrender. But we would prefer to live in peace. Surely you can see that this struggle is going to be a calamity for us both?'

'And you, of course, try to place the blame for the conflict squarely on us. That, I'm afraid, won't do. Long before the armada was thought of the empire was suffering from your armed incursions, your attempts to interfere with imperial chron integrity—'

'And we were suffering from the impudence of your missionaries,' retorted Wirith Freeling hotly. 'You evidently do not appreciate what your religious aggressiveness means to us. And apart from that, there was always your patent desire to see us as a part of your territories.'

Haight shrugged gloomily. 'Your intransigent attitude towards the true faith renders it a duty to bring you the light of the Church.'

'We have our own religion, the religion of the Risen Christos! We want none of your – of your—' Freeling was sputtering with indignant rage.

Ortok Cray raised a hand. 'Patience,' he murmured to his colleague. 'This is not the time for quarrels and recriminations. This is the time for explanation.'

He turned to face Haight once more. 'You complain of our earlier attempts to interfere with Chronotic history. But I wonder if you realize the reason behind those attempts? Our endeavours to make our case plain to your government at Chronopolis have always been thwarted, since your Church refuses to accept our representatives there.'

'Well, now I am your prisoner and you can say what you like.'

'Precisely. The point at issue concerns the Century of Waste. Our cultures are separated by a period of a hundred years when the Earth is uninhabitable. The origin of this is presumably known to you.'

'Some war in the hinterland of Node Seven,' said Haight reflectively. 'Node Seven is the empire's frontier. We have not yet consolidated ourselves in the stretch of time succeeding it. Indeed, it may be left for that to be accomplished by the natural advance of the node.'

'That's right: a war which left the Earth desolate. In point of fact this was established in orthogonal time well before time-travel was introduced at what you call, I believe, Node Six. But do you not see what this means? *During that war mankind was wiped out.* History came to an end at that point until, by some random movement in the strat, there was a historical mutation that led to the invention of time-travel. The future Earth was then colonized by migrants from the past. Thus it transpires that time-travel is the instrument of mankind's survival.'

'So? All this is recognized. Time-travel came as a gift from God, to redeem mankind from its own destruction. That is the entire basis of the true faith and the justification for the Chronotic Empire. You have told me nothing new.'

'Except that we do not regard the invention of time-travel as an act of God, but never mind about that.

Do you not see the implications? The annihilation of mankind took place before the Chronotic Empire had begun to establish itself throughout time. The course of history was quite different then. The migration to the future took place when the empire began to expand – and more particularly when the Church of San Hevatar established itself as the one true church. Do you now see what I am getting at?'

Haight merely frowned, but the truth struck Aton forcibly. 'You are refugees!'

Ortok Cray nodded. 'We, or rather our ancestors, were religious dissidents who were driven out of the empire in the early days. We established ourselves here, beyond the empire's reach – at that time. Hence our proud independence and our dislike of your Church.'

'None of this explains your impudent forays into our territory,' complained Haight broodingly. 'If you wished to be left alone, why did you draw our attention to you?'

'Because the empire's hold on the structure of history is increasing,' Ortok Cray reminded him. 'We have every reason to fear the Historical Office. If nothing is done now, then in about fifty years' time the Hegemony will disappear from history.'

'How do you know that?' Aton said, puzzled, and ignoring his lack of entitlement to join in the discussion.

'Time is not static,' pointed out the Hegemonic minister. 'The nodes proceed forward at a steady rate, overtaking events that are already established in the future. If the node contains some Chronotic mutation or has been altered in some way, then events ahead of it will also change as it approaches. And this means that the Chronotic Empire, even while maintaining its fixed rear at the Stop Barrier, will continue to grow into the future – quite apart from further conquests by timeships. At the moment the events leading to the disastrous war that wiped out mankind are still intact. But Node Seven is already encroaching on them and eventually will overtake them. The Historical Office, naturally, will want to delete this war. There will be no general destruction, no Century of Waste.'

'A change we should all applaud, surely,' Aton commented. 'To annul such a terrible happening does not seem at all bad.'

'*We want the war to be fixed in time for ever.*'

They were all taken aback by the ferocity of the minister's words.

'If there is no war,' Ortok Cray continued quietly, 'if the Earth is not depopulated, then the disciples of the Risen Christos can have found nowhere to settle themselves on fleeing the persecutions of your Church – or, at best, can only have been absorbed into a more friendly population, whatever that population might be. The future will have a new, completely different history. The Hegemony will never have come into existence at all.'

Commander Haight came to his feet and paced the lounge, frowning. 'Once time-travel becomes an established fact of life such temporal upheavals become inevitable,' he commented. 'Only the continued existence of the empire is absolutely guaranteed. Yes, I can see that you have good cause to fear us.'

'We do not agree that the continued existence of the empire is a certainty,' Wirith Freeling snapped. 'The empire is contingent, like all the other things existing in time. That *time-travel* cannot vanish, once having been invented, is true, no doubt, but not the empire. Time-travel came before the empire.'

'The two are indissolubly linked.'

'Let us not argue theology,' Ortok Cray put in. 'You have your religion, we have ours. We believe we can destroy your empire, even though we destroy ourselves in doing so. These are our demands: the Chronotic Empire must limit itself in time and must not intrude into the period containing the annihilatory war. You have a thousand years, be content with that. Let Node Seven continue without you, do not extend your authority beyond its current generation.'

Haight stopped short and looked at the two Hegemonics with controlled fury. 'Do you expect His Chronotic Majesty to agree to terms like that?'

'We wish him to examine the situation and to recognize the delicacy of our own position. Also, that the present course will destroy us both.'

'Then I will not answer you, since the answer belongs to His Majesty.'

Minister Ortok Cray acknowledged this with an inclining of his head.

'We would welcome a meeting between our respective representatives,' he said. 'Some arrangement tolerable to us both would be better than total war. If your side is willing to take part in talks, send a timeship broadcasting an appropriate message.'

'I will convey your requirements.' Haight's tone was sardonic, almost sarcastic.

'Then we thank you. Please let us know if you need anything to make your ship timeworthy. I think we can expect you to be on your way in, let us say, ten hours?'

Haight nodded. Ministers Ortok Cray and Wirith Freeling made some parting gesture that was strange to him, and swept sedately from the room.

When they had gone, Commander Haight stroked his chin for a few moments, then looked thoughtfully at Aton.

'I can see allowing you to wear the emperor's uniform has done the trick,' he said slowly. 'You are a veritable model of rationality.'

As Aton made no reply, Haight turned to Anamander. 'Well, our enterprise has come to a surprising conclusion, eh, Colonel?'

Seating himself at the table, he carefully deactivated the *Lamp of Faith*'s emergency self-destruct.

7

'It's hard to say what it is, or what it's like,' Aton muttered. 'There are really no words to describe it. All the words of our language refer to three-dimensional orthogonal time.'

'Are the experiences still in your memory? Are they vivid?'

'Yes, but they tend to fade, to become . . . recast so as to resemble ordinary experiences. Such as what you might see on a strat screen.'

Commander Haight sighed deeply. 'That figures. A strat screen interprets the substratum in terms of sensory criteria. One might well expect the brain's memory banks to do the same.'

They were heading back towards Chronopolis, Node One, accompanied by the *Song of Might*, and were already deep inside the empire's historical territory. Haight had been kept busy, first attending to repairs to the *Lamp of Faith* and then negotiating a homeward course, the journey to the frontier being under escort by a squadron of Hegemonic Tower-class ships. But the moment he had been able to take a rest from his duties he had hurried to his quarters to question Aton closely on the nature of the strat.

'Nothing has a single nature,' Aton said. 'Everything merges into everything else; there are a billion aspects to everything. Nothing exists as an object; all is flux and motion.'

'Hmmm.' Haight listened carefully to the words, fixing his gaze on Aton's face. It was as if he was trying to find in Aton's steady eyes some glimpse of what those eyes had seen.

He was somewhat disappointed by the results of his experiment. Aton's descriptions had been fairly lucid but resembled technical descriptions such as one might find in text-books. They did not convey the *essence* of the experience.

Aton's return to normalcy was also something of a disappointment to him. He turned, stretched his weary limbs, then stepped to the cocktail bar and poured himself a stiff slug of gin. After brief hesitation he poured one for Aton too and pushed it across to him.

'I have not had my money's worth,' he said with a grim smile. 'Interfering with your hypnotic instructions should at least, I would have thought, have produced some interesting psychological disorder. But here you are as healthy as apple pie.' He reflected before knocking back his gin. 'Perhaps next time I should try an ordinary criminal type who will have no mental discipline.'

Aton had a question of his own. 'Commander, do you think the representations the Hegemonics have made to us will influence policy in Chronopolis?' His face wore a worried frown.

Haight looked at him in surprise. 'Don't be a fool, Captain. The emperor's will is inviolable.'

'But, sir—'

'I would probably not even bother to deliver such pathetic pleas,' Haight told him irritably, 'had not the Hegemonics inadvertently given us such valuable information at the same time. My orders were to seize the distorter or to sacrifice the mission in the attempt. But that business about its origins is most peculiar, don't you think? One can only think that there is high treason in the realm. The historical background to the Hegemony, too, should prove most useful, though I should think the point about the advance of Node Seven is something the Historical Office is already alive to.' He gave a loud, braying laugh. 'See how invincible is the empire! No wonder the Hegemonics are in a panic. There's no way they can win!'

'In that case, would it not be advisable to hold back the armada, and gain our ends by subtler means?'

'That would not end the provocations of the Hegemony. It would only give them more time to work their mischief. And besides, the Church has declared the enterprise a holy crusade. The Church being infallible, its edicts cannot be reversed.'

Aton became depressed as he realized the inevitability of what Haight said.

'I shall report the full conversation to the emperor personally,' Haight mused. 'It will make little difference. Of greater interest is the news that the Hegemonics spring from our own dissidents. That, too, offers possibilities of eliminating the Hegemonics by tracking down these dissidents *before* they flee – though where time-travel's concerned such a course of action is not guaranteed to be effective. In any case I doubt that it will be considered.'

'Why not?'

'The Church wants converted souls, not annihilated souls. The purpose of the armada is to save men, not to destroy them.'

Aton brought himself to attention, aware of the import of what he was about to say.

'I agree with the Hegemonics, sir. The only important thing is that the war should be brought to a stop. We are headed on a course of mutual disaster.'

Haight, in the act of filling his glass again, glanced up sharply. 'You are way out of line, Captain. You have forgotten your role. *You have performed your duty.*'

As he performed the trigger phrase lifting the hypnotic block on the implanted death urge, Aton went dizzy. Something inside his mind struggled madly for expression. But he clamped down on it. There was a mental convulsion, a struggle. Then calm.

'What happened?' asked Haight softly.

Aton had closed his eyes. He opened them. 'You were supposed to keep me alive for not more than an hour. I've been here for more than three days. The death command has lost its force.'

'A hypnotic command should be permanent.'

'The hypnotic component is not a command, only a suggestion. It depends for its force on immersion in the strat. That experience is three days old.'

Haight nodded. 'I thought this might happen.' He toyed with his tumbler, his expression becoming curious. 'You know, men have been pulled out of the strat after falling into it, and they don't recover. Though there have been some cases I couldn't speak for, taken into the care of the Church to spend the rest of their days in monasteries. Poor devils.'

'This is the second time I've seen the strat. I saw it for the first time when the *Smasher of Enemies* went down.'

'You think that might have acclimatized you, eh?'

'Possibly, sir.' Haight's obsession with the strat, Aton saw, was a growing one. For his part, he was eager to return to the former subject of conversation.

'Sir, we must try to make the emperor understand the seriousness of the situation. *The war must be brought to a stop.*'

'*We* must? Did you not just now hear me pronounce sentence of death on you? Or are you trying to save your skin?'

'I am not trying to save my skin. It is your doing that the normal procedure has . . . misfired. But I am still willing to submit to execution, if you will grant me one last wish.' Aton spoke evenly, with increasing urgency.

'And what is that?'

'Let me be present at the interview with the emperor. Let me put the Hegemonics' case as they would wish it to be put. Frankly I do not think that you will do so.'

'You accuse me of misrepresentation?'

'Sir, I believe the empire is in danger, deadly danger. You understand the havoc that can be wreaked by the time-distorter – and we have not even seen it used at full power yet! – but your instinct is that of a warrior: to fight, to defeat the enemy. Yet to take a detached view, the Hegemonic cause has some slight justice in it. The issues at stake are not worth the strain we will be putting in the structure of time.'

Haight took a step towards Aton, dangerous emotions chasing themselves across his face. 'You want to sell out to the enemy!'

'We *must* reach an accommodation with the Hegemonics! Or else the empire itself may be destroyed!'

The commander stared at him incredulously. 'Hah! So you really think the empire can be brought down! Why, the empire's resources are inexhaustible! Other powers in time have at the best but one node to draw on. The empire has seven! That means seven times the industrial might, and seven times the manpower, of any enemy we might face. And our strength will grow.' He shook his head. 'No, the empire cannot be defeated.'

'You speak of orthogonal time. I have seen the strat. You have not. All we have can be wiped away in the blink of an eye.'

'You add heresy to your crimes,' Haight said with increasing virulence.

'Is that your only response – to take refuge in doctrine?' Aton replied, in a voice thick with disappointment. 'It is clear that with you for a messenger the emperor can gain no clear idea of what the Hegemonics intend.'

Haight sneered, looking him up and down. 'Who are you to lecture me?' he retorted. 'Your offers and arguments are all tricks to help yourself! Let *me* tell *you* something – something of service! True, even emperors can make foolish mistakes. What is Philipium but a foolish old man? But that is not important. Something more surrounds the Ixians and welds the empire together. That something is *service* – the ideal of service to the empire! Men give their lives to this ideal, it is the empire's main strength. And what of you? What do you understand of this strength?' Haight's voice rose to a roar. 'You are a traitor, a criminal, a coward! But now you face *me*, a loyal servant of the empire!'

Aton stood pale-faced but erect while the commander raged. 'I had been undecided as to what to do with you,'

Haight said more quietly, 'but now I think I will kill you anyway.'

Aton skipped back. His hand darted into his tunic and came out with a small hand beamer he had found in Haight's stateroom.

'I am set upon a course, Commander. I will not give up, at least until I have spoken with Colonel Anamander. Perhaps he agrees with me.'

'And perhaps he does not. It makes no difference, but in fact he does not.' Haight stared contemptuously at the beamer.

Aton was pointing the gun uncertainly at Haight. 'Keep your hands where I can see them, sir.'

'I need no gun. I have a weapon pointed directly at your heart: your own vagus nerve.'

Aton's eyes opened wide.

'Your information is probably incomplete,' Haight continued. 'You have conquered the compulsion to pronounce the trigger-word, evidently. But it is not necessary that you should pronounce it. It is only necessary that your nervous system should *hear* it. And I, as the receiving officer, know what the word is.'

Although his finger tightened on the stud of the beamer, Aton found that he could not, after all, fire on his commanding officer. He staggered back yet another step.

'*Vom.*' The word dropped from Haight's lips like a dose of poison.

And Aton's nervous system reacted instantly. Brain cell after brain cell fired in response to the signal, spreading the message in a web of pending death. Aton sought to clamp down on the impulse, to dampen it before it could reach the vagus nerve, sometimes called the suicide nerve because of its ability to initiate cardiac arrest on instructions from the brain.

His heart gave a convulsive leap and missed several beats. Aton staggered, the gun slipping from his fingers. He was vaguely aware of Haight looking on, half in satisfaction, half repelled.

Then the scene before him vanished, for a split second – a split second that was an eternity long. And so, for that same split second, did orthogonal time.

He was back in the strat, transposed there spontaneously by his nervous system somehow and experiencing its impossibilities all over again.

And when, almost immediately, he phased back into Haight's lounge, the cabin bore its former flat, two-dimensional appearance. But this time he was far from being mentally incapacitated. He felt strangely young, strong, and omnipotent, as if he could fly while others were earthbound.

Vom. The word had no danger in it now. Its fearful virulence had been expunged from his mind.

'What – Did something happen just then?' Haight whispered. For a moment he had seemed to see Aton surrounded by an aura of near-invisible flame.

'Yes. Your word won't work against me either. I have rid myself of it.'

He paused. He still did not understand what was happening to him, at least not entirely. He only knew that it was surprising, incredible and yet logical.

'Commander, you have wondered why the empire requires a time-courier to die. I think I can tell you.'

'Oh? Why?'

'It is because he becomes like a god.'

'A god.' Haight chuckled derisively. 'Well, you may have broken the psychological conditioning, but let's see how well you fare against hot energy.'

He had unflapped his waist holster and now he drew his clumsy-looking hand beamer, larger than the toy-like weapon Aton had discarded. With slow deliberation he clicked off the safety and aimed the orifice at Aton's chest.

Aton had time for a hasty valediction.

'Commander,' he gasped, '*I also am a loyal servant of the empire.*'

Then he seemed actually to see the dense microwave beam, made visible by its accompanying dull red tracer waves, advancing through space towards him.

And Commander Haight gave a hoarse cry. For Aton had vanished completely from his cabin. He had been plunged back into the strat.

As he fell through the unending plenum of potential time Aton wondered why – and how – his nervous system had rescued him. Had it been a survival response, an instinctive reaction against threatened death? Or had his subconscious mind, still obeying the suicide command in some perverse fashion, welcomed and anticipated that death, precipitating him into the strat through over-eagerness?

As to how his body had gained this power, he could only guess. Presumably it was connected with the unique combination of his recent experiences. How it was accomplished, considering the heavy equipment and intense energy that was normally required, he could not say. But one thing was sure. He was no longer as others were. He was a four-dimensional man, able to transpose spontaneously through time.

And no longer was he a despairing mote tossed about by the currents of the strat. This time he was not robbed of the sense of sequential time that was his brain's birthright; he carried his own weak ortho field with him. Because of this his mind maintained its natural rationality. His perceptions had learned to handle the supernal contents of the strat in a way that did not cause his ego to blow a fuse.

Previously the strat had engulfed him, and half drowned him. That was why his consciousness had taken refuge in experiencing his life over and over: it had been the only familiar element in his surroundings. He could, if he wished, choose this refuge again, but he did not, because this time his consciousness was not overwhelmed and in his new condition, with his brain no longer scrambled by endless unintelligible monstrosities, the strat took on an entirely different appearance.

Fire. That was the nearest he could come to describing it. He was in an ocean of eternal fire, whose flames consisted of the myriad half-creatures whose existence was, as yet, only potential. The flames blasted and trembled, whirled and rolled, swelled and receded.

This, he knew, was not the strat as it was in reality; this was the interpretation his newly adjusted perceptions put upon it. The fire hurtled and withered everywhere; it was a five-dimensional sea that could not be understood any other way.

If he turned in a certain direction he could see what appeared to be a vast leaden wall. Upon it, as upon a huge mural, ran scenes of an amazing variety and richness. It was the surface of the strat. The realm of existential, orthogonal moving time from which Aton came. The real, solid world. And if he wished he could gaze upon this world and see what took place there.

But instead he was hurtling pastwards – pastwards, that is, in orthogonal terms – at a terrific rate, bent upon a mission that was only gradually becoming clear to him.

His trajectory, however, was to be interrupted. Suddenly, looming ahead of him, he saw a form that did not belong here. Like himself, it moved in a bubble of orthogonal time, but it was larger than he was. Much larger.

Briefly he recognized it as it swept past him: a step-tiered office block travelling taller end sternwards, the company name *Buick* written hugely along its side in graceful silver script. It was an internodal chronliner.

He would have passed it by, but apparently the section of his nervous system that controlled his new-found powers had its own autonomic responses. As the ship's orthogonal bubble touched him he phased precipitately out of the strat and found himself in a new, unexpected situation.

He was standing, still in his captain's uniform, in the chronliner's main lounge.

Nervously Inpriss Sorce sipped her drink, her eyes flicking here and there around the lounge like the wary eyes of a bird.

She spent most of the time in the big lounge. There were always plenty of people there, and bright lights. She was short of sleep because she was reluctant to stay long alone in her cabin, where she feared unwelcome visitors. Instead she had learned to live on nervous energy. At the same time she knew that she would have to learn to break this habit when she reached Revere, where she would spend much time alone – hopefully safe and unobserved.

Captain Mond Aton noticed the frightened girl as soon as he took stock of his surroundings.

Surveying the spacious, well-appointed lounge, glancing at the faces of the passengers, he discovered that along with the ability to travel through time at will went another gift. Insight. Either his awareness or his senses had been heightened; he seemed able to guess instantly what thoughts and feelings lay behind the faces he saw. Human personality was an open book to him.

But even without this clarity of perception the young woman's condition would have been no secret. He recognized her look as that of a hunted animal. He had seen that particular look only once before in his life, and that had been on the face of a man with whom he had been slightly acquainted. At the time it had been a puzzle to him. Later the fellow had been found murdered in an imaginative, bizarre fashion that bore all the hallmarks of the Traumatic sect.

Cautiously he moved towards the girl and sat down at her table. A waiter approached. Having no money, he waved him away.

'Where are you bound?' he asked the girl. 'I haven't had a chance to ask you before.' She would not find the question strange: chronliners called at all nodes en route and they were now, he believed, somewhere between Nodes Four and Five. The ship probably had two or three stops to make.

Her reaction, however, was far from reassuring. She shrank instinctively away from him. In her eyes Aton seemed to see the thought: Who is he? What does he want? Is he following me?

She's terrified of strangers, he realized.

Seeing that she was afraid to answer the question he let it pass, covering up her confusion with a stream of chitchat while he looked around the lounge, wondering who it was she was so badly frightened of.

He spoke of his experiences in the Time Service, talking in such a way that few responses were required of her. He felt her eyes on his face and gradually she seemed to relax a little. If his guess was correct it would be hard for her to trust anyone, but he hoped he might inspire just a little confidence.

To test out his theory he mentioned the time he had found Traumatics aboard his ship. She gasped. He sensed her body tense, go rigid.

'They are extremely unpleasant people,' he said.

She nodded dumbly.

'Listen,' he said gently. 'I think you ought to tell me what's worrying you.'

She looked away. 'Nothing's worrying me. What makes you think it is?'

'If you don't mind my saying so, it does show, enough for me to notice, at any rate. I've seen it before.' He paused. 'It's the Traumatic sect, isn't it?'

Her lower lip trembled. She nodded again.

'Have you really seen it happen before?'

'Only once. To a friend of mine.'

In a rush of words she told him everything. The three visitations, her desperate efforts to escape, to get lost. Finally her decision to migrate to another province of the empire.

He could see that it was a great relief to her to be able to tell someone. It also showed just how desperate she had become, for she could hardly imagine it was safe to talk to a stranger. Probably the uniform had helped. The Time Service was greatly esteemed. Few people knew that chronmen were perversely prone to the Traumatic heresy.

'So now you hope to settle in Revere?'

'Yes. In Umbul, probably.'

'Ah. The holy city.'

'I thought that perhaps – perhaps—'

'Yes, I see.' Her hopes were plain. She thought that perhaps the Traumatic sect stayed clear of Umbul, birthplace of San Hevatar, of the Church, and in fact of the whole Chronotic Empire.

He looked down sombrely at his hands folded neatly on his lap. 'Citizeness Sorce, I am sorry to have to tell you this but you have been doing everything the Traumatics want you to do. This is their play, part of their ritual. The sacrificial victim must not be killed outright but must be captured and allowed to escape in the nick of time – by luck or his own efforts, so he thinks. Then captured again, allowed to escape again, on and on. The purpose is to make the victim aware of his, or her, situation and of the fact that he is being hunted, so as to produce a particular psychological state. This continues until his will is entirely broken and he actually co-operates in the final ceremony.'

Inpriss Sorce's brown eyes widened pleadingly. 'Then I haven't shaken them off?'

'No.'

'Oh!'

Her hands flew about agitatedly. Aton thought she might be near a breakdown. In that case the Traumatics would not be far behind her.

'Help me!' she cried. 'Somebody must help me!'

'I'll help you. Calm yourself.'

She gazed at Aton, studying his face. 'You will?'

'I hate these people as much as you do.'

'Is that why you're going to help me?'

'I'd help you anyway.' Aton's eyes narrowed as he saw a man enter the lounge and walk to the bar with a swaggering gait. His jaw clenched.

The man was Sergeant Quelle!

'Stay here and don't move,' he told Inpriss. 'I'll be back shortly.'

The gunnery noncom uttered a grunt of startlement, his sharp face becoming a grotesque mask of disbelief, when Aton joined him at the bar.

'What the hell are you doing here? I thought—'

'You thought I was safely dead,' Aton supplied. 'More to the point, what are *you* doing here?'

'Me? Why—' Quelle gave a weak, hysterical laugh. He was, Aton noticed, wearing civilian clothes. 'Just taking a spot of leave, Captain. Well-deserved leave. I'm on a cruise. I've got a medal now, you know. All of us have who got off the *Smasher of Enemies*. Except you, of course,' he added thoughtfully. He gulped down the drink he had just bought, nearly choking on it. 'Did you get a reprieve, Captain?' he asked quaveringly. 'How did you get here?'

'Suffice it to say that I am here and that I can now remember all that took place on the *Smasher of Enemies*.' Aton watched the look of agony that appeared on Quelle's face. 'How many of your friends are with you?' he asked.

'Eh? I've no friends here, sir.'

'You're lying. I happen to know who it is you are pursuing.'

Quelle's glance flicked involuntarily to Inpriss Sorce, who sat watching anxiously from across the lounge. 'I don't know what you're talking about.'

Perhaps Quelle was alone after all, Aton thought. Perhaps he was merely shadowing Inpriss Sorce and others would take over when the ship reached Umbul. But the gunnery sergeant's shiftiness and deceit was so plain that nothing could be taken as certain.

'Are you going to turn me in, sir?' Quelle asked mildly, inspecting the bottles stacked against the bar.

'Yes.'

'Then why haven't you done it before?' Quelle turned to him, smirking. 'You know what I think, Captain? I think you're an escaped prisoner. I don't know how you did it, but the fact you're here shows you did. There's a courier dispatch chamber waiting for you in Chronopolis, isn't there? Maybe I should turn *you* in. Because whatever you say it's still your word against the testimony of *eight witnesses*.'

Aton stepped closer to the man. His hand darted inside Quelle's jacket. As he had expected he found a tiny beamer, small enough to fit into the palm of a hand.

No one around them had noticed his sudden movement. 'Let's go and see the security officer, Quelle.'

Quelle stood his ground for a moment. Then, at an insistent nudge from Aton he reluctantly preceded him towards the exit.

Although unfamiliar with the layout of the civilian timeship, Aton found the security office without difficulty. Quelle made no attempt to escape or to move against him, and Aton reflected that the Traumatic had made a good point. Back in Chronopolis his own story would carry little weight. But that did not matter; somehow or other he would rescue Inpriss Sorce from the Traumatic sect's attentions.

In the security office was a middle-aged, long-jawed man in the blue uniform of the Buick line. Aton pushed Quelle in ahead of him.

'Officer, I am Captain Aton of the Third Time Fleet,' he announced. 'This is one of my men, Sergeant Quelle, whom I must ask you to place under close arrest. He is a criminal, a perjurer and a heretic, a member of the Traumatic sect, and he is currently engaged in hounding one of your passengers with intent to murder her.'

The officer looked from one man to the other, his face impassive. But behind that impassivity Aton caught feelings that were unsettling – recognition of Quelle, dismay at the whole proceeding.

'Serious charges,' said the officer. 'One moment, I'll call my men.'

He pressed a button. Almost immediately two security guards appeared at the door. Uneasy now, Aton turned to face them.

'He has my beamer,' Quelle said quickly.

A numbing, stinging shock struck Aton in the neck and spread down to his shoulders and arms. The beamer slipped from his nerveless grasp; his arms hung uselessly. He swung around clumsily and saw the security officer holding the numb-prong with which he had half-paralysed him.

The door slammed shut. All four men crowded around Aton, pushing him back. 'What on Earth happened?' the officer snarled at Quelle.

'He knows about me,' Quelle said in a surly tone. 'He's supposed to be dead; we thought we'd fixed him in Chronopolis. Hulmu help me, I nearly dropped when I saw him in the passenger lounge just now.'

'Does the girl know about you too?'

'I don't know.'

'You'd better stay out of her way. We can't let this get to the captain.'

Aton made a lunge for freedom, kicking with his feet, butting and shoving with his body. Before he could gain the door they had restrained him and held him in a corner where he panted in quiet fury.

Quelle swaggered in front of him. 'It's not only the Imperial Time Service that's host to the Cult of Hulmu, Captain. We Traumatics make much use of the internodal facilities.'

'What shall we do with him, Quelle?' the security officer asked.

'Maybe we could use him,' one of the guards said in a caressing voice, looking Aton over in a way that was incongruous coming from this burly, blue-jowled strong-arm man.

'Don't be a fool, he hasn't been pointed.'

'He's no problem,' Quelle said gleefully. 'He may have been my captain once, but the truth is that now he's a condemned convict who's escaped from the Courier Service. We can get rid of him without anybody asking questions.'

'Good. We'll put him through the garbage chute.'

Quelle cackled, eyeing Aton with undisguised hatred. 'I'm sorry about this, Captain, speaking as one chronman to another. But you see how it is – dog eat dog.' He darted a look at the security officer. 'I hate to do this to my own superior officer, you understand.'

'You traitor,' breathed Aton. 'You're worse than scum.'

'Don't you go saying that, now.' Quelle seemed genuinely hurt. 'I'm a good chronman. Religion is one thing, the Time Service is another. Why, as soon as my leave is finished I'll be riding out with His Chronotic Majesty's armada!'

One of the guards checked the corridor outside to ensure it was empty. The officer gave Aton another dose of the numb-prong so that he could give as little trouble as possible. Then they were dragging him along the passageway.

After a few yards they opened a grey-painted door and proceeded through narrow service passages, safe from the eyes of either passengers or crew. Aton knew that for the moment attempts at resistance were useless, and bided his time. Presently, close against the outer wall of the ship, they came to an area littered with cardboard boxes and tubs of rubbish.

The mouth of a big cylindrical chute, with a covering lid clamped shut, projected from one wall and was accompanied by several large steel levers. The two guards gripped Aton's arms tight.

'You tried to put me in the strat once, Captain,' Quelle murmured. 'It's my turn now, I reckon.'

Aton struggled weakly. The security officer pulled on one lever; the chute's lid swung open. Aton was swung off his feet and inserted into the smelly cylinder, upon which the lid closed up over him to leave him for a moment in darkness, his feet pressing upon some further obstruction down in the chute.

Then this too, a second valve, slid open. He heard a clicking, grating noise and then the chute's hydraulic rams swept down on him, clearing the chute. He was pushed at speed through the ship's wall, through the limit of the containing orthogonal field, back into the strat.

Supernal fire burned all around him. Looking back, Aton saw the chronliner receding into the futureward – the plusward, in chronman's jargon – direction.

The fate of anyone else thrown into the strat would have been clear. They would sink deeper and deeper into mere potentiality, into the Gulf of Lost Souls. If, as a time-courier, he had failed to reach his target that would have been his fate too, once he lost momentum.

But now he had nothing to fear from such a horrendous ending – if ending it could be called. He could move through the strat at will, by the mere wish.

His intention was to return to the chronliner where he would continue his efforts to help the Traumatics' frightened quarry, the unfortunate Inpriss Sorce. When he willed himself to follow the timeship, however, another, deeper urge in him took over and instead he moved with accelerating speed minuswards – into the past and towards Chronopolis. His sojourn aboard the chronliner had, it seemed, been but an accidental interruption of his journey.

For it was slowly becoming clear to Aton that his subconscious mind, not his waking thoughts, was controlling his destiny. His subconscious mind had discovered, under duress, the secret of time-travel. And now it was sending him, at near-courier speed, on a mission *to save the empire*!

To one side the shimmering leaden wall of the ortho-world flashed by. He knew that he could phase himself into that world anywhere he liked, choosing any of the millions of locations and scenes that the endless screen presented.

But he passed them all by. Prompted by his inner urgings, he had a definite destination in mind.

Chronopolis. Node One. The Imperial Palace.

After what seemed like a long time the majestic vision of the empire's administrative centre swung up before him. He sped closer, seeing it expand as upon a holo cinema screen. Then he phased himself into actual, orthogonal time.

Archivist Illus Ton Mayar, a slender wispy figure standing alongside the stocky detective Perlo Rolce, exhibited
some awkwardness as he delivered his final report to
Prince Vro Ixian.

When informed that the investigation he had ordered
was complete, Vro had answered peevishly: 'It has taken
you long enough!' and had turned his back on them to
gaze into the holocast of the empty mausoleum.

'An undertaking of this kind *does* take time, Your
Highness,' Mayar told him apologetically. 'It was with
the greatest difficulty that I was able to include it in our
work programme. The tragic events befalling the empire
have practically overloaded the capacity of the archives.'

'Yes, all right. What have you to tell me?'

'Perlo Rolce's suspicion has been vindicated. The body
of Princess Veaa has disappeared in a causal hiatus.'

'And what is that, exactly?'

'Put simply, a dislocation in time. A failure of cause
and effect to match up. In practical terms, Princess Veaa
was transported to Node Six and, presumably, hidden
there. Later a crack in time appeared; all events leading
up to a certain point – in the city of Umbul – were
wiped away. Normally this would lead to the body still
being back in Chronopolis, never having been removed.
Instead the effect of the now-nonexistent cause remains:
the body remains where it was hidden.'

'But with the trail leading to it eradicated,' Rolce put
in.

Prince Vro nodded his understanding. 'All this would
have seemed incredible only a short while ago. Now it
seems commonplace.'

Mayar murmured in agreement. The attacks from the
Hegemony had intensified. Not only were whole continents undergoing existential deformation but the empire
now seemed riddled with cause-and-effect cracks, some
of them large enough to present enormous administrative
difficulties. Sometimes it seemed to Mayar, from his

unique standpoint, that the structure of time was about to come crashing down like a shattered vase.

'It's like magic,' Vro said wonderingly. 'She's been spirited away with no one doing it.'

'That's what it amounts to, Your Highness,' Rolce said stiffly.

'Well.' Vro's voice became brisker. 'What can you do to find her?'

'The temporal discontinuity has been mapped, Your Highness.' Mayar produced a thick scroll and opened it, laying it on the table. It was so large that it covered the whole surface.

Vro stared perplexed at the chart, written in the esoteric Chronotic symbolism used by the Achronal Archives. Mayar explained that the vertical grid bars referred to time-units, though whether to minutes, days or months he did not say. He pointed out the jagged, wandering line that staggered through the neat layout like an earthquake crack.

'Here is the path taken by the discontinuity. Now, the issue revolves around Rolce's information that the body was secretly taken aboard the chronliner *Queen of Time*. Later this gilt-edged information was contradicted by the direct observation – and this has been verified by agents equipped with orthophases – that the body was *not* taken aboard. This anomaly suggests that time had mutated in a nonuniform way, leaving traces in the environment of both versions of history. Typical of a causal hiatus. The body is neither in Chronopolis, nor was it removed from Chronopolis. The perfect dilemma.

'Now what became of the princess during the *first* version? There are six stops where the *Queen of Time* could have off-loaded the body, presuming it was not discharged into the strat in transit. We reason that the body must have been taken off the ship before the hiatus occurred, otherwise it would still be here in Chronopolis and indeed might still be resting in the mausoleum; there would be no anomaly. On the other hand, it had probably been offboard for only a short time when the hiatus occurred. Transition from one resting place to another would seem to offer the most likely circumstance for the dislocation of the cause-and-effect relationship.'

Mayar paused to catch his breath. This argument had been worked out between himself and Rolce, and it had cost them considerable mental effort.

'Now look again at this discontinuity line,' he resumed. 'We find that it answers our deductions in every respect. It comes very close to intersecting the point in space and time when the chronliner was due to arrive at Umbul, Node Six. To be precise, it intersects Node Six just five hours after the *Queen of Time* docked.'

'Umbul,' breathed Vro. 'The Holy City.'

'We conclude that Umbul is where the princess was taken, and probably is where she still lies.'

'Archivist Mayar has even pinpointed the streets and buildings through which the discontinuity passed,' Rolce informed in a dry voice. 'It sounds incredible. Nothing, an investigator's void, and then, suddenly, clues begin again. The trails starts out of thin air.'

The prince rounded on him. 'You believe you can take up the trail again – in Umbul? You can find my beloved Veaa using your normal methods?'

'If our conclusions are correct, Your Highness, I feel every confidence.'

'Then you and I will both depart for Node Six, Rolce. I will order my private yacht to be readied tonight. Go, prepare yourself. Your instruments, your gadgets, whatever you will need. Can you manage it alone? Or do you need your agents?'

The detective shifted his feet. 'One or two men, perhaps.'

'Whatever you need. Go, now. Return as soon as you can.'

With a bow the detective departed. Prince Vro flung himself into a chair and lounged there, relaxed. For the first time in many months his manner was almost cheerful.

'Well, Archivist, I hear your establishment has been moved into the strat. A wise measure, perhaps.'

'It was deemed so, Your Highness.'

'And so how does it feel to visit the world of we mortals?'

Prince Vro's tone was amicably sardonic; in point of fact Mayar found the necessity for the visit far from pleasant and he longed to return to the safety of his vaults. His department's deployment into the strat had increased the sense of separation and isolation pervading the archives, and he had had to conquer a very considerable fear in order to make the trip to the Imperial Palace. Nothing but a command from a member of the imperial family was enough to persuade him to venture forth these days.

'It feels unsettling, Your Highness. The world is in a far from happy state. It has lost stability. Who can tell what will happen?'

'So you still feel it is all a dream, eh? Perhaps you feel you only wake from this dream when back in your archives.'

'Something like that.' Mayar licked his lips. 'Your Highness, since you are going to accompany Perlo Rolce in the search for Princess Veaa, let me entreat you to take care. The Traumatics are highly dangerous people. They are afraid of no one.'

Vro laughed. 'Why, I had thought you were well on the way to becoming one yourself!'

The archivist looked puzzled. 'I, Your Highness?'

'But of course! Surely you realize that all this gloomy talk of yours about time being a dream, and that only the strat is real, is part of the Traumatic heresy? That it conflicts with the doctrine of the Holy Trinity? You should be careful who you speak like that to. If Arch-Cardinal Reamoir were to—'

'I hadn't thought of it like that,' Mayar muttered uncomfortably.

'Probably, like me, you have no time for religion. And of course you avoided the misfortune of receiving a prince's education. I know every aspect of Church doctrine by heart; it was drummed into me from infancy.'

'My work is more scientific than religious,' Mayar admitted. 'I was brought up in the tradition of the Church, of course, but I cannot say I have made a study of heresies. It is not encouraged in a high official.'

'Just as well, or you would probably be too frightened to indulge in your present freedom of thought.' Vro swung a leg negligently from the arm of his chair. He seemed amused. 'You are definitely heretical. Compare your frame of mind with the Church's teaching on the Holy Trinity. God is the Father, the world of orthogonal time is the Son, and the strat is the Holy Ghost, by means of which the Father creates the Son. According to the Church the orthogonal world is real, palpable, actually existing, while the strat, or Holy Ghost, is less real because it is spiritual and potential. It's a sort of median between the real world and God, who transcends reality.'

'I know my catechism,' Mayar muttered, a trifle put out by the lecture. Vro, however, continued. He enjoyed such discussions; although he was privately an atheist, theology fascinated him.

'Your own beliefs come closer to those of the Traumatics,' he repeated to Mayar. 'The world is unreal, or relatively so, and the strat is real. According to them the world is created by Hulmu, their god who dwells in the deeps of the strat, and he creates it by projecting it on to a screen, exactly as in a cinema. Its entire purpose is to comprise a sort of picture show for him. That's why their emblem of the creation is a hologram projector and why one of their ceremonial names for Hulmu is "the Projector Operator".'

'Strange that an organization with such horrible practices should support them with so philosophical a doctrine.'

'Oh, the cult of Hulmu is not new. It is at least as old as the Church. Some say it challenged the Church for supremacy in the early days.'

'You mean it sprang from an independent source?'
Mayar frowned. 'I always thought it was founded by
renegades.'

'The origin of the Traumatic sect isn't quite clear,'
Prince Vro admitted. 'But the Church's own doctrine
has been modified over the years. In the beginning it
was somewhat closer to the Traumatic beliefs. God was
deemed to dwell in the uttermost depths of the strat.
The Holy Order of the Chronotic Knights even organized
deep-diving expeditions to try to find God, but they all
came to grief. Later the Church's theology became more
sophisticated and now it is taught that God cannot be
found in any direction accessible to a time-ship. Seeking
for him by entering the deeps of time is regarded as a
trap for the ignorant, for it harbours not God but the Evil
One.'

'Hulmu.'

Vro nodded. 'Officially the Traumatics are devil-
worshippers. Hulmu is identified with the Adversary.
It's rather interesting that even the Church doesn't dismiss the sect as simple foolishness. In the Church's eyes
Hulmu really exists, though he deludes his followers into
believing him to be the creator.'

'Then the soul of Princess Veaa is in mortal danger,'
mumbled Mayar, and instantly regretted his words.

Vro's face clouded over. 'Yes, Archivist,' he said softly.
'But I may yet save her. Like a knight of old, armed and
ready, I shall go forth into the future!'

Aton materialized behind a pillar in the main court of the
inner sanctum.

While vectoring in on the spot he had glimpsed the
multitudinous activities of the palace. He had glimpsed
Emperor Philipium himself, holding audience with nobles, ministers, civil servants, and military commanders.

The court itself had an air of tension and excitement,
as though something was about to happen. Aton stepped
into the open, looking about the sumptuous place with

interest. There was much coming and going. All around him was the buzz of conversation.

Accustomed to a more austere life, Aton found the colour and luxury disconcerting. He was wondering how to achieve his object – an audience with the emperor – when an oval-faced young woman wearing the tiara of an Ixian princess caught him by the arm.

'Good evening, Captain. You're new here, aren't you?'

Hastily Aton bowed, frantically trying to place her from pictures he had seen of the imperial family. The trouble was that the family was so large. But he thought he recognized her as Princess Mayora, one of the emperor's own children.

'Are you going to be with the armada?' she asked, not giving him time to speak. 'But of course you are! A handsome fellow like you wouldn't let himself be left behind. Isn't it exciting? To fight for one's religion!' Her eyes sparkled.

Aton was about to frame a reply when a hush fell on the gathering. Through the padded doors came a procession; the emperor, noticeably tottering and with his right arm shaking visibly, was partly supported by servants. Behind him walked some of the dignitaries with whom he had recently been conferring. Close to the emperor, like an ever-present shadow, was Arch-Cardinal Reamoir, head of the Church. Something like triumph was on the arch-cardinal's face. Philipium's eyes, too, displayed a beady, unnatural brightness.

Everyone present bowed.

Philipium's weak, reedy voice rose to address the court. 'Our tribulations soon will be at an end,' he announced. 'All vessels of the armada have successfully finished their trials and are fully provisioned. In a few days the enterprise will begin!'

His words were greeted with cheering and applause. Philipium advanced through the great chamber, a path spontaneously appearing before him, until he faced the gold panel that took up a large section of one wall.

'*Imperator!* Grant us audience!'

The gold panel slid up. From out of the deep recess the massive machine-emperor slid out on its castors.

Aton stared, entranced. So this was the *Imperator*, the enigmatic construct that stood even higher than the emperor himself in the exercise of authority. And yet Aton had never heard of a single edict that had issued from it. In practical terms most people believed the *Imperator*'s power to be nominal only.

Philipium repeated his words to the humming machine. 'Give us your approval of this plan,' he added. 'Confirm its outcome, that our confidence may be justified.'

The humming sound emanating from the *Imperator* intensified and broadened, changing into a vibrant baritone voice.

'The enemy of the empire grows powerful. The struggle will ensue.'

Silence.

'Speak on, mighty *Imperator*!' Philipium urged. 'Grant us the wisdom of my fathers!'

This time a grating tone entered into the magnificent voice. It spoke falteringly, as if in distress.

'*The struggle will ensue!*'

'In your omniscience, grant us the boon of knowing that the outcome is certain, *Imperator*.'

But already the crenellated structure was retreating into its interior chamber. The gold panel slid down into place.

'Well, what do you make of that, Reamoir?' Philipium turned to his confessor, a frown on his narrow features.

'The *Imperator* is always cryptic, Majesty,' Reamoir murmured, 'but one thing is without doubt: it instructs us to continue with our plans.'

'Yes, that is so. That is so.'

Philipium was assisted to a throne, cushioned and moulded so as to give comfort to his weak frame, where he reclined, speaking occasionally to those who approached him.

The chatter of the court started up again.

Aton turned to Princess Mayora and in his urgency was nearly insubordinate enough to seize her by the arm. 'Your Highness, I must speak with your father. Will you help me?'

'What is this?' She smiled at him gaily. 'You have a petition? You are most importunate.' She leaned closer, becoming a shade more serious. 'Have a care. Father can be a crotchety old thing and is sometimes impatient with trifles.'

'This is no trifle, Your Highness. I cannot put the matter through the proper channels. But as an officer of the Time Service I feel it my duty . . .' He trailed off, realizing the impossibility of explaining who he was and how he had got here. 'If you could help me into His Majesty's presence I will risk the rest myself,' he murmured.

Somewhat curious, she sauntered towards the throne, beckoning him to follow. As they came near, he heard the emperor talking to his eldest son, the future emperor Philipium II.

'Not two hours ago a courier arrived from the dispatching station at Barek – from Commander Haight, no less, who put in there *en route* to Chronopolis. He has returned without the distorter but with the offer of a truce from the Hegemonics. It seems they want to parley for peace. That's a good sign they know how hopeless their situation is.'

Philipium II laughed. It was a reedy, dry laugh. He had inherited his father's manner of speech, as he had much else about him. 'Rather late for that now!'

The emperor nodded with satisfaction. 'No doubt our retaliatory attacks have taught them what's in store for them. Also they must have gained some intelligence concerning the might of our armada.' He frowned. 'Haight discovered something about the distorter, too, but we shall have to wait until he arrives here for his full report.'

Aton and the princess were now mingling with the courtiers surrounding the throne. Boldly Aton stepped forward to confront the emperor and prince.

'Your Chronotic Majesty!' he said in a loud voice.

Both men turned to look at him. Philipium II appeared cold and supercilious, the emperor merely startled.

For one instant Aton looked into his ruler's tired, feverish eyes and knew that his mission stood no chance of success. Behind those eyes was . . . nothing. The emperor was dead inside. There was nothing but bigotry, prejudice, set patterns of thought. Even if Aton were to persuade him of the truth of his story, which seemed unlikely, nothing at this stage could possibly cause him to alter his decision.

Aton glanced from him to the younger Philipium, and again from him to Arch-Cardinal Reamoir, who was hovering as always by the emperor's side. As before he found that his new perceptions laid bare their inner natures. In Philipium II there was only a blind arrogance that was a sort of later version of his father's unctuous religious humility. And in Reamoir there was ambition of truly shocking proportions: ambition that was prepared to sacrifice whole worlds, to cheat, lie and kill in the pursuit of personal and religious aims.

He stood, tongue-tied and white-faced, as the awful realization struck him.

'What is it, young man?' Philipium said sharply. 'Who are you?'

'Captain Aton of the Third Time Fleet, Your Majesty.'

'Then you should be helping defend the frontier. On leave, are you? Why?'

'. . . The action for Gerread, Your Majesty,' Aton said after a momentary effort.

'Ah, yes. Take courage, young man. Eventually we shall regain Gerread, together with all the other possessions that have been lost since.'

An official slid through the circle and murmured something in the emperor's ear, who then turned and began a conversation with someone else. No one took any notice of Aton. His rude intrusion had been forgotten.

Princess Mayora accosted him as he slipped away. 'Well, I don't think much of that!'

'I suddenly realized how foolish my course of action was,' Aton said ruefully.

'Rather belatedly, don't you think?' The princess eyed him with growing inquisitiveness. 'What was your petition? Can I help?'

'I think not, Your Highness.'

Awkwardly aware of his bad manners, Aton made a perfunctory bow and walked stiffly away. He felt desolated. Here was the centre of the empire and everyone around him was hell-bent on destruction. Impending calamity was tolling like a great bell.

It seemed that his mission was impossible.

Or almost impossible.

Hours later the court chamber was deserted and in half darkness. A shadow slipped through that darkness, pausing and listening to the sleep of the huge palace.

At length Aton stopped before the dully gleaming gold sheet that hid the *Imperator*.

He had spent the intervening time wandering through the inner sanctum or just sitting brooding in one of the libraries. No one questioned his presence. It was assumed that anyone who had managed to enter the sanctum had a perfect right to be there.

'*Imperator*,' he called in a hoarse voice, afraid to speak too loudly in case he was heard from outside the chamber. 'A loyal servant seeks audience.'

He had no idea whether the machine-emperor would respond to any voice but Philipium's. But it was worth a try.

Nothing happened, and he called again. '*Imperator*. The empire is in danger!'

Miraculously the golden panel withdrew towards the ceiling. From the dark cave came the whine of an engine and the rumble of castors. The *Imperator* rolled majestically into view, a strange sheen playing over its matt surface. A scarcely visible light seemed to flicker between its four corner towers.

'*Who has dared approach?*'

The thrilling full-bodied voice, even though at low volume, filled the hall. The experience of facing the *Imperator* alone was strange and frightening. The machine radiated charisma. Aton, conscious of its majestic relationship with the empire, felt small and insignificant.

'I am Captain Mond Aton,' he announced. 'Late of the Third Time Fleet.'

The *Imperator*, hummed and clicked. 'Sentenced to death for cowardice and dereliction of duty. Placed at the disposal of the Courier Service. Dispatched to the receipt of Commander Haight on the thirtieth day of the fifth month of this year.'

'The facts are as you state, *Imperator*. However I am still alive, as you can see.'

'Poor little tool of broken time . . .'

'*Imperator*, I have just returned from the Hegemony,' Aton said. He launched into his tale, describing Commander Haight's experiment, their meeting with the Hegemonic ministers, and his subsequent discovery of his new powers. Throughout, the *Imperator* made no interruption except for the continuous humming that swelled and receded in volume.

Finally, with complete frankness, Aton related the intransigence of the emperor and of the advisers who surrounded him. 'You are mightier even than the emperor, *Imperator*,' he said. 'Command that the empire make peace. Draw back from this suicidal course.'

'All must be as it has been.'

Aton puzzled over the words. He had heard that the *Imperator* rarely expressed itself in plain speech.

'The enemy of the empire is the enemy of mankind,' said the *Imperator*. 'Fight, Aton. The power is yours alone.'

'*Imperator*, I do not understand you. Can you not explain what I am to do? Your meaning is not clear.'

'We live in dreams and walk in sleep. All that is real is unreal.'

Suddenly Aton heard footsteps behind him. Approaching out of the gloom came a young man wearing a short cloak of deep purple. The face was that of an Ixian, but unlike most of that brood, the eyes had a steady percipience and the man's whole bearing an uncharacteristic lack of vanity. As he came closer Aton recognized Prince Vro.

'An incredible story!' said the prince.

'You heard?'

'Forgive my eavesdropping,' the other said with a shrug. 'I merely happened to be passing. It was a scene I could not resist. Yes, I listened to every word.'

A rumble caused Aton to whirl around. The *Imperator* was withdrawing into its chamber. The golden panel closed and left them in silence.

'I must say I think you're wasting your time petitioning that machine in there,' the prince told him affably. 'Nobody has ever got any sense out of it, and in my opinion never will for the simple reason that our much-vaunted *Imperator* is quite insane.'

Aton must have looked shocked, for Prince Vro laughed softly. 'Well, is it any wonder, my friend? Infused with the brains of all the emperors! If my father is anything to go by, it must consist of lunacy piled on lunacy.'

He clapped Aton on the back. 'We are somewhat exposed here. I was on my way to supervise the readying of my time-yacht, in preparation for a certain romantic quest. Come with me. Afterwards we can talk in my quarters.'

With a last despairing look at the *Imperator*'s dwelling, Aton followed.

Prince Vro's chill and morbid apartment intensified still further Aton's feeling of desperation. While looking over the yacht the prince had explained his great loss to him, describing the steps he was taking to recover his beloved.

Yet despite the prince's bizarre preoccupation, Aton saw him for a man of rare intelligence by the standards of the Imperial Palace. It was a relief to be able to talk to him.

'Hmm. This certainly explains the rule about the disposal of couriers,' Vro remarked, lounging in an easy chair and dividing his attention between Aton and the empty sarcophagus in the wall hologram. 'Evidently people exposed to the strat are liable to develop a natural time-travelling ability. The Church wouldn't like that.'

'Then that means I'm not the first,' Aton pointed out. 'The phenomenon must already be known. Where are the others?'

'It is, no doubt, a closely guarded Church secret,' Vro said. 'Chronmen who are pulled out of the strat are generally put in the care of secluded monasteries and are never heard of again. Officially that's because they're mentally deranged. Now we know there's more to it, eh, Captain? We can be sure care is taken to see they never realize their powers. You'd better watch your step or you might find yourself forcibly enlisted as a monk.' Vro smiled faintly.

Aton reflected. 'Did you mean what you said about the *Imperator*?' he asked.

'Of course. It's a demented machine, no more. That's why it's only a figurehead. My father can't quite believe it's not rational, of course. He treats it as a totem and consults it from time to time. But it never says anything meaningful.'

'Then will *you* help me, Your Highness?' Aton pleaded earnestly. 'You, at least, seem to understand what the present situation will lead to. Can you not try to persuade your father?'

'I?' Prince Vro chuckled. 'Affairs of state are far from my interests.'

'But how can you ignore them at a time like this?'

'I care only for my beloved Veaa,' Vro said, gazing pitifully into the mausoleum. 'Let the world perish, it's nothing to me.'

Aton sighed deeply.

'As for my father the emperor and his enterprise against the Hegemony,' Vro went on, 'that old lunatic could never be moved by anything I say to him anyway. I have not spoken to him for three years, yet he still expects me to command a wing of the armada! He will be disappointed. I shall not be here. I shall be away, into the future, to rescue my beloved and make her mine again!'

Without warning a change came over Vro's face. He leaped to his feet and appeared to be listening intently.

'What is it?' asked Aton in alarm.

'Can you not sense it?'

Aton became quiet and indeed did seem to sense something. A swelling that was inside him and outside him, in the air, in everything. Then he momentarily blacked out. When he came to, he was aware of a loss of consciousness lasting a split second.

Prince Vro went rushing about the room examining everything, peering into the mausoleum, studying his face in a mirror.

'What happened?' Aton asked in a subdued voice.

'That's the third time they've got through. Nothing's changed here anyway. But then, I wouldn't remember . . . not unless the change was discontinuous, perhaps not even then.'

'The Hegemonics? They can strike even here?'

Vro nodded. 'Usually they are beaten off, occasionally they manage to focus their projector for a second or two. Chronopolis has undergone a few minor changes, so the Achronal Archives tell us. I wonder what it is this time.' His lips twisted wryly. 'It could be for the best. Maybe my father has had some sense mutated into him.'

This revelation of how hard the Hegemonics were attacking was the most depressing thing Aton had met with so far. He laid his chin on his hands, thinking deeply. At length he decided upon something which had been brewing in his mind, but which he had not dared to think about up until now.

'You can see why my father is so keen to get the armada under way,' Vro remarked. 'Much more of this and there won't be any empire left.'

'But once the armada is launched everything will get worse!' Aton protested. 'Both sides will let loose with everything they've got. The Hegemonics will use the time-distorter at full aperture!'

Vro did not seem interested. 'What are you going to do now, Captain? You ought to give it some thought. It's dangerous for you here. Once someone realizes who you are they'll make short work of you.'

'I haven't stopped trying yet. The emperor won't listen to me. The *Imperator* won't. There's still someone left.'

'Who?'

'San Hevatar!'

Vro grunted. 'Him! What do you expect him to do?'

'I don't know. The whole empire springs from him. Perhaps he can change everything. Perhaps he could even suppress the invention of time-travel.'

'And wipe out the empire from the beginning?' Vro's voice was soft with awe.

There was a tight pain in Aton's chest. When he spoke, his tone was leaden. 'It sounds strange, doesn't it? I, a committed servant of the empire, talking of annulling the empire. The ultimate in treachery. But I can see no other way. It is not just the empire that's at stake now, it's mankind, perhaps time itself. Mad the *Imperator* may be, but one thing it said is true: the enemy of the empire is the enemy of mankind. Perhaps madmen – or mad machines – can see clearly what saner men cannot.'

'Your vision is certainly grandiose.'

'With no communication through time each node would live separately, undisturbed. There would be no Chronotic Empire, but neither would there be any time-distorter, any Chronotic war, any strain on the fabric of time. Who can say what will remain when it finally rents open?'

'And no Holy Church,' Vro reminded him. 'I wonder what San Hevatar will have to say to that.'

Aton turned to him. 'You tell me you are heading for Node Six in the morning, Highness. Have you room for me aboard your yacht? Can you drop me off in the hinterland?'

'I thought you could travel through time at will.'

'Not quite at will. I have already tried. It seems my nervous system only asserts the ability during an emergency, or under certain kinds of duress.'

'Well, it seems the least I can do,' Prince Vro murmured, 'to aid in the annihilation of the empire.'

9

The origin of the Chronotic Empire was, to some extent, obscured in the haze of recurrent time. It had taken place at a point in time that now lay between Node Five and Node Six – between Barek and Revere – about fifty years into the hinterland of Node Five. But two nodes had swept over the spot since the earth-shaking discovery attributed to San Hevatar. The empire had had three hundred years or more of nodal time, as apart from static historical or orthogonal time, in which to establish itself.

And during that nodal time the soul of San Hevatar had, of course, traversed his life several times, as had that of everyone around him. The world in which he lived had changed much in the course of those repetitions. The original San Hevatar would not have recognized it. Largely because of his own efforts, he was now born into a world where time-travel and the empire were already facts.

Most history books inferred that the Ixian family had already been the rulers of Umbul when San Hevatar placed the secret of time-travel at their disposal. Prince Vro told Aton, however, that he believed this to be a distortion of the truth. It was unlikely that the city of Umbul itself had existed in the beginning. As far as he could judge, the Ixians had not been kings or rulers, but the owners of a giant industrial and research conglomerate where San Hevatar had worked as a scientist. They had seized their chance to indulge their wildest ambitions, conquering past centuries, always moving pastward, where the technology was inferior to their own.

For his part San Hevatar had been a man with a vision. He had given a religious meaning to his discoveries and had found the past a fertile ground for his teachings. He had founded the Holy Church, thus giving the burgeoning Chronotic Empire a unifying culture.

Eventually the Ixians had realized that, once it was let loose on mankind, time-travel, which they had used so successfully, could also work against their interests. It would be particularly dangerous if time-travellers were to penetrate the empire's rear, travelling into the past beyond the empire's control and working changes there – changes which inevitably would influence the present in ways not planned by the Historical Office. They determined to fix a date in time beyond which time-travel could not be introduced. To this end the stupendous Stop Barrier had been built, consuming one-third of the imperial budget and rendering the past impenetrable to time-travellers. One day it would be moved back to bring yet more of history under the empire's control, but for the moment it remained both the pastward limit on the empire's expansion and its rearward protection.

Umbul, on the other hand, was much too close to the futureward frontier to be entirely safe from marauders from the future. A new imperial capital, Chronopolis, had been built close to the Stop Barrier, at what was designated Node I (although now another node, Node o, lay between it and the barrier), protected by nearly the full extent of the empire.

So San Hevatar, prophet and God's special servant, now lived a life of relative quietude away from the mainstream of events. But he continued, in each repetition of his life, to make the crucial discovery of how to move mass through time, paradoxically even while the evidence of that discovery was all around him *before he had made it*. It was as if his inner being performed this act as a sacred rite: the central, essential rite of the Church.

Captain Aton meditated on all this as Prince Vro's yacht crossed Node Five. 'Where in San Hevatar's life cycle would you like to intervene?' Prince Vro asked him politely.

It would be no use approaching the prophet when he was an eager young man, Aton thought. Someone on the verge of a momentous discovery would hardly be persuaded to abandon it. Aton needed to talk to a man who had time to reflect, who would be old enough to make a sober judgement.

'At about fifty years of age,' Aton requested.

'So late? That is a quarter of a century after the gift of time-travel. If your object is to annul the empire I would have thought, perhaps, a few decades earlier.'

'That is not really my object,' Aton said with a smile. 'It would, after all, be asking too much. But if San Hevatar were, perhaps, to appear at Chronopolis and speak against the war, then I am sure his word would carry more weight than that of all the emperors put together.'

'Maybe. If His Eminence Arch-Cardinal Reamoir does not declare him a heretic!' Vro laughed caustically.

The cabin of Prince Vro's yacht was not large (nearly all the vehicle's mass being taken up by its powerful drive unit) and with six passengers, three of whom were Perlo Rolce's assistants, Vro had been obliged to dispense with his crew and attend to both navigation and piloting himself. He typed some instructions into the yacht's computer and made adjustments in accordance with the figures it gave.

Rolce and his men, trying not to appear inquisitive, kept glancing at Aton surreptitiously. They could hardly believe what was happening.

The yacht slowed down as it approached Aton's target. Vro became fretful.

'I am at a loss to know where to phase into ortho,' he said. 'To tell the truth I am reluctant to do so at all. As you know, civilian timeships are forbidden to materialize anywhere between nodes, and I am not keen to make myself conspicuous. I'm afraid I shall have to land you somewhere quiet, Captain, and that could put you many hundreds of miles from San Hevatar.'

A strange look came to Aton's face. 'There's no need to phase in at all,' he told Vro. 'Just open the cabin door and let me out.'

Perlo Rolce surged to his feet, his hard face displaying most uncharacteristic shock.

'Your Highness!' He and his staff plainly thought Aton was insane. Prince Vro waved him back. 'It's all right, Rolce. We know what we're doing.' But even he looked at Aton in a puzzled, doubting way.

'You're sure of this?' he asked.

'As sure as a swimmer knows he can enter the water.'

Vro went to a cupboard and took out a flat box-like gadget attached to a belt. 'You'd better take this orthophase.'

'Thank you, although I'm not sure I shall need it.'

Aton strapped the device around his waist. Returning to the pilot's seat, Prince Vro watched the computer count-down while glancing at a small strat screen. 'Right. We're about there.'

'You'd all better face the wall,' Aton advised. 'Open the door, Your Highness.'

Vro tapped out the safety sequence on the computer keyboard. With a hum the door slid open. Beyond it, outside the ortho field, the strat billowed and swirled.

Aton steeled himself and leaped right into it.

After the door had closed again the five men remaining in the cabin turned and stared after him, not speaking.

The Manse of San Hevatar lay in a great park in the south-west of the city of Umbul: a quieter, more sedate Umbul than it would be at Node Six a hundred and twenty years hence. The park was dotted with shrines and religious monuments. The approach road that wound through the town was lined with churches, and that stretch of it that crossed the park was strewn every day with rose petals by order of the local bishop.

For all its magnificence the manse itself still bore traces of the research laboratory from which it had been converted. The limestone cupolas floated in places above rectilinear structures of glass and steel. An outhouse contained the powerful transformers, fed by underground cable, that had once provided energy for the scientists' experiments.

Like a ghost Aton observed all this as he approached from the strat. He phased into orthogonal time in a circular lobby, paved with mosaics, surrounded by balconies, and surmounted by a dome of frosted yellow glass.

The murmur of voices came from one side. Padding towards the sound, Aton found himself peering through the open door of a chapel. Two figures knelt before the altar, one wearing the prophet's mitre permitted to San Hevatar alone. The other was an older man, perhaps seventy, a small bent figure with a wrinkled face and bushy eyebrows.

Aton could not hear the words of the prayer or service which San Hevatar was intoning with feverish intentness. The older man was acting as his assistant, speaking the responses and holding a chalice of holy wine into which the prophet dipped his fingers, anointing both himself and the other.

Presently their business was finished. Both men stood, San Hevatar straightening his voluminous cope, and came away from the altar. It was then that San Hevatar saw Aton. He strode towards him.

'An officer of the Time Service!' he said wonderingly. 'And may I ask how you got in here? No permissions were given for today, and I have been informed of no unwarranted intrusions.'

'I made my own way here, Your Holiness, I have journeyed through time to see you. I feel that the information I have is so important that you must hear it.'

San Hevatar looked about him. 'You came through time? I see no timeship. I still do not understand how you entered my manse unobserved.'

'I came by my own power, Your Holiness. My brain has learned to propel me through the substratum.'

San Hevatar's eyebrows rose. He indicated a door to his left. 'In here. We will talk.'

When Aton had finished, San Hevatar's expression changed not at all.

'Your power is not entirely unknown,' he murmured. 'It was at one time the Church's intention to create a body of time-travelling sainted knights. But the gift is unreliable. One cannot initiate it at will. Conversely one never knows when it will spontaneously show itself. It appears to answer to the subconscious mind, not to one's thinking self. In that respect it resembles other legendary powers of the saints, such as levitation, the ability to talk to animals, and so on.'

'That is what I have found, Your Holiness.'

'And that is why the Church has kept it a secret. Anything that cannot be controlled is dangerous. There is another reason also. You must beware, Captain.'

'Holiness?'

'All chronmen fear the strat. You may think you have conquered that fear because you believe yourself safe in it. You are not. Eventually your power will fail and the strat will claim you. You will drown in the Gulf of Lost Souls, as have others who thought they had become supermen.'

Already Aton was beginning to feel that he would be disappointed for the third time. Even in middle age San Hevatar's face was striking. Full, sensuous lips, large soulful eyes, and an appearance of enormous self-collectedness that was somehow selfish rather than benevolent. It was the face of a fanatic. Aton could already guess what was coming.

'Your Holiness, the matter I have touched upon. You must agree that the Church, the empire, everything that has been achieved stands to be destroyed if the war continues. Instruct your Church in the foolishness of this Armageddon. The emperor is a deeply religious man; he would obey any command that came from you.'

San Hevatar smirked ever so slightly. He turned and glanced at the aged assistant who also sat with him, as though sharing some private joke with him.

'Have you so little faith?' he said quietly. 'The Church, the empire cannot – *must not* – be destroyed. It is eternal. The armada is God's plan. The Evil One must be fought. Mankind must be saved.'

As he uttered the last words San Hevatar seemed to find speech increasingly difficult. To Aton's amazement he passed his hand over his eyes and seemed to be in distress, rocking to and fro.

'Fight the enemy of mankind, Captain Aton!' he gasped as though in a trance. 'Conquer his minion! All is not as it seems!'

Aton was fascinated to hear the prophet coming out with words almost identical to those of the *Imperator*. Then San Hevatar seemd to recover himself and become once more self-composed. He stood up.

'Your concern, though bordering on the heretical, is commendable,' he said smoothly, as though unaware of his words of a moment before. 'It deserves a reward. It would be possible for me to have your sentence of death commuted. We have a certain monastery where by means of special techniques your dangerous gift can be unlearned and your nervous system returned to normal. Of course, it would be necessary for you to pass the rest of your life in seclusion, as a monk. You know too much to be returned to public life.' He nodded. 'Spend the night here and think it over. Rilke will look after you.'

Suddenly Aton said, 'What do you know about a man with jewels for eyes?'

He did not know why the image had come to his mind so abruptly, but the prophet's mouth opened and his face went ashen.

'You have *met* him? Already?'

'Yes.'

San Hevatar's expression closed up. He reminded Aton of an insulted woman as he swept from the chamber, his long cope rustling.

The old man regarded Aton for long moments with tired eyes. 'My name's Dwight Rilke,' he said, standing and offering his hand. 'Come along with me, I'll find you a room.'

Aton had slept for a number of hours when he was awakened by the sound of the door opening. He sat up. At the same time, the light came on.

Dwight Rilke entered the room, looking stooped, defeated and very tired. 'Sorry if I'm disturbing you, Captain, but I want to talk to you,' he said. He found a chair and sat down close to Aton, then licked his lips before speaking again in a dry, ancient voice.

'Listen, I've been doing some hard thinking,' he said. His eyes, though tired, were almost unnaturally bright. 'San Hevatar isn't really capable of responding to what you've been saying, you know. He's too deep into his role . . . the whole weight of the empire is on him. I'm the one you should have been talking to, because I'm the one you've convinced.'

Aton felt a stir of interest. 'Just who *are* you?'

'Me? I was Hevatar's assistant, you know.'

'Yes, I can see that.'

'No, I'm not talking about this religious stuff. I *was* his assistant; his scientific assistant. We were on the project together.'

'*The* project?'

'Yes. Would you like to see it?' Rilke rose. 'Come on, I want to show it to you. You don't mind, do you?'

He waited while Aton quickly dressed. Then Aton followed him through the passages and courtyards of the still brightly lit manse. Cowled monks and comforters stood guard here and there, some wearing handguns strapped over their habits. Rilke ignored them all, however, and halted before a door apparently made of solid lead. He took a big iron key from beneath his cloak and inserted it in a keyhole. There was a loud click, and the door swung open.

'Here you are, this is where it all began.'

They entered what Aton, after first taking in the profusion of heavy-duty equipment, realized was a high-energy physics research laboratory. This, he supposed with a feeling of awe, was the centrepoint of the whole empire.

Carefully Rilke closed the door behind them.

'So this is where San Hevatar discovered the secret of time-travel!' Aton breathed reverently.

'Him? He didn't discover it,' Rilke told him flatly. 'I did.'

Aton stared at him blankly. 'You?'

'Hevatar developed it, but I made the initial discovery.' Rilke's face softened, and he began to reminisce. 'We were a team. Hevatar was the leader, Absol Humbart and myself were his chief assistants. There was a lot more equipment in here in those days. There were particle accelerators, high-energy plasma chambers, and so forth. But we weren't even thinking of time-travel then. We never dreamed it was possible. We were investigating the nuclear binding force of baryons, that was all. One day I thought of a new way to isolate pi-mesons. When I set up the apparatus, by chance a surge gate malfunctioned and there was a sudden rush of power. Suddenly I found I had discovered a way to accelerate pi-mesons faster than light.'

The old man looked around the laboratory as if remembering. 'It was an accident, a million-to-one shot. From then on, Hevatar took over. Naturally he grabbed something like that with both hands, and he explored it from all angles. Before long he had discovered the most important consequence of the effect I had produced: that it could be used to move mass through time. From then on there was no stopping him. He takes all the credit for it now, of course, but none of it would have happened if I hadn't carried out that one experiment.'

'You must feel proud.'

'Do I? For a long time I did. But lately it frightens me. We get all the news here; we're privileged in that respect. History is being ripped apart. It's like seeing the end of the universe, but no one seems to realize that time itself can collapse and no one wants to stop it. I opened a real Pandora's box when I made that experiment. And when you came this afternoon I realized that everything had gone too far.'

'What happened to this other man – Absol Humbart? Is he dead?'

Rilke turned away and muttered something Aton could barely catch. 'We've spoken of him already. Let's not go into that.'

Aton reflected bitterly that of the only two people to share his view of the situation, one was too obsessed with his insane love for a corpse to care and the other was this weary old man.

'I'm glad that you at least agree with me,' he told Rilke. 'But there seems little we can do.'

'Isn't there? There's something *I* can do. Something I can try to do, at least. I can go back in time, prevent any of it from happening.'

'You can do that?'

Rilke led him to a large dull-brown cabinet that at first Aton had taken to be a cupboard. 'This is a functional time-machine. The very first, in fact.' He opened the door. Inside Aton saw seats, a control panel.

'You really think you stand a chance of influencing Hevatar's – or your own – younger self?'

Rilke's smile was wintry. 'Hevatar has never been influenced by anybody. As for myself, I was an eager young pup and I certainly wouldn't have passed up the chance to make a crucial discovery, not for anyone. Besides, there's something you need to understand. We didn't know the empire existed in those days. It's strange, isn't it? Time has changed such a lot. Past, present and future have all changed. But there's one thing the empire and Church are very careful to see doesn't change. They are careful to preserve the vital event that led to the creation of the empire. San Hevatar and myself were brought up under special conditions and weren't allowed to know that there already was time-travel. We worked for the same company, Monolith Industries, that presumably we had worked for before anything had altered. But not until we had unearthed that one secret of how the time-drive works was the truth gradually revealed to us.' He smiled. 'It was like coming out of a dream. In a way we'd known all along; there was plenty of evidence for it if we had cared to piece it together. But we never had. The answer is, of course, that we were psychologically constrained in some way.

'And that's why,' he finished briskly, 'my younger self would never believe me if I went to him with such a wild tale.'

'It's logical,' Aton commented. 'The Historical Office would want to avoid paradoxes in anything as important as that. But you mentioned another assistant, Absol Humbart. Presumably he was put through this procedure too?'

'Did I mention Absol Humbart? No, he wasn't there,' Rilke said vaguely. 'Maybe he was in the earlier repetitions.'

The point didn't seem worth pursuing. 'So what *do* you propose to do?' Aton asked.

The old man produced a heavy hand beamer from under his cloak. 'Kill myself,' he said simply. 'It's the only way. Kill the young Rilke before he makes that experiment in isolating pi-mesons, then none of this can happen. There'll be no empire, no Chronotic wars. The world will be as it was before time-travel was invented.'

'And how was that, do you think?'

'I don't know. Nobody seems to know any more.'

'Kill yourself,' Aton said woodenly. 'Are you really prepared to do that?'

'Somebody has to do something. I can't think of any other way, and besides I'm really responsible for what's happening.' His face creased. 'It's taken me six hours to reach this decision. Now I've taken it, I know what to do.'

'Paradoxes,' Aton murmured. 'If you kill your earlier self, then you'll no longer be alive to kill yourself.'

'We'll just have to let that sort itself out.' Rilke jutted out his jaw ruminatively.

'Why have you taken the trouble to tell me all this?'

'Piloting the machine is a two-man job. One to navigate, one to steer. If anything happens to me you'll still be able to get back, though. It's programmed to retrace its course automatically.'

'If you succeed,' Aton mused, 'there won't be any question of coming back. There'll be no time-travel. As a matter of fact, I probably won't exist. Few people now living will.'

'True. Well, what about it?'

Dwight Rilke's self-sacrifice did not surprise Aton or occasion any particular admiration in him. The issues at stake were so awesome that the fate of any individual shrank to insignificance. Rilke was clearly not aware, however, of the other side of the coin; if the world returned to its original state, humanity would become extinct in a few hundred years.

But, in fact, Aton was certain that the reversion would not be anything like as complete as the aged scientist imagined; otherwise he would not for a moment have contemplated letting Rilke carry out the scheme. Rilke's understanding of Chronotic mutations was evidently crude and simplistic. He did not realize that the original world had been so deeply erased that it could probably never reappear. Something else, resembling it in many features perhaps, would assemble itself out of the jumble the Chronotic Empire had made of time.

Which meant there was a good chance the annihilatory war that had made a desert of Earth would never take place. Mankind would survive even without time-travel.

'All right, I'll be your navigator,' he told Rilke. 'But it's your show.'

He followed Rilke into the narrow cabin and examined the controls. They were antiquated, but he recognized them as the forerunners of the timeship controls he was used to.

Rilke closed the door and busied himself preparing for the journey. The drive unit started up with a whine, and Aton realized it was more powerful than he had first thought.

He studied the navigator screen. Rilke, mumbling to himself, phased them into the strat.

The Umbul of Node Six was a place of slender towers whose smooth walls, straddled at the base, curved up to end in knife-edge peaks. It was a place of boulevards and curiously intricate passages that wound around the base legs of the soaring buildings. Inpriss Sorce ran through these passages in blind panic.

She had been in Umbul for a day and a half, during which she had not slept. She had found nowhere to live, nowhere to earn money. She had been too busy running.

On the chronliner she had searched desperately for the handsome young Time Service officer who had promised to help her. He was nowhere to be found and she could think of only one explanation: the Traumatics had already murdered him. Neither had she seen the man he had left the passenger lounge with.

But the officer's warning was not lost on her. The Traumatics were playing cat-and-mouse with her. She could not escape them and they would kill her when they were ready.

When the chronliner docked she had fled into the city. She soon discovered there was nowhere she could go. As she stepped off the disembarkation ramp a man had emerged from the crowd and smiled at her.

It had been Rol Stryne!

She had run past him, but he hadn't tried to stop her. Since then either he or the other man, Velen, had seemed to appear everywhere.

Now her nerve had finally cracked. She ran up to strangers in the street. 'Help me, please help me!' But they shouldered off her hysterical pleas. Once or twice she mentioned the Traumatics, but that only made the response even more hostile. The Traumatics were a secret power, here in Umbul as elsewhere, and there was scarcely a citizen who would knowingly cross them.

Inpriss collapsed on to a bench, sobbing.

A man sat down beside her.

'You see, baby, it just isn't any good to fight it. Go along with it, it's better that way.'

She looked up open-mouthed into the lean, predatory face of Stryne.

'You just have to co-operate,' he told her soothingly. 'Then the hunt will be over.'

Suddenly she was like a rabbit hypnotized by a stoat. Her eyes were glazed. 'You want me to come with you willingly,' she said in a flat, empty voice. 'That's why you let me go before. Because I wasn't willing.'

'That's right, honey. You understand now.' He flashed a knowing glance at Velen, who was standing nearby, and made a signal to the helpers, who had been keeping track of the woman for them and were hovering in the background, to disperse.

She had broken and would obey them. Stryne knew how to recognize the signs. In a way he was slightly regretful it was ending so soon. Many victims kept up the chase for years. He knew of one, a man, who had been pursued for two decades before submitting.

'Hulmu is the only true reality, sweetheart. You'll find that out soon. You're going to him.'

She closed her eyes.

'Come on, Inpriss. Let's go.'

Meekly she rose and walked with the two men, clutching her satchel. She was in the grip of some-thing she had never felt before: a resignation so strong it overpowered her. It wasn't as if they had broken her will. It was as if her will had changed, so that she agreed with what they were going to do to her, simply because she couldn't see any other fu-ture.

'You see, honey, by the time we get to this stage we're doing you a favour,' Stryne told her as they walked. 'Just imagine if we didn't sacrifice you for some reason or another. Every time your life repeated you'd have to go through all this again. But this way your life won't repeat. Your soul will go to Hulmu. You'll never have to endure the pursuit again.'

'Where are we going to do it?' Velen asked eagerly. 'Somewhere nice and quiet? We could hire a hotel room.'

'We have to go to the main temple,' Stryne informed him. 'The Minion himself is taking an interest in this case. He'll be watching.'

'The Minion? Wow!'

'Yes, he's one, your Highness. I was right.'

In Prince Vro's suite in the discreet, extremely select Imperial Hotel a man was stretched out on the floor. The oblong plates of the field-effect device stood on either side of his head. Perlo Rolce fiddled with the device's knobs, watching a small screen with a greenish tint across which dim shapes flickered, while one of his men knelt by the prisoner holding a pain-prong.

Progress had been much quicker than even Vro had hoped. Rolce had started by visiting the street where Archivist Mayar believed the causal hiatus might have occurred. While using a map to help him look out the likely routes where the body might have been taken, he had noticed some activity an untrained person would not have observed. In his own words the place was 'crawling with snoopers'. Rolce had taken a chance and his men had performed a routine but efficient street kidnapping.

'Why should so many Traumatics be on the street?' Vro asked with a frown, sipping a liqueur.

'That's easily answered, Your Highness. This man's part of a pursuit operation. They are harrying some poor devil through the city till he drops.'

He nodded to his assistant to apply the prong again, repeating his question to the prisoner. The Traumatic gave a long gurgling scream and squirmed on the thick pile of the carpet, and Rolce kept watch on the screen, stroking his chin.

He had long found that a field-effect device coupled to long jolts of unbearable agony provided an almost foolproof method of interrogation. The subject might discipline his mind so as to prevent the answers the inquisitor sought from forming there, but pain broke down this discipline. While his attention was preoccupied with pain, images and information flooded into the body's electrostatic field automatically, quite against his will.

'He doesn't know anything about Princess Veaa,' Rolce declared at length. 'But he knows the address of their chief temple here in Umbul.'

'So what do you recommend now?'

'The princess might be in the temple, or nearby. At any rate someone there should know what has been done with her.' Rolce cogitated briefly. 'Our best bet is to act quickly and decisively, before the Traumatics have time to suspect anything amiss; the disappearance of one of their members, for instance, might alert them to trouble. I suggest a raid on the temple, perhaps assisted by the police or by members of the Imperial Guard stationed here. Even if the princess is not on the premises we are very near the end of the trail.'

Vro gestured floorwards. 'And what of him?'

'If the majordomo can be depended on to dispose of a corpse . . .'

'Have no fear. The standards of service in this hotel know no limit.'

'In that case . . .' Rolce bent low, taking from his pocket a rubbery cylinder which he applied to the prisoner's head. The struggling Traumatic went limp as the weapon turned his brain to jelly.

'Now, Your Highness, I propose that we make our move with the least possible delay.'

Inpriss Sorce was privileged to be sacrificed with full ceremony upon the altar of Hulmu, in the Umbul Temple itself.

She stared as if hypnotized at the representation of Hulmu's Impossible Shape. Here it was not an abstract sculpture but a hologram mobile that writhed and twisted. Stryne noticed her fascination and seized her chin in his hand to forcibly avert her gaze. If one stared at it too long one's eyes began to move independently of one another and sometimes did not right themselves for up to an hour.

As the accredited pursuers, Stryne and Velen had the right to perform the ceremony with no other Traumatics present. A camera had been set up so that the Minion, founder and leader of the Traumatic sect, could watch from another part of the temple.

'Do you believe in Hulmu now, honey?' Stryne asked Inpriss.

'Yes,' she said weakly. And she did. Evil as powerful as theirs could not be founded only on imagination. Something real had to exist behind it.

'He does exist, you know,' Stryne assured her. 'The God of the Church, *he* doesn't exist. We are all Hulmu's creatures. He projected us on to the screen of time, so he could watch us. Mmmmmm.'

The two men moved about the room adjusting the various apparatuses it contained. 'Strip off, Inpriss,' Stryne said.

Obediently she removed her clothes.

'Fine. OK, lie down on the altar.' His voice became caressing.

They began the ceremonies, going through the Compounding of Villainies, the Plot and Counterplot, the Scriptwriter's Diversion. To indulge themselves, though it was not obligatory, they both performed the Ritual of Mounting for the second time, offering up the orgasms to Hulmu as before. Sex and death always went well together.

The devices around them hummed and clicked, many of them performing symbolic functions secret to the sect. Eventually, at their prompting, Inpriss began to speak the responses herself. This was most important. The victim's co-operation had to be genuine.

Stryne and Velen knew that Inpriss had reached a stage of resignation quite divorced from reality: a state that was almost euphoria. If they did their job properly this would be followed by a return to cold realism, a new appreciation of the horror of her position. That was what made the euphoria so useful: the subsequent mental agony was that much greater.

Velen flicked a switch. A chill, urgent vibration undulated through the room. It acted on Inpriss Sorce like cold water. Her eyes widened and came into focus. There came a pause in the Traumatics' chanting.

'What will happen to me when my soul is in the gulf?' she asked in a quivering voice.

'You will be Hulmu's to terrify and torture as he pleases.' Stryne's voice was harsh and brutal.

Suddenly she was shaking all over, her naked limbs knocking uncontrollably against the altar table, and Stryne knew she was ready – in the state of terror required by the ritual. One that would multiply the natural death trauma a hundredfold.

To verify it he consulted one of the monitoring instruments that were arranged around the altar. Her fear index had passed the hundred mark.

Yet he knew that her obedience remained unconditional; her mind had given up believing in any kind of escape.

Finally he switched on an apparatus resembling a miniature radar set. From its concave scanner bowl a mauve effulgence crossed the room and bathed Inpriss Sorce in a pale flickering aura.

This device was probably the most essential of the sect's secrets. The method of its manufacture had been imparted by the Minion himself, who was said to have received it direct from Hulmu. The gadget ensured that during the death trauma the soul would be detached altogether from the body it had clung to for so long. No longer would Inpriss Sorce return to the beginning of her life and live again. She would sink bewildered into potential time, to be seized by Hulmu and enjoyed by him.

Stryne nodded to Velen. They had already decided to accomplish Inpriss's exit by means of slowly penetrating knives. They picked up the long shining weapons.

'Arch your back. Lift your body upwards,' he ordered.

Inpriss obeyed. Her belly and breasts strained up off the table to meet the downpointing knife points.

Slowly the knives descended.

In the prototype time-machine Aton and Dwight Rilke spoke little to each other until they approached the end of their journey. Rilke was meticulous about the final vectoring in. He knew to the minute where he wanted to go.

The laboratory they emerged into was the same one they had left, but less tidy, better equipped, and obviously a place of work rather than a carefully preserved museum. Its sole occupant sat at a workbench with his back to them, poring over some papers and oblivious of their arrival.

Aton viewed this on the time-machine's external vidscreen. Rilke picked up his beamer. He was trembling and there was perspiration on his wrinkled face.

'You're afraid,' Aton said quietly.

The other nodded. 'Not for me. For *him*.'

'How do you see your past self? Is he like someone else? Or is he still *you*?'

Rilke did not answer the question. 'You stay in here, Captain,' he said. 'This is something I ought to do, nobody else.' He paused, then opened a fascia panel beneath the control board. Another beamer was in the small compartment.

'He has a gun too,' he told Aton. 'One shooting lead slugs. Maybe he'll kill me instead. If so, you'd better finish it. Think you can?'

'If I have to.'

Rilke opened the sheet metal door and stepped out. Hearing the sound, the young Rilke turned. Aton saw a steady-eyed young man in his thirties who was less confused than most would have been by the sudden appearance of the bulky cabinet.

'Who are you?' he said sharply after a long time. 'How did you get here?'

The elder Rilke was close to collapsing with the emotion of the moment. 'I am your elder self, Dwight,' he cried in a shaking voice. 'And I'm here to kill you!'

The other looked startled and then, surprisingly, laughed. 'You lunatic!' he leaned over and held down a switch. 'Security? I have an intruder.' Then he turned back to the old man. 'Now why should you want to kill me?'

'Because in a few years you are going to discover something that will turn the world inside out. Look at me, Dwight, don't you recognize me?'

Aton was wondering why Rilke was prolonging the scene instead of getting it over with. Then he understood. Rilke could not bear to see his younger self die in ignorance. He had too much respect for himself.

And that self-respect was liable to prove fatal to his intentions. The young Rilke was astute. He glanced from Rilke to the time-machine as if prepared to take the old man's words seriously. Then he suddenly stood and crossed to one of the cupboards lining the walls of the laboratory and produced from there a hand weapon made of a bluish metal.

Old Rilke, who had kept his beamer out of sight up to now, pointed it and fired. From his shaking hand the beam went wide. The younger man dodged out of the way, turned, pointed, and fired his own gun.

Two loud bangs shattered the air of the laboratory. There was no visible beam but something whanged off some metal support struts. Old Rilke, it seemed, hadn't been hit. He took his beamer in both hands and held down the beam on continuous – a rarely used ploy since it exhausted the power pack. Before it faded the dull red ray scythed across the younger man, who toppled to the floor.

Aton came to the open door of the time-machine. Rilke let fall his beamer. His face sagged.

'It's done!' he said hoarsely. 'It's done!'

Aton stared with interest at the living paradox.

And then what life there was in Rilke's eyes went out. He collapsed to the floor as if every string holding his body together had been cut. With amazing rapidity the flesh began to dry up and shrivel. In little more than a minute nothing remained but a skeleton covered with parchment-like skin.

The paradox was resolved. If the time element was taken out it was a simple suicide.

In moments the security men would be here. Aton gazed around himself once more, marvelling at his continued existence. Then he moved back to the control board.

Experimentally he depressed the automatic retrack stud.

The drive unit started up with a whine and instantly phased the time-machine into the strat.

He sat passively while it carried him back to the starting point, his thoughts subdued. Through the still-open door he could see the naked strat and the conjunction of that with the orthogonal interior of the cramped cabin was one of the oddest things he had ever seen. It occurred to him that there was a way he could control, to a limited extent, his time-travelling ability. He could take a timeship into the strat, open one of its ports, and jump out to go where he pleased – if his subconscious did not take over for him. He could jump out now if he liked. But he decided to see the thing through, and after a while closed the door. From time to time he did some navigational checking to make sure the automatic pilot wasn't being blown off course by Chronotic vagaries, but everything seemed to be functioning normally.

When the machine phased back into orthogonal time San Hevatar was standing in the laboratory looking pensive. Aton stepped calmly out of the cabinet.

'Where have you been?' San Hevatar asked sombrely.

'Trying to straighten out time,' Aton said with a cynical twist of his lips, dispensing with the customary deferences. 'Your assistant Rilke suddenly became one of *my* disciples and thought he could cancel out everything that happened since you and he worked together. But he was wrong.'

178 The Fall of Chronopolis

Concisely he related what had taken place. San Hevatar was not in the least embarrassed by the disclosure that it had been Rilke who discovered the basic principle behind the time-drive. He merely remarked that for purposes of religious mythology it was better that he, founder of the Church, should be the man to take the credit and that he, in his humility, should attribute it to a direct revelation from God.

'I suspected it would turn out like this,' Aton finished. 'That's one tenet of the Church that's apparently true. Once invented, time-travel stays invented. Rilke's sacrifice was unavailing because paradoxes don't alter anything.'

San Hevatar nodded thoughtfully. 'I always considered that the Historical Office's protective attitude towards the crucial God-given event is unnecessary. Chronotic history is much too ravelled to be undone so easily. The very fact of time-travel weakens from the outset the unique relationship between cause and effect, even when movement is only from node to node. So now, we have time-travel without its ever being invented. Truly wondrous.'

'And truly disastrous,' Aton said. 'Rilke couldn't wipe out the empire, but the Hegemony can. And probably mankind with it.'

The prophet was staring at Aton with a terrible burning intensity. '*You are he!*' he gasped abruptly. 'You are the one! I know you!' He passed a hand across his eyes and swayed as though suffering from dizziness.

'What are you talking about?' Aton demanded harshly.

'Forget my small deceptions,' San Hevatar said with a weary smile. 'Despite those, I am still a prophet of God and occasionally I see through the veil.' His voice became dreamy. 'You are our hope, Aton. You are God's champion, His sword, to fight the enemy of Church and empire.'

A dizziness came over Aton also as he heard the unexpected words. Then, from deep within his mind, he seemed to feel an urgency, a summons. He struggled against the feeling and tried to frame a reply to San Hevatar.

But it was no use. The subconscious part of his nervous system was asserting itself again.

Aton phased into the strat.

He went hurtling futureward – plusward, in chronman's language. All around him flamed and roared the supernal fire of the strat. As he went, that fire burned into him and he realized that his personal ortho field was down. He was soaking up transcendental energies, was becoming multi-dimensional in his nature and powers.

Because he was fused with this fire, because he maintained no subjective sense of passing time, the journey to his new destination involved no duration. He was vaguely aware that he was skimming at tremendous speed close under the silvery lead screen of orthogonal time. The events on the screen raced past him in a blur of motion.

Then the screen swayed as he slowed down and approached a certain location on it. He found himself looking into a room in a tall building in Node Six. Two men, one lean and feral, the other pudgy and bland, stood over a naked woman who lay on a cloth-draped table, her back arched. In their hands were gleaming daggers which they were bringing down slowly and deliberately towards her white body. All around stood humming, clicking, droning instruments.

Coming closer, Aton knew where he had seen the woman before. She was Inpriss Sorce.

He phased into orthogonal time.

To the two Traumatics it seemed as if he had emerged from the Impossible Shape of Hulmu, for he materialized between it and the altar. They stumbled back with cries of fear, convinced for a moment that their god had appeared to them. Aton was surrounded by a shining halo of iridescent colours. The energies with which he was saturated pulsed and flashed as he moved.

Then they regathered their courage, and, deciding in their confusion that Aton was after all but human, moved in to attack with daggers extended.

A dazzling cloud of pure power, like a charge of ball lightning, shot from Aton's chest and enveloped Styrne, who fell dead.

Velen halted in his stride and stood looking stupid, the knife held awkwardly in his hand. His attention wandered perplexedly between Stryne and Aton. A second power charge soared towards him and he died soundlessly.

Aton stepped softly to the girl. She still lay quivering with back arched, eyes closed, little grunts of exertion coming from her throat as she awaited the knife thrusts. As gently as he could, he put an arm under her shoulders, raised her to a sitting position, and told her to open her eyes.

She looked at him blankly. 'You're safe now,' he said. But it was plain she was in deep shock. Someone who had been subjected to her experience could remain a psychiatric case for years.

He put his hand to her brow. Subtle powers flowed from his palm into her brain. He could sense her every thought, every crevice and receptacle of her mind. Into those hollows he sent healing influences as his thoughts flowed into hers.

Eventually she stopped shivering and became normally alert and calm. 'Thank you,' she said.

'Get dressed. We're leaving.'

While she hurriedly pulled on her garments he prowled around the room, contemptuously knocking over the still-active items of equipment. When he came to the holo camera he cursed himself for not having noticed it before, but disconnected its lead.

He knew that he was at the back of the building and on the third floor. He opened the door and peered out. Glancing back to make sure she was ready, he signalled her to follow him. Together they ventured into the corridor.

On either side were doors, from some of which came the sound of murmurs or muffled chanting. Aton led Inpriss to a staircase. Confident of his ability to deal with all comers, he set off down it, leading her by the hand.

On the second floor a door opened a few yards along the corridor and a bony-faced figure wearing a preoccupied look stepped out. Aton pulled up sharply at the sight of him.

'Sergeant Quelle!'

Quelle looked up, jerked out of his reverie, and plainly could not believe his eyes. His lips mumbled something inaudible. He seemed rooted to the spot. Then, with an inarticulate cry, he turned and tried to claw his way back through the doorway.

Aton raised his free hand and pointed with his index finger. From the finger issued a tight, brilliantly white ray that struck Quelle on the back of the skull. Along the ray passed images: a succession of images at the rate of billions per second. A few of them were marginally visible to Aton and Inpriss, rushing along the narrow beam like a superfast comic strip.

The heretical sergeant fell headlong to the floor, his brain overloaded and burned out by the unnaturally high rate of impressions that had been forced into it.

More Traumatics crowded the doorway in answer to Quelle's cry of alarm. Aton released more power balls in their direction, feeling exultant in his newly acquired might. Inpriss simply watched, her disbelief totally suspended by everything she had been through.

Again he led her down the stairway, but now the building was coming to life. He heard the sound of running feet, of doors opening and slamming.

Aton was puzzled. Could all this activity be on account of him? Not, he reasoned, unless they had been observed by remote, which could not have been by means of the camera in the altar room or they would have been intercepted before now.

One floor further down his question was answered. Here the staircase descended to a lobby opening out from the building's hotel-like front entrance, whose doors had been forced. The lobby was filled with the toques, plumes and grim faces of the Imperial Guard. The temple was being raided.

The guardsmen spread out through the building, trotting past the two fugitives as they mounted the stairs. The captain of the invading force put a bullhorn to his lips.

'The building is surrounded. There is no escape. Come down and surrender to the forces of the law.'

As soon as they appeared Aton and Inpriss were seized and hustled urgently down to the lobby. Aton found himself face to face with Prince Vro Ixian, who was accompanied by the stocky Perlo Rolce.

The prince, enwrapped in a purple cloak, presented a picture of youthful hauteur. He raised his eyebrows on seeing Aton.

'But that the question might provoke a lengthy answer,' he said, 'I would ask what you are doing here.'

'Highness, the lady with me is one of the Traumatics' victims,' Aton replied. 'I beseech you to guarantee her safety. She has suffered much at their hands.' In a lower voice he murmured: 'She needs careful handling.'

Vro gestured impatiently to the guardsmen who held the two in their grip. 'It's all right, they are no Traumatics. Release them.'

Inpriss immediately curtsied, apparently overawed by the presence of royalty. Vro acknowledged her with a just-perceptible movement of his head, but his eyes softened.

'Did they abduct you too, my dear? Never fear, you are under the protection of the House of Ixian now. This nest of villains will be cleaned out. Here, let my officer take care of you.'

He called over the Captain of the Guard. As Inpriss was led away, she looked back imploringly at Aton. He smiled and nodded to her, trying to reassure her.

Prince Vro turned back to Aton. He could not help but notice a change in him since he had last seen him. There was something godlike about the handsome young officer. His eyes were stern and flashing; his whole being seemed charged with life and energy.

'We are here looking for my beloved Veaa,' he told Aton. 'I would appreciate your assistance. Have you acquainted yourself with the layout of this den?'

'I'm sorry to disappoint you. I arrived here only in the last few minutes. But I have killed three Traumatics in that time.'

'Easy,' Prince Vro objected, 'I want them alive.'

They walked together up the staircase and through the house. Aton watched as Vro's detective and his assistants questioned the Traumatics who were brought to them, using a combination of torture and field-effect device. Most were eliminated after a minute or two; Rolce did not become interested until he interrogated one of the two women to be found.

She was a tough-faced woman of about fifty whose ragged hair bore streaks of grey. 'She knows something,' Rolce announced as she lay between the plates of the device. 'I'm getting images.'

Vro peered close. On the monochrome screen flickered the shadowy spectre of a young girl in a coffin. 'Veaa!' he cried in a choked voice.

'The prong, long and hard!' snapped Rolce.

The female Traumatic screamed and drew in breaths in hard noisy gasps. 'I'll talk!' she begged. 'I'll talk!'

'Let her talk!' commanded Prince Vro.

'That's not necessary, Your Highness. Information is more reliable when obtained by field effect.'

'Let her talk!' roared Vro. He leaned close. 'You know of Princess Veaa. Was her body brought here?'

'Ye-e-e-s.' The woman's lips twisted lasciviously. 'An imperial princess! The Minion thought her soul might be retrievable. That it was suspended in the strat.'

'And was it?'

'No. She was good and dead. Properly dead. Her soul had gone back to the beginning, like everyone else's.' Her face registered disgust.

'So what did you do . . . with the body?'

'Kept it. For a trophy.'

'Is it here in the temple?'

'No.'

'Then where?'

'Don't know.' She shrugged. 'In the city somewhere.'

Rolce ascertained that she was telling the truth. And as more interrogatees were put under the device, Vro grew more and more fretful. Many of them knew of Princess Veaa. But no one seemed to know where she had been taken.

'Don't despair, Your Highness,' Rolce comforted him. 'She's been here, that's certain. It's a routine matter to trace her from here on.'

Aton decided to explore the temple and left them to it. It was fairly quiet now, but the Imperial Guard would have their work cut out to winkle out everyone in a building so large. There were probably a hundred hiding places. Aton made his way upstairs towards the area where he had found Inpriss. Perhaps, he thought vaguely, he could find what Prince Vro was looking for.

He opened all doors he came to as he went. He saw altar rooms, storerooms filled with enigmatic equipment, rooms for mysterious purposes. In some of the rooms people huddled in corners and stared at him fearfully. He did not envy them; the Church was not kind to heretics.

Venturing down a deserted corridor he heard a strange mewing sound from behind a door. Aton hesitated, then opened the door slowly and slid inside.

Standing with its back to him was a fat, shabby, slope-shouldered figure holding in pudgy hands a mirror-like object whose surface crawled and shimmered with unrecognizable shapes. The mewing seemed to be an expression of pleasure or amusement as the man gazed into the roiling surface.

At Aton's entrance he put down the mirror and turned to face him. Aton confronted a being straight out of a nightmare, a nightmare he had endured only recently.

The man with jewels for eyes!

The crystal-filled sockets flashed and glittered in a multitude of colours. The face was pudgy and covered with a film of sweat. The slobbery mouth was agape with mirth.

'Come in, Captain Aton, and close the door!' welcomed the creature, its voice giggly and cheerful. 'I have been waiting for you!'

Aton felt an urge to retreat, to get away. 'Who – what – are you?'

'I? Do you not know? I am Hulmu's Minion, chief of all his worshippers!'

'But you are not human.'

'Not human? Indeed I am! A little extended, perhaps, but that is because I am Hulmu's pet, his little favourite. Like you, I am familiar with the strat. I have been all the way down to Hulmu, to let him sport with me. From time to time he gives me little presents and gadgets. He gave me these eyes, all the better to see in the strat with.'

'Hulmu is real?' Aton became aware of a peculiar, offensive odour the Minion gave off.

'Oh, indeed! Do not doubt it. He gave me the time-distorter, all the better to wreak havoc with.'

'The distorter? It comes from *you*?'

'Correct. Surprised?' The Minion lolled his head disclaimingly. 'I don't use it much myself,' he drawled. 'I have an arrangement with the Hegemonics – purely out of the goodness of my heart, of course. When they want to raid the empire, I lend it to them. Afterwards I take it back for safe-keeping. They tried to keep it for themselves once. They still don't know how I got it back!' He chortled.

'There is only one?'

'Only one. It's enough.'

'Why don't they try to make another?'

'Can't. They might have tried to analyse it, I dare say. No human being will ever make a gadget like my time-distorter. Only Hulmu is clever enough for that.'

'But why? Why should you want to destroy the empire?'

'Why not? It's all part of Hulmu's plot and counterplot. He is the scriptwriter, is he not? He projects us, does he not?' The Minion's giggles became hysterical. 'How does it feel to have an audience?'

Aton felt dirtied by this creature's presence. Surely, he thought, the Traumatics' creed cannot be literally true. When he compared this giggling monster with the sedateness and calm reason of the Church . . .

The Minion seemed to read his mind. 'Oh, the cult of Hulmu is very old. A little bit older than the Church, even. I should know, I started it! Before I became Hulmu's Minion I was Absol Humbart! But those other fools, San Hevatar and Dwight Rilke, rejected Hulmu, the genuine creator. They founded their silly church.'

Grinning, the Minion came towards him with tiny mincing steps. Aton determined to destroy the loathsome creature if he could. He ejected energy from his body, sending rays and waves against the shambling figure. The Minion laughed. His own body began to pulse, shedding sparkling rainbows all around. He seemed to regard it as a game. Their contest filled the room with fantastic forms of light, but neither was hurt in any way.

'I was wiser. I gave myself to Hulmu. He gives me my little toys, and I help him to get what he needs – souls in death trauma!'

They both left off wasting energy in firework displays. Suddenly the sound of booted feet came from further along the corridor. The Imperial Guard were on their way.

'Come, friend Aton,' the Minion hissed. 'Come to Hulmu!'

With surprising agility he bounded forward and seized Aton in his arms. Fetid breath wafted across Aton's face, but before he could react, the Minion had phased into the strat, *taking Aton with him.*

The Minion was amazingly strong. Aton could not break loose from his embrace. Down they sank, spiralling and plummeting, down, down, down. The four-dimensional screen of orthogonal time was left behind. Left behind, too, were the upper reaches of the strat where what was potential already bore some resemblance to what was actual. They went down, down, into the deeps where potentiality had less and less prospect of becoming actuality – that is, of materializing on to the orthogonal world – and had less and less in common with its forms. The pressure was frightful. They sank into gloomy six-dimensional regions where nameless things lurked and waited in the murk. Aton felt brooding hatred as they passed by; the potential quasi-beings sensed that he and the Minion came from the upper world and experienced a writhing envy.

The descent was timeless and Aton seemed temporarily to lose the will to free himself. Then he began to feel the presence of a vast, overpowering intelligence.

Hulmu!

Hulmu was something impossible. A six-dimensional, non-existent shape that lashed and danced in all directions in frantic convolutions. He was lord of this region; all bowed to him.

A voice he could almost smell spoke in Aton's mind.

'Know me and surrender your being.'

In that instant it came home to Aton with a certainty and conviction he could not analyse, who the enemy was, that had been spoken of by the *Imperator* and San Hevatar.

The enemy of the empire was not the Hegemony. It was not even the Traumatic sect, or the Minion.

It was Hulmu.

He could not define the ultimate evil that was Hulmu. He only saw, as if in a vision, that the struggle was relentless and would continue until victory was gained by one side or the other.

With newly regained strength Aton lashed out. The Minion sought to restrain him, but he broke free and soared upwards like a bubble, out of the reach of Hulmu's lashing tentacles. Other powers snatched at him but he knew he was safe.

Up, up, up.

10

Aton was semi-conscious for the latter part of his ascent to the realm of materiality. He did not fully recover until he had already phased into ortho.

His subconscious mind had brought him to familiar territory. He was standing in the deserted court chamber of the Imperial Palace's inner sanctum, Node One. It was night and the chamber was only dimly lit.

Silence prevailed everywhere.

After some moments he saw a lone figure seated on a couch and stepped closer.

It was Inpriss Sorce.

'Inpriss?'

She looked up. 'You're back!'

'How did you get here?'

'Prince Vro's men brought me. They said I'd be safe here in the palace. I'm under imperial protection.' A note of pride entered her voice as she said the last. She smiled. 'It's certainly a different type of life from what I'm used to.'

'But it can only have been minutes ago that I last saw you.'

A slightly wary look crossed her face. 'It's been nearly three days.'

Three days. Had he been that long in the gulf?

Shaken, he glanced at a wall clock and frowned.

'Where is everybody? Surely they don't retire this early?'

'They're all in the churches and chapels, praying. The armada has set out.'

So matters were coming to a climax. And his mission had failed.

Disconsolately he paced the great hall. He tried to imagine the pace of events beyond the bounds of the palace in the eternal city and throughout the mighty time-spanning empire. Did he fancy he heard the structure of time creaking like the timbers of a crippled ship?

Unexpectedly there came the whirring of motors. The *Imperator* rolled out from its hidden compartment and towered over the man and the woman.

'My servant, Captain Aton,' the resonant voice murmured.

'*Imperator*.'

'It was a stirring sight, Captain. Powerful timeships, seemingly without number, coming one by one up the procession ramp to be presented to the people and blessed by the Arch-Cardinal Reamoir, before phasing into the strat. Now the three main wings are joining formation from the nodes where they were built. Very soon the Hegemony should feel their presence. If it does at all . . .'

'May God go with them, *Imperator*,' Aton replied dully.

'If it does at all,' repeated the *Imperator* fatalistically. 'The Hegemony is also gathering all its forces. It knows the last card has been called. For the past few days it has been using the time-distorter at full aperture.'

'*Imperator*,' Aton said eagerly, though it now seemed rather late for this information, 'the time-distorter belongs to the Traumatic sect and was given to them by the being they call Hulmu.'

The machine-emperor's continuous hum undulated thoughtfully. 'Orthogonal time is breaking up, Captain. If you were to journey through the empire now you would not recognize it. For the past two days it has been impossible to phase into Nodes Three and Four.'

Aton was aghast. '*What*?'

'Nothing intelligible exists there. Orthogonal time has become totally deranged in the area. The strat is like an ocean in many respects, Captain Aton. The features we call the nodes are the regularly spaced ripples on the surface that hold the orthogonal world together. But there can be deeper waves that can overthrow everything. Tidal waves that tear the world of reality apart.'

Aton noted that the *Imperator* spoke more lucidly than on an earlier occasion. But if it had recovered its sanity it had done so belatedly. The picture it drew was frightening.

'What will happen?'

'What has happened will happen.'

Back to cryptic utterances, Aton thought in disgust.

Inpriss had crept forward to join them. She looked up overawed at the *Imperator*, which she could only have known as a semi-legendary ultimate authority. Her hand touched Aton's sleeve as if seeking comfort.

Aton happened to glance to his right and with bulging eyes saw the east wall curve inward as though it were a wall of water. In seconds the heaving structure righted itself and stood rigid, but he knew the signs of spatio-temporal deformation.

'Are we under attack?' he asked sharply.

'The whole empire is under attack. Time is under attack.'

Those were the last words the *Imperator* spoke before the great darkness descended on them all and expunged them from reality.

They returned still carrying the memory of their previous existence. 'What happened?' said Aton.

'The empire was annihilated,' said the *Imperator*, 'and then put back.'

The entirety of the strain being put upon orthogonal time had been steadily building up into a wide-scale wave motion originating deep in the substratum. Eventually it had climaxed in a sort of tidal wave. The Chronotic Empire, and everything associated with it, was swept away.

But the giant time-storm was by no means over. On the contrary, the oscillations were building up and becoming more violent. As the wave entered the second half of its cycle the empire reappeared, almost exactly as when the wave had overtaken it.

But not quite.

There were innumerable small changes. And the difference between these and normal Chronotic mutations was that the inhabitants of the empire were aware of them.

Prince Vro Ixian had at last achieved his heart's desire. Following leads found in the Traumatics' temple in Umbul, the detective Perlo Rolce had traced the body of Princess Veaa to a rundown house in the outskirts of the city. Prince Vro, arming himself and taking only Rolce with him, entered the house and found it uninhabited.

Methodically he went through the dwelling room by room. In the second floor back he discovered a chamber draped in white silk. An open coffin of pinewood lay on a dais, and in the coffin, as beautiful as a pale rose, was the embalmed corpse of the young princess.

'My dearest, my beloved Veaa!' Vro swept towards the coffin.

And in that moment the tidal wave of potential time overcame the material world and swept everything away. The world came back in what, to the actors in it, could have been only an instant. But Vro was aware of the hiatus and understood what it implied.

In the coffin Princess Veaa opened her eyes, moved her head, and slowly sat up.

Vro gave a wild cry. 'Veaa!' he shrieked.

'Vro!' Her shriek was no less mortified.

The two stared at each other in utter horror.

In the court chamber everything was more or less as before. Inpriss Sorce clung tightly to Aton.

'Will it happen again?' Aton asked.

'The wave has but receded for a moment. The turbulence is still building up. When it returns there will be no reprieve. All will dissolve . . . permanently.'

The *Imperator* clicked and hummed. Suddenly there was a muted whine, and a part of its matted surface opened. Aton saw a tiny room within, illuminated, its walls padded.

'Get inside, quickly,' the *Imperator* ordered.

The command's urgent tone brooked no inquiry. Hastily Aton and Inpriss crowded into the small space. The door closed up behind them.

The rolling goodesics of the substratum, summoned up from the deeps, had hit a resonance that nothing could withstand. As the mighty preponderance of Chronotic potentiality smashed against the empire for the second time, the edifice that had been built up with such care was not temporarily annulled merely, but torn apart, and the materiality of the fragments dissipated beyond recovery. The screen of orthogonal time was, itself, ripped to shreds.

Seconds before this happened the *Imperator* had phased into the strat. Aton, reading the move on a small instrument panel with which the tiny cabin was provided, was only mildly surprised to learn that the machine-emperor possessed this ability. He heard the strained drone of the modest drive unit as it battled against the dangerous turbulences.

Where was the *Imperator* taking them?

So it had happened. The one thing uniquely feared by achronal archivists had finally come to pass.

Phased permanently into the strat, the Achronal Archives were the one department of Chronopolis's administration to survive. The archivists now saw the fullest justification of their cult of isolationism. The emotionally shattered men and women prowled around the vaults, touching one another for comfort, caressing the humming casings that contained the computer store of all that had taken place in the vanished Chronotic Empire.

All around them lay nothing but the strat. *There was no orthogonal time*. The time-storm, of unprecedented proportions, had eliminated it, and potentiality reigned supreme. There was no actuality, except for this one little isolated bubble.

The in-turned atmosphere of the sepulchral establishment, always noticeable, now intensified by the minute. Chief Archivist Illus Ton Mayar knew that in short order it would develop into group insanity. But he did not think that any of them would live to see that happen. Very soon the archives would melt into the strat like sugar in water. Their existential support – the whole material background from which they had sprung – had been taken away. They persisted now only by virtue of strat time, which did not match one-for-one with orthogonal time.

Mayar was sitting alone in his private room when there was a hammering on the door and an excited shout from one of the senior archivists.

'There's something approaching through the strat!'

Mayar hurried to investigate. He arrived at the loading bay just in time to see the imposing bulk of the *Imperator* materialize there.

All present fell to their knees. A door in the side of the *Imperator* clicked open and a man and a woman, the man dressed as a captain of the Time Service, stepped out.

Mayar watched the apparition with astonishment. 'God be praised!' he managed to say. But he still did not dare to hope.

The man and the woman stepped towards him, but before he could speak again the *Imperator* had once more vanished.

And in the Invincible Armada, swaying its way through the disturbed and roiling strat, there also dawned the realization of the empire's destruction.

Prince Philipium, Grand Admiral of the Armada, enthroned in the majestic bridge in the titanic flagship *God's Imposer*, froze as though paralysed. His face was almost green with shock.

There could be no mistake. From all parts of the huge armada the message was the same. The instruments revealed that the concept of order and religion which everyone on board was sworn to serve was irrevocably gone.

To the commanders surrounding Prince Philipium the news brought varied emotions. Sick anger, sinking fear, stony grimness, defiant hatred.

'We are ghosts!' uttered Prince Philipium in a voice hollow with grief. 'What can we do? The empire is vanquished!'

'Ghosts we may be, but we shall still live for a while,' growled Commander Haight. He tried to calculate how long it would be before the armada faded away and lost all vestige of materiality, now that it had no existential support. It could be hours or days.

'One thing is still left to us,' he urged. 'Revenge! Let us ensure that of the Hegemony, too, nothing remains!'

Exultant shouts greeted his words. Prince Philipium, his eyes staring but devoid of life, gave the orders.

The ghost armada moved forward only to find that its quest was needless. The Hegemony had gone down along with the empire. The ships that it had put into the strat, however, persisted like those of the armada itself. The two forces locked on to each other and began to battle. There was no question of phasing into ortho to fire their weapons – there was no orthogonal time any longer – and the strat torpedoes were too ineffective to satisfy their blood lust. Instead the ships sought to destroy each other by collision. The conflict raged on, fed by despair and hatred.

Aton found he could strike little cheer from the Chief Archivist and his assistants. They seemed unable to recognize that the existence they knew had, in fact, vanished and that they would shortly die. In what Aton found a morbid manner they preferred to go about their duties and spent as much time as possible lovingly going over recorded scenes of bygone days and endless lists of names, places and events.

Neither was he able to answer any of their questions. But two hours later those scanning the surrounding strat reported that an object was again approaching.

For the second time the *Imperator* materialized into the loading bay.

'Aton, my servant!' it boomed.

Aton stood before it stiffly. 'I am here, *Imperator*.' Then he added, 'Where have you been?'

'Into the far future. My mind is clear now.'

The *Imperator* seemed larger, more powerful, more majestic than it ever had before. 'The time for your greatest service to the empire has arrived, Captain Aton.'

'I do not understand, *Imperator*. There is no empire.'

'What has been will be. If you are victorious.' The machine-emperor paused. 'The Minion thinks he has won. He has recovered the time-distorter from his Hegemonic tools and now plans to use it again for another purpose.'

'*Imperator*! What is there to talk about?' Mayar interrupted brokenly. 'All is gone!'

Impatiently Aton cautioned Mayar to keep silence. The *Imperator* hummed loudly. 'At present potential time, alike to primordial chaos, has drowned the world of real time,' it resumed. 'The Chronotic storm, however, is abating; soon orthogonal time will form again on the gulf's surface, like a skin forming on a liquid. If allowed to congeal without interference, it is impossible to say what that new world will be like. That is where the Minion intends to come in. He will use the time-distorter to project a world agreeable to Hulmu, his master. That must not be. You must fight him, Aton. You must take the distorter away from him.'

'But I don't think I can, *Imperator*,' Aton said. 'I have already learned to my cost that the Minion is strong.'

'With the help of religion, you can defeat him.'

Without warning a wide-angled beam of light shot out from the *Imperator* and bathed Aton. Immediately an extraordinary flood of thoughts and feelings flooded his mind, all connected with the religion in which he had been brought up. Prayers, catechisms and hymns such as he had been taught as a child seemed to sing in his brain.

The emotion engendered by this experience made him feel humble. Objectively, he recognized the use of a thought ray similar in principle to a field-effect device, except that it worked in reverse. The *Imperator* was reminding him of his religious training. But why?

'The Minion approaches. Come.'

Once more the door to the inner chamber in the machine's metal side opened. Aton hesitated.

Then he entered. The *Imperator* phased into the strat and went speeding down, seeming to know where to go. After what felt like a long wait, Aton became aware that it had killed its velocity and was idling. The door opened, and through it he could see the strat, spreading and convoluting before his tortured eyes.

The message was clear. He ventured into the strat.

He saw the Minion almost immediately, soaring up from the deep, carrying the big tube-like device Aton had seen once before. As Aton came closer he saw the jewel eyes flash and glint through the supernal fire that surrounded them both. The Minion's mouth was agape and raucous laughter issued from it.

'Ha ha ha! You want my little toy! Oh, no! This time Hulmu will have *you*!'

Aton moved in to the attack.

The Minion pointed the tube. Vapours gushed forth and Aton felt himself being wafted away, his four-dimensional form deformed and eroded. With difficulty he evaded the vapours, and then he closed with the Minion and wrestled bodily with him.

The Minion had more than one shape! Limbs and extruberances shot out from him in all the directions of the five-dimensional space in which they fought. Aton found himself encaged in a living organism of roots, limbs, and branches.

He himself was not without resource. With a supreme effort he caused every cell of his body to discharge the transcendent energy it had gained by immersion in the strat. There was a sort of explosion, an uncoiling of the immaterial continuum, and he was free.

But he was weakened. And then, before he could take stock of himself, he was imprisoned once more.

This time he seemed to be transfixed or encaged in

brilliantly coloured glass or crystal. There was a sudden shift, and then he knew he had been transferred to a similar, but second prison.

He was inside the Minion's eyes, being flashed alternately from one to the other!

Laughingly the Minion ejected him and hovered jeering. His ability to alter him in size gave Aton a real appreciation of the greater power of his enemy. He began to despair.

'Hee hee hee! First I will reform the world, and then I will take you down again to Hulmu, poor little captain!'

Tenaciously Aton circled, and then moved in again.

Through his brain was running a prayer, one he had known since he was a child. Something within him was urging him to say this prayer aloud, and when he came near the Minion again, he sent the vibrations of the words spearing into the strat.

'Holy Father, bringer of comfort, deliver us from the enemy of time.'

That was all, but surprisingly the Minion recoiled as if in horror. Aton pursued him, speaking the prayer over and over again.

'Holy Father, bringer of comfort, deliver us from the enemy of time. Holy Father, bringer of comfort, deliver us from the enemy of time.'

The Minion shrieked with pain. He flashed out and writhed in a million illusory shapes, running the full gamut of his evil energies in an uncontrolled spasm. The prayer seemed to reduce him to a condition akin to the effect of nerve gash on a normal nervous system. Aton dived in and seized the time-distorter. The Minion struggled briefly to retrieve it, then fell back.

Then the Minion suddenly fell headlong into the gulf at extraordinary speed. 'Hulmu! I have failed you again! Ohhhhhh . . .'

And Aton had carried out the orders of the *Imperator*.

The *God's Imposer* was junked.

The huge ship had run head-on into countless enemy vessels. Smaller craft it had swatted like flies. But finally the total of those collisions had proved crippling. The twisted and shattered hulls of upwards of a dozen Hegemonic vessels were embedded in the *God's Imposer*, and the giant drive units now were silent.

'The ortho field won't last long, sir!' gasped an ensign. 'It's down in parts of the ship already.'

'Then kill yourself, you little fool, like the others are doing,' growled Commander Haight, 'Me, I'm not hanging around like a trapped rat.'

And in fact the bridge was littered with suicides, including Prince Philipium. No one had bothered to use the ship's many life rafts or strat suits. But Commander Haight was not on the bridge. He was down in the guts of the ship, just within its outer wall. And the ensign was stationed at one of the ports that, had the armada succeeded, would have been pouring troops on to the ground.

'There's something I've always wanted to experience,' Haight grated out, 'and now I'm going to. Open the port, Ensign.'

'But, sir!'

'You heard me, you young squirt. It's an order. *Get that port open!*'

Trembling, the ensign turned his back to the port and operated a series of switches. The port whined slowly open, dilating iris-fashion. The safety cover went up.

Pressing his forearm against his eyes so that he would not be struck unconscious and fall to the deck, Commander Haight flung himself at a run into the strat.

'To understand what has happened,' said the *Imperator* to Aton, Inpriss Sorce, and the assembled archivists, 'it is necessary to understand the nature of time and the origin of Church and empire.

'Orthogonal time is reality. But reality cannot continue to subsist by itself. Like every structure in the universe it requires a certain kind of feedback on itself to remain steady. It requires something against which to rest itself, to react upon, otherwise, if it simply existed in a void, it would soon collapse into nothing.

'This something is the temporal substratum. The strat is, if you like, aberrated reality; it provides the feedback that keeps real time stable, or relatively so. As such, it is potential, not actual, and less than real.

'The deeper one goes, the less like reality the strat is. In the uttermost depths are forms of quasi-existence inconceivable for us! And they are only there at all because somewhere – in orthogonal time – is the authentic existence from which they are degraded.

'The quasi-beings in these depths have a terrible hunger for authentic existence. But they are unable to emerge into it because they are too far removed from its nature. Some of them, however, are immensely powerful in their own realm; such a one is Hulmu.

'He is the enemy of mankind.'

'I had thought Hulmu was just a superstition on the part of the Traumatic sect,' Mayar said hesitantly. 'I hadn't even believed the Church when it identified him with the Evil One.'

'He is genuine and we have been fighting him for countless aeons. The empire is much older, in terms of eternity, than you think.'

The *Imperator* hummed meditatively. 'Until the discovery of time-travel the existential world was safe from such monsters. There was no possibility of their touching orthogonal time. Then, in some unique accident of history, a man called Dwight Rilke hit on a flaw in the structure of the world. He discovered that there was a way whereby matter could be moved through time.

'From that instant the universe of actuality was in danger. And that danger manifested almost immediately. During the early experiments there was an unfortunate accident whereby one of the assistants fell headlong into the temporal substratum. This man was Absol Humbart, later the Minion. He was caught by Hulmu, who realized that the weakening of orthogonal time offered him an opportunity to claw his way up and become real. But still it was not easy. In order to gain a foothold Hulmu needed first to acquire sufficient reality, in order to transfer himself to the surface.

'For this Absol Humbart promised souls! If Hulmu could devour enough souls that had lived in orthogonal time, then he could erupt into our world and establish himself there, satisfying his enormous hunger to become real!

'But the driblets he has been given are not nearly enough. His strategy has only one object – *to be able to absorb the death trauma of mankind, past, present, and future!* Only by devouring every man, woman and child who ever lived, or will live, can Hulmu gain the wherewithal to climb out of his pit, claim the Earth and eventually, perhaps, the galaxy. To this end he and the Minion scheme, trying to create a situation that will bring about the death of humanity in special circumstances. If the Minion could have employed the time-distorter just as orthogonal time was reforming, he might have achieved this. The distorter is an instrument no man could have conceived of; its construction requires the powers of a god.'

The *Imperator* paused to allow them to digest its words.

'You say we have fought this beast for aeons,' called a brave archivist, 'but the empire itself has not existed that long.'

Something resembling a laugh issued from the machine. 'The empire has risen, fallen, and risen again, countless times. All that will be has been, again and again and again. Always, at this point, we have managed to foil Hulmu; always we have managed to resurrect the empire by the same means that he destroyed it. The process has, I estimate, gone through the cycle one billion times.

'But I have not completed my tale. How did the empire arise? It was no accident. Of those involved in so rashly presenting mankind with time–travel one, San Hevatar, saw the danger. He knew that the evil Traumatic sect had to be countered. He founded the Church to fight Hulmu. He designed the rituals of the Church as a weapon and a bastion against Hulmu. That is why, Aton, your prayer was so effective against the Minion; it is especially constructed to contain vibrations he cannot endure. If it were not for the Church, all might have fallen victims to Hulmu by now.'

'You say this,' pointed out Aton seriously, 'but the San Hevatar I have met did not strike me as being aware of it.'

'He was not. Perhaps the first time around he was. But now, after so many changes and resurrections, we move through our parts as if in a dream. Did you know that you must fight the Minion? Even I did not know, I only remembered flashes, like San Hevatar. Most of the time I am completely insane, as your friend Prince Vro tells you. I am insane, and know only these lucid periods when the empire has vanished. Then I travel into the far future to visit the civilizations there, and everything becomes clear.'

'The future people,' Inpriss objected, 'why don't *they* help us to fight Hulmu?'

'They cannot, and in any case they do not believe in Hulmu. They know only that the secret of time-travel is the most dangerous secret in the universe, that if it is not controlled it can destroy time. That is why they want the empire continually to rise and fall in its war with the Hegemony; it is history's warning to man-kind. There are no Chronotic empires in future ages; men are too afraid. But if the example of the empire were not before them then they might forget and begin to tamper with time.'

'And you,' said Aton. 'Who are you? *What* are you?'

'I am the oldest part of the empire. I began life as an administrative computer in the physics laboratories of Monolith Industries. I took part in the original discoveries concerning pi-mesons. When the struggle with the Min-ion began I played a leading part in it. Gradually I was extended and increased my intelligence. Now I and the Minion are the main actors in the drama. He has an advantage because he is coached by Hulmu. With every cycle he grows stronger. We, too, must grow stronger,

Aton! I could not tell you how often you have fought the Minion!'

'One billion times,' Aton said dryly.

'No, not so. No one could be expected to endure that for so long. Every so often fate changes the champion who challenges him. Once it was Commander Haight; now he has been relieved of the duty and knows nothing of it. Next time it may be you, or it may be another. I cannot tell. But someone always arises with sufficient power to struggle against him. And always I am here to see that he does so. Eventually, perhaps, I will have evolved sufficiently to play the role myself.'

The *Imperator*'s hum grew louder. 'You must understand that of the world as it was before the empire arose nothing remains. Even the calendar is different. Dwight Rilke's discovery was made in the twenty-fourth century of their era; and the Stop Barrier was eventually placed in what was their fifteenth century, before a technological society had even developed.'

'You speak of resurrecting the empire,' said Mayar, still puzzled, 'but how can that be? How can it possibly be accomplished?'

'In the same way that the Minion hoped to accomplish a world fit for Hulmu to live in. We have Hulmu's time-distorter. Hulmu misled the Minion when he represented himself as the creator and projector of the images on the screen of time; he is not that, merely an impotent spectator. Nevertheless his time-distorter can, to an extent, achieve creation.'

The *Imperator* rolled forward and stood over those present in an almost menacing fashion. 'The strat, just before the film of orthogonal time forms, is like a supersaturated solution waiting to be seeded. The time-distorter is designed to feed vibrations into that solution, and from those vibrations a world will grow. Here we have all the components to recreate the empire. We have the Achronal Archives with their detailed knowledge of the empire. The rituals of the Church themselves are the basis whereby the essence of the empire can be restored; San Hevatar intended them that way. We have the time-distorter to project all this on the newly forming orthogonal world, and we have myself, *Imperator*, to operate it!'

With a small sharp explosion a section of the *Imperator* fell away to reveal a neat concavity. 'Long ago I equipped myself for this task. Fit the distorter into this space. Jack into me the output leads from your archival computers. Quickly, there is little time! I will re-create all the original conditions, the starting point from which the empire will burgeon! All will be foreordained! The war with Hulmu must continue eternally!'

Inpriss Sorce gave a little cry. 'Must I go through it all again?' she quavered.

'There may be variations,' the resonant voice said in a near-whisper. 'Perhaps next time you will live in peace. Perhaps, too, some other officer of the Time Service, not Captain Mond Aton, will become familiar with the strat and be called upon to fight the Minion. Only one thing is certain; if the empire falls and cannot be reformed, then mankind falls to Hulmu, and monsters crawl out of the deeps of potential time to claim the Earth.'

While the machine spoke, the archivists were busy doing its bidding; the *Imperator*'s word was law.

And when at last the time-distorter was triggered and mighty energies began issuing from its mouth, and when at the same time they all began to fade out of existence, Aton, holding Inpriss's hand, felt in the depths of his being that this was not the end, that he would be called on, once more, to be a servant of the empire, and that the war, truly, was eternal.

11

'These pi-mesons certainly are tricky fellers,' said Dwight Rilke.

'Tricky as hell,' agreed Humbart.

Rilke threw down his pencil and leaned back. Vague thoughts and ideas drifted through his mind, all related to the main problem: how to isolate pi-mesons in a stable state, for long enough and in sufficient quantity to do something with them.

His gaze fell on the computer across the room. Its unusual bulk was due to the fact that it incorporated its own compact nuclear power unit as insurance against the erratic electricity supply. The civil disturbances were becoming more pronounced of late and the computer did most of the administrative work for the branch.

Rilke had decided on a nickname for the machine, because of the imperious way it delivered data.

He would call it *Imperator*.

The door opened. One of the staff girls came in with a sheaf of reports.

'Thank you, Miss Sorce,' Absol Humbart said.

Collision
with Chronos

1

Rond Heshke wondered if there would ever be victory without arrogance. Banners, everywhere banners.

On the raised forecourt of Bupolbloc, world head-quarters of the Bureau of Politics, they hung to form a gigantic grille, like an array of sails a hundred feet tall. Even though the last of the wars against the deviant subspecies – the campaign against the Amhraks – had been won twenty years before, these banners were still redolent of military glory. And still there were the annual parades, the rousing speeches, the braying documentaries on the vidcast.

The War to Win Earth: that was what they had called it. But now Earth was won – irrevocably won for the True Man – and privately Heshke thought it was time the paean of triumph was played down.

He crossed the forecourt, intimidated by the immense red-and-black canvases, which swallowed up all visitors like ants. In point of fact Bupolbloc was the most impressive of the many fine buildings in the administrative sector of Pradna, soaring up for over a thousand feet of serried glass frontages, and it exuded a sense of power that soon overshadowed Heshke's disrespectful thoughts, making them seem sacrilegious. He entered the spacious foyer and checked his destination on the office plan.

He took an elevator to the twentieth floor and then walked through seemingly endless corridors. All around him passed the tall, handsome men and women of the Titanium Legions, the self-styled Guardians of Earth who currently had succeeded in attaining political supremacy over humanity. Wearing sleek uniforms in black and gold, all of impeccable biological pedigree, they cast disdainful glances at Heshke which he chose not to notice. He accepted that any military elite was apt to revel in its own superiority; he was, after all, but a paunchy, middle-aged civilian who, insofar as anyone could these days, took no interest in politics. His concern was with the past, not the future.

The twentieth floor lay in the precinct of the Bureau of Propaganda and the office he had been summoned to was the Archaeological Office – Bureprop (Arch.). He arrived in good time and was kept waiting only ten minutes by the pretty, coolly efficient secretary before being ushered in.

Titan-Major Brourne rose to greet him, smiling jovially.

'Good to see you, Citizen Heshke! Sit down, won't you?'

Behind Brourne stood a younger man Heshke did not know: a pale, supercilious-looking captain with a deformed left eyelid – an unlikely defect to find in a Titan, and which gave him a disconcerting, quizzical expression. Heshke could only suppose that he made up for the deformity in other qualities, or he would never have been permitted to enter the ranks of the Titans.

'This is Titan-Captain Brask, Citizen,' Brourne said by way of introduction. 'I've called him to our meeting for reasons which will become plain later.' He sat down and leaned back, placing his large hands squarely on the table. Brourne was a solid-looking man, somewhat too broad for his height, and his tub-like bulkiness was accentuated by the crossed black belts of his uniform. He had thinning brown hair that had once been thick and luxurious, brown eyes and a face that, having seen much and enjoyed much, was now beginning to soften under a new career of desk-work. Heshke preferred him brisk and businesslike rather than jovial, as now. His cordiality always was an introduction to something else.

Heshke's gaze drifted to an archaeological chart that covered the wall behind the two men. It was a good professional piece of work, even if too much biased in favour of the particular interpretations the Titans put upon historical findings. It clearly showed the periodic rise and fall of civilization, the persistent pattern of all human history. He was still staring at it when Titan-Major Brourne spoke again.

'Well, Citizen, and how is progress at the ruins?'

'I can't speak of any new developments, if that's what you mean.' Heshke fumbled uneasily with his briefcase.

The Titan-Major's voice became heavy and unaccommodating. 'What you're trying to tell me is that there's been no progress.'

'You can't always depend on progress to follow a straight line,' Heshke answered defensively. 'The first thing to learn about the alien interventionists is how complete their destruction was, how nearly all their traces were erased. In a sense we are lucky that sites like the Hathar Ruins exist at all.'

Brourne rose from his desk and paced to and fro, his face becoming serious. 'Victory is ours, but it must be consolidated,' he intoned. 'The history of the Fall and of the Dark Period must be fully researched and documented, if we are going to be able to give future generations a correct historical perspective.'

Titan-Captain Brask continued to gaze on the scene as if from some superior viewpoint while Brourne held forth. 'We've beaten the deviant subspecies – but they were always the lesser threat. I don't have to tell you what the greater threat is, or how crucial your own area of research is, Citizen Heshke. You know just what the nature of a future struggle would be; we must never again allow ourselves to become vulnerable to an attack from space.'

He stopped pacing and looked directly at Heshke once more. 'Our present ignorance is unacceptable. It has been officially decreed that progress in the research into the alien interventionists is required.'

Heshke did not know how to answer him. He wished he was back at the alien ruins, quietly going about his work with his colleagues, not here in this office being browbeaten by Titan officers.

'In that case new sites will have to be unearthed,' he opined. 'I would go so far as to say we've already got most of what we can from Hathar.' How much can they expect me to deduce, he thought, from empty stone ruins and a few nonhuman skeletons? It really was extraordinary how few artifacts had survived.

For the first time the younger Titan spoke. His voice was precise and condescending.

'We do not rely only on your efforts, Citizen. We have our own archaeological teams – and they, let me say, are producing better results than you are.'

Yes, they would, Heshke thought. Because the Titans already had an ideology, a creed. It was easy to dig up a few remains and recruit them in support of already constructed doctrines. But Heshke thought of himself as a scientist and a scholar, not as an ideologist, and he took facts simply as facts. As far as the alien interventionists went there was altogether too little information to form a complete picture.

Oh, the broad outlines were clear enough, all right. About eight hundred years ago the powerful and mature classical civilization had suffered a total, cataclysmic collapse. The subsequent Dark Period had lasted nearly four centuries, and only since then had civilization been built anew.

But it was also evident that another civilization, not of the Earth, had established itself here side by side with the human one some time during the past thousand years. It also had been wiped out – but much, much more completely. That a civilization could be eradicated so completely was puzzling. The actual age of the ruins it had left behind it was still in dispute, but to the ideologues of the Titanium Legions the inference was unavoidable – the old human civilization had died in a gigantic struggle to save Earth from the intruders. Though it had succeeded in its mission, the effort had been too much for it and had left it too weak to survive.

The argument was plausible. The alien remains showed every sign of having been destroyed in furious warfare, and nearly everyone accepted that the war between the two races had taken place. But as for the second premise

. . . Heshke's eyes strayed back to the archaeological chart on the wall. The collapse of classical civilization was hardly a unique event in history. Rather there had been a whole series of such collapses at intervals separated by about two millennia, as if human civilization was inherently incapable of supporting itself, time and time again falling under its own weight. Some extremists among the Titans attributed this pattern to successive waves of alien invasion, but there was no evidence to support the idea.

And neither, despite exhaustive efforts on the part of Heshke and numerous colleagues, was there really decisive evidence to show that the last, classical civilization *had* in fact disappeared under the onslaught of alien attack. To Heshke's mind the picture was more one of the rapid internal decline covering about a century and culminating in final violent collapse. Furthermore, there was an inexplicable lack of reference to the aliens in most of the records so far unearthed. Nevertheless he found himself having to accept the Interventionist Theory, with some reservations, even if only on the grounds of probability. After all, the aliens had been there, and they might have used weapons whose effects were not now discernible.

He hesitated, then opened his briefcase and took out a set of glossy photographs. 'I wasn't sure whether or not to show you these. They're quite interesting in a way . . .'

He passed the photographs across the desk. Brourne and Brask bent to inspect them. They were pictures, taken from various angles, of the alien ruins where he had his camp.

'These came into my hands a short while ago,' he explained diffidently. 'They were passed on to me by a colleague making a study of the old town of Jejos – it's due for demolition, you know. We think they were taken about three hundred years back, probably by an amateur historian of the time. At first we thought they would be instructive; however . . .'

He dipped into his briefcase again and passed over more photographs. 'These are modern pictures, taken from the same angles for comparison.'

Brourne looked from one batch to the other in puzzlement. 'So?'

Heshke leaned across the desk. 'See this conical tower here? Even today it's in fairly good shape, as you can see. Yet in the old photograph – the one three hundred years old – it's missing, except for a crumbled base.'

Brourne snorted. 'That's impossible.'

'Yes, obviously,' agreed Heshke. 'There are other anomalies too – crumbled walls, generally deteriorated stonework; in fact if we were to believe these photographs it would mean that the ruins are in better condition – are – *newer!* – today than they were three hundred years ago.'

'So what do you make of that?'

Heshke shrugged. 'Apparently, for some reason, the pictures have been touched up and generally faked to make the ruins seem older than they were.'

'And why would anyone want to do that?'

'I haven't even the beginning of an idea. But that's what must have happened. There's no other explanation.'

'Obviously.' Brourne's voice was sarcastic, and Heshke felt stupid for having raised the matter at all. 'And that would seem to negate their historical value,' the Titan-Major continued, staring intently at the pictures. Finally he handed them to Brask. 'Have copies made of all these,' he said.

The fakery, Heshke reminded himself, was extremely well done. The old yellow prints gave him quite an eerie feeling.

Brourne coughed and returned his attention to Heshke. 'We are wondering if you have sufficient enthusiasm for the task that has been entrusted to you?' he asked, sending a chill down Heshke's spine. 'Perhaps you fail to appreciate the urgency of what confronts us. Remember that the research you're doing has more than one motive. There is the need for scientific knowledge, of course – the need to know as much as possible about the great war our ancestors fought with the aliens, so as to give our political attitudes a firm historical basis. But there is also another reason. Already the aliens have tried to steal Earth once: who knows when they might try again? We have to know where they came from, we have to know whether they might still be lurking out there in space. *We have to know about their weapons.*'

Brask entered the conversation again. Into his icy blue eyes came a glint of steel, making their oddness all the more striking. 'Have you heard the latest theories about how the deviant subspecies arose? It has always been a mystery as to why they should arise when they did, when the natural course of evolution is quite plainly in the direction of pure-blooded True Man. Radioactivity from warfare cannot be the answer, because the nuclear weapons used in the classical era were radiologically clean. Well, it has recently been discovered that the Earth's magnetic field wards off high-powered particles coming in from outer space. If this field were interfered with so as to allow the passage of these particles the rate of biological mutation on Earth would increase to an unnatural level. Such a situation is consistent with the growth of deviant species.'

Heshke frowned. 'But *could* Earth's magnetism be interfered with?' he asked doubtfully.

'Theoretically – yes. We don't know precisely how, but we're working on it, naturally. I think there can be little doubt what happened – the deviant subspecies are the products of an alien weapon whose object was to destroy our genetic purity – to pervert nature itself!'

Brourne nodded his agreement. 'We know for a fact that not only man was involved. Several breeds of dog existing today, for instance, were not in existence a thousand years ago.'

Heshke ignored this dubious item of reasoning. 'If it could be established that Earth's magnetic field *did* undergo changes at the appropriate time, then that would largely substantiate the theory,' he ventured. 'But even then – could it not equally have been one of our *own* weapons that did it?'

Titan-Captain Brask's response to this suggestion was indignant. 'Would True Man have jeopardized the blood of the future? The idea is absurd, inconceivable. The interference can only have come from a non-human source, and the enemy that produced it may still exist, preparing himself for a fresh assault. We may yet be called upon to defend not only Earth, but our very genes!' And he fixed Heshke with an icy stare.

'And so there you have it, Citizen Heshke,' Brourne resumed in a tone of deadly seriousness. '*Now* do you see why our archaeological work is of such importance?'

Wearily Heshke nodded his understanding. The endless ideologizing of the Titans fatigued him, yet he had to admit the urgency of their demands. Unpleasant though their practices sometimes were, they were a necessary force.

And at the moment a chill more penetrating than their veiled threats had entered his loins. The picture of alien fingers meddling with man's genetic heritage was a vision of pure horror.

'You're right, absolutely right,' he said in subdued tones. 'We need to call on all our resources to meet a threat as big as this. Yet to be honest I don't see what I can do that I'm not already doing. The Hathar Ruins *are* just about played out. I don't think I can draw any more fresh conclusions without fresh evidence.'

The two Titans glanced at one another. Brourne nodded, and instantly the atmosphere seemed to relax.

'We're aware of your difficulties,' the Titan-Major said, 'and we have some news for you. In another part of the world a discovery has been made that you don't yet know about. We want you to take part in a field trip.'

A feeling of relief swept over Heshke. He was not going to be purged after all!

Traditionally suspicious of everyone, the Titans had been baiting him, sounding out his attitudes to make sure he was the right man for the job. Evidently it was something they couldn't use one of their own people for – Heshke was well aware that they would have liked to dispense with the services of civilians altogether, but they couldn't. Titan scientists, if left to their own resources, too often seemed to fall down in the last analysis, tripped up by their attachment to prejudicial theories. Heshke was the foremost authority in his field and they needed him and men like him.

Often he had wondered what he would do if, appallingly, he was offered a Titan commission. To accept or to refuse both had the aspect of suicide.

'The trip is extremely unusual in nature,' Brourne continued. 'I must warn you that there is a certain degree of danger involved.'

Heshke blinked. 'Physical danger?'

'Yes. Not the sort of thing an archaeologist usually has to face, I know, but . . .' Brourne shrugged, waving his hand casually.

'No, no, not altogether,' Heshke became excited. 'As a profession we're always prepared – unknown regions, and all that. Where will we be going? Into a dev reservation?'

'I'm sorry, the details are top secret at the moment. You'll be briefed in good time.'

It had to be a dev reservation, Heshke thought. Where on a conquered, controlled planet could there be a risk to life and limb except in one of the special regions where a few surviving deviants were allowed to survive for purposes of study? The Titans must have made an important find there – perhaps a hitherto unknown alien settlement.

'Surely you can give me some indication?' he persisted. 'I'd like to have some idea of what to expect.'

Brourne hesitated, an unusual gesture for him. 'One of our teams has found an alien artifact in good condition. In working order, in fact. It's a more significant find than anything else we've ever turned up . . . I'm afraid I can't tell you more. The truth is I'm not allowed to know much myself. But you must be prepared to be called away on short notice.'

He came to his feet again, signalling that the interview was at an end. 'Well there it is, Citizen. I'm glad to see you so enthusiastic. I hope we can depend on you to do your damnedest for us . . . for humanity . . .'

Heshke rose, made a curt bow, and left.

2

Squat conical towers.

Throughout the world these were the features of alien architecture to survive more than any other, probably by reason of being the most difficult for time or man to dismantle. The ruins Heshke and his team were studying sported plenty of them.

He arrived back at the site at sunset. The Hathar Ruins, as the site was called, was one of the most important of out-worlder remains, and one of the best preserved. More typical were the expanses of fused glass where cities and settlements had been destroyed by nuclear bombardment. The Hathar Ruins had not sustained an atomic hit, but they had suffered extensive damage from less powerful weapons; nevertheless they still exuded a rich aura of a bygone race. Crumbled walls, curiously curved and rounded, wavered towards the sky. The short conical towers seemed to sprout everywhere and at all levels. It was hard to believe that the aliens had been on Earth for a comparatively short time – which had to be the case if history made any sense at all. This settlement, and even more so the larger settlements dotted around the world, were clearly built to last.

The team was just finishing its day's work of carefully sifting earth. Heshke hurried over to the finds tent, hoping to see some new artifact, perhaps even a document in the cryptic alien script that no one, so far, had deciphered. As usual, he was disappointed. In the North Sector, in the large building popularly known as the Cathedral, someone had uncovered a glass object of which there were already scores of samples. It was believed to be a common domestic article used for squashing fruit.

That, in essence, was most of what they had. Simple articles of common use, elementary tools, some furniture. From skeletons they had a fair idea of the aliens' physical appearance. But the advanced technology, the machines, equipment, records – virtually the whole apparatus of a tremendously advanced species – had all gone in the frenzy of annihilation in which the men of the past had torn through everything alien, burning and pulverizing. A few rusted, mangled machines had been found, but not enough to reconstruct even approximately what the outworld technology had been like.

Heshke did not blame the men who had carried out this destruction – they had seen their planet despoiled, their society wrecked – but in retrospect it was an unintelligent move.

He could not wait to see the functional artifact that Brourne had promised.

He was watching a young teamster clean the fruit-squasher, when there was a movement behind him. He turned to see Blare Oblomot, his chief assistant.

'Well, Rond,' Blare said breezily, 'what did the Titans want?'

Heshke coughed, looking nervously at the teamster. He took it for granted that someone on his team was a Titan 'watcher', and it made him feel uncomfortable. He jerked his head towards the exit.

'How about a drink in your place?' he said once they were outside. As they walked towards Blare's quarters he noticed that the camp seemed abnormally quiet and even

Blare seemed slightly uneasy. That was odd: the tousle-haired, raffish archaeologist usually had an unshakable confidence.

Blare lifted the flap of his tent for Heshke to enter. Seated at the small wooden table, he poured them both glasses of wine.

'The Titans have been here today,' he announced. 'Asking questions. Practically interrogating everyone, in fact.'

Heshke started. 'What kind of questions?'

'Political, what else?' Blare shrugged, looking away. 'You know, I think I feel the cold wind of a purge coming on. They wanted to know a lot about you, too.'

Heshke put down his glass, feeling suddenly numb. So far he had managed to keep Titan influence at the site minimal. He had seen what happened when the Titans put in their own teams to work alongside civilian diggers: they soon dominated the entire project; scientific objectivity was the first casualty. He didn't want that here.

At the same time the calculating coolness of it struck him. The Titans had wanted to investigate the project while he, its leader, was absent. Why?

'What did they ask about me?' he demanded.

'They seemed to want to find out whether you are . . . on their side, for lack of another way of putting it. Are you, Rond? What's going on, anyway? Are we being taken over?'

Slowly Heshke shook his head. 'No . . . it's something else.' He was silent for a few moments. 'My God, it must be something big,' he muttered wonderingly.

'What, Rond?' Blare looked at him curiously, the light of the lamp playing over his sharp features. 'Well, you know my views. I don't mind telling you I had a fright today. I think I'll have to get out.'

Heshke blinked. 'Don't be ridiculous, Blare. There's nothing to worry about. They're checking up, that's all. They've made an important find, and they want me to help them . . . I shouldn't really tell you anything, but hang it all, I don't really know any more than you do. They've found an alien artifact and I gather they're excited about it. Anyway, it entails a field trip. I don't know where to, except that it's probably somewhere in a dev reservation.'

Blare was frowning. 'Really? Why only probably?'

'Well, there's some danger involved. That's all they would tell me.'

Blare grunted. 'Dev reservations are pretty quiet places these days, you know, except for when the Titans go storming in. You may not be going to one.'

'Well, perhaps not. I just wanted to reassure you that there's no purge coming, that's all.'

'Thanks for your concern, Rond, but . . . I still think I'd better go. I got the impression this afternoon that something more is brewing. I don't feel safe here any more.'

Heshke stared at him. 'What on Earth are you talking about, Blare?'

The other moved uneasily and took a gulp of wine. The movement of his head cast grotesque shadows on the canvas of the tent, the lamp being set on the table beside them.

'I'd better be frank – hang it, I feel I can trust you, if no one else. You know my sympathies – you know there's a political opposition. I think the Titans are on to me, and if so you know what the outlook will be if I hang around much longer.'

'*On* to you?' Heshke echoed uncomprehendingly. 'But of course there's a political opposition – there always is! It's hardly a crime to belong to it. Not unless you mean . . .'

His voice trailed off. He had known Blare Oblomot for years. Like Heshke himself, he was one of the foremost experts in his field, though younger and less experienced. Heshke also knew of his contempt for the Titans, of his somewhat anarchistic-liberal views. But he had always put that down to a kind of freakish waywardness – no, not freakish, he corrected himself hastily; freakish was an unfortunate word – to a kind of charming and frivolous individuality. But not as a serious defiance of . . .

His thoughts, like his voice, trailed off.

Blare was speaking wryly. 'There's always a point where opposition becomes incompatible with good citizenship. What is legitimate, even if disapproved of, in peacetime becomes treasonable in a state of war. Figuratively speaking we're still in a state of war. So there comes a time when one has to make a hard and cut decision. I made mine some time ago.' Blare rubbed the side of his face. Heshke noticed the fatigue in his eyes – did the Titans have that effect on *him*, too?

'Blare – you're not telling me that you're one of . . . *them*.'

Oblomot nodded. 'Yes, I'm afraid so. I was pushed into it step by step, really, by the Titans themselves. Their grip has tightened, not relaxed, since the Deviant Wars. Their ideas have taken on an even more intransigent form, so that even some thoughts would infringe the legal code today, if there was some way to monitor thoughts. So when you belong to a secret organization pledged to fight the Titans by any means whatsoever and which believes the *so-called* deviants should be allowed a place in the world—'

'Blare! What are you saying!'

Oblomot shrugged again. 'You see? Even you can't approach a thought like that. And yet you like the Titans scarcely any more than I do.'

Heshke's shoulders sagged. Here was his old friend Blare Oblomot confessing that he was a race traitor; that he was secretly a member of the despised underground that during the last war had actually *helped* the Amhraks. It just didn't bear thinking about; his bewilderment was complete.

He forced himself to speak mildly, calmly. 'One can make many criticisms of them, of course,' he said, 'but the Titans aren't the source of their ideology – they are merely its chief instrument. And that instrument is *necessary*, Blare. Earth has to be defended; so does the correct evolutionary lineage – I'm astounded if you can't see that.'

'Defending Earth against an alien invader is one thing,' Oblomot rejoined. 'We haven't had to do that – this civilization hasn't had to do that. It all happened centuries ago. As for the rest—' He shook his head sadly.

Although he felt he had had enough of arguing for one day, Heshke could hardly allow such wild contentions to pass unchallenged. 'But it's all part of the same thing!' he protested. 'The blood that flows in the veins of the Titanium Legions is the same blood that flowed in the men who flung back the invader. The threat is the same, the task is the same – to have and to hold the planet Earth!'

He was, he knew, spouting Titan slogans, but that didn't worry him. This was part of the creed he would never seriously have doubted.

But Oblomot merely looked sardonic. 'The blood in the veins of the deviant species is the same, too. We're all descended from Classical Man.'

'Yes, but—'

'I know what you're going to say. That we alone carry the unchanged line of Classical Man and hence constitute True Man – the others are aberrations leading away from the "natural" line of evolutionary development. Well, it *is* true that we're closest to Classical Man, in physical characteristics, anyway. And probably in mental characteristics too, I grant you that.'

'Then there you are. That *is* what I'm saying.'

'Yes, but what does it mean? Just because we resemble an old type doesn't mean that newer types are somehow wrong. I and my friends aren't opposed to evolution, Rond. We're trying to *save* evolution from being stopped, from being cut short – because that's what the Titans are doing. Nature's method is diversity – always to be radiating out into new forms. The Titans are destroying all new forms and imposing a rigid uniformity. Believe me, we'll all be victims in the end.'

Heshke found these new ideas frightening. 'The Titans believe the deviants were caused by an alien weapon that affected mankind's genes,' he said.

'Yes, I've heard that type of theory before. Perhaps it's true. Or perhaps it was one of our own weapons. But so what? All these mutation-inducing influences can do is speed up evolution, compressing into centuries what otherwise would have taken tens of millennia or longer. The subspecies we've been dutifully annihilating would have developed sooner or later anyway.'

There was an awkward silence. Heshke shook his head, sighing deeply.

'I still say only one race can occupy the Earth,' he said sombrely. 'For heaven's sake, how do you expect us to react to an all-out attack by the Lorenes?'

Oblomot nodded slowly. 'In that particular case, I agree with you. The Lorenes were an even more aggressive species than we are; they had to be wiped out – they were a strain this planet just couldn't afford. But we didn't stop there, we went on to all the others. The Lorenes were a danger, yes – but the Amhraks?' He smiled. 'No, Rond. And as for the Urukuri, they were scarcely able to put up a fight. As a matter of fact I think it's stretching a point to call them subspecies at all. They merely have exaggerated negroid characteristics and an exceptionally placid disposition.'

'Think of the dangers of miscegenation. Of our blood becoming contaminated with Urukuri or Amhrak blood.' Heshke shuddered slightly. 'Imagine your daughter being raped by one. They *have* raped our women, you know.'

Oblomot rummaged for a fresh bottle in a nearby cabinet. It was as if he were pretending not to hear Heshke.

At last he said heavily: 'Have another drink, Rond. I don't blame you for thinking like that, because Titan propaganda is very good and everybody is infected by it. To your mind it even appears perfectly rational, that's how good it is. But it's wrong.'

Sipping the newly filled glass, Heshke said with a note of petulance: 'Well, why are you unburdening your soul to me? Aren't you afraid I'll report you?'

'No, I trust you. Basically you're just not the Titan type. I wanted you to know why I'm leaving. When things get bad – which they may – I want you to understand that *there is an alternative*, that Titan thinking isn't the only option for our species.'

He raised his glass as though offering Heshke a toast. 'To the future.'

'Where will you go?' Heshke asked idly.

'In hiding for a bit. I have friends.' Oblomot drained his glass. 'Sorry to make a "race traitor" of you, old man.'

'That's all right,' mumbled Heshke, waving his hand in embarrassment. 'You know I could never bring myself to inform on you, Blare.'

Lacking the energy to meet Oblomot's arguments, he left after a few more drinks and made his way to his own tent. It was night now; the full moon was out, casting a cold, eerie radiance over the ruins. He glanced up at the shining satellite, thinking briefly of the Titan outposts there, lonely sentinels guarding the approaches to Earth, watching the outskirts of the solar system for the return of the invader.

Then for the millionth time he turned his full attention to the ruins themselves. Even without moonlight there had always been something ghostly, unearthly, about them – he couldn't quite put his finger on it, but he had always put it down to the fact that they were, after all, of alien origin. On the short stroll to his tent he placed his hand on a time-worn wall. It was chill – yet, in his imagination, the phrase *living rock* came to him. The stone did indeed seem to carry the ghost of life, as if redolent of the beings who had shaped it. He reminded himself of the inexplicable photographs and shook his head in despair. Towers and walls reconstructing themselves over the centuries. What incredible hoax had the faker tried to perpetrate?

In his tent, he went straight to bed, his conversation with Oblomot tumbling over and over in his mind. Yes, he told himself, the Titans *were* masters of propaganda. But the propaganda was about real things, not about the fake things – not like those photographs. Its strength lay in its appeal to a primeval urge of nature. *Blood and soil.* It was a rare man who could resist it.

And he, too, was of that blood, and of that soil.

He was awakened just before dawn by the whine of hoverjets.

Blearily he rose from his camp bed and peered through the tent flap to see two hoverjets bearing Titan insignia settle squarely in the middle of the camp. Two others remained in the air, standing off just outside the ruins.

It was a frankly military style of approach. The airborne helijets were in a guard posture, and carried glaring searchlights which cast the scene in vivid relief.

Hurriedly Heshke dressed and went outside. A traversing searchlight beam hit him full in the face, transfixed him for a moment or two, then moved on. When his vision returned to normal he saw that two Titan noncoms were striding towards him.

'Are you Citizen Heshke?' one demanded. He nodded.

'Come with us, please.' They turned and strode off, leaving him to straggle after them.

The slim figure of Titan-Captain Brask stood by the nearer hoverjet. 'Good morning, Heshke,' he said in a supercilious but not unfriendly voice. 'We did warn you to be ready. Unfortunately it seems we need you somewhat sooner than we thought we would.'

Heshke said nothing, his brain still slow with sleep. 'Is there anything you need to bring with you?' Brask asked politely. 'Books, notes, charts? Well, we can supply anything you want, anyway.'

He turned. Blare Oblomot was approaching, walking slowly between Titan escorts. In the background Heshke saw some of his helpers emerging from their tents to stare curiously, white figures in the pre-dawn darkness.

'Is my assistant Oblomot included in this project too?' he queried.

Brask gave a short, sharp laugh. 'Oh, we know all about him. He's got a different destination.'

As he came near, Oblomot gave Heshke a half pleading, half I-told-you-so look. Brask made a violent gesture with his arm.

'Take him to Major Brourne at Bupolbloc Two. Heshke comes with us.'

Heshke watched his friend being put aboard the second hoverjet, feeling sick inside. Bupolbloc Two, he thought. He hadn't known there was a Number Two; hadn't known that the building he had visited just yesterday was only Bupolbloc One.

Suddenly he reminded himself that his small personal belongings and toilet requisites were still in his tent, but he decided against returning to collect them. Brask looked impatient, and anyway the Titans were very efficient at providing details like that.

Numbly he climbed into the hoverjet. They surged upward and whined away to the north.

Suddenly there was a glare of light and the sound of an explosion from one of the other helijets, the one carrying Blare Oblomot. Heshke gasped with shock, and saw the flaring skeleton of the jet plummeting earthward in the darkness.

Brask jumped to his feet, cursing. 'The fools! Didn't they know enough to check him? He must have been carrying a suicide grenade!'

Heshke tore his gaze away from the blaze on the ground and gaped at him. Brask gave him a sidelong glance.

'You don't know about those, do you? The underground has been using that trick quite a lot lately. Saves them from interrogation and takes a few of us with them.'

Unsuspected vistas seemed to be opening up to Heshke. 'I . . . no, I hadn't known.'

'Naturally, you wouldn't. It's not advertised on the media, and we have ways of discouraging rumour. Yes, there is an organized underground and your friend Oblomot was a member of it. You didn't know that either – or did you?' Brask's odd, quizzical gaze darted towards him.

'No, I hadn't known – not until tonight,' Heshke murmured.

They hovered over the spot for a few minutes, watching the wrecked jet burn itself out. Finally one of the three remaining jets put down beside it. The other two continued the journey as the sun rose, whistling towards a destination that still had not been divulged to Heshke.

3

At the city of Cymbel they transferred to a fast intercontinental rocket transport. On board Heshke was given breakfast, but Brask said little during the two-hour journey. Once he went forward to the guidance cabin to receive a radio message and returned looking pensive.

They had chased the twilight zone on their five thousand mile trajectory, so it was early morning when they arrived at their destination. The rocket transport put down at what was evidently a private landing strip. A car drove up to take them to a low, massive concrete building a few hundred yards away.

Once inside the building Heshke found himself confronted with the usual Titan combination of efficiency and bustle. The corridors literally hummed – he didn't know from what source. Symbols whose meanings he did not understand signposted the way to various departments. He turned to Brask.

'What is this place?'

'A top secret research station.'

'Is the artifact here?'

Brask nodded. 'That's why this centre was set up – to study the artifact.'

Heshke's eyebrows rose. 'Then how long ago was it found?'

'Just over five years.'

'Five *years*? And you've kept quiet about it all that time?'

Brask smiled distantly. 'Patience, Citizen. You'll understand everything shortly.'

They came to a heavy door guarded by two armed Titans. Brask presented a pass; the door opened with the sigh of a pneumatic lock.

Beyond the guarded door the atmosphere was quieter and more calm. 'This leads to the main research area,' Brask told him. 'I'll introduce you to your new colleagues shortly. They begin the day here with an ideological session – would you care to drop in on it? It must be nearly over now.'

Resignedly Heshke nodded. Brask led him down a corridor and they entered a small auditorium. An audience of about two hundred white-smocked men and women faced a large screen which illustrated a commentary by means of a succession of pictures.

The visualization, Heshke noted, was skilled and professional. The scene at the moment was a soulful one of the sun setting over the forest-clad hills; in the foreground a deep blue sea lapped against a rocky, encrusted shore.

But smoothly the picture merged into a slow collage of viruses and soil bacteria. The sudden transition from the expansive world of forest, sea and sun to the invisible, microscopic world at the boundary of life was, Heshke thought, effective. It caught his attention right away, and he listened with interest to the mature, persuasive voice that accompanied the vidtrack, knitting the brief scenes together into a coherent whole.

'Here we have the *germinal essence*,' purred the voice
on the audtrack. 'In these primary particles of life the
spirit and essence of the planet Earth has concentrated
all its being. By means of a mighty distillation from the
potentiality of rock and soil, sun, ocean and lightning,
were created these seeds of all future things. From this
moment Earth, which before was barren, has produced
DNA; and from this DNA, like a giant rising from the
sea, there inevitably springs in due season the culmination
of the entire process: the entity for which all the rest of
Terrestrial life is but a platform. This is known as the
culminating essence, or the *human essence*.'

The pictures that illustrated this speech were swift and
dizzying. The virus forms vanished; momentary images
of DNA helices, dancing chromosomes and dividing cell
nuclei appeared one after the other, interspersed with a
swift procession of diverse living species as the stages of
evolution unfolded.

At the end of the sequence, to coincide with the speaker's last words, appeared the image of a young, naked
male, godlike both in proportion and feature (and posed
no doubt by a suitable Titan). The figure stood with arms
outstretched, light streaming around his silhouette from
a point source in the background, slowly fading into a
picture of Earth swimming in space.

'It follows,' continued the voice soberly, 'that evolution
is *not* a series of arbitrary accidents but a *whole process*,
tending towards a predestined end. It follows that by
nature Earth produces but *one* supreme species, this being
her destiny, and it follows that this is a law holding for
all planets throughout the universe. Earth is our mother,
our home, our sustenance. From Earth's soil we draw our
blood. We are her sons; no one shall take her from us.'

With a sonorous orchestral chord the screen went
blank. Heshke was fascinated. Blood and soil, he thought
again. There was much in the lecture that, paradoxically,
was both appealing and repellent: the mysticism, the bla-
tant Earth-worship, the belief in destiny. But who knows,

he thought, there might be something in it. Perhaps evolution *does* work like that.

The audience rose and filed out silently. Brask nudged Heshke. 'Now you can meet the people you'll be working with.'

Three members of the audience stayed behind, going over to a small table at the back. Brask and Heshke joined them.

Two of the men had the armbands and precise bearing of Titans. The third was a civilian, standing out from the others by reason of his sloppy slouch. He had a habit of glancing furtively around him, as if wishing he were somewhere else, and his mouth was twisted into a permanent expression of sardonic bitterness.

Brask made introductions. 'Titan-Lieutenant Vardanian, Titan-Lieutenant Spawart, Citizen Leard Ascar. Gentlemen, this is Citizen Rond Heshke.'

All made brief bows.

'Are you gentlemen archeologists also?' Heshke asked as politely as he could, since he did not recognize their names.

'No, we are physicists,' Leard Ascar said shortly. His voice matched his face, ironical, mocking.

Brask motioned them to chairs. 'It's time to put you into the picture, Citizen,' he said to Heshke. 'I hope you're able to absorb strange facts at short notice, because you'll need to.'

He flicked a switch on a small console on the table. The big screen lit up, but for the moment remained without a picture.

'We told you earlier that we had discovered an alien artifact in working order. You probably imagined it had been found in a dig or something of that sort. In point of fact it was discovered lying in the open on a grass field, quite accidentally, far from any known alien remains. Moreover it was obviously of very recent manufacture.'

He flashed a picture on the screen. The background was as he had described: a grassy meadow, with a line of trees in the distance. Lying in the foreground was a silvery cylinder, rounded at both ends and with dull, rather opaque-looking windows set fore and aft. A Titan stood by it for size comparison, revealing it to be about seven feet in diameter and about twelve in length.

'As you see, it's a vehicle of some sort,' Brask continued. 'Within were two aliens who appeared to have died shortly before of asphyxiation. As these were our first complete specimens they have increased our knowledge of the enemy to quite an extent.'

The screen blanked for a moment and then flicked to another picture. The cylinder had been opened. The two occupants, seen partially because of the awkwardness of handling the camera through the opening, were strapped side by side in narrow bucket seats. They were small furry creatures with pointed snouts and pink mole-like hands, being perhaps the size of young chimpanzees. After a few seconds the picture flickered and the same two corpses were shown more completely, pinned to a slab in a Titan laboratory.

Despite his excitement, Heshke found time to be pleased that the specimens resembled quite closely the reconstruction that had been attempted from skeletons.

'So it was a spaceship,' he said.

'That was naturally our conclusion, to begin with. But we were wrong. Only gradually, by experimenting with the vehicle's drive unit, were we able to piece together what it did.'

Heshke noticed that the physicists were all looking at the floor as though hearing the subject talked about embarrassed them.

'The equipment aboard the vessel used a principle completely unknown to us,' Brask went on. 'Movement through space – through comparatively short distances of space, not interplanetary space – could in fact be achieved as a by-product, but that was not its main purpose. Its main purpose is to move through time. The artifact we had stumbled on is a time machine.'

The physicists continued looking at the floor. Heshke let the bombshell sink into his mind.

Time. A time machine. The archaeologist's dream.

'So they're from the past,' he said finally, staring at the picture of the alien time travellers.

Brask nodded. 'That would be the assumption. Presumably they developed the means of time travel during the final stages of their sojourn on Earth, but too late to do them any good. We can only hope the secret is not known on their home world, but frankly I think we would have felt some effect from it if it was.'

'Yes, indeed,' Heshke muttered. 'The whole thing is – frightening.'

'You've said it,' Brask responded.

Heshke coughed nervously. 'This field trip I'm going on,' he said after a pause. 'It's a trip through time?'

'Perhaps. Perhaps not.'

'I don't understand.'

Brask looked at Titan-Lieutenant Vardanian. 'Would you care to explain?'

The tall Titan physicist nodded and turned to Heshke.

'You'll appreciate that we had no intention of risking our only time machine in reckless jaunts. We've spent five years of hard work trying to grasp the operation of the time traveller so that we could duplicate it. Finally we completed our own operational traveller – so we thought – and have made some trips in it. But the results are such that we need your expert advice; we're no longer sure that our traveller works properly.'

Heshke didn't understand what he meant. The Titan turned to the screen, reached for the control box and eliminated the image of the dead alien pilot. 'Watch carefully. I'm going to show you some pictures our men took.'

A flurry appeared on the screen, then an impression of racing motion as if some colourful scene were swinging wildly to and fro and passing by too swiftly to be grasped properly. After some moments Heshke discerned that the only stable element in the picture was a sort of rim on the upper and lower edges; he realized the this was the rim of another screen or window through which the camera was taking the sequence.

He found it hard to believe that all this was really happening. Here he was seeing pictures from the past while an efficient, intelligent Titan officer calmly explained something he would have thought to be impossible. It made even the death of Blare Oblomot seem a shadowy, dream-like event.

Suddenly the picture stilled. They looked out over an even landscape, the sun high in the sky. In the middle ground stood clumps of ruins stretching for several miles. Though so corroded and overgrown as nearly to have blended into nature, to Heshke's trained eye they clearly showed their alien origin.

'The Verichi Ruins, approximately nine hundred years ago,' Vardanian said quietly. 'Not what you would expect, is it?'

No, thought Heshke, it certainly wasn't. Nine centuries ago the Verichi Ruins – ruins in the present century, that is – should have been in their prime: an inhabited, bustling city. He watched an armoured figure stumbling about some heaps of stones. 'It's more like what they'll be nine centuries in the future,' he agreed. 'Maybe you were headed in the wrong direction?'

'Our conclusion also, at first,' Vardanian told him. 'Initially we made five stops, all inside a bracket covering two centuries. We failed to find any living aliens at all, merely ruins such as you see here. However, it didn't take long to ascertain that the wars of collapse – the death-throes of classical civilization – *were* in progress simultaneously with the existence of these ruins. So we *were* in the past after all.'

'But that doesn't make sense,' Heshke objected, frowning.

'Agreed. According to everything we know there was a large alien presence at the time of the wars of collapse.

Could we be wrong? Could the alien presence have been much earlier? That would explain the dilapidated condition of the ruins – but it would *not* explain their much fresher condition today. Frankly, none of the historical explanations make much sense. So we were forced to draw other, more disappointing conclusions: that the time traveller was playing tricks on us, that we weren't travelling through time at all.'

'You're beginning to lose me. Where *were* you going?'

Vardanian gestured vaguely, as though searching for words to express thoughts he only understood as abstract symbols. 'There are some peculiarities about the time-drive that suggest other possibilities. In order to work at all it has to be in the presence of a wakened consciousness; an unmanned, automatic time traveller simply wouldn't move. So a living pilot is one of the essential components. Bearing this in mind, we were able to formulate a theory that the traveller – the one we have built, at any rate, even if not the alien one – fails to move through *objective* time. It enters some region of "fictitious time", and presents to the consciousness of the observer elements from both the past and the future blended together, probably drawing them from the subconscious imaginations of the pilot and passengers.'

'It's all an illusion, you mean?'

The other nodded doubtfully. 'Roughly speaking, yes. Though the time traveller obviously does go *somewhere*, because it disappears from the laboratory.'

Heshke noticed that throughout the latter part of this explanation Leard Ascar scowled and muttered under his breath. Vardanian glanced at him pointedly. 'That, with one dissenting vote, was the explanation we had adopted until yesterday.'

'And then you showed us those photographs,' Brask put in. 'That upset things somewhat.'

Yes, the photographs. The pictures that showed the Hathar Ruins three centuries ago, and showed them in worse condition than they are today. The pictures that obviously – perfectly, clearly, obviously – were faked. The pictures that could not possibly be true.

'It was too much of a coincidence,' Brask said. 'Here was independent, objective evidence of the findings that *we* had thought were subjective and illusory. We immediately dispatched the time traveller to Hathar at around the time these photographs were presumably taken, and took a corresponding set of photographs from the same viewpoints.' He opened a drawer underneath the table and withdrew a sheaf of glossy prints. 'Here are copies of both sets. Check them: you'll find they match, more or less.'

Heshke did as he was told, looking over the prints. One set was in colour, the other – the old ones – in monochrome. He pushed them away, feeling that he was being surrounded by too much strangeness for one day.

'Yes, they look similar. What does that prove? That you *did* travel back in time after all?'

'Yes,' said Leard Ascar fiercely, speaking for the first time.

And the other Titan, Spawart, also spoke for the first time. He adopted an expression of meticulous care, choosing his words slowly. 'It may not necessarily mean that. We can't really take these photographs as substantiating our own findings. They *could* have been faked. Or, knowing now that time travel is possible, they *could* have been displaced in time, owing their origin to our future. There are a number of possibilities which do not rule out a malfunction in our time traveller.'

Yes, thought Heshke. Someone sent a package of photographs from three hundred years in the future to three hundred years in the past – a hop of six hundred years. That could have happened. But why?

It was useless to speculate. There could be a thousand bizarre, trivial, or unguessable reasons.

'Gentlemen,' he said, 'I'm finding this all just a little bit too bewildering. Do you mind telling me exactly why I'm here?'

'Yes, of course,' said Brask solicitously. 'We hadn't meant to call on your services until we had ironed the defects out of our time-drive system, but these photographs have thrown us somewhat into confusion. So we want you to take a trip back to the Hathar Ruins of three hundred years ago.'

'Why?' Heshke asked.

'Well—' Brask hesitated. 'We're working in the dark at the moment. Our most pressing need is to know whether our present capacity to travel through time is objectively real or merely illusory. The psychologists tell us that if it is illusory then there will be anomalies in the structures that appear to exist outside our own time – much as a dream fails to reconstruct reality with accuracy. There would be something to distinguish the ruins in the second set of photographs from the *real* Hathar Ruins.'

Heshke glanced again at the two sets. 'They don't look much different to me.'

'Agreed. But perhaps there's a difference the pictures don't show. Now you know the Hathar Ruins better than anyone: they're your speciality. We just want you to go back and make a study of them; see if you can throw any light on the mystery.'

'Those are pretty vague directives.'

Brask shrugged. 'Quite so. But Leard will be going with you; perhaps you can work something out together.'

Heshke contemplated for a few moments. 'This travel into a "fictitious past": it would be like a descent into the subconscious mind, wouldn't it?'

'Possibly so,' Titan-Lieutenant Vardanian said. But Leard Ascar gave vent to a derisive guffaw.

'Take no notice of all this nonsense, Heshke,' he said waspishly. ' "Fictitious past", my eye! The time-drive works!'

'Then the ruins . . .?' Heshke enquired delicately.

Ascar shrugged and then seemed to retreat into himself.

Heshke turned to Brask. 'When do we go?'

'As soon as possible. If you feel up to it, today.'

'I'll need recorders, and a few tools.'

The other nodded. 'We've anticipated that. I think you'll find we have everything you could require.'

'You mentioned danger . . .'

'Only because the unit is relatively untested. That's the only source of risk.'

'Apart from other aliens?' Heshke queried. 'This business makes their technology look pretty formidable.'

'Yes, but not necessarily in all-area advance of our own,' Spawart replied. 'After all, we were able to copy their time-drive. That would indicate that we have comparable ability.'

'That is, provided we *have* copied it,' Brask rejoined, giving the other a sharp look.

'Of course we have!' snapped Ascar.

Heshke first inspected his equipment, and then was given a private room in which to rest. He slept for a couple of hours and then lay on the couch thinking over everything he had learned.

The expedition, he gathered, was to comprise four men in all: himself, the physicist Leard Ascar, and two Titan technical officers to pilot the time traveller. Departure was timed for midafternoon, and as the day wore on his nerves began to fray.

Shortly after lunch had been brought to him he was visited by Leard Ascar, who had spent the morning working on the time apparatus.

'Hello, Heshke, feeling nervous?' the sour-faced physicist said.

Heshke nodded.

'No need to worry. It's all quite safe and painless really. This is my third trip.'

'How long will the journey take?'

'We can manage a hundred years per hour. So say three hours there, three hours back.'

'We're rather a long way from Hathar, aren't we – in spatial terms, I mean?'

'No problem. While we're travelling through time – strictly speaking we're travelling through *non*-time – we can manoeuvre over the Earth's surface at will. We'll land slap on top of our target.'

'From here to Hathar in three hours.' Heshke mused. 'That's not bad at all. This time machine would make quite a good intercontinental transport, then?'

Ascar laughed shortly. 'You're quick on the uptake, but no, it wouldn't. You have to trade space for time. To travel to the other side of the Earth you'd have to traverse about a hundred years. I suppose you could do it by moving back and forth until you matched destinations in space *and* time, but after you'd finished messing about you would have done better to go by rocket.'

Ascar fumbled in his pocket, brought out a crumpled tobacco roll and lit it, breathing aromatic smoke all around. Heshke noticed that his eyes bulged slightly. 'Mind if I sit down? Been working on that damned time-drive all morning. I'm kind of tensed up myself.'

'Sure, be my guest.' Ascar took the room's only chair and Heshke sat on his bed to face him. 'I'm rather curious . . . how does the time traveller work?'

Ascar grinned. 'By detaching "now" from "now" and moving it through "non-now".'

Heshke shook his head with a sigh. 'That means absolutely nothing to me.'

'It wouldn't have to me, either, before we found the alien machine. And not even then for a long time. But I understand it now. That's why I'm sure the Titans are wrong with this cock-eyed notion of "subconscious time" or whatever.' Ascar puffed on his roll as if tobacco were the staff of life. Heshke realized that the man was even more nervous than he was. 'I'm sorry, Heshke, it's just that I think this whole jaunt is a waste of time. The time traveller does what we intended it to do: to travel, objectively and in reality, back and forward through time. And I'm the one to ask because it was *me*, in the end, who cracked the problem. *They'd* still be fumbling.'

'What's this, professional jealousy?' Heshke smiled.

The other waved his hand and looked annoyed. 'Why should I be jealous? The Titan scientists are good at their work – on straightforward problems. Give them a premise and they'll take it right through to its conclusion, very thoroughly. But where creative thinking is called for they tend to fall back on their ideology – and we all know what a lot of bull that is.'

Heshke looked around uneasily, wondering about hidden microphones. 'I never thought I'd hear anyone talk like that in a Titan stronghold,' he said.

The physicist shrugged. 'They tolerate me. I've been with this project from the start, five years ago. Things were more easy-going in the old days. I'm sick of it now, though.'

'Oh? Why?'

Ascar sneered. 'I've built them their time traveller and they say it does not work, just because they don't like what they've discovered in the past. They're disappointed that the aliens didn't seem to have played any part in the wars of collapse, that's what it all comes down to. And we've hardly even done any exploring yet. Maybe the aliens *were* around, somewhere or other.'

'You sound bitter.'

Ascar pulled on his roll. 'Just tired. Five years spent trying to understand time has unhinged my mind. Take no notice of my grumbling, Citizen. It's all part of my personality syndrome.'

'But the ruins,' Heshke reminded him. 'If we were to take the evidence at face value they are growing *newer* as time passes, instead of older. That just can't be, can it?'

Ascar shrugged. 'How the hell would I know? Nothing looks impossible to me now I know that time's mutable, that the individual's "now" can be detached from absolute "now". There must be an explanation.' He smiled. 'How about this? Thousands of years ago the aliens flew over here and planted some seeds – special kinds of seeds. Ever since they've been slowly growing, not into plants or vegetable matter but into structures of stone and metal. The ruins we see are like trees maturing over centuries into full-blown houses, cities, castles and whatever. When they are fully grown the aliens will come down and live in them.'

Heshke laughed, thinking over the idea. He was tickled by Ascar's quick imagination, by his readiness to face impossible facts and draw daring inferences from them. 'But there are skeletons, too,' he reminded. 'The seeds wouldn't grow those.'

'Why not? Maybe a few skeletons were included to fool future archaeologists.' But Heshke could see that the physicist wasn't being serious.

There was silence for a while. Ascar smoked noisily and shuffled his feet, staring at the ceiling. He seemed to have become unaware of Heshke's presence.

'Has any attempt been made to contact people in the past?' Heshke asked then. 'Probably they could answer a good many of our questions.'

'Huh?' Ascar's attention jerked back into the room. He stared at Heshke with glazed eyes. 'Oh. Oh, you don't know about that, do you?'

'Don't know about what?' asked Heshke in some exasperation.

'About what it's like in the past. You can't talk to the people there because they don't hear you. They don't see you, either. What's more you can knock them down and they don't react in any way at all, just lie there squirming and eventually get up again. It's as if they were robots going through motions which time has already ordained.'

Heshke stared at him.

'Oh, I know it sounds weird,' Ascar said with a wave of his hand, 'but that's how it is.'

'Do you mean they have no consciousness?'

'They act like they have no consciousness. Like robots, predetermined mechanisms,' Ascar repeated.

'That sounds . . . sort of dream-like. Are you sure the Titans couldn't be right?'

'Oh no, it accords with my theory of how the time traveller works very well. You've probably read fictional stories about time travel and got your ideas of time from them. They always make the past or the future sound no different in essence from present time; but we know now that they're very different indeed.'

The physicist finished his tobacco roll and threw away the end, groping in his pocket for another. Heshke gave him one and helped him light it. 'How?'

'I'll explain. Think of the universe as a four-dimensional continuum – three dimensions of space, as is our ordinary experience, and an additional dimension which we call time, extending into the infinite past and the infinite future. If we take the moving "now" out of the picture we could just as easily call it a universe of four dimensions of space. So now we have a static four-dimensional matrix. That's basically what the universe consists of, but there's one other factor: the fleeting present moment, sweeping through the fourth dimension like a travelling wave.'

Heshke was no physicist but he had read widely and to some extent was already familiar with what Ascar was saying. He nodded, picturing it to himself. 'The "now" that we seem to be trapped in, being moved on from one moment to the next.'

'That's right. What is this "now"? Does anything exist outside it? For centuries the philosophical question has been whether the past and the future have any existence, or whether only the present that we experience has existence. Well, we've found out the answer to that question all right: the past and the future *do* exist, but they have no "now". In effect, they have no time. No differentiation between before and after. They're both dead, as it were.'

'So that's why the people in the past act like robots?'

Ascar nodded. 'The travelling "now-wave" has passed them by. Consciousness can only exist in the "now" – somehow or other it appears to be a function of it.'

'This time-wave – what does it consist of?'

'We're not really sure. Some form of energy that travels through the four-dimensional continuum like a shock wave. We know its velocity: it travels with the speed of light. And as it goes it has the power to make events happen and to organize matter into living forms. You know in olden times they used to talk about the "life force"? This is the life force.'

A thought occurred to Heshke. 'You say there's no time in the past. But what if you went back in time and changed something? What happens to the past as it was *before* you changed it? There'd have to be a kind of time there because there'd be a *before* you changed it and an *after* you changed it . . .' He broke off in confusion.

The physicist grinned. 'What you're talking about used to be called the Regression Problem, and it exercised us too when we first realized time travel was possible. Actually, in a slightly different form, it's an ancient philosophical riddle: how can time pass without having another "time" to pass in? One instant "now" is at one point and the next instant it's at the adjacent point, passed on to the next event, and so you seem to have a "before" and an "after" associated with the same moment – one where "now" was there and one where it wasn't.'

'Yes, I think that's what I mean,' Heshke said slowly.

Ascar nodded. 'These paradoxes have largely disappeared now that we're able to make on-the-spot observations. Theorists used to posit an additional fifth dimension to accommodate these changes, but we know better than that now. The universe is indifferent to all artificially imposed changes, as well as to where "now" is situated. It doesn't distinguish between one configuration and another: therefore any changes you make don't alter anything.'

Heshke didn't understand him. 'But there's still the old riddle, what if I went back and murdered my father before I was born . . .?'

'It would probably turn out that your father was somebody else,' Ascar said acidly. 'Joking apart, if you did succeed in "killing" your father, you'd find that he was still alive . . . later. Cause and effect, as we understand it, only takes place in the travelling now-wave – what we call the Absolute Present. We've established that experimentally. Elsewhere the universe behaves indifferently, and if you *do* force changes on the past, then the consequences die away instead of accumulating.'

'You're beginning to lose me,' Heshke said slowly. 'I find it hard to grasp . . . that even when tomorrow comes I shall still be here today, smoking this roll . . . only I won't be aware of it.'

Ascar rubbed his jaw and yawned tiredly. 'That's it: you've got it exactly. Now we are here; shortly the Absolute Present will have moved a few minutes further on, taking our consciousness with it. But the past doesn't vanish, it's merely that you can't see it – just as you can't see the future yet, even though it exists up there ahead of us. The time traveller acts like a lever, detaching a fragment of the present and moving it about independently. If that fragment has your consciousness attached to it you can then see the past, or the future.'

'How far have you been into the future?' asked Heshke suddenly.

Again Ascar looked sour. 'Only about a hundred years, no further. There's no point.'

'Oh? Why not?'

'Because do you know what you find in the future? Just an empty desolation! There are no living forms – no people, no animals, no grass, no birds or trees or anything. Not a virus or a microbe. Just one second futureward of where we're sitting the world is void of all life, and these chairs we're sitting on are empty.'

Horrified, Heshke blinked at him. Ascar smiled crookedly. 'It's logical, if you think about it. There's life in the past, even if it does behave like clockwork, because the now-wave has already swept over it and the now-wave creates life. But it hasn't reached the future yet. Everything we've constructed out of inorganic matter – our buildings, our machines, and so on – are there, but without the hand of man to maintain them they fall into a state of decay. And as for the substance of our own bodies, that's dust, just dust.'

And Heshke sat contemplating that vast, dead emptiness.

4

The Titan time traveller was considerably larger than its alien prototype. Instead of the latter's cylindrical form it had a cage-like structure, being square at both ends and ribbed with louvres. One end contained the cabin for the crew and passengers, the other the bulky drive machinery. It did, however, borrow some features from the alien design: the windows were of a thick nearly-opaque material possessing the quality of image-control, capable of being adjusted so as to admit or block light, and the control system copied the alien concept in its entirety.

Initially the machine's departure from the present was assisted by a second, even larger apparatus from whose maw it currently projected like a tongue, but once dispatched it flew under its own power and had no contact with the home base. This fact was nagging at Heshke's consciousness as he tried to fight down his fears and allowed himself to be helped into the stiff combat armour the Titans had insisted he wear.

'Are you comfortable?' the young com-tech asked.

He nodded, though he was far from comfortable since

the leather-like suit restricted all his movements.

For some minutes the Dispatch Room had been filled with a loud whine as the launcher was warmed up. Ascar was already in his suit, as were the two technical officers who were to pilot the time traveller. Ascar beckoned him forward.

'All set? Your gear all ready?'

'It's on board.' Not that he anticipated using much; he didn't really know what he would do when he reached the ruins.

'Then let's take our places.'

He followed Ascar into the time traveller. The cabin was comparatively large, about nine feet by nine. He sat down beside the physicist, strapping himself in. The tech officers came in, wearing their combat suits with more grace and style, and settled into the pilots' seats in the front of the cabin. The whine from the Dispatch Room was cut off as the door slid shut: the time traveller was soundproof.

Heshke's muscles knotted up. The tech officers murmured to one another and through microphones to the team outside. A raw, fuzzy hum arose to their rear.

One of the Titans half turned his head to speak to them. 'We're away.'

Was that all? Heshke's stomach untensed itself. He felt no sensation of motion; but through the semi-opaque windows he saw a runny blur of motion and colour, phasing wildly to and fro as though the vehicle were pursuing an erratic course.

'Home,' Ascar said to him. 'We're leaving home.'

Heshke looked at him quizzically.

'Well of course it's home!' the other scowled impatiently. 'Don't you know what I mean? Haven't you any vision?'

'I guess not.'

'I mean we're leaving the Absolute Present. That's home to us. The only place in the universe where conscious life exists. Just think of all past time, stretching back and back into eternity. The further back you go into it the further away you are from the brief intersection where life exists, until you would be like a ghost, a brief fragment of time in a timeless abyss . . . and the same if you go into the future. Doesn't that get through to you?'

Ascar's eyes were bulging and there were tiny beads of perspiration on his brow. 'Is that what going back in time is like for you?' Heshke asked quietly. 'Like falling into an abyss?'

'That's what it's like – a chasm without a bottom. And we're descending into it.'

Suddenly Heshke understood Ascar. The man was afraid, for all that he had reassured Heshke. He was afraid that something would go wrong and they would be cut off, unable to get back to the world of life and time.

He had too vivid an imagination; and he was getting a little melodramatic. Heshke wondered if the physicist's five-year-long obsession had left him mentally unbalanced. After all, it was an awesome subject to have preying on one's mind.

Heshke himself still found the explanations of time and non-time too abstruse to be grasped properly; his mind spun when he tried to think it through. He found it hard to understand why the travelling wave of 'now', that is, of time, should be at one particular place at one particular *time* . . .

No, that wasn't it, either. Being where it was was what *made* time . . .

They passed the rest of the journey in silence, Ascar slouching in his chair, insofar as the combat suit would let him, and occasionally muttering to himself. Three hours passed; and then the tech officer warned them that they were coming in to land.

A gong sounded. The blurred, racing images that had almost lulled Heshke to sleep ceased, but he couldn't see anything definite through the thickened windows.

Ascar released his safety strap and invited Heshke to do the same. 'Come and have a look out of the window,' he said, 'you might like to see this.'

Heshke followed him and peered through one of the frosty windows. Ascar turned a knob and the plate cleared.

Outside was a scene reassuringly pleasant and familiar. Judging by the position of the sun it was mid-afternoon. Beneath a blue sky stretched greenery: a savannah interspersed with scrawny trees. And nearby, recognizable to Heshke despite the intervening three centuries, were the Hathar Ruins, broken, crumbled and moss-covered.

'Notice anything?' Ascar said expectantly.

And Heshke did notice something. A raven was flying across their field of view – or rather, it was not flying. Close enough for every feather of its outspread wings to stand out distinctly, it was hanging in mid-air, frozen and motionless.

'It's not moving.' he murmured in wonderment.

'That's right.' Ascar seemed secretly gleeful. 'We're at a dead stop. Halted on one frozen instant.'

A thought occurred suddenly to Heshke. 'But if that were so we wouldn't be able to see anything. Light would be frozen, too.'

Ascar gave a superior smile. 'A clever inference, Citizen, but a wrong one. There's no such thing as frozen light – its velocity is constant for *all* observers, which is the same as saying it's not properly a velocity at all. Few laymen understand that.'

He gave a signal to the pilot. 'Just the same, for practical purposes we need to explore an environment with all the features of our own, that is to say one that moves.'

The pilot did something on the control panel. The raven bolted into action, flapped its wings and flew away. The savannah stirred in the breeze.

'Now we are travelling futureward at the rate of one second per second: the normal rate of time we are used to. This rate will persist automatically. We can go outside now.'

The door hissed open, allowing fresh air into the cabin. Heshke moved to the rear of the cabin, picked up a movie vidcamera, a satchel of tools and a specimen bag. Then he followed Ascar into the open air.

There could be little doubt of it. The photographs dug up in Jejos weren't faked; there was no coincidence, nothing that could account for them in accidental terms. They were pictures of the actual ruins he and Ascar stood in the midst of now.

Beyond them, on a grassy knoll, stood the time traveller, guarded by one of the Titan technical officers. The other officer had taken up a nearer position just outside the ruins and was scanning the landscape for signs of danger. God knew what kind of danger there could be here in the middle of nowhere, three hundred years back in limbo, but there he stood in the textbook standoff position.

It was hard to believe it: hard to believe that they *were* three hundred years into non-time. The air brought to Heshke's nostrils all the freshness of summer, the sun shone down, and everything looked peacefully normal.

'Are you absolutely sure?' Ascar asked.

'Absolutely. I know these ruins like the back of my hand. I've been studying them for years. These *are* the Hathar Ruins, as I would expect them to be three centuries *after* our time. We *must* be in the future.'

'No, we're in the past.' Ascar was frowning, a scowling frown of great agitation.

'Well . . .' Heshke put his hand on a weathered alien wall, feeling the almost subconscious thrill he had noted so often. 'Then we're up against a paradox that would seem to support the Titan theory: that the past and the future have got mixed up somehow and nothing we see is real. But I have to say that personally I feel forced to reject even that theory. These remains are too perfect, too solid and incontrovertible in every detail. They *have* suffered three centuries of physical decay from the ruins of my time, and they have decayed exactly as I would expect.'

'But we *are* in the past,' Ascar insisted.

Heshke shouldered his vidcamera and shook his head sadly. 'Come over here,' he invited.

Clambering over the mossy stones, the physicist followed him into a grid-pattern of low walls which had the appearance of once having been a set of rooms. The archaeologist crouched down beside a wall where he had earlier pulled away a patch of moss.

'This clinches it,' he said, looking up at Ascar. 'See these grooves?'

Ascar stooped. The sharp sunlight glinted on little fronds of moss, on dirt and sparkling stone, and made shadows in a number of short trenches cut in three blocks of stone, surrounding a third.

'Yes.'

'I myself helped to cut those grooves. We suspected there was an aumbry behind here – a cupboard cut in the wall. And we were right. Afterwards we replaced the sealing stone. Here, give me a hand.'

He took a couple of jemmies out of his tool satchel. Ascar helped him to lever away the slab. It came after a little effort, being not as thick or as solidly entrenched as it looked. Heshke shone a little light into the cavity thus revealed and moved aside so that Ascar could look.

'I'll bet a year's pay there's some writing in there. See if you can find it.'

Ascar poked his head into the entrance. The recess was larger than its door suggested and smelled damp, but it was free of dust. On the opposite wall were some large letters, neatly cut with a powered stone inscriber.

'Skeleton thirty-one,' he read slowly. 'Glass vessel four hundred eighty-nine.'

Heshke chuckled. 'That's right. I inscribed that message myself. It was to record what we had found in there and their catalogue numbers.'

Ascar stood up and took a deep breath.

'Well, there's your proof,' Heshke told him. 'Right now we are standing *after* our time, *not* before.'

'Well, you're the expert,' Ascar said amiably. 'I can't argue with that.'

The time traveller surged forward, and Heshke relaxed, idly watching the flurry of shapes and colours through the windows and listening to the fuzzy hum of the time-drive. For the first part of the journey back to the research centre he had tried to talk to Leard Ascar; but the physicist had retreated into himself and now sat staring with glazed eyes at the floor, either stupefied or engaged in deep meditation.

He had asked the pilots that he be allowed to release the safety straps, since they appeared to be superfluous and made the journey even more tedious, but they had refused, explaining that the machine was liable to a sudden lurch if a rapid change in direction was called for.

He wondered how his report would be received by the Titan controllers of the research centre. Already he had communicated his findings to the pilots. They were well-trained and understood the implications. But with typical Titan superciliousness they'd made no comment.

Half resentfully, he stared at their broad, uniformed backs. These Titans had killed his friend Blare Oblomot, he reminded himself. He realized now that he had gone around anaesthetized since that event, as if in a dream . . . it was a happening he just hadn't been able to take in properly. But then Blare, by his own admission, had been a traitor; inexplicably, a traitor . . .

A gong rang out, in a different tone from that which had heralded the approach of their outgoing destination. The pilot spoke up for the passengers' benefit.

'We're approaching Absolute Present.'

Ascar jerked his gaze up from the floor. Just then the co-pilot murmured something to his colleague, who glanced down at the other's section of the instrument panel.

'Citizen Ascar, we appear to have a malfunction on the Absolute Present register,' the pilot announced in a puzzled tone.

'Eh?' Ascar released himself from his straps and bounded forward to peer closely at the designated instrument. From where he was sitting Heshke could see it: a large strip-dial that had commenced to flash as the gong sounded. A marker moved steadily across it in a count-down towards zero: the travelling wave of time.

But now the marker was quivering and behaving erratically, first darting towards the zero and then retreating from it. 'Without that register we'll find it difficult to synchronize back into "now",' the pilot warned.

'Malfunctioning, hell, it *must* be in order,' Ascar growled.

'It gives impossible readings,' the Titan corrected meticulously. 'It's obviously an instrument failure.'

Ascar froze for a moment. 'Not impossible,' he said slowly. 'It's detecting the presence of real time, but not strongly enough for it to be absolute time. Hell, we ourselves carry a small fragment of time with us – *as does every other time traveller*!'

He stepped to a window and tuned it to near-transparency, peered through it briefly and then crossed the cabin to do the same on the other side. There, pacing them so as to stand out steadily against the kaleidoscope-like flurry, was a cylindrical shape rounded at both ends.

It duplicated perfectly the alien time traveller that had been shown to Heshke on film.

Cautiously he released his straps and joined Ascar at the window, peering fascinated through the glowing pane. He became aware that behind the dulled windows of the alien traveller there were undoubtedly eyes, alien eyes, that were watching them.

'Great Mother Earth!' one of the Titans swore softly.

Ascar swung around. 'For God's sake man – don't let them track us to the Research Centre!'

The Titan understood him perfectly. 'Back to your seats!' he ordered. But Heshke was still not secured properly when the traveller gave a sickening lurch and raced off into whatever other direction might conceivably exist – Heshke was confused on that point for the moment. He just saved himself from being toppled on to the floor and fastened the straps.

The Absolute Present register was flaring more brightly. 'We shall synchronize with the present on a distant part of Earth, and make our way from there to the Centre by conventional means,' the Titan announced. 'By that means we may hope to evade alien detection.'

'No,' said Ascar. 'Keep going.'

'What for?' the other said sharply. 'Our orders are to return to the Centre forthwith!'

'Keep going – on into the future.' Ascar's voice was trembling with excitement. 'There's something I have to find out,' he said. 'Something we *all* have to find out. So keep going!'

The pilot glanced over his shoulder, perturbed – as Heshke was – to see the physicist so in the grip of passion. 'Are you suggesting that we depart from the flight plan, Citizen? That can *not* be allowed! Any suggestions you may have will have to be put before the controllers.'

'Yes, Titan ideologues who can't see the facts even when they're held up in front of their faces!' Ascar snarled, apparently in fury. 'They'll delay, delay, delay – by then it might be too late! Mankind will be finished!'

Ascar had again stood up. Heshke was alarmed to see that he had produced a gun from somewhere in his combat suit. With a cry Heshke also scrambled free of his straps and staggered forward, recklessly intending to tackle him. But at that moment Ascar lunged, seizing a handgrip on the control panel and swinging it far over. The time traveller accelerated wildly and overshot the Absolute Present to hurtle wildly futureward. The accompanying jolt sent Heshke reeling. He fell, hit his head violently against the arm of a chair, and blackness overwhelmed him.

He came round to find himself back in his seat, lolling against the straps. His head ached abominably. But the pain was soon forgotten in the horror and shock of what he saw.

The co-pilot was lying against one wall, evidently dead. The other Titan was disarmed and stood against the opposite wall, warily watching Ascar who was nonchalantly piloting the time traveller while keeping an eye on him.

'Uh – what happened?' Heshke rasped.

Ascar spared him a glance. 'Welcome back. I'm afraid there was a scuffle. Lieutenant Hosk got shot. Wasn't really my fault.' He spoke the last in a surly mumble.

Heshke paused. 'And the alien time traveller?'

'We lost it.' Ascar gave a tight, sinister grin. 'I've been pushing this ship to its limit – close to a hundred and fifty years per hour.'

The words 'You're mad' died in Heshke's throat.

'Where are we now?'

'Nearly four hundred years in the future.'

Heshke lay back in his seat, trying to fight off a feeling of hopelessness. Ascar's mind had evidently snapped under the strain. He and the pilot would have to be patient and await their chance to overwhelm him.

'The future? What do you expect to find there?' he asked, stumbling over the words. 'You said yourself it's all dead and empty.'

'The facts are staring us in the face,' Ascar replied. 'That's the mark of the true scientist, isn't it, Heshke? To take facts as facts even if they conflict with theory, and draw the most obvious deductions from them. That's what we've been failing to do.'

'What facts are those?' Heshke glanced nervously at the Titan, who was watching Ascar warily.

'Chiefly, the plain fact that the alien interventionist ruins are *ageing backward in time*. If we take that at face value, then their source lies in the future, and we're going to track it down.'

His words were interrupted by the sounding of the gong. The Absolute Present register began to glow, for the second time this trip.

'There she blows!' crowed Ascar.

The Titan's jaw dropped. He stared at the register as though unable to believe his eyes.

'But we're four centuries away from Absolute Present!'

'Four centuries from *our* Absolute Present.'

'There *is* only one,' the Titan insisted emptily. 'Your own equations say so . . . you to whom we owe the secret of the time-drive . . .'

'Well, I can't be right all the time,' Ascar said, rather bleakly. 'What do you think I was doing for three hours while we made the journey back – just sitting there with a blank mind?' He snorted. 'Oh no, I was going over those very equations you seem to regard as sacrosanct . . . and it occurred to me that I might not know as much about time as I had thought, and that the equations could be wrong. So I began to imagine a number of other possibilities. What if the Absolute Present *isn't* unique, as I had formerly assumed it to be? Perhaps there are other waves of time, separated from our own by millions of years, by millennia – or only by centuries. Perhaps there is a regular series of them, forming the nodes of a cosmic wave frequency vibrating through the universe. Whatever the truth, I discovered that if I amended the equations to make room for any of these possibilities then the basic principle that makes the time-drive work remains unchanged . . . so the theoretical structure had to give way . . . even if the Great Earth Mother has to give way too . . .'

While he spoke Ascar had been deftly flying the time traveller, dividing his attention between the instruments and his two hijacked passengers. His gun was never more than an inch or two away from his right hand.

He continued ramblingly. 'And what if one of those other time waves was travelling *in the opposite direction* to our own? Not proceeding from the past into the future, as we understand time, but from the future into the past? The very words past and future tend to lose their meaning in such a context . . . Whatever lies behind one's direction of motion is the past and whatever lies in front of it is the future . . . *There it is!*'

His last words were a shout, an excited squawk. The Absolute Present register had zeroed in and stood slightly on the other side of zero.

Ascar turned a knob, tuning the windows to transparency. 'Take a look,' he said. 'We're at time-stop.'

Slowly Heshke rose and approached one of the windows.

It was Earth, but it was not Earth. The sky was blue, with white clouds hanging majestically in it. The sun was of a familiar size, colour and radiance. But there the resemblance ended. True, there was grass – green grass . . . but it was an olive green shot through with mother-of-pearl colours, and all the other vegetation was discreetly non-Terran; the trees – twisted, writhing things – bore no resemblance to any Earth tree that had ever existed as far as Heshke knew.

These trees, growing on the slope of a grassy eminence where Ascar had set them down, did not detain his attention for long. Briefly he noted an unrecognizable flying thing, frozen in midair as had been the raven, and then he flooded his vision with the incredible scene that was set out below.

The Hathar Ruins: but not the ruins that Heshke had studied for so many years, and not those still further back down the centuries. This was the Hathar site as it had been in its prime: an intact, inhabited settlement. He drank in the clean-cut, sparkling conical towers, the large buildings, the Cathedral (whose purpose he still did not know), the tenement-like masses of smaller rooms, the plazas, the roads . . .

It was all as he had constructed it in his imagination so many times. Alien, but *alive*. A bustling, living habitation of a non-human people.

And those people thronged Hathar. Furry, sharp-snouted, standing in triangular doorways and walking the streets and squares. But they were caught in mid-motion like a stereo still photograph: the traveller was not moving in any direction in time.

'The alien interventionists!' breathed the Titan officer. Both he and Heshke had forgotten their tacit agreement to jump Ascar.

'Correct. But they are not interventionists, though they are alien in a sense.'

The Titan clenched his fists. 'So we have been mistaken all along. The enemy is attacking from the *future*. That must be where he made his landings on Earth.'

'No, no,' said Ascar, adopting a tone of uncharacteristic patience. 'Watch this: I'm putting us in motion again at the biological rate of one second per second.'

He made an adjustment. The scene came to life. The clouds sailed across the sky, the trees moved, the aliens walked through streets and squares.

'They're walking backward,' said Heshke blankly.

And so indeed they were. The whole scene was like a motion picture thrown into reverse. 'That's because we've adopted the time sense normal to us,' Ascar explained, 'but it's not normal to *them*. Now watch what happens when I put our machine into reverse at the same rate – one second per second.'

Again he made an adjustment. They all watched through the windows while the scene rewound itself and went forward, the alien creatures walking naturally this time, with a rolling gait, their posture not quite as erect as that of a human being. '*This* is their normal time-sense,' Ascar told them, 'the reverse of ours. *Now* do you see it? These creatures aren't alien to Earth. They're Terran.

They evolved here, millions of years in our future. By the same token, we are in *their* future. The Earth has two completely different evolutionary developments on it, separated in time and associated with separate time-streams — time-streams moving in opposite directions. *And they are on a collision course.*'

The shock that affected Heshke and the Lieutenant, once they understood this news, lasted some time. They stared for long moments without speaking.

'But the Earth Mother,' the Titan stuttered.

Ascar gave a harsh laugh. 'Earth Mother!' He made the words sound like a curse.

Heshke turned to Ascar and gestured with his thumb through the window. 'Aren't we too exposed? What if they see us?'

'They can't see us. We're not synched on their present moment; we're pacing a few minutes behind it.'

'Collision!' gasped the Titan. 'It's inconceivable! What will happen, Ascar?'

Ascar laughed again, this time horribly and savagely. 'Can't you envisage it? The converging time processes are now only four hundred years apart, and already we've become aware of one another. Each will make massive preparations to destroy the other.' His eyes shone, as though he were privy to some dreadful vision. 'And while the time-waves are yet centuries apart an indescribable war of annihilation will be in progress. Each civilization, on seeing the constructions of the other rising magically in its midst, on seeing them become *newer* with each passing year, will grow more and more fearful. Both sides will find themselves trying to manipulate *the same materials* from different points in time! But everything will be in vain — for what will happen when the two time-streams actually collide? Can anything survive such a shock? Annihilation, that's what will happen. Annihilation, followed by the cessation of all time . . .'

With an effort the Titan broke free from the spell of

Ascar's words. He drew himself erect.

'There's no time to lose: the High Command must be made aware of the situation immediately.'

'Yes, that's where our duty lies.' Ascar was trembling with nervous reaction. He drew back from the pilot's seat, leaving his gun where it was, and wiped his brow with a shaky hand. 'Take over, Lieutenant.'

The Titan seated himself at the control panels and made calibrations. He appeared to have recovered his composure completely and spoke with authoritative self-righteousness.

'It has to be admitted that you've rendered mankind a service, Citizen Ascar. Nevertheless when we return to Absolute Present you will be charged with disobeying orders and with murdering a Titan officer.'

'Leave him alone, for God's sake,' Heshke pleaded worriedly. 'Can't you see he's insane?'

'Yes, insane,' muttered Ascar. 'Who wouldn't be . . . five years alone in that place. Who wouldn't be? The strain . . . knowing I was the only man on Earth who could solve the problem . . . who could give humanity the secret of time travel . . . I wasn't sure I could do it. The enemy had an advantage over us. We had to take away that advantage or perish . . . now we're going to perish anyway.'

The fuzzy hum of the time traveller rose in volume as the machine picked up power and glided away from its position to go surging pastward. Heshke settled down for the journey, reassured by seeing the tall Titan once more at the controls and by Ascar's apparent lapse into inactivity.

For about an hour they journeyed in silence. Heshke began to doze, but was awakened by a hoarse cry from the pilot, accompanied by a sickening lurch. The pilot was taking evasive action.

Heshke observed that the Absolute Present register was again flickering. The pilot cleared the windows to transparency to reveal the shape of a pursuing enemy

time machine. Ascar shouted incoherently; at the same
time they sustained a shuddering shock and seemed to
go into a kind of spin.

Heshke became dizzy. When his head cleared the cabin
was motionless, but leaning crazily, and a large hole had
been torn in its side. Behind them the drive-unit gave out
a ragged, injured buzz.

Somehow it came as a surprise to Heshke to find that
the alien time traveller had been armed.

'Damn!' moaned Ascar. 'Damn!'

Heshke got to his feet. The Titan officer was already
peering out of the smoking hole in the side of the cabin.
Heshke joined him and saw, in midair, a cylindrical
shape half materialize, shimmering, and then fade away.
He shrank back momentarily; then, when the officer
stepped cautiously to the ground, he followed him and
stood staring around.

If death was the absence of life, then Heshke had
never imagined such an expanse of death. The landscape
stretched all around them in a grey, sterile tableland,
featureless except for some hills in the west and some
tumbled ruins to the north. There was not a blade of
grass nor anything that moved. And dust, everywhere
dust – Heshke had never conceived of so much dust,
unless it was on the surface of the moon.

Ascar scrambled out of the cabin after them, his face
gone ghastly pale. 'The drive's ruined!' he exclaimed in a
strangled tone. 'That bastard knew exactly where to aim
for!'

His glance darted around helplessly. 'You asked me
about the future, Heshke – well, here it is. The future
that time hasn't reached yet. And we're stranded in it!'

That was what he was afraid of, Heshke thought.

'We've failed,' said the Lieutenant in a stricken voice.
'Our comrades will never hear our report now.'

'It doesn't matter, you fool,' Ascar snarled. 'Life on
Earth has exactly two centuries to run – then *everything's*
finished.'

Blood and soil, Heshke thought. *Blood and soil*.
They all stood staring at the dead landscape.

5

Far from Earth, the ISS – Interstellar Space Society
– known to its inhabitants as Retort City floated as
if transfixed in the blackness of space, approximately
mid-way between Altair and Barnard's Star – that is, as
far from any celestial body as it could manage. It took
its name from its appearance, which was that of a double retort, or hourglass, but long and elegantly shaped.
Retort City was, in fact, a city in a bottle, its outer skin
being transparent and having a glassy sheen. An observer
watching from the void would have discerned within the
glass envelope a sort of double spindle, this being the
general plan of the city's internal structure, and would
have seen through a muted blaze of lights an intermittent
movement as the internal transport facilities passed up
and down.

The city had a history of about five thousand years,
having lived it uneventfully for the most part. Probably,
its rulers thought, there were other ISS establishments
somewhere within a hundred light-year radius of Sol, all
surviving fragments of long-vanished Earth civilizations,
for at one time the idea of forsaking life on planetary
bodies and taking to artificial cities in the interstellar void
had been a fashionable one. But they did not know this for
sure, and felt no urge to comb space for their lost cousins.

Colloquially the two halves of the ISS were known as
the Lower Retort and the Upper Retort – terms with
social, rather than spatial, implications. Officially they
were the Production Retort and Leisure Retort. And
no one, except newborn babies, ever passed from one
retort to the other.

Or almost no one.

Hueh Su-Mueng shut down his machine and stood for a few moments looking abstractedly around him at the work area: a large, spacious hall filled with rows of machines, some like his own, some different. The next shift was already beginning to wander in; some of the men stood around chatting, others looked over their spec sheets or started up their machines, already becoming absorbed in their work.

Most of Su-Mueng's shift had already gone. He was about to follow them when a young man, a few years older than himself, stopped by with a smile.

'Hello, Su-Mueng. There's nothing much doing in my section today. Got anything you'd like me to be getting on with?'

Su-Mueng hesitated. He had been finding his current job interesting and had intended returning tomorrow to continue it – had, in fact, been postponing the final stage of his *other* project so as to be able to complete it. He glanced down at the half finished assembly of finely-machined components: a new type of calibrator for some unguessable instrument wanted in the Upper Retort.

'Oh, all right. You can carry on with this,' he said resignedly. He pulled out the spec sheets and explained the details and where he'd got to. 'There's no hurry,' he added. 'Deadline's more than a month away.'

The other man nodded, looking eagerly over the work. 'It's always like that on these slow cycles. I hate it when we're so slack.'

Su-Mueng walked away and discarded his work-gown in the locker-room, washing his hands and face and using a refresher spray on himself. The hormone-laden mist settled on his skin and in his nostrils, making him feel fresher and brighter and washing away the weariness that comes from long hours of effort.

Then he strode away and down spiral staircases to the elevators, a slim, elegant youth. His mind began to buzz

with thoughts and the excitement of his secret rebellion
. . . but in the elevator that sped towards his domestic
level his encountered Li Kim, an old friend he knew from
training school, who pressed him to enjoy a short game
of ping-pong. Not being able to think of a good reason
to refuse, Su-Mueng left the elevator with him and they
proceeded together to the nearest recreation hall.

Kim invoked two cans of beer from a dispenser and
handed Su-Mueng one. They strolled through a gallery of
gaming machines, then past the entrances to the theatres.
Farther on there was a thumping noise against the wall
from some fast-action physical game in progress – batball,
most likely.

Ping-pong, Su-Mueng thought. That's what we get
down here. They don't play ping-pong in the Upper
Retort. By Almighty Time, the games they play there!

But even ping-pong, the way it was played in Retort
City, was interesting enough, workers' game or no. They
secured a table and Su-Mueng took up his bat. The table
was concave, like a wide, shallow bowl, divided by a thin
screen of aluminium. Li Kim drained his beer, grinned,
took up the ball and served.

They sent the ball ricocheting back and forth a few
times. Kim was good, as Su-Mueng had discovered on
many past occasions. The curved surface, of course, made
a quick eye and hand all the more necessary; but that was
not all.

Su-Mueng almost missed a return, just caught it, and
hammered the ball over the left-hand side of the screen.

On crossing the divide it vanished in mid-air.

Kim vanished, too. But an instant later the ball came
rocketing back at Su-Mueng and Kim, also, sprang back
into view at the centre of the table.

This development demonstrated the speciality of Retort City: the ability to manipulate time. The table was
divided into time-zones each of whose present moment
was marginally out of phase with the others. More than
quick reflexes were required – one needed to be almost

psychic to anticipate where the ball would be returned from, or when. The phases could be adjusted so as to give a longer or shorter time difference, or more esoterically, rotated so that, for instance, the ball would be returned to the left and mysteriously come back from the right. It was even possible for the ball to be returned *before* it had been delivered.

And it was easy for the workmen of the Lower Retort to be technically extravagant with such toys. Technology was, after all, their life.

Kim was in fine form, flashing in and out of existence faster than Su-Mueng could follow or anticipate him. He might have done better if his mind had been on the game, but as it was his moves were confused with other thoughts. Kim won the first match and stood grinning at him.

'Same again?'

Su-Mueng laid down his bat. 'Some other time, maybe. I don't think it's an even contest the way I'm playing today.'

'Time-chess then? Each row on a different time gradient?'

Su-Mueng shook his head. Time-chess required such concentration, such a phenomenal memory, that he wouldn't have stood a chance.

'Oh. You want to relax more, maybe? A show? Or some girls?'

'Thanks, Kim, but there's something I want to attend to at home. I think I'll be getting along.'

'Sure. Don't let me stop you. Well, in that case I'll be getting along too.'

Kim waved him a cheery goodbye and went bounding towards the gaudy awning of a trampoline emporium. Su-Meung left the leisure area and continued on his way home.

Kim could never understand, he thought, what was on his mind. And his intentions would have left him aghast. Probably no one but himself *could* understand,

and that went for either side of the divided city. People never did understand what was outside their experience, and for everyone but himself the other retort up – or, in the reverse case, down – the shaft was little more than a theoretical concept . . .

The elevator swept down, past endless tiers of factories and workshops, past amusement emporiums and domestic precincts. Finally Su-Mueng left the elevator and made his way through a maze of tiny streets until he came to a neat little house merging with a dozen others in a jumbled, interlocking design. He put his thumbprint to the key and went inside.

His grandfather sat at a table drinking a glass of fizzy mineral water. He was not really so very much older than Su-Mueng (so demonstrating another aspect of Retort City's mastery over time); to be precise he was twenty-six years older.

Su-Mueng gave him a perfunctory greeting, drew a meal from the dispenser, sat down and began to eat the synthesized rice, curried chicken and bamboo shoots.

'Interesting job today?' his grandfather asked, eyeing him speculatively. Su-Mueng nodded abstractedly. 'Not bad.' It still surprised him, even ten years after, how much casual conversation in the Lower Retort centred on work. The social system really did function as it was meant to: everybody down here had an obsessive interest in production, in making things. He was interested, too – after all, it was interesting – but with him that was not all. He did not neglect the wider vision that was denied to these . . . servants . . .

He shovelled down the food and sat back, brooding. His grandfather switched on the wall screen. A technician was explaining how to set up a time delay circuit – a circuit that really did delay time, running a tiny fraction of the travelling 'now' through a recurrent phase. Su-Mueng, already familiar with the technique, looked on without interest. Later there would be crude dramas, comedy shows, and so forth.

His resentment welled up. 'You should see the kind of thing they screen in the *Upper* Retort,' he suddenly said, loudly.

With a faint groan his grandfather turned to him, smiling derisively. 'You're not going to start *that* again, are you?'

'But, Grandfather, wouldn't you *like* to see what it's like up there?' Su-Mueng asked. 'Believe me, it's so *different*. They live so much better that we do . . . everything's so *luxurious*. You ought to see it.'

The older man laughed gently, tolerantly. 'Your father certainly has something to answer for,' he chuckled. 'You tell me they live better – I don't think so.' He made a wry face. 'No work, nothing really productive. Life would seem useless. I like it better here.'

Yes, Su-Mueng reflected, that was precisely the secret of how the system was able to perpetuate itself: neither side of the spirit city envied the other. The inhabitants of the Leisure Retort were scarcely aware of the workers who served them, and the workers, in their turn, regarded the participants in the aesthetic leisure culture as idle drones who would probably have been happier doing something useful.

One might have expected that over the passage of centuries *some* sort of resentment would have built up. But Retort City had neatly circumvented this possibility, by the practice known as the Alternation of Generations – a weirdly democratic principle that for cunning and ingenuity was probably unique. For while the work and leisure classes were strictly segregated, their separation was on a non-hereditary basis. Each babe was taken from its mother a few hours after birth and transported to the opposite retort, usually to be reared by its paternal grandmother – who previously had surrendered her own child . . . now the babe's father or mother.

The arrangement was made even more perfect by virtue of the fact that the double exchange could be made simultaneously, even though in real terms a time lag of decades was obviously involved. This was because of the flexible phasing of the two retorts in time. *On the same day* that a couple parted with their new-born child, they received that child's own offspring . . . their grandchild.

It all had a simple, basic ethic: a man might be fated to spend his entire life in the Production Retort, but he had the satisfaction of knowing that his children enjoyed the luxury and sophistication of the Leisure Retort. Conversely, an inhabitant of the Leisure Retort who was obliged to send his children to a life of work and discipline in the Lower Retort was compensated by being able to educate his grandchildren in their stead.

In practice, however, such a rationalization was unnecessary. Family attachments were weak; people harboured no feelings for the children they never saw, and experienced neither envy nor pity in regard to their lot. In centuries there had been no questioning of the social order, and very few defections.

'Come, now,' Su-Mueng's grandfather chided, noticing his continuing long face. 'Life's all right here, isn't it? Don't worry your head about life *up there*. Let *them* live it. This is good enough for me.'

Su-Mueng didn't answer. Yes, he thought, it all ran perfectly – as long as the two cultures never met.

Which was why it didn't run perfectly with him.

For he was a product of one of those few defections, the only one, to his knowledge, in recent years.

His father was Hueh Shao, once an official of high rank – a cabinet minister, Su-Mueng believed – in the Leisure Retort. There must have been something badly maladjusted about Hueh Shao, for in a society where for centuries everyone had been faultlessly conditioned into accepting the long-established custom, he had been unable to bear the thought of sending his newborn son down into the Lower Retort. He had broken the law, secretly keeping the babe and representing it as his grandson sent up from below.

It seemed incredible that the deception could go undetected, let alone that Su-Mueng's absence from his proper place could go unnoticed, but somehow Hueh had managed it for ten full years. Then his crime had come to light. And the law was the law: there could be no exceptions. Su-Mueng, having been raised in what was probably the most refined culture the galaxy had to offer, and despite his tender years, had been sent down to live with total strangers in a different, cruder environment.

The first few years had been nightmarish; and though he had eventually adjusted to some degree, he had conceived a burning sense of resentment against the divided form of society.

And his father – the son of the man who sat opposite him – had been punished. Was still being punished.

He glanced at his grandfather, realizing that he was something of an embarrassment to the old man. He had arrived too late, like a messenger from another world.

They had no right to do that, he thought. They should have let me stay where I belong.

He got up from the table and slid aside one of the screens that divided their small dwelling, entering his minuscule home workshop. From a slender cradle he picked up a model of Retort City he had made: two bulbous glass vessels, cinched in the middle with a metal girdle, glittering within like a tinselled tree of metal components.

He had spent the best part of two years working on that model. It was not, in fact, a model – that was simply a disguise. It was a machine. He had put his utmost into it, all his skill, all his ingenuity and patience. One thing they did in the Production Retort was train you well.

This device was going to help him go back where he belonged, to his father.

He spent the next few hours checking it over with the instruments on his workbench. Eventually he heard his grandfather retire to his sleeping mat, followed by his gentle snoring. Su-Mueng made one last test, then slipped to his own cubicle where he changed into a loose, flowing tunic with a high collar. Then he put his model of Retort City in a cloth bag and left the house.

Minutes later he was on a high-speed elevator heading for the transport end of the Production Retort, the great metal girdle through which all commodities passed to their destinations in the other half of the city. He swept past scenes that, in most circumstances, would have been fascinating: great shining structures of steel, aluminium and titanium that comprised an ascending industrial process terminating in the delivery area.

No one paid any attention to him when he left the elevator and picked his way across the shunting yards where big cylindrical carriers were pushed through the metal neck into the other retort. He went up a narrow passage, little used, that passed behind the main control junctions. He went through a series of doors and soon was in semi-darkness, climbing a spiral staircase that went up and up interminably.

A good deal of poring over maps and schematics, and a good deal of exploring, had gone into his discovery of this route. There were in fact several such routes: the area between the retorts was riddled with service access passages. All one needed was patience and the right equipment.

At length he came to the top of the staircase and into the galleries surrounding the massive coils that ringed the interior of the metal girdle between retorts. Already peculiar sensations assailed his body, warning him that he was approaching the influence of the stupendous field of variable time that separated the two societies. There was a feeling of tension across the bridge of his nose; his eyes went slightly out of focus; and his heart gave a cautionary jump.

If he had smuggled himself into one of the freight containers and got himself carried through that way, the steeply graded time difference would have killed him whatever precautions he took. This way, threading himself through the surrounding machinery like a needle through half a dozen holes, he stood a good chance. He took the fake model out of the bag and touched some studs fused on to its base. Within, a ragged pattern of subdued lights, amber, green and white, glowed.

He touched the studs again, making adjustments. The model had now taken control of his personal 'now-moment', protecting him from the ravages of the energies in the giant coils; it would synchronize him more gently with the gradient, hopefully making the transition without injury to himself.

He went forward. He was in a place which, though cavernous, was so chock-full of machinery that it seemed like a solid mass. He squeezed between cabinets and stanchions, the hum of the machinery becoming louder in his ears. Once or twice he paused to make further adjustments to his device, and eventually the instrument told him what he already guessed.

He was through the time barrier – synched with the time of the Leisure Retort.

There could be little to stop him now. He continued worming his way through the time-control apparatus, and finally was able to switch off his gadget altogether. But here he came to a slight difficulty. There were no maps or schematics of the Upper Retort available where he had been living for the past ten years. He had hoped that the receiving area would be, to some extent, a mirror image of the delivery area and that therefore there would be a descending staircase in a corresponding position to the one he had come up by. But where was it?

He searched, and located, not a staircase, but a small riding platform. This took him beyond the region defined by the metal girdle; he was in the Leisure Retort.

Below him stretched the retort's receiving area for all the goods supplied by the city's willing slaves. It was a shunting yard pretty much like the one he had left, except that everything appeared to be under cybernetic control and the canisters were already being broken open, their contents being transferred to smaller trolleys for dispatch to ten thousand different destinations.

Su-Mueng swung himself down from a gantry and strode confidently forward. He had nothing to fear. No one would stop him or question his presence; no one questioned anyone in the Leisure Retort.

And as he walked he already noticed, with a feeling of excitement, the difference between here and the place he had just left. The *air* was different; he had ceased to notice, during his long years as a worker, that everywhere in the Production Retort the air smelled faintly of oil and namelessly subtle industrial substances. Here there was only a faint suggestion of perfumes, of anything that pleased the senses.

Many times he had reconstructed in his mind the layout of the retort. He decided that he would not delay, but proceed immediately to execute his mission.

The next half hour was, to him, delirious. He passed through the gorgeous gardens and concourses that had grown faint in his memory. Past the people who went calmly, serenely, about their unhurried business – unfettered by any regime to timetable, but given to the abstracted, civilized pursuits of art and philosophy, of every kind of cultured subtlety. Here was life at the peak of refinement, a life incomprehensible to those in the Production Retort who had not been educated to appreciate it. But Su-Mueng *had* been so educated, and then it had been torn from him. As the aura of the Leisure Retort seeped into him his existence down below began to fade to the aspect of a dream . . . Su-Mueng pulled himself together. He could not say how long he might manage to stay here, and he was bent on a task that to him was of great importance.

He entered a quiet part of the retort that was used chiefly as a precinct of government. No one accosted him as he walked through the fresh-scented corridors, decorated in shades of orange and lime green, that led to a group of apartments terrible to his memory: the place where his father was incarcerated.

Ten years ago he had witnessed the beginning of Hueh Shao's imprisonment. The Retributive Council had ordered that horror, in acknowledgement of the seriousness of his offence. Su-Mueng was not surprised to find the environs deserted; all would shun such a place.

The lock on the door was a simple one, though it could not be opened from the inside. Su-Mueng took a small device from his carrying sash, and after a little experimenting sprung it. Stepping inside, he found himself in a glass-walled foyer looking into the offender's prison: a dwelling-place something like that in which Su-Mueng and his grandfather had lived, but larger and much, much more luxurious. It appeared to be untenanted. Su-Mueng examined a panel set into the rear wall of the foyer, replete with strip-dials, access sockets and so forth. He took his time-phase controller out of the bag he carried, waved it in front of the panel and observed the interior of the glass vessels, touching one or two of the external studs.

Then he picked up a microphone and spoke into it, trying to keep his voice calm and unemotional.

'Honoured father,' he said. 'I know that you can see me, although I cannot see you. I am your son, Su-Mueng. I have returned to release you, if I can.'

He put down the microphone and returned to the wall panel; on one end of the model city was a metal plate which he placed against the panel. Magnetic bubbles circulated in the plate, inducing control currents in the apparatus within the wall.

He would never be made to believe that his father deserved the punishment that had been inflicted on him. The Retributive Council had sentenced him to solitary confinement in past time. He was out-synched – his personal 'now-moment' back-graded to minutes, possibly only to a few tens of seconds, behind the common 'now-moment' of the Leisure Retort. His solitude could not have been more complete, and was scarcely mitigated by the concession that he was not permanently confined to his apartments – being permitted during certain periods to wander within a restricted area – for everyone's time was ahead of his; he could see them, but they could not see him, or hear him, or respond to him. He was like a ghost, moving among people who ignored him.

The mind of man, thought Su-Mueng, could not have devised a crueller exile.

The lights within the glass bottle flickered and raced. Suddenly the apartment shimmered and the artificial retarded time-field was abolished. There stood Hueh Shao, staring at him amazed, but like Su-Mueng forcing himself to adopt an attitude of dignified restraint.

The ex-minister bore a strong resemblance to his own father in the Production Retort – they were, in fact, of about the same age, a little under fifty – but the similarity was modified by the difference between the customs of the respective communities. He wore a long, wispy goatee beard and neatly cultivated mustachios that drooped down on either side of his mouth. The eyebrows were plucked, curved upward at their outer ends, and showed traces of cosmetic. The greying hair was carefully combed back, but was considerably longer than the cropped style affected down below.

He continued staring with steady eyes while Su-Mueng unlocked the inner door and stepped into the apartment.

'My son,' he said, 'what foolishness is this?'

And Su-Mueng stared back, unable to speak, unable to explain what foolishness it was. Incredibly, his thoughts had never ranged beyond this moment: the moment when he set the old man free. His father, a revered elder individual of intelligence and resourcefulness, would surely know what to do, his subliminal thoughts had told him.

Only now did he realize that those thoughts were the thoughts of a ten-year-old boy, arrested at the moment when the law had torn him away from that father. His childish adoration had never died. And only now, as he faced Hueh Shao, did it come home to him that his father was as helpless and resourceless as himself.

6

A hush fell on the gathering in a quiet room in a derelict back street. Sobrie Oblomot stared at the tabletop, slightly embarrassed by the sympathy he felt emanating from the others.

'Sorry, Oblomot,' the Chairman said, somewhat awkwardly. 'But at least your brother died like a comrade. Went out with a bang. And took four Titans with him.'

'That's not as self-sacrificing as it sounds,' said Sobrie stiffly. 'I'd commit suicide as well, rather than face what those bastards have waiting in Bupolbloc Two.'

The Group Leader from Kansorn nodded. 'The Titans have been coming down hard lately. I admit I wake up sweating sometimes. I never go without my s-grenade, either.'

'I concur,' said the man sitting next to him. He wore a mask and spoke through a voice modifier, being a person of such public prominence, and besides this of such importance to the League, that his anonymity was deemed essential.

'The League is reeling under the Titans' blows,' he said. 'Nearly three hundred people arrested in the past few months. The antipodean networks are practically destroyed. If this continues I fear for our whole cause.'

The depression of the League members was palpable. The Chairman shuffled his feet and spoke more forcefully.

'There is less cause for alarm than many of you think,' he told them. 'The reprisals are a sign of our growing strength, not of our weakness. Remember what a low ebb we were at twenty years ago – at one time the Panhumanic League was down to about fifty members.' He smiled ruefully. 'Its very name was a joke. That was during the wars. But, after a long period of peace, we've been able to expand our activities and increase our influence. It was inevitable that there would be a Titan reaction to our successes.'

'That's true,' the Kansorn Group Leader said. 'Our problem is how we're going to meet it. Everything depends on our riding out the storm.'

The Chairman nodded. 'And that brings me to the main item of our remaining business. At the last meeting it was suggested that League membership should be barred to people of mixed blood. The reason for this, you will remember, was to protect our public image—' he spoke as if the words were distasteful to him – 'so that we should not be characterized, as we have been, as an organization of "squalid freaks and sub-men". I take it we have all considered the motion?'

'I'm against it,' answered one voice with passion. 'It runs counter to all our ideals. It suggests that we too consider other subspecies of mankind to be inferior. We shouldn't play the Titans' racist game.'

'I'm for it,' said the member from Kansorn, 'merely on the grounds of tactics, as stated.'

'How many of our people *do* have mixed blood?' Sobrie asked suddenly.

The Chairman answered. 'The statistical department gives a figure of twenty per cent. A significant proportion – one which can give weight to anti-League propaganda.'

'Propaganda is the least of our worries,' grumbled the Kansorn Group Leader. 'The Titan campaign against mixed blood is gathering pace, too. These half-breeds and octoroons give them a road leading right into the heart of the League. By moving against one, they move against the other.'

'These people also see the League as their protection,' Sobrie pointed out. 'If we expel them, we can hardly count on their loyalty. We'll be twice as exposed as before.'

'There's another aspect to the business,' said the voice that had spoken previously. 'Are we also to discontinue our contacts with the dev reservations?'

After a strained pause, the Chairman said: 'We may, in any case, have to scale down our activities in the reservations. Titan supervision of these areas is so strict that they're becoming weak points in our networks – a number of agents have been apprehended trying to pass in or out. Even the imprisoned peoples have become wary of our approaches. Many of them have given up all hope of freedom and merely want to be left to live as best they can.'

Several members snorted in disgust. The idea of any kind of future at the mercy of Titan hatreds, of Titan scientists and land-utilization experts (always pressing to contract the already small areas 'lost to True Man') was, to their minds, ridiculous.

They turned to the masked man, whose opinion, despite his anonymity, carried great weight. He pondered.

'The benefits to be gained from such a drastic step would probably not be great enough to justify the defying of our principles,' he stated finally. 'In the long run, it would do little to dispel the legend of the Dark Covenant.'

Yes, thought Sobrie Oblomot, the Dark Covenant: the incredibly subtle, fantastically detailed scheme to destroy True Man that had supposedly been created hundreds of years ago by the combined evil geniuses of all the deviant subspecies then extant. The League was fairly sure that no such document, nor any document or plan even vaguely approximating it, had ever existed. But the beliefs that had grown up around it were elaborate and fascinating, and they were encouraged by the Titanium Legions. Popular belief had it that the Panhumanic League itself was but part of one of the Covenant's contingency plans, following the initial failure to exterminate True Man altogether and replace him by nature's mistakes . . . by the Earth Mother's mutants, sports and abortions.

It was the kind of inanity that made Sobrie Oblomot despair that the League could ever achieve its aim of bringing rationality to civilization.

While the argument went on his thoughts returned – as they had returned every few moments since his hearing the news – to his brother Blare. Suicide, he thought bleakly. Gone in the glare of a fiery explosion when arrested by Titans. It would look fine in some annals after the battle was won, or on a monument in a better world. But here, in the squalor of an underground struggle, it seemed merely . . . bleak.

Blare had been an active member of the League for only a short time, and Sobrie was eaten up with guilt because it was he who had put his brother there. His hints, his persuasion, his appeals to reason, had won Blare over to the side of subversion. Not that it had been very difficult, but just the same Blare was too much of an ingenuous idealist, too much of a moral simpleton, to be successful in his work. Sobrie could see that clearly now. He shouldn't have pushed him into it. It shouldn't have been Blare who went up in that s-grenade. It should have been him, Sobrie.

The Chairman called an end to discussion and held a vote. The motion was narrowly defeated.

There was more discussion on tactics. It was decided to break up some groups and to scatter their members to various parts of the globe, where they were to remain inactive until further orders. The Chairman ended with a brief item.

'This is connected with your brother, Oblomot,' he said. 'As you may know, he was working with Rond Heshke, the famous archaeologist, on the alien ruins at Hathar. It seems that on the night your brother died, Heshke was taken by the Titans as well.'

'I didn't know he was connected with the League,' Sobrie frowned.

'He isn't. As far as we know Heshke is an upright citizen who holds a certificate of racial purity. We've learned that he was taken to Cymbel and put on board a private rocket transport. We're not sure, but we think the transport landed in the Sarn Desert.'

'So?' Sobrie stared at him.

'The Titans have a secret research establishment there,' the Chairman divulged. 'They guard it so jealously that we haven't been able to find out what goes on in the place. But the fact that Rond Heshke may now be on the staff would confirm that it's connected with the alien interventionists in some way.'

'And the aliens are also of interest to us,' murmured Sobrie, nodding.

'Correct. We, as much as anyone else, would like to know who they were, where they came from, and what kind of beings they were. It's possible that racial fanaticism on Earth results from the antagonism between man and the alien. If so, our psychologists say that fear of the alien will have to be rooted out before hatred of other subspecies dies away.'

Heads nodded. This theorem was known to them all. It did not, in fact, take a psychologist to be able to see it.

'I mention this only because we'd like more information, and it's proving hard to obtain directly,' the Chairman ended airily. 'Pass the word through your networks: does anyone know of any supplies being sent to the Sarn Desert? If so, what sort of supplies? By the way, the situation is made to look more interesting by the dramatic way Rond Heshke was suddenly picked up from Hathar.'

The masked man gave a hollow laugh. 'That means nothing. The Titans love drama.'

'Yes, perhaps—' The Chairman turned suddenly as the door opened behind him, a pistol leaping into his hand.

But it was only the guard. 'There's a report of Titan patrols in the area, Chairman. Thought you had better know.'

'Thank you. You'd best get away, and tell the street observers to do the same.'

The door closed behind the guard. 'We'll wind it up now, for safety's sake,' the Chairman ordered quickly. 'Is anyone without a cover?'

Sobrie held up his hand. Being an artist, he was generally obliged to travel without being able to supply any particular reason. The others would all have equipped themselves with business or personal cover-motives for being in Cymbel. Most of them would be attending the World Economic Integration Conference Preliminary Hearings – the reason why Cymbel had been chosen for this meeting.

'Right, you leave first,' the Chairman ordered. 'If the guard's still here ask him to guide you past the patrols, and leave the city right away.' He glanced around the table. 'You'll all be notified of the next meeting.'

Without ceremony Sobrie left the room. The others would follow at ten-minute intervals, the masked man leaving last of all.

The guard had already vanished. Sobrie checked the alley outside, then slipped from the derelict building. He strode quickly, almost running, until he reached the narrow defile that gave out on to a main thoroughfare.

The Titans had probably cottoned on to the fact that planet-wide conventions were a good opportunity for clandestine meetings, he thought. The Chairman would have to think of something else.

He saw one or two uniformed Titans about, but guessed that most of them were in civilian clothes. It was not hard to spot the tall, fair-haired young men by the cold, supercilious way they scanned the faces of passersby. Probably there were some people known to them that they were hoping to find.

He forced himself not to cringe as he walked by them. He was still worried by his obvious association with his own brother. But that had been weeks ago, and there had come no knock in the night. He could only presume that he had covered his tracks well. And the one track he had not covered, Blare had covered for him. With an s-grenade.

He arrived at Cymbel's large transport field and bought a seat on the next rocket to Sannan. He had over an hour to wait, so he had a drink to calm his nerves, then decided the reception lounge wasn't the best place to be hanging around. He went into the district adjoining the field, wandered around for a few minutes and went into a public drinking lounge. After a couple more drinks he felt better.

There was really nothing to be afraid of, he told himself. The Chairman was simply being overcautious – a wholly admirable strategy. The Panhumanic League hadn't gone through over a century of experience without learning how to survive.

Several drinks later the rocket roared off from the transport field with Sobrie aboard. During the two-hour flight, arcing up above the best part of the atmosphere, he tried to sleep; but his head ached and he thought constantly of his brother.

It was an autumn evening when the rocket planed down into his native city of Sannan. It was a beautiful city, untouched by the dev wars. Rows of apartment blocks marched across the skyline, shining with muted colours in the slanting sunlight. Challenging them for prominence were the domes and towers of cathedrals, once centres of the old religions for which Sannan had been famous. These religions had been discouraged and were practically defunct now; the cathedrals were used for Titan pageants and for ceremonies revering the Earth Mother.

He left the transport field, his head clearing slightly in the fresh evening air, and took the tubeway to his own district. With a feeling of sanctuary he walked into his apartment, into the welcoming presence of Layella, the woman he lived with.

There were times when Sobrie felt weary of everything, weary of the cause he lived for, and felt tempted to give way to the persistent social pressure and to think: to hell with it, let's just live comfortably. What does it matter what happens to those others? That was how everyone else thought. The Titans, after all, are only working for the good of us, of real people. It can't be helped what happens to *those others*.

But then he would look again at Layella and renew his faith. She was one reason why he would probably never, not at any price, give up the cause. For Layella was of mixed blood.

Racially impure. Part Amhrak.

The percentage was not large – she herself did not know if it came from a grandparent or a great-grandparent, or even if some recessive genes had happened to come to the top – and because of her skilful use of cosmetics it passed unnoticed by the average citizen. Sobrie, by long loving acquaintance, was familiar with the differences and was eternally fascinated by the off-beat beauty they gave her. She had the small head and rounded cranium of the Amhraks – though not to an exaggerated degree – and the round, soft eyes, which she contrived to flatten a little with eye-paint. One dangerous feature was her ears, and therefore she kept them hidden beneath her hair, which was a soft, neatly cut shell of orange. Her skin shade was wrong, too – tending slightly towards Amhrak red – and for this she used a skin dye.

Other small differences in body proportion and stance she accentuated away by attention to her dress.

Provided life was quiet and uneventful she was safe. They could not marry, of course, since to be legally married both parties were required to obtain racial purity certificates, but otherwise no one of average percipience would know her apart from a True Woman.

But Sobrie knew – they both knew – that she could never pass muster if examined by the anthropometricians, the Titans' racial experts. They would come along with their tapes and calipers. They would measure her nose, her cranium, a hundred and one bodily measurements. They would apply a chemical to her skin to bleach away any dye and measure the skin-tone with a colourometer. They would take some hair to test for disguised crinkliness. They would strip her and observe the configuration of her bones when she walked, when she sat on a chair, and if they wanted to be exhaustive they would take a retinal photograph and run a chromosome test.

But more probably, he thought, they would do scarcely any of those things. They would not have to hunt so far to identify her. Some of these race experts, so he had heard, were real masters who by their own boast could 'tell blood at a glance'. They would take one look at her, and tell her to walk across the room, or else put a chair in the middle of the room and make her sit on it, noting the position of her buttocks. And they would know. And they would take her away and give her a painless injection, or perhaps worse, send her to the Amhrak reservation.

He flung himself down on a couch, exhausted by the content of the day, and waited while she brought him a soothing bowl of soup. Then he told her about Blare.

Her sympathy, thankfully, was not embarrassing, as that of his League comrades had been. She knew his moods and his needs, as if by an instinct. She sat beside him, a hand touching his thigh, and said little.

He drank the soup quickly and leaned back with a doleful sigh.

'Layella,' he said with difficulty, 'we must part.'

Her eyes widened with alarm. 'Why?'

'It's getting too dangerous.' He sought for words to make her understand. In some ways she was strangely oblivious to the danger that had surrounded her, almost since birth. Just like Blare, he thought, with a sudden feeling of surprise.

He had steadfastly refused to let Layella join the League herself, though from their conversation she knew a good deal of his business with them – he was unable to refrain from sharing that side of him with his mate. But he had become more and more aware that he himself comprised the greatest threat to her existence. If he was pulled in, she would have no chance of escape.

'I don't want more people to go down on account of me,' he said bluntly.

'*More* people? What do you mean?'

'Don't you see why Blare killed himself?' he said, looking up at her and trying to keep the note of agony out of his voice.

'You would all have to,' she soothed. 'It's necessary.'

'No, no, you don't understand.' He clenched his fists. 'Blare is – was – not the suicidal type. He would have hung on for as long as he could. He's an optimist. He wouldn't have killed himself right away – and yet that's what he did. Almost as soon as they picked him up, before he could really have known how much they knew. He did it for *me*. So that he wouldn't be able to betray *me*. If it comes to that, I was the only person he could have betrayed. He had no direct connection with anybody else.'

Both were silent for long moments. 'You see why we must split up,' he said heavily. 'We've taken risks for far too long. I don't want to be the cause of your death, too.'

'You're Blare's brother,' she pointed out. 'If they were suspicious they would have been here by now.'

'How do we know they're not watching?' he rejoined. 'Still, we're a large family, and scattered. They may not suppose a connection. But that's not the point. They're still liable to get *me* some day. That's why you must go.'

'No,' she said with firmness, taking his arm. 'You're my . . . husband, or whatever. I'm staying with you, to take whatever comes.'

He stood up abruptly and paced the room, looking out of the wide window at the lights of the city, coming on in clusters and masses in the gathering dusk. 'What a mess,' he said, feeling his fatigue. 'Those goddamned Titans – causing all this tyranny. There's nowhere you can go in the whole world and live like a free man.'

'It's not really their fault,' Layella said mildly, her expression open. 'True Man, as they call it, probably didn't start all this. It was probably the Lorenes.'

'No, it wasn't the Lorenes,' said Sobrie agitatedly. 'It was even before that. It was the aliens – their invasion started all this insanity. But for them, the races of mankind would probably be living in peace together. Before the aliens came, they probably *did* live in peace together.'

She came over to him and stood behind him, her arms around his waist. At his back he could feel her voluptuous breasts, her head on his shoulder. From where he was standing he could see through the door into his small studio, littered with canvasses and plastic composites. Many of the paintings were of Layella. He thought bitterly of the studies of her he did not dare to paint, for fear that someone might see them: paintings of Layella without disguising cosmetic, in the nude, betraying the proportions between torso and hips. He thought of the children they did not dare to have, for fear of what might become of them.

Everything seemed hopeless. Nothing would be achieved in his lifetime; all the gains made by the Panhumanic League, important though they seemed within the League itself, were objectively trivial. Sobrie remembered what the Chairman had reiterated so many times: that they were working towards a goal that could not be achieved for several centuries; that their sights must be set that far ahead.

'Listen,' Layella said. 'I couldn't stand it if we parted. It would be too much of a blow for me. Leave the League if you like, if you can't stand it any more. We'll go away somewhere where we won't be traced to our life here. Not that I'm asking you to. But don't send me away.'

'All right,' said Sobrie. 'Stay if you insist. If you can accept what it might mean. But I won't leave the League. The League comes before everything.'

The meeting that took place far away, in a great castle some miles outside the city of Pradna, was far removed in style from the furtive sessions of the Panhumanic League.

The Titanium Legions were well-advanced in pomp; each high-backed chair bore a nameplate of titanium edged with gold, engraved with the name of its occupant. The table around which the chairs were set was of mahogany with inlaid platinum, while the walls were hung with tapestries depicting inspirational themes: representations of the Earth Mother with her strong, upright son; scenes of past glory – crucial moments in historic battles.

The Legionary Council of Generals convened once a year as a matter of course, or whenever Planetary Leader Limnich dictated. As he entered, all the Council members were at their places with eyes closed, deep in one of the spiritual exercises they all practised, especially during their sojourns at the castle. Planetary Leader Limnich insisted on these practices among his generals; he knew them to be proven strengtheners of the will. They had been handed down from ancient times – but only to a privileged few – by True Men deeply experienced in spirituality.

'Attention.'

Limnich spoke the word quietly but incisively as the big oak doors closed with a barely audible thump behind him. He was a man of below average height for a Titan, pale-faced, with a receding though blue-jowled chin, bulbous cheeks, and fish-cold eyes behind the large round lenses he preferred to more fashionable contact lenses.

The generals opened their eyes with a snap, summoned from their meditation, and stood to attention while Planetary Leader Limnich seated himself at the head of the table. Then, stiffly, they seated themselves again.

'Good evening, gentlemen,' greeted Limnich in a distant, but conversational tone. 'You must be wondering why I've convened the Council at this particular time, when our annual retreat together is so near. As you may guess, there's news of import. But first, I'll hear your reports.'

One by one the generals gave a brief résumé. The accounts were no more than recapitulations – each man commanded a vast area of activity and his real reports were massive documents handled by computers. But Limnich was never one to skimp on ritual. He bent his head to give closest attention to the remarks dealing with the pursuit of the Panhumanic League and the hunting down of racially impure persons, numbers of which still existed in normal society, even years after the last of the deviant wars.

'The work is long and arduous, but its conclusion is inescapable, gentlemen,' he commented. 'It must be prosecuted with unremitting vigour. Earth's destiny is dependent on a one hundred per cent purity of racial stock . . . but now to the main burden of my information tonight . . .'

In the dimly lit chamber, whose illumination was supplied by shaded cressets, his voice fell to a dramatic murmur, the tone of voice he used on his extremely rare vidcasts – Planetary Leader Limnich was the most powerful man on Earth, but he was the power behind the throne, not the man on the throne itself. Ostensibly his title referred only to his command of the Titanium Legions. There was a World Racial President, a civilian, whom the Legions were sworn to protect. But in actuality Limnich handled nearly all practical affairs, and made nearly all important decisions, though frequently after conferring with the President.

'You all know of the work being undertaken at the Sarn Establishment, and of the discoveries that have been made there,' he said, placing both hands on the table and directing his gaze at the shining mahogany.

'You were all informed, by secret memo, of the mysterious disappearance of our first functional time travelling machine, together with Chief Physicist Leard Ascar and archaeologist Rond Heshke.

'The loss of Ascar is a blow to our efforts, since his genius was instrumental in developing time theory, but luckily developments had already reached a stage where we were no longer dependent on him. We were able to bring our Marks Two and Three machines into use fairly quickly, and a search was undertaken for the expedition that failed to return. It was established that the expedition had actually landed at its destination. But although the whole of the route covered in the flight plan was thoroughly searched, as well as its environs and possible alternative routes that might have been taken in an emergency, no sign of the machine itself could be found.'

He paused, lifting his eyes to glower through his lenses like some frightening goblin. 'We formed the conclusion that the machine had been intercepted by alien interventionists, and its occupants kidnapped.'

A tremor of consternation went around the table; backs stiffened. This was the stuff of which nightmares were made – the nightmares they had all experienced at some time since childhood, of strange beasts that dragged their victims into the abyss. And there was no abyss more bottomless, or more unknown, than that of time.

'Taking account of the possibility that the prisoners might be made to reveal the whereabouts of the Sarn Establishment, I immediately ordered the dispersal of its activities around the globe and the rapid building-up of our time travelling capabilities. With a determined allocation of resources, it was possible to bring to completion about twenty apparatuses and in the ensuing weeks a good start was made towards a more complete exploration of our time environment.

'Early on, one of the time machines was fired upon while in flight and destroyed. I had, however, given orders that the machines were only to travel in squadrons

of three or more. The victim's companions gave chase to
its attacker and pursued it *into the future*, where they lost
track of it. Later, more signs of the aliens' presence were
found, and revealed a situation of utmost danger. It seems
that the aliens are extremely active in time, not only in the
past, and in our present, but in the future also.'

'The *future*, Leader? But how can that be?' One of
the burly Titan generals, a man in his sixties, turned to
Limnich in puzzlement. He was like many of these older
Titans who had been born and bred in the deviant wars.
His life had been one of conquest and heedless force,
and he had difficulty in understanding these abstract
concepts.

Limnich himself recognized his generals' limitations in
the context of the modern world. Some of these old-time
soldiers, he told himself, would have to be phased out.
They would need to be replaced by younger men of
greater sophistication. Men who understood theory, as
well as the necessity for action.

'There is increasing evidence that the enemy has
established a massive base some centuries in the future,'
he replied. 'Presumably he believes himself to be out of
the reach of retaliation there – *but he is wrong!*' His pale
fish-like features suddenly burning with passion, Limnich
thumped the table with his fist. 'Gentlemen, what I am
trying to tell you is that we must once again put ourselves
on a wartime footing. The second confrontation with the
alien, which we have suspected would come one day, is
imminent.'

And the gleam of excitement that followed his words
swept aside any incomprehension that might have bedev-
illed the Titanium Council. Here was one thing they did
understand – and gloried in.

War!

'You will set to work in all your sectors to bring industry up to the pace of wartime production,' Limnich told
them more calmly. 'Specific blueprints will be issued
shortly, when we've trained sufficient technical teams

in the new science of time manipulation. I've already taken the steps that will lead to the creation of time travel equipment on a large scale. This will result in new battalions being raised for the Titanium Legions: battalions trained and equipped to wage war across the centuries.'

He paused again, and launched into the evocative language he could never resist on such occasions. 'Mother Earth is once again calling her offspring to her defence. We must gird our loins, muster our strength, and strike before we're overwhelmed by the alien onslaught that we must assume is being prepared. There's no time for rest: we're entering upon a new era of conflict.'

Limnich rose to his feet, paused with dignity while the assembly too rose, and arms shot out, hooking themselves with clenched fists in the Titan salute. Then, without a further word, he turned and walked quietly from the chamber.

7

Up until the second day the inevitability of death was something Heshke's mind had been unable to encompass. Stubbornly his thoughts had kept running in the same grooves as before, as though he were going to continue to live.

The second day was when their water ran out. The Titan tech officer, Lieutenant Gann, had suggested that they go searching for more, but Leard Ascar had ridiculed the idea.

'What for?' he sneered. 'We'll probably find water – but one thing we won't find is *food*. We're on a dead planet.' He stroked his pistol. 'I'll tell you what I'm going to do. When I start to get too thirsty I'm using this.'

And yet, though Ascar constantly licked his dry lips,

his voice became cracked and he complained plaintively of thirst, he still had not killed himself. Heshke believed he knew why: the man's incredible brain was still at work, determined to wrest as much knowledge as possible from the enigma of time before he died.

They had dug a shallow grave to bury the dead Titan and now sat in the shade of the wrecked time traveller, talking desultorily. At first Lieutenant Gann had dwelt on the failure of their mission; but Ascar reassured him.

'It will only be a matter of weeks before they start sending out more probes. The truth will come to light. They're a thick-headed group, but it will penetrate in time . . . to start preparing for the holocaust.'

Heshke shivered at the other's matter-of-fact acceptance of the calamity to come. 'Then what chance have we of being rescued?' he enquired.

'None; don't harbour any hope on that score. They've got a whole planet and centuries of time over which to look for us. It's impossible.'

'But they will find the alien civilization?'

'Yes. Not as quickly as we did – it won't occur to them the way it did to me – but yes.'

'But they might get shot down the way we were.'

'Probably the first few will. Then they'll realize what it's all about, send out armed machines, and so on.'

Lieutenant Gann came into the conversation, speaking in a hollow voice. 'What we've discovered is almost too horrible to think about. This head-on collision you speak of – it's incredible! Are you *sure*, Ascar?'

'I don't understand it at all,' Heshke admitted. 'What are they, a time travelling civilization? Have they found a way to make their whole society travel in time?'

Ascar shook his head. 'It's even more than that. It's a whole biota – a world of biological life – that's unconnected with our own. I think it's a natural phenomenon, not an artificial one. Plainly, our own present – our own time-stream – is not unique. There are two of them – at least two – sweeping towards one another through four-dimensional space. When they meet it will be like God clapping his hands together, with all living creatures caught in the middle . . .'

'You make it sound like the end of the universe!'

The physicist shrugged, then sighed. 'Probably not. The end of time, maybe. I don't know; I just can't figure it out.'

'Something else bothers me,' Heshke continued after a pause. 'The other civilization is supposed to be only four centuries away from our own. But from the state of their remains, such as the Hathar Ruins, I would say they were *definitely* abandoned more than four centuries ago. It's hard to date these things, but an age of eight hundred, maybe even a thousand years, would strike me as more reasonable. It's an anomaly.'

Despite his discomfort, a weird smile came over Ascar's features. 'As a matter of fact that was one of the clues that turned my mind in the right direction. There are two ways that things can decay. They can decay with the progress of the Absolute Present – just normal entropy. But there's another kind of decay: the decay that sets in beyond the margin of the travelling time-wave – decay in non-time. Where the constructive forces of the present moment leave off, decay sets in. And at first entropy acts much more rapidly than in the present. So as you travel into the future things are falling to pieces very quickly. That's why living forms vanish altogether, for instance.'

They all pondered his words. 'Of course,' Ascar added casually, 'as the now-wave draws closer things magically reconstruct themselves, as it were.'

Heshke framed a further question, but before he could speak he was astonished to hear a whining sound from above. They all glanced up, and what they saw made then shout incoherently and cringe back in sudden fear, seeking the useless shelter of the time traveller.

Against the blue of the sky a metallic shape was falling rapidly towards them. They all fumbled for their weapons. Heshke was debating the futility of fleeing when the oncoming missile, with extraordinary agility, braked and came to a landing only a few hundred yards away.

'Looks like those damned aliens are back to get us,' Ascar said through gritted teeth.

The Titan laid a cautionary hand on Heshke's arm. 'They mustn't take us alive,' he said evenly. 'It's our duty to die by our own hands.'

'Yes, of course,' Heshke muttered.

But they all delayed the fatal moment. Heshke fingered his gun, secretly fearing to put a bullet through his own brain. Ascar snarled and stepped out a pace or two in front of the others, facing the vessel defiantly and hefting his weapon.

He's going to try to take one or two of them with us, Heshke thought, admiring the man's irrational courage. Perhaps I should do the same.

It surprised him that the machine standing out in the desert bore no resemblance to any of the time travellers he had seen. Vaguely, it reminded him of a space shuttle. It had an ovoidal shape and stood on its tail, supported by piston-powered legs. Just like something a human engineer would design that landed from space, he thought.

His perplexity was increased when a hatch opened and down stepped human figures. Ascar let his gun sag in his hand, while Lieutenant Gann started forward, his sharp features creasing into a frown of scrutiny.

'I'll be damned!' Ascar exploded.

Heshke started to laugh weakly. 'And you said we wouldn't be rescued.'

'Shut up!' snapped Ascar irritably.

And Heshke did stop. The men who came towards them were *not* wearing either Titan uniform or Titan insignia. Neither, for that matter, did they wear the familiar combat suits.

There were three of them (three of them, three of us, Heshke told himself with relief; they must be friendly) wearing what appeared to be light, one-piece garments without badges or symbols of any kind. On their heads were simple bowl-shaped helmets each sprouting a feathery antenna. And as they came closer they held up their hands palms outward, smiling and speaking in strange, singsong voices.

Heshke put up his gun; their friendly intent was obvious. Now he could discern their faces . . . Their skin was sallow, virtually yellow; their cheekbones were unnaturally high, their noses somewhat flat, and they were slant-eyed . . .

Heshke felt a long moment of uncontrollable nausea.

Beside him Lieutenant Gann drew in a loud, shuddering breath.

'Devs!'

Ascar fell back to join them, his pistol wavering. 'Who the hell are those animals? Where did they come from? What are they doing here?' He stared wildly, half out of his mind.

There could be no doubt about it. The newcomers were not of the race of True Man. True, their points of physical difference did not make them as grotesque as some of the races mankind had fought recently, but even so anyone with even a smattering of racial science could see that they were beyond the pale of true humanity as defined by Titan anthropometricians. In other words, they belonged to a deviant subspecies.

A loud report banged in Heshke's ears. Lieutenant Gann was firing, his face hard and determined. One of the devs spun around and fell, holding his arm where he had been hit.

Heshke drew his gun again, confused but thinking that he, too, should help fight the enemy. As it was he was given no time to fire. The two unhurt devs dropped to one knee and took careful aim with objects they held in their hands, too small for him to be able to see properly. He felt a momentary buzzing in his brain, before he lost consciousness.

Awareness returned suddenly and clearly, like a light being switched on. Nevertheless Heshke knew that there had been a lapse of time.

The strange surroundings took a few moments to become familiar with. He lay, half reclined, on a sort of chair-couch, in a room that was long and narrow, decorated at either end with burnished gold filigree. He was alone except for a yellow-faced dev who stood by an instrument with a flat grey screen, and who gave Heshke a distant, rather cold smile.

'You – all – right – now?' he asked in a weird, impossible accent, pronouncing each word slowly and carefully.

Heshke nodded.

'Good. Solly – stun.'

Heshke studied the offbeat face that belonged to his slim, youthful captor. These devs reminded him of something . . . They were not representative of any modern subspecies, but he believed he had seen something like them in photographs of subspecies long exterminated. What had they been called? Shings? Chanks? It had been only a small grouping, in any case. It was perplexing to find them operating a time traveller – or spaceship? – now.

'Where are my two friends?' he demanded.

The other listened politely but did not seem to follow him. Apparently his grasp of the language was limited.

Nothing bound him to the chair-couch; he stood up and approached the dev threateningly. 'What have you done with my friends?' he said, his voice rising to a shout.

The dev staved him off with a gesture; an elegant, flowing gesture.

'You – have – nothing – fear,' he said, smiling broadly. He pointed to a table on which stood various articles: a pitcher, a cup, plates of food. Then he sauntered away from Heshke, opened a door Heshke had not noticed before, and left the room, closing the door behind him.

Heshke went to the table and sat down on the chair provided, inspecting the fare with great interest. From the pitcher – in passing he noticed its almost glowing glaze, its light, almost fragrant yellow colour, its fine shape – he poured a lemon-coloured liquid into the wide-brimmed cup and drank greedily. It was delicious; heavenly, unsurpassable lemonade. He drank again, and only then did he pause to examine the excellent craftmanship involved in the cup. It was of a feather-light, bone-like material, but so thin and delicate that it was translucent. It had no decoration; its whole form was so perfect that it needed none.

He realized that he had fallen into the hands of a people who knew how to gratify the senses.

Next, being ravenously hungry, he attacked the food. It was a mixture of spiced meat, vegetables and a near-tasteless mass of white grains he couldn't identify. At first he was disappointed to find the meal only lukewarm – he liked his food hot – but the flavours were pleasing and he gulped it swiftly down.

Afterwards, his stomach satisfied, he felt much better. He could not altogether quell his alarm at having fallen into the hands of devs – but after all, this was such a totally mysterious situation.

And he was alive – and, hopefully, would remain so. Things were much better than they had been a short while ago.

He sat brooding, exploring the room with his eyes. Its shape was pleasing, he realized. A ratio of – four to one? Hardly the proportions he would have chosen, but somehow it worked; it was aesthetic. These people, dev or not, were artists.

He remembered Blare Oblomot, and felt a sudden pang for that rebel's protestations regarding the deviants. Poor Blare.

He became aware of a murmur of energy, barely audible through the floor. The room suddenly seemed to shift, to tilt. Then it became steady again.

Of course. He was in some kind of vehicle.

He paced the room, which was lined with horizontal slats of a honey-brown material, and stopped before the instrument the dev had been standing beside when he awoke. It was mounted on a pedestal, like a washbasin. As he came near, its flat grey screen glowed with neutral light; words appeared.

YOU ARE EN ROUTE TO INTERSTELLAR SPACE

The characters were neat, but functionally inelegant. There followed a diagram consisting of dots, some heavily, some lightly scored, superimposed by a series of concentric circles. An arrow left the centre and stabbed slowly out, jerking several times towards empty space.

Heshke guessed it to be a star map, but he was no astronomer and it meant nothing to him.

For a minute or two he waited, but the screen offered no further information. Just the same, he felt overawed. The civilization to which he belonged could not undertake interstellar travel, though all the planets as far out as Saturn had been fairly well explored. It came as a blow to his sense of racial superiority to find these devs so advanced. Automatically his mind began seeking some explanation, one which would permit the fatal flaws of intellectual or spiritual inferiority with which all dev races were supposed to be cursed.

Deep in thought he roamed the room. Absentmindedly he tried the door the dev had left by, pushing it and then pulling on a ledger set into the panel. To his surprise it slid open easily, vanishing into the wall.

He peered into an empty corridor, slatted with honey-coloured ribs as was his room, and hesitated. Had the dev mistakenly forgotten to lock him in? After a few moments he slipped out and proceeded along the corridor, feeling absurdly guilty and exposed, glancing all around him and expecting to be recaptured any second.

The corridor came to an end in a circular junction from which radiated other corridors. He hovered near the wall, peeping down each one in turn. Then he stiffened; a dev was striding out from a corridor to his right, unseen until this moment.

Heshke decided instantly not to put up any resistance and turned to face the dev, his arms hanging limply by his sides. The dev's stride broke for a moment and he looked at Heshke, his face speculative, interested. Then he raised his hand in what appeared to be some kind of greeting, nodded curtly and strode on past him.

Heshke looked after his retreating back, astonished.

'Citizen Heshke!'

Startled, he turned. The voice was Lieutenant Gann's. He came towards him down yet another corridor, at a near-run.

'Thank Earth I've found you,' the Titan said breathlessly. 'I was afraid they'd done something with you.'

'You're free too?'

The other nodded. 'So's Ascar. These fiends don't seem to care; we have the run of the ship.'

'But why?'

'Who can say? A dev mind is bound to be devious, devilishly twisted. Probably they want to study us, catch us off our guard.' He glanced around them, at walls, floor and ceiling, evidently seeking out spying devices.

'Where's Ascar?' Heshke asked.

'In his room. He's gone into a sulk, just sits there and won't co-operate.'

Heshke looked carefully into the Titan officer's sharp face. He saw signs of nervous strain. Gann was intelligent, well-trained, but he was under pressure: in the very maw of hell, by his own doctrine.

'Let's keep moving,' Gann said in a mutter, nudging his arm. 'Probably they can't pick us up very well while we're on the move.'

He guided Heshke down another of the corridors, pacing swiftly and talking in a low, furtive mutter.

'Keep your voice down,' he warned. 'Don't give them any more help than you have to.'

'What have you found out?' Heshke asked.

'We're heading into interstellar space. Presumably this ship is equipped both with time-drive and some kind of interstellar-drive – but we always knew the aliens must have something like that. This disproves Ascar's theory, anyway: his theory that the alien interventionists are indigenous to Earth.'

'Aliens?' Heshke queried. 'But . . .'

Gann shot him a glance. 'Isn't it obvious? *These devs are working with the aliens*. It would be just like them, too. They must be taking us back to one of the alien home bases.'

Yes, thought Heshke, to Gann it would make perfect sense. It would enable him to resurrect his belief in the Earth Mother; to clear her from the charge of infidelity, of having given birth to two legitimate sons.

Doctrine apart, it made a certain kind of sense to Heshke, too.

'How can we be sure?' he said doubtfully. 'Couldn't the devs themselves be responsible for all this?'

Gann didn't answer for a moment but glanced around him, gesturing with his hand. 'I don't think so, Citizen. You've seen this ship, what a high cultural standard it has. I don't believe devs could have produced it. Besides, they would have had to invent the time-drive all by themselves, and that requires genius. Degenerate races don't have that kind of intellectual genius. Cunning, yes – but not genius. No, Citizen, the aliens are behind this.'

Again, the Titan tech's reasoning sounded plausible. Heshke hurried to keep up with his swift strides. But, he thought, if Gann was right then that suggested that there was a conspiracy of cosmic proportions directed against True Man . . .

Gann nudged him again, directing him down a side turning. They passed through a sort of foyer, or salon, where a number of devs stood before a large wall screen on which enigmatic schematics processed. They discussed quietly among themselves, and paused only momentarily to glance up as Gann and Heshke passed them by.

Gann remained silent until they were once more walking down an empty corridor. 'Don't you know who these people are?' he said, his voice rising slightly. 'No, perhaps you wouldn't . . . but I had plenty of instruction in race identification in training college.'

'No,' Heshke said, 'I don't know who they are.'

'They're Chinks,' Gann told him. 'The last group of them was supposed to have been exterminated five hundred years ago. Quite an interesting strain, as devs go. Tradition has it that their cunning was almost superhuman.'

'*Super*human?' repeated Heshke wonderingly. 'And yet you deny them intellectual ability?'

'It's more of an animal cleverness raised to a high degree. In devs the intellectual faculty is always perverted in some way, producing bizarre sciences and practices, yet it can involve extreme subtlety – in fact there used to be a saying: "the fiendishly clever Chink."'

Heshke found the phrase amusing and smiled, at which Gann shot him a sharp glance.

'It's no laughing matter. And you wouldn't think so if you fell foul of a Chink puzzle.'

'A Chink puzzle? What's that?'

'One of their weapons, capable of incapacitating the nervous system. Just some kind of ingenious contraption made of wire or bits of metal, apparently. But whoever it's given to is instantly confronted with insuperable problems and riddles of such a nature that the mind is totally paralysed. The worst of it is that he can't be released until the puzzle is solved, which only a Chink can do.'

With a deep sigh, Heshke decided that perhaps his amusement had been too facetious, after all.

'As you can see,' Gann concluded, 'these people are natural candidates for alliance with the aliens. Perhaps they were allied with them all along.'

'Well, what are we going to do now?'

'Our duty is somehow to seize this ship if we can and take it back to Earth – and to the Absolute Present.'

'But how?' said Heshke, overawed at such audacity.

'I don't know yet. I haven't finished reconnoitring. But there doesn't seem to be a very large crew.'

'But even if we did take control – which doesn't seem possible to me – how would we fly it?'

'I can pilot a time traveller, and the alien version is basically the same as our own. We can manage it with Ascar's help, even if I have to kick co-operation out of him.'

The Titan stopped abruptly. They were in a broad passage – a sort of gallery – one side of which was covered with silk screens adorned with delicate, trace-like figures of men, women and willow trees. The brushstrokes were sparse, economical but expansively eloquent.

'Well, that's the picture,' Gann said. 'We may as well get back to our rooms now. I haven't eaten yet and I'm hungry.'

'Didn't they give you any food?' Heshke asked him in surprise.

'They left food of some kind. But I discovered the door was unlocked and decided action was more important. I've been all over the ship.'

So that was why the Titan was so much ahead of him, Heshke thought. The man's devotion to duty was total.

'I don't think I can find my way,' he said.

'I'll show you. Or else you can come back with me. It's probably not safe to talk in our rooms, though.'

Heshke allowed the Titan to guide him through the corridors and to explain the general layout of the ship, which Gann had grasped in remarkably short order. Just before they parted, Heshke turned to face him, raising his finger as though bringing up a point of debate.

'You speak of Chink puzzles. I'm still wondering why they're content to let us wander around like this to plot and scheme. How do we know we're not on the *inside* of one of those puzzles, being manipulated?'

And the bleak, stubborn look on the face of the Titan showed that he, too, had entertained this thought.

It was hard to tell time on the Chink ship. The meals did not arrive regularly; they arrived as ordered. One had only to press one of the studs on the grey-screened pedestal and in a very short time a cheerful, smiling Chink would arrive, bearing a tray piled with the strangely spiced food.

Lieutenant Gann ate but sparsely and devoted all his time to finding a way to seize the ship, a project in which Heshke, none too willingly, was embroiled. They soon abandoned, however, the ban on discussions in their rooms. Heshke had grown tired of charging through corridors with the indefatigable Titan – and besides, he pointed out, the Chinks on the ship appeared to understand very little Earth language. Probably the rooms weren't bugged at all.

Experimentally they tried stating some outrageously violent intentions, but their captors failed to come charging in as Gann had expected.

Both Gann and Heshke made efforts to talk to Leard Ascar. But the physicist seemed to have retreated even further into himself and barely acknowledged them. He ate vast quantities of the Chink food, calling for one dish after another, and seemed to relish Gann's disgust for his exotic tastes.

'Your ideas are all screwy,' he growled when Heshke tried to talk some reason into him. 'And so are your theories.'

Heshke was taken aback. One could not help but have respect for Ascar's penetrating intellect, whatever the state of his mental health might be.

'I'm surprised to see you take this attitude,' he admonished. 'I thought you were as anxious to see the aliens defeated as anyone.'

Ascar merely shrugged, scowling derisively, and continued engorging steamed rice in rapid spoonfuls.

They returned to Gann's room. 'Plainly we can't count on him to help at first,' the officer conceded reluctantly. 'Nevertheless I don't think he'll refuse us technical assistance when the time comes. We'll just have to tackle the dangerous part by ourselves.'

Heshke, whose enthusiasm for the venture was less than he cared to admit, sighed. 'I don't see how we're going to manage anything. Just us against the whole ship!'

'It's our duty to try, whatever the odds. Besides, if we fail it will still remain our duty to kill ourselves before this ship reaches its destination. *We can't allow them to interrogate us.* So we have nothing to lose.' Gann looked grim. 'We'll have to kill Ascar, too.'

'Very well. So what now?'

'I've evolved a plan.' Gann reached into his tunic and drew out a sharp-bladed knife.

'Where did you get that?' Heshke asked, astonished.

'From the ship's kitchen. I wandered in there, and managed to pick it up before they shooed me away.'

'It's still not much,' said Heshke doubtfully.

'It's not all. Wait.'

He unbuttoned his tunic and pulled up his shirt, then probed a spot on his abdomen, just under his ribs, with his fingers. 'Feel there.'

Heshke obeyed. He felt a hard lump under the skin.

'Something the Chinks don't know about,' Gann said, with a note of satisfaction. 'A vial of nerve gas.' Suddenly he thrust the knife at Heshke. 'Here.'

'What?' Heshke blinked.

'Cut it out!'

Though squeamish with distaste, Heshke complied. Gann lay down on the chair-couch and took the cuff of his sleeve between his teeth. Heshke plied the knife, uncomfortably aware of the other's pain.

Fortunately the capsule was only just below the skin. It had been cleverly grafted in, so that the skin showed no trace of surgery. Heshke wondered whether all Titans were similarly equipped. Probably they were, he thought.

It was like all the other thoughtful touches of Titan elitism: the blood-group tattooed on the inside of each man's arm, for instance.

The capsule came out easily, an egg-shaped spheroid slippery with blood. 'Thanks,' Gann gasped. 'I could have done it myself, but I was afraid I'd make a mess of it.'

'You're bleeding quite a bit,' Heshke commented.

Gann looked around, snatched up a cloth that covered a small table and tore a strip off it with strong hands. He passed it around his waist, binding up the wound.

'That'll do for now. This is our plan of operations, Heshke.' Gingerly he took the capsule, wiping off the blood. 'Our first requirements are, one: weapons, and two: command of the control room. Now, most of these Chinks don't seem to carry weapons, but you've seen those ones dressed differently from the others – wearing blue jackets with high collars?'

Heshke nodded.

'I've reason to think that they do. They're probably officials or troops of some sort. There's always one of them standing guard outside the control room. You'll walk up to him and engage his attention. Then I'll come up behind – right?' He brought up the knife, going through the motions of grasping a man from behind and cutting his throat.   •

His stomach turning over, Heshke nodded.

'Right. Then we'll take his gun, and chuck the gas capsule into the control room. It's very quick acting, but disperses after about half a minute, so we'll be able to take over. If anyone does come charging out before the gas gets him, we can simply shoot him.'

'And what do we do then?'

Gann frowned. 'Then, I'm afraid, we'll have to improvise. There'll still be the rest of the crew to deal with. But we'll be in a good position – at the nerve centre of the ship, and with plenty of weapons at our disposal. At least they'll know they've been in a fight.'

Murder isn't my business, thought Heshke as they made their way towards the execution of Gann's plan. I'm an archaeologist, a middle-aged archaeologist. I wish there was some way out of this.

But there wasn't.

In a way their being devs made it easier; not like killing True Men.

But even killing a dog was unpleasant.

The thoughts were still spinning around in his mind when they came to the last intersection before the control room. Gann touched his elbow encouragingly and slipped off down a side passage.

Heshke continued on until he arrived at the demilune where some swing doors gave entrance to the control room. There was always a Chink standing here, like a commissionaire before the door of an expensive hotel. At the sight of him Heshke froze, momentarily paralysed. The Chink was so young, so affable-looking.

The young Chink turned and saw him, apparently noticing the stricken look on his face. Lieutenant Gann hove into view on the other side, a tall, comparatively sinister figure. He surreptitiously motioned Heshke to get on with it; Heshke took a step forward.

And then, impatient with Heshke's hesitancy, Gann sprang. He hooked an arm around the Chink's neck, forcing his head back to expose his throat to the knife. Heshke's eyes bulged; he couldn't look, he couldn't turn away.

But just as the worst was about to happen something, a sliver of light, darted from the ceiling and struck Gann in the back. Scarcely any change of expression came over the Titan's face; his body went limp, collapsing to the floor and nearly dragging the Chink with it.

The Chink recovered his balance and stared down at the body, his eyes wide with consternation. Then he flung open the swing doors and shouted something in a high-pitched, singsong voice. More Chinks came running from the control room, looking first at Gann and then at Heshke and chattering to him, their faces expressing commiseration, concern, regret.

One of them took Heshke by the arm and led him into the control room. He gazed blankly around at it, at the curved control panel sweeping by on either side, at the flickering screens whose rapidly changing images meant nothing to him.

His guide stepped up to one of the panels and began punching something out on a keyboard. After a pause words appeared on a screen over the Chink's head.

Ship programmed protect itself. Very sad friend die. Should have warned. So sorry.

Heshke nodded dismally, turned and walked back into the demilune, where a small crowd was still collected. For some reason Ascar arrived. He stood looking down at the dead lieutenant, his expression unreadable. Then he suddenly gave the Titan hooked-arm salute.

'Salute to a brave officer,' he said wryly.

'He *was* a brave officer,' Heshke answered.

'Yes, I know.'

Heshke felt unutterably weary.

He returned to his room and remained there for the rest of the voyage. He felt defeated, but oddly the death of Gann did not affect him as much as he might have imagined.

And neither did he kill himself. He had come to the conclusion that Ascar was right: Gann had been too presumptuous concerning the people who had rescued them from non-time. There was nothing substantial to indicate that they were hostile at all.

He slept, ate and slept, ate and slept until he felt rested. Eventually a Chink came and took him to the control room again. Ascar was already there; he gave Heshke a glance and a nod. He seemed to be familiar with the control room, as if he had made himself at home there.

The Chink pointed to a screen, and Heshke suddenly understood. He was being shown their destination. He stared entranced at the glittering shape, like an elongated hourglass, that hung suspended against ebon space, backed by hard, shining stars. A touch of the old apprehension came over him. Was this some alien stronghold, –

Or what was it?

8

Watching through the transparent wall of his spatio-temporal observatory, Shiu Kung-Chien saw the ship return from Earth and dock in the nearby sphincter. He could pretend no enthusiasm for the event; the ship's drive interfered with his apparatus and until the docking was completed he was obliged to suspend his current experiment.

He spent the time sitting patiently, drinking green tea and contemplating the dark, star-clouded universe all around him. He derived a satisfying feeling of insignificance from regarding it thus; a feeling that, as an organic, thinking being, he was a stranger in it. For it was an infinite expanse of non-time, a universe that had been made, in the first instance, without any time at all. Here and there localized processes of time had started themselves up, mostly weak, some quite powerful, proceeding in all directions, at all angles to one another. Occasionally they even met. They were accidental, small-order phenomena of limited period, but because of them life was able to exist.

On Earth, the most unhappy circumstance that could happen in the whole of existence had arisen: two distinct time-streams associated with the same planet. What was more, they were on a direct, head-on collision course.

Not that events of this nature were impossibly rare, especially in galaxies where the forces of *yin* and *yang* were so much out of balance as to cause numerous time-systems to arise. It was one good reason, in fact, for living in interstellar space, away from the traffic, as it were. Even so, Retort City itself had suffered a near-miss some centuries ago – a glancing blow by some entity travelling obliquely to its own time-direction. Shiu Kung-Chien still maintained contact with this entity: actually it was the object of his current experiments.

Pouring his third cup of fragrant tea, he noted that the space-time-ship had now slipped through the sphincter. No doubt the Earth passengers it carried would be full of hysterical pleas for assistance and he foresaw a tiresome time ahead. Personally he had opposed offering Earth any help at all, on the grounds that it might involve the full capacity of the Production Retort and cause inconvenience, particularly with regard to delays in the delivery of equipment he had ordered for his own work. But the other members of the Cabinet, out of some sort of filial respect for the planet where mankind had been bred, had disagreed with him.

The meter by his side informed him that the incoming ship had shut down its engines. He rose, beckoning his cybernetic servitors.

'The area is clear. Let us begin.'

The machines rolled across the work area to make final preparations. But Shiu Kung-Chien was interrupted yet again by a gentle introductory tone from the observatory's entrance door. Into the observatory came the sedate figure of Prime Minister Hwen Wu.

'Welcome to my retreat, honoured colleague,' said Shiu Kung-Chien in a voice that bore just a trace of exaspera-tion. 'Your visit is connected, presumably, with the arrival of the ship from Earth.'

The other nodded. 'One of the passengers, it seems, is a scientist of some repute – no less than the brain behind the Terrans' recent discovery of time travel. He is hungry for knowledge. He'll certainly demand to speak at length with you.'

Shiu Kung-Chien tugged at his beard and cursed. 'So now I must waste my time conversing with barbarian dolts! Can you not give him someone else to vent his ignorance on? There are plenty of people adequate for that.'

Hwen Wu affected surprise. 'Let us not be discourteous, Kung-Chien. I am told that, judging by the character of the man, he'll insist on meeting our foremost expert in the field, and that is yourself.'

'Oh, very well. But can't it wait? I'm in the middle of something important. I'm about to re-establish contact with the Oblique Entity.'

'Indeed?' Hwen Wu clasped his hands within his voluminous sleeves. 'I thought it had passed out of range?'

'So it had, using former methods. But this new apparatus of mine uses the principle of direct, all-senses contact.'

'Is that not a trifle dangerous?' Hwen Wu enquired delicately.

Shiu Kung-Chien shrugged.

'There's no particular hurry concerning the Earthman,' the Prime Minister admitted after a pause. 'He still has to be put through language indoctrination. Would the experiment be compromised if I were to stay and . . .'

'Watch by all means,' Kung-Chien told him, 'though there'll be little to see.'

The servitors signalled that all was in readiness. Shiu Kung-Chien, Retort City's greatest researcher into the phenomenon of time, entered a glassy sphere which, though transparent from the outside, encased its occupant in apparent darkness. He murmured something, his words being conveyed to the cybernetic controller.

Hwen Wu gazed placidly on the scene. He saw the scientist go rigid, as though suddenly paralysed. His eyes stared sightlessly, his ears were without sound, even his skin no longer felt the touch of his garments or the pressure of the floor under his feet. His body remained, but his senses – and therefore his mind – had been transferred hundreds of light-years away in a direction which no telescope could show: obliquely in time.

'What shall we do, Father?'

Ex-Minister Hueh Shao looked at Su-Mueng, realizing with a pang what a handsome young man his son had become.

'Do?' he repeated in astonishment. 'This is *your* enterprise. What did you intend?'

Su-Mueng answered lamely. 'I had hoped for your guidance, Father. Perhaps we could escape from the city, go to Earth.'

'Mmm. Possibly, but I doubt it – and you obviously know nothing of the conditions there. We'd be unlikely to survive.'

No matter; that had been the lesser of Su-Mueng's hopes. Vaguely, he had envisaged he and his father making a fight of it together. Suddenly getting over his initial stupefaction, he rose to the occasion and spoke with new resolve.

'Then return with me to the Production Retort. It's honeycombed with little-used areas, deserted spaces. I'll find a hideout for you there.'

'What, exchange one prison for another? Where's the advantage in that?' The older man frowned.

'No, that's not it.' Abruptly the real issue that lay before him crystallized in Su-Mueng's mind; the heat of passion entered his voice. 'There's work to be done. We must work to overthrow the structure of society!'

His father stared at him as though he had gone mad. 'Do you know what you're saying?' he exclaimed in a shocked whisper.

'But isn't that why you committed your crime and tried to save me from my fate?' Su-Mueng rejoined. 'Do you not feel the injustice of our way of life? One part of the population being forced to content itself with production, otherwise enjoying only crude entertainments, while the other part leeches off this work force?'

'But we're maintaining the highest state of civilization!' spluttered Hueh Shao. 'The arts and the sciences have been carried to the peak of sophistication here in the Leisure Retort, to say nothing of the graciousness of our life-style. How could we devote ourselves to this if we had to spend time producing material things for ourselves?'

Su-Mueng was taken aback by this response, which was not what he had expected. 'The inhabitants of the Lower Retort could also enjoy what we have here, if they were given the opportunity,' he said. 'It's unfair that it should be denied them. *All* should share, in production as well as in higher things.'

'But then neither production nor refinement could be carried as far,' his father replied with a wave of his hand. His voice fell, became sombre. 'I confess that my motives in keeping you in the Leisure Retort were purely selfish. I'd wanted my son to live as I'd lived. No feeling of a general injustice entered my mind – that, presumably, would only occur to someone who saw both sides of the divide.'

'Then come down to the Lower Retort and see for yourself!'

Hueh Shao sighed. 'It seems that I set in train more than I dreamed when I hid you in my secret apartments. Social revolution, now!'

'Are you agreed, then? If we leave quickly perhaps no one will learn of your escape for some time.'

'They know of it already,' Hueh Shao told him, indicating the panels by the door. On one of them an amber light glowed. 'The time-displacement machine has reported your interference of it.'

Su-Mueng whirled and gasped. Running to the panels, he pulled free the model of Retort City he used as a time-control and brandished it vigorously.

'Quickly – before they get here. Perhaps I can out-phase us with this – make us invisible!'

Hueh Shao's face was a mixture of sadness, pity and regret. He followed his son into the corridor outside the apartment, where Su-Mueng fiddled desperately with his time device, producing a chiaroscuro of flickering lights.

'There!' he pronounced with satisfaction. 'We're back-phased a full half minute. If we move fast we can be in the Lower Retort within the hour.'

Again Hueh Shao hesitated, and then seemed to come to a decision and nodded, moving with Su-Mueng through the scented passages, staying within the field of his gadget. Su-Mueng walked rapidly, excitedly, but even before they left the section they encountered what the older man had known they would encounter, but which he had optimistically supposed they would not.

It was a rare sight in the Leisure Retort: four citizens in the garb of law enforcement officials, looking oddly severe in the tight-fitting blue and high collars, coming along the corridor with calm self-confidence.

Their leader carried a small cylinder which he held before him like a torch. Even as he noticed this Su-Mueng felt a wave of dizziness and realized with dismay that he'd been phased back into normative time. His hand darted to his double retort, but then went limp as he recognized the greater power of the other's instrument.

The leader looked from one fugitive to the other, a hint of recognition crossing his features. 'Would you kindly accompany us?' he asked politely. 'Regretfully, we must presume that you're in infringement of a city ethic.'

The blue-jacketed men turned and retraced their steps, leaving their prisoners to follow them of their own accord. Su-Mueng was sick to think how futile all his work had been.

From the moment when they passed through the ship's outer doors and into the incredible space city, a phantasmagoria of rich impressions greeted Rond Heshke and Leard Ascar. The ship they had been travelling in, Heshke realized, was austere and functional compared with the voluptuous standards of these people.

The air was invigoratingly fresh and laden with captivating scents. They had emerged from some kind of dock into which the ship, apparently, fitted snugly; and the spectacle before them was bewildering in its complexity. Level gave way to level and split-level; screens and interrupted walls ran hither and thither with the complexity of a maze, offering glimpses of gardens and parks arrayed in riotous colours.

The place breathed the essence of luxury. Blooms and delicate orchids flowered everywhere, springing from walls and ceilings. It was like being in some primitive conception of Heaven.

A Chink led them through a low archway and gestured to them to be seated in a carriage that appeared, to Heshke's astonished eye, to be made of green jade. The carriage moved silently along meandering pathways, giving Heshke a chance to observe the people of the city. Their styles of dress were varied; most common among the men, however, was a long, flowing silk robe with enormous sleeves. The older men generally affected long, sparse beards, adding yet more strangeness to their slanted, scarcely human features.

The dress of the women was much more diverse. Some swathed themselves in voluminous silk, others wore short, revealing split skirts or scarcely anything at all, and all wore flowers in their invariably black hair. Despite his natural revulsion for devs, Heshke gazed fascinated at their alien beauty, and at the graceful, sedate fashion in which both they and the men carried themselves.

More and more his 'educated' attitudes as regards deviant subspecies were coming crashing to the ground. It was impossible to claim now, as Lieutenant Gann had, that all this was the creation of extraterrestrials. Quite obviously these Chinks had a superb sense of beauty – something which, in Titan doctrine, only True Man possessed. He thought of Blare Oblomot, who would not have been at all surprised by it.

Ascar, he reflected, had been right yet again: their ideas had been all wrong. And Ascar was certainly no underground sympathizer. He turned to him to make a comment; but Ascar was taking no notice whatsoever of his surroundings. He sat looking blankly at his lap, his face wearing his customary sullen scowl.

It just doesn't get through to him, Heshke thought wonderingly. He's all intellect – he's blind to everything that isn't abstract.

The carriage entered a set of vertical guide rails that took it up, amid masses of perfumed foliage, to another level. Here there were no more gardens; the prospect was that of an endless summerhouse whose apartments were partitioned by flimsy, movable screens, exquisitely decorated. At their conductor's request they left the carriage and walked a short distance through this open-plan habitat. Heshke noted the sparsity of furniture; indeed, too much furniture would have entirely spoiled the light, airy effect. Everything here in this city, it seemed, was arranged to provide perfect harmony.

They rounded a corner and came to a stop in a fairly small room where a tall, bearded man regarded them with cold detachment. On a table beside him were several bowls and an assortment of slender needles, some gold, some silver. Unrecognizable apparatus stood on the other side of the table, while on the wall behind was an apparently normal television screen.

The old man uttered some quiet words, and with much dignity motioned Heshke to recline on a nearby chair-couch.

Heshke did so with reluctance, and then felt a sudden panic as the Chink took up one of the long slender needles. All his repugnance of devs came flooding back, and his mind filled with fears of hideous, infinitely cunning tortures. Seeing his terror, the old Chink paused, head inclined.

Ascar spoke, struggling with unfamiliar syllables. To Heshke's boundless admiration he had actually succeeded in picking up a few phrases of the impossibly difficult language. He listened to the Chink's reply, spoken slowly and clearly for his benefit.

'Relax,' Ascar said then to Heshke. 'He's not going to hurt you. It's some sort of processing. They're going to teach us the language.'

Partially reassured, Heshke leaned back. The oldster approached, muttering something, and touched him just behind his ear. Where his fingers touched, Heshke seemed to go numb. Then the Chink applied the needle he was holding; from his action Heshke knew that he was inserting it under the skin, deeper and deeper.

Into his brain!

He fought not to feel frightened. The Chink, with the assurance and solicitude of a skilled doctor, used about a dozen needles on him in all, in various parts of his body: chiefly around his head, neck, hands and arms. But as the treatment progressed a curious soothing feeling overcame him and his fears vanished. Finally the oldster stepped away and returned a few moments later, slipping some earphones over his ears and some goggles over his eyes which plunged him into blackness. He heard the snap of a switch.

And Heshke fell instantly asleep.

He awoke, he did not know how much later, to find the old man deftly pulling the needles from his skin. Ascar, too, had just finished his treatment. He rose from a second chair-couch, smiling sardonically at Heshke.

'Excellent,' said the old man. 'And may you both be honoured guests in our city.'

He had spoken in the singsong Chink tongue – and yet Heshke had understood it.

'This is really remarkable!' he exclaimed. But the other waved his hand.

'You're still speaking in your own language,' he intoned. 'Try to find the *other* tongue in your mind – and speak again.'

Puzzled, Heshke tried to do as he was instructed,

turning his attention inward as he spoke. 'I was merely praising the effectiveness of your treatment,' he said. 'I'd like to know how you did it.'

And then, while he was speaking, he found it: the 'other tongue' – lying alongside his own in his mind, ready to seize his larynx and tongue and to express his thoughts, as automatically and faultlessly as he used his own language. His last few words came out in the language of the Chinks.

It was strange at first – like being able to switch to another vidcast channel at will.

The old man smiled politely. 'The principle is quite simple,' he explained. 'A computer-programmed language course was fed into your mind at high speed while you were unconscious, so that for every word or phrase of your own language, the speech centre of your brain now contains the equivalent word or phrase of our language.'

'That's pretty impressive,' Ascar interjected, also speaking flawless Chink. 'I've never heard of anything like that before. I wouldn't have thought it was possible – not in such a short space of time, anyway.'

Heshke listened fascinated to the way the foreign syllables flowed off Ascar's tongue – and was just as fascinated at his ability to understand them.

'The brain's capacity to absorb information at computer speed is not, I believe, known to your people,' the old man admitted. 'We're able to achieve it with the assistance of an ancient technique called acupuncture.' He indicated the needles that lay on the table. 'By inserting these fine needles at particular points under the skin we're able to deaden or stimulate the nerves selectively. By this means we open the requisite pathways to the brain so that it's able to assimilate data at a much faster rate than normally – and there are also many other uses for acupuncture.'

'But that seems such a primitive way of going about things,' Heshke commented, staring at the needles. 'Your apparatus is hardly sophisticated.'

'The technique depends more on knowledge and skill than upon technology,' the old man replied. 'It is a very old practice, but it's been vastly refined and extended by us here in Retort City. It's said to have been invented originally by the ancient philosopher Mao Tse-Tung, who also invented the generation of electricity.' The Chink smiled tolerantly. 'But these legends are not, of course, reliable; they also tell of him driving out the evil demons Liu Shao-Chi and Lin Piao.'

Ascar grunted and cast a sarcastic glance at Heshke. 'You're right – history tells nothing but fairy stories.'

Heshke ignored the gibe. 'I take it your people have a reason for bringing us here,' he said to the old man. 'When will we learn what it is?'

The other sighed. 'Ah yes, very distressing. But that's not my province. You'll have to meet representatives of the Cabinet – perhaps even the Prime Minister himself. Have patience.'

'Patience be damned,' growled Ascar, finding Retort City curses not strong enough for his liking. 'When am I going to meet your physicists?'

In view of the seriousness of the offence, Prime Minister Hwen Wu himself presided over the court. With him sat two lesser ministers, and at a table to one side were the court's advisers, experts in logic and law.

Hueh Shao was brought in first and offered green tea, which he refused. He pleaded guilty to attempting to break his confinement, and added that he had intended to go into hiding in the Production Retort, where he would be helped by his son. His voice betrayed an inner weariness, as he spoke quietly and calmly.

Hwen Wu found the proceedings disturbing to his inner peace. There seemed to be only one possible judgement that could be made in the case of the man who once had been his close friend.

'One further statement I wish to put before the court,' Hueh Shao continued, 'and that is that my son Su-Mueng should be absolved from guilt. It was with my encouragement that he agreed to guide me to the Lower Retort, and in so doing he was prompted by filial duty – he looks upon me as other men look upon their grandfathers. Furthermore, his entire aberration springs from my own actions. But for my former crime he would have lived happily and blamelessly as a production worker, with no knowledge of any other life. In my opinion, any punishment inflicted upon him would be unjust.'

A logician raised his hand, was recognized and rose to speak.

'The accused commits an inconsistent statement with his tale of how he induced his son to guide him down to the Production Retort,' he said in a low, melodious voice. 'The facts are these: Hueh Shao and Hueh Su-Mueng *were* apprehended while leaving the area where Hueh Shao was incarcerated. Hueh Shao admits to this. But as regards his statement of his intentions, Hueh Shao must certainly *have known* that he and his son would be apprehended before leaving the Leisure Retort – although Hueh Su-Mueng, possibly, did not. Hueh Shao couldn't have intended to do something which he knew to be impossible, and therefore his intentions were otherwise.'

'And what were his intentions?' Hwen Wu queried.

'Taking everything into account, it would appear that Hueh Su-Mueng appeared unexpectedly in his father's apartment and released him from his time-displacement. Hueh Shao was then in a quandary; he knew his son's scheme to be impossible to execute, and that his son was laying himself open to severe punishment. From that moment on his foremost intention became to spare his son from his punishment – remember the unusual bond that exists between these two, unnatural though it might seem to us. He pretended to fall in with Hueh Su-Mueng's plan, in order that he might thereby represent himself as its part-instigator and remove some of the guilt from his son's shoulders.'

Hwen Wu turned to the accused.

'Do you admit to this version of events?'

Hueh Shao nodded; the logician had mercilessly exposed his motives.

'Hueh Shao's following statement, however, stands up to examination,' the logician continued. 'Hueh Su-Mueng's aberrated state of mind *is* to be laid entirely at his door. But whether we should conclude from this that no punishment devolves upon the younger man is an entirely different matter. One cannot dismiss the principle of personal responsibility so lightly.'

The Prime Minister listened carefully to these pronouncements, considering them from all angles. Finally he turned to the accused again.

'I find you guilty of co-operating in your own escape, but not of instigating your escape,' he said. 'Your actual infringement, in this particular instance, of a city ethic is not an enormous one, but that's not the issue before us here. The issue is that your original crime, one of truly serious proportions, has surfaced again. You've created an individual of apparently irremediable criminal tendencies – already, in his preliminary statements, your son has expressed himself as being totally opposed to the social structure.'

He fingered the tendrils of his beard, contemplating. 'Your crime is unforgivable because it strikes at the roots of society,' he proclaimed. 'If allowed to gather force it could destroy the civilization we enjoy here in Retort City. Nevertheless, your sentence was a lenient one, initially, because it was the first case of its type to occur for many centuries. We must now withdraw that leniency. I regret that I must sentence you to loss of life.' He looked calmly at Hueh Shao. 'Do you agree with the sentence?'

Hueh Shao nodded. He could almost see what was in the Prime Minister's mind. The sentence was not merely on himself; it gave Hwen Wu a way of punishing Su-Mueng without directly punishing him. The principles of fairness and justice were both satisfied, even though they were in conflict.

'Then let the sentence be carried out immediately.'

Hueh Shao turned and walked out through a door to his right.

A minute or two later Su-Mueng took his place before the court. He listened to the formal charge, pleaded guilty, but in his following statement firmly absolved his father of all guilt in the matter.

Meantime, in a nearby room, Hueh Shao relaxed into a chair-couch and was handed a bowl of refreshing green tea.

The bowl was of the most delicate porcelain and its embossed design, a mere tracery when touched by the fingers, was of a style he particularly admired. He sipped the tea, enjoying its fragrance. A feeling of numbness, not particularly unpleasant, came over his limbs as the poison in the tea took effect. He laid the bowl down on a nearby low table, the tea still unfinished, and quietly died.

In a cold voice Hwen Wu accepted Su-Mueng's plea and explained the verdict and sentence that had just been passed on his father. 'The sentence,' he added, 'will by now have been carried out.'

Su-Mueng's reaction to this news inflicted the whole court with a faint feeling of revulsion, for it demonstrated the emotional bond that existed between two men who should never even have known one another. Su-Mueng went deathly white and sagged as though punched in the stomach. He recovered himself with difficulty, drawing himself erect, his face still grey, and looked Hwen Wu straight in the eye.

'Damn you,' he said in a strangled voice. 'Damn you all. Your whole system is evil – and one day it will be destroyed . . .'

The President of the Court nodded. 'We're acquainted with your opinions, and of their causes. We're aware also that your attitudes are intractable, which raises the problem of what we're to do with you. Punishment is inappropriate, because insofar as punishment is deserved it's already been inflicted in the form of your knowledge that your actions have led to your father's death. We cannot permit you to live in the Leisure Retort, since that would transgress the law; yet if we return you to the Production Retort, which is your proper place, you'll no doubt continue to cause trouble. So the question remains, what are we to do with you . . .?'

9

Leard Ascar had been obsessed, from an early age, with only one question.

The question of time.

He could remember the day – it had been his tenth birthday – when the full force of the enigma had first struck him. The dilemma, the paradox, the impossible, irreconcilable paradox. The transient present, moving from a past that vanishes into a future that appears from nowhere. And even more perplexingly, what he later came to know as the Regression Problem: how can time 'pass' without having 'time' to pass in?

These enigmas drove out all his other interests. He read everything he could understand on the subject, and then studied physics and mathematics so as to understand what was left. He was precocious, ahead of his class in all the subjects he took. He never made any friends, but could have had a brilliant career in almost any branch of physics, had he not preferred to devote himself to unsuccessful, self-financed researches into the nature of time. Among more conventional minds he gained a reputation as a crank, an oddball, and his experiments had regularly ground to a halt for lack of any further money.

Then he had come into contact with the scientific establishments of the Titanium Legions and they, to give them their due, had made it possible for him to continue his work. Following the victories over the deviant subspecies there had been a splurge of boastful expansionism in the sciences, a feeling that True Man could achieve anything. Not only Ascar but real cranks, near-psychotics with the most extraordinary and fanciful theories, had been allotted funds to bring their ideas to fruition. And so he had made some small progress until that incredible day when the real nature of the captured alien vehicle had become evident.

That day had been a climax in Ascar's life. A second climax came on the day he was introduced to Shiu Kung-Chien, the foremost expert on time in a city that had mastered nearly all its secrets.

That he had been trained to regard individuals of Shiu Kung-Chien's race as subhuman did not bother him. He would gladly have sat at the feet of a chimpanzee if it could have taught him what he wanted to know.

He sat across from the master physicist, beside whom, on a lacquered table, was a pot of the steaming green tea the man never seemed to stop drinking. Around them was Shiu Kung-Chien's observatory which, so he understood, explored both space and time: on one side a curving, transparent wall giving a view of empty, sable space, on the other a neat array of apparatus whose functions Ascar could not divine.

Shiu Kung-Chien himself Ascar would not have picked out among his compatriots – but then these Chinks all looked alike to Ascar. His dress and appearance were modest: a simple, unadorned silk gown tied at the waist with a sash, the long, silky beard worn by many of his generation. But his fingernails, Ascar noted, were unusually long, and painted. It seemed that Shiu did almost no physical work himself; all the equipment he used, though designed by him, was constructed elsewhere, and thereafter was set up and attended by the robot mechanisms that now busied and hummed at the other end of the observatory.

'Yes, that's quite interesting,' Shiu Kung-Chien said. He had been listening politely while Ascar tried to give him a rundown on his own ideas and what had led up to them. They'd been forced to resort to verbal descriptions – Ascar's own equations, as it turned out, were adjudged near-useless by Shiu, and those he offered instead were incomprehensible to Ascar. Seemingly the type of mathematics he used had no equivalent in Ascar's experience, and even the acupuncture assisted language course was of no help.

Ascar folded his arms and sighed fretfully, rocking back and forth slightly on his chair. 'Up until recently my mind was clear on the subject. I thought I'd got to the bottom of the age-old mystery. But since I discovered *another "now"* – another system of time moving in the opposite direction – I've been in confusion and don't know what to think. The picture I'd built up is really only credible if the Absolute Present is unique.' He shot Shiu a hard glance. '*You* tell me: is the universe coming to an end?'

Shiu's seamed face showed amusement and he chuckled as if at some joke. 'No, not at all. Not the universe. Just organic life on Earth. To be more precise, *time* is shortly due to stop on Earth.'

He waved a hand and a cybernetic servitor rolled forward with a fresh pot of tea. 'You know, you haven't quite disposed of the Regression Problem, although you appear to think you have.'

Ascar frowned. 'Let's make sure we're talking about the same thing. The Regression Problem points out the apparent impossibility of passing time. It's defined thus: take three consecutive events, A, B and C. One of these events is occurring "now" and the other two are in the past or the future. Let's say that B is "now", so that A is in the past and C is in the future. But there must have been a time when A was "now" and B and C were in the future, and likewise there will be a time when C is "now" and the other two are in the past. So we can draw up a table of three configurations of these three events, giving nine distinct terms in all. But we can't stop there: if we did there'd be three simultaneous "nows", and there can only ever be one "now". So we must select one of these configurations and assign our own "now" to it – this gives us a second-order "now" related not to a single event but to a dynamic configuration of all three events: the one containing the real location of "now". But we can't stop there, either. Each one of the three configurations can in turn claim a second-order "now", by virtue of the fact that the "now" is moving. So we have to draw up a new table where the first table is repeated three times, the A-B-C groups number nine, and the single events themselves are permutated to twenty-seven, all this being encompassed by the third "third-order now". The process can be repeated to the fourth-order, fifth-order, and *ad infinitum* time.'

Shiu waved his hands at Ascar, suddenly impatient with the exposition. 'I'm fully conversant with all the arguments,' he said. 'But what made you think you'd resolved the paradox?'

'Well,' said Ascar slowly, 'when we actually travelled into the past and into the future and discovered there was no "now" there, I simply assumed that the whole argument was fallacious. The facts showed that there *was* no regress.'

'But did you not bother to ask yourself *why* the regress did not occur?' said Shiu acidly. 'No; you merely rushed in like a schoolboy and forgot about the matter.'

Ascar was silent for long moments.

'All right,' he said, 'where did I go wrong?'

'Your basic mistake was in presuming time to be a general feature of the universe,' Shiu told him, bringing out his words carefully and emphatically. 'You imagined the Absolute Present as a three-dimensional intersection of the whole of existence, traversing it everywhere simultaneously, much like a pickup head traversing a magnetic tape and bringing the images it contains to life. Agreed?'

'Yes,' said Ascar, 'that's a pretty good description.'

'But don't you see that if you adopt that picture then *the Regression Problem remains*?'

'No,' Ascar answered slowly, 'because the time intersection passes each instant only once—'

He stopped suddenly.

'Yes, you're right,' he resumed heavily. 'I can see it now. There'd have to be an infinite number of identical universes, one for each instant in our own universe, varying only in that the Absolute Present – the time intersection – was in a different part of its sweep. Every instant, past, present or future, would at this moment have to be filled by an Absolute Present somewhere among those universes.'

'And beyond that,' Shiu continued for him, 'would have to exist a further set of universes numbering infinity raised to the power infinity, to take care of the next stage in the regression. Already we're into *trans*finity.'

Ascar nodded hurriedly. 'All right, I accept that. I also accept that the facts have shown my model to be wrong. *So what's the truth?*'

'The truth,' said Shiu, 'is that the universe at large *has no time*. It's *not* "now" everywhere simultaneously. The universe is basically, fundamentally static, dead, indifferent. It has no past, no future, no "now".'

He refilled his teacup, allowing Ascar to interrupt with: 'But there *is* time.'

Shiu nodded patiently. 'Localized, accidental phenomena without overall significance. Processes of time *can* begin over small areas, usually associated with a planet, though not always. They consist of flows or waves of energy travelling from one point to another: small, travelling waves of "now". Philosophically it's explained thus: the universe issued from the Supreme as an interplay between the forces of *yin* and *yang* to form a perfect, dead-locked harmonic balance. Occasionally these forces get a little out of balance with one another here and there, and this causes time energy to flow until the balance is redressed. As such a wave proceeds it organizes matter into living forms in the process we know as evolution.'

'So time is a biological phenomenon, not a universal one?'

'Rather, biology is a consequence of time. Biological systems aren't the only phenomena it can produce. There are – many variations. But life and consciousness can arise in the moving present moment and be carried along with it.

'You can see now why time travel is comparatively easy,' Shiu went on. 'We merely have to detach a fragment of the travelling "now-wave" and move it about the real static world of non-time. It comes away quite easily, because it's local energy, not part of a cosmic schema.'

'Yes, and we've found that you need a living presence to make a time machine work,' Ascar agreed. 'That would follow, too.'

'Only because your machinery is primitive. In Retort City we can dispatch inanimate objects through time as well.'

'Yes . . . I see . . .'

Ascar strained to grasp in entirety the vision Shiu Kung-Chien was presenting to him. 'So let's put this together,' he said with difficulty. 'The universe consists of a static four-dimensional matrix—'

'Not four-dimensional,' Shiu corrected. 'Your whole theories about dimensions are erroneous: there are no dimensions. But if you want to use them as a descriptive tool, that's all right. In that case a six-dimensional matrix would suffice to describe all the possible directions that exist. Time-waves, when they arise, can take any one of these directions – from our point of view, forward, backward, sideways, up, down, inside-out – directions impossible to envisage. But the wave-front always abstracts, as it proceeds, a three-dimensional environment to anyone who is inside it. And it always creates, for an observer trapped in it, a past and a future.'

'And the Regression Problem,' Ascar reminded him. 'What happens to that?'

'There is no Regression Problem. The problem only arises when time is thought of as an absolute factor in the universe. But it's an incidental factor only, a triviality. The universe as a whole doesn't notice, is indifferent to, time, as well as to all the phenomena such as living creatures which it produces. Therefore there's no contradiction about before and after, past and future, or the moving moment. There is, as far as the universe is concerned, no change; non-time swallows it all up without a whisper.'

Considerately, Shiu gave Ascar time to mull this over. The Earth physicist placed his chin on his hand, gazing at the floor.

'And so this is what's happened to Earth?' he said finally. 'Another time-system has taken root on it, creating another process of evolution . . . but travelling in the reverse direction to ours. And they're going to collide.'

'Correct,' affirmed Shiu in a neutral voice.

'I still have difficulty with this. With the idea of time travelling in reverse, but producing the same effects as our own time. I've been used to regarding physical laws, such as chemical reactions and the laws of thermodynamics, as working only one way. The laws of entropy, for instance . . . that would seem to give time a definite direction irrespective . . .'

'That's because you're accustomed to looking upon time as an absolute function. To take the law of entropy – the law that disorder increases with time – the time-wave itself produces this effect. There are two contrasting modes in every time-wave: first, the tendency towards increasing disorder, and second, the tendency towards increasing integration, which results in biological systems. These tendencies are due to the *yin* and *yang* forces which are present in the time-wave, but battling against one another instead of harmonizing. *Yin* brings the tendency towards integration, and *yang* brings the tendency towards disorder. When they cease to war with one another, time dies away.'

'But that's not how it's going to be on Earth?'

'No. Your civilization is most unfortunate, as also is the civilization which is going to collide with yours. It will be a violent, catastrophic conflict between irreconcilable powers – the weirdest, most fantastic event, perhaps, that can happen in this universe.'

'What will happen?'

'Almost certainly the end result will be that time will cease. The two wave-fronts will cancel one another out in a sort of time explosion.'

'What I really meant was,' Ascar said, avoiding Shiu's eye, 'what will it be like for the people on location – caught on the spot when the wave-fronts come within range of one another?'

'You want to know what it will be like?' Shiu said. 'To a certain extent, I can show you.'

He rose and walked towards the other side of the laboratory, making for a transparent sphere about eight feet in diameter. 'Retort City once suffered a similar incident.'

Ascar sprang to his feet and joined him. 'And you survived?' he exclaimed.

'It wasn't quite as disastrous as it will be with you,' Shiu told him mildly. 'For one thing, the angle of approach was small – the entity we encountered was moving obliquely to us through time, not in head-on collision as will be the case with you. For another, we gained an advantage from our situation here in interstellar space. We were forewarned and were able to move ourselves, so that there was no actual physical contact. Neverthelesss the wave-fronts *did* interfere with one another, and the effects were extremely unpleasant. It's the closest we've come to annihilation.'

He halted before the transparent sphere. 'At the time some all-sense tapes were made of the event. Do you have all-sense recording on Earth?'

Dumbly Ascar shook his head.

'As its name implies, it gives a record covering all the senses – all the external senses, and besides that the internal senses as well, such as body feeling, and so on. Where the senses are, the mind is; therefore you won't be able to distinguish the experience from the real thing.'

He turned to his guest. 'I'll play you one of these sense-tapes if you like. I warn you it will be somewhat disturbing.'

'Yes, yes,' Ascar said eagerly. 'I want to know what happens.'

Shiu nodded, his expression withdrawn and unreadable and directed Ascar to enter the sphere by a narrow hatchway which closed up behind him. Once Ascar could no longer see him he smiled faintly to himself. He was unexpectedly pleased with the Terran visitor; despite his barbarian origin he was proving to be an apt pupil.

From within, the walls of the sphere were opaque. There was dim light, by which Ascar saw a chair fixed to the floor. He sat on it, and as he did so the light went out, leaving him in pitch-darkness.

For a few moments nothing happened. Then light sprang into being again. But he was no longer in the glass sphere. He was sitting in a similar chair in a typically light, airy room in Retort City. The air carried a mingle of faint scents, and from somewhere came strains of the jangly, hesitating music that was popular here.

He stared at the room's fittings for a while before he began to see that there was something odd about his surroundings. The proportions of the room were wrong, and seemed to become more wrong by the second. The angles of the walls, floor and ceiling . . . they didn't add up, he realized; they were an impossible combination, as if space itself were altering its geometry.

The music, in the middle of a complicated progression, became stuck on one chord which elongated and prolonged itself, wailing and wavering unable to escape its imprisonment in one moment of time.

Ascar watched with bulging eyes as a slim vase left the shelf on which it stood and moved through the air on an intricate orbit. This in itself was not so amazing; but the vase itself was deforming, going through a variegated procession of shapes. Finally Ascar found that he was looking at the vase transformed into a *four-dimensional object* – something akin to a klein bottle, impossible in three-dimensional space, with no inside, no outside, but comprising a continuous series of curved surfaces all running into one another.

He felt stunned to think that not only could he visualize such a figure but he was *actually seeing it*.

Everything else in the room began to deform in the same way. Alarmed, Ascar tried to rise from his chair – but couldn't. Dimly, he tried to remind himself that he was being subjected to a recording, not an actual event; presumably the sense-tapes inhibited the power of movement in some way. Soon he stopped even trying, for the deformations, quite horribly, were acting on him, too.

Ascar let out a long, howling scream. *Pain – Pain – Pain*.

Then the room collapsed and was replaced by something indefinable. Ascar became aware of his nervous system as a skein, or network, floating like a rambling cloud, without tangible form, drifting through a multidimensional maze. Nothing was recognizable any more, and neither was there any proper sense of time. But his nerves, perhaps because the intruding time field had compromised their chemical functioning, were signalling pain: agonizing, sharp, irresistible.

And into his consciousness was intruding something that, it seemed, was imminently going to end that consciousness. *Thump, thump, thump*, it went, like a living heart, or like a hammer that had his soul on the anvil.

Around him, his surroundings seemed to crystallize into some sort of form for a few moments. He saw more than the room in which he'd been seated: he saw a whole section of Retort City, deformed into bizarre non-Euclidean geometries so that its walls were no longer impediments to vision. Trapped in that nightmare were thousands of people, themselves transformed beyond semblance of humanity, like flies in a sticky jungle of spider-web: protruding through walls, floors and ceilings, combined with pieces of furniture, broken up into fragments of bodies still connected by long threads that were drawn-out nerves.

Then the city was on the move again, folding, distorting, sliding together like some shapeless, living monster from the ocean's ooze.

Shiu Kung-Chien, watching a monitor of the tapes on a small screen set into the sphere's pedestal, chose that moment to cut the playback, before there was any risk of Ascar suffering psychosomatic damage.

He switched on the sphere's internal light and opened the hatch. Leard Ascar staggered forth, his face haggard and his breath coming in gasps.

'I think that will do,' Shiu said mildly. 'It gets worse, but we don't want to make a psychiatric case out of you.'

'It gets worse?'

'Yes. What you experienced were the effects of the initial approach of an alien time field. By the time it was all over our population had actually been decimated. We might not have got off so lightly, had the Oblique Intelligence itself, being also able to manipulate time, not taken steps to alter its direction.'

Ascar hung on to the edge of the hatch. 'And this is what it's going to be like on Earth?' he wanted to know.

'Oh, on your planet it will be incomparably worse than anything that happened here. Ours was merely a glancing blow, scarcely more than a close passage. What it will be like for you is scarcely conceivable.'

'Holy Mother Earth!' whispered Ascar hoarsely.

10

Hwen Wu's cabinet ministers sat gazing impassively at the two Earthmen, their expressions mild, faintly supercilious. Rond Heshke found this detached look, which the people of Retort City invariably wore, somewhat unnerving. It was as if they weren't really interested in one at all.

'So you understand, I hope, the situation that faces your planet,' Hwen Wu said calmly, conversationally, as though he were discussing how they might spend an idle hour or two. 'We in Retort City have been aware of it for some months, ever since Shiu Kung-Chien made a chance survey in that direction. That's why we put a space-timeship in orbit around Earth to make detailed observations.'

'How come our people never detected your ship?' Ascar asked sharply. 'Our tracking stations keep watch on the whole solar system.'

'Its orbit was elliptical in time, I believe,' the Prime Minister told him, 'swinging not only around the planet in space but also from the past to the future and from the future to the past. Your surveillance stations would never have picked it up.'

'Ingenious,' Ascar murmured to himself.

Hwen Wu continued. 'Recently we decided to offer Earth what assistance we could afford. For this, since we're racially unacceptable to your ideology, we needed emissaries your government would trust. That explains your presence here in Retort City: our observers watched your tragic journey through non-time and decided you'd be most suitable. You're both eminent personages on Earth and were already to some degree acquainted with the facts.'

'What is it you want us to do?' asked Heshke.

'Merely return to Earth and make representations to your government, advising them of the facts and the help we can offer.'

'And just what form of help is that?' Ascar demanded, frowning doubtfully.

'The only solution for your civilization lies in the style of life we've adopted,' Hwen Wu said. 'By that, I mean a life in space, lived in artificial cities. You must get off the planet before the disaster strikes.'

Heshke was aghast. 'But that's practically impossible. We can't possible take *everyone* off!'

'Not everyone, true. But we'll be able to help you. Our productive facilities are as great, if not greater, than those of your civilization. We're able to put our Production Retort – the lower half of our city – through cycles of time, so that it can go through several production periods where an Earth factory would go through only one.'

'We'll show you how to construct your space cities,' an aged, venerable minister put in, 'and add our resources to your own.'

Hwen Wu nodded in agreement. 'The two time systems won't meet for generations yet. We should be able to establish, perhaps, two hundred million people in space. It might even be greater, but—' he waved a hand negligently – 'we'll also be making a similar offer to the civilization which unhappily is to be in collision with yours, and probably the Production Retort will be working to capacity.'

'Two hundred million people – that's only a fraction of the population of Earth.'

'But enough to allow your culture to continue, surely. We're motivated, in part, by a desire not to see interesting cultures destroyed needlessly.'

'Interesting cultures?' echoed Heshke in bewilderment. 'But do you not realize that by the norms of *my* culture *you* are biological perversions? Freaks? And should be exterminated? And you want to help *us*?'

'Your religious beliefs don't influence us in any way,' replied Hwen Wu in his usual cold but cultivated voice. 'We're swayed by reason, by what's possible, but not, I hope, by passion.'

'It won't work,' said Ascar, an acid, final note in his voice. 'The Titanium Legions just won't hear of it. The Earth is a goddess to them. They won't desert her in any circumstances.'

'I fear Ascar may be right,' Heshke sighed. 'Is there no other way? You're masters of time: can't you do something to prevent the collision from taking place at all?'

'You ask the impossible,' Hwen Wu said. 'We're not masters to that degree! We're able to control a time field large enough to cover this city, yes – but one so large and powerful as either of the two on Earth? It would be like trying to move the Earth itself. Is that not so, Leard Ascar?'

'So Shiu Kung-Chien informs me,' complied Ascar dully.

'And what if my government *does* refuse?' Heshke asked.

Hwen Wu gave a small, delicate shrug. 'Then that's their affair. We'll take no further interest.'

He rose to his feet and waved his hand, signalling a cybernetic servitor. The machine rolled to a flimsy screen door and slid the panel aside.

'You won't return to Earth alone,' Hwen Wu said. 'One of our people will come with you, naturally, as our liaison. If your mission is successful he'll stay on Earth to help to co-ordinate our joint efforts.'

Into the room walked Hueh Su-Mueng.

Heshke reclined on a low couch, wiping his brow with ice cubes wrapped in a cloth. His head ached and he was tired. He needed a long rest; he was scheduled to leave for Earth tomorrow.

Tomorrow and tomorrow and tomorrow . . .

Time's illusion.

Nearby was a decanter of a light, peach-tinted wine, of which Heshke had taken a draught. It was refreshing on the tongue and had an invigorating effect, but he was in no mood to drink any more of it.

Ascar, however, sloshed it back with gusto. 'I think it's very bad of you,' Heshke reproved him, 'to back out at a time like this. In spite of your past actions, which have been awful enough, I'd have expected you to show a greater sense of responsibility, in the circumstances.'

The physicist had announced that he wouldn't be returning to Earth with Heshke. Shiu Kung-Chien had accepted him as a pupil; he washed his hands of Retort City's entire scheme for the sake of an academic career under the great master.

He guffawed to hear Heshke's protest. 'You know what the Titans are like,' he said. 'The whole enterprise is a lost cause. I'm too old to back any more lost causes – you're quite capable of conducting the fiasco by yourself.'

Perhaps he's right, Heshke thought to himself. I've suffered enough mental upheavals myself lately. Someone as unbalanced as Ascar probably *would* react by turning his back on everything, his whole race, his whole planet.

Not that Heshke could count himself as a racist any more. As an archaeologist, he had taken good care to delve into Retort City's version of Earth history. Theirs wasn't archaeological inference, it was recorded fact. And the fact was that there never had been an alien interventionist invasion, never had been such a thing as True Man. Human civilization had risen and fallen into barbarism again and again of its own accord, that being its pattern. The elders of Retort City claimed that theirs was the only system that wasn't subject to that pattern, the only one that could preserve itself for millennium after millennium. As for the deviant subspecies, Heshke knew now that Blare Oblomot's version of their arising had been the correct one. It was a natural tendency for species to radiate into diverse subspecies. Usually, when there was global communications, so much interbreeding took place that the different strains all merged. But some time ago, after one particularly violent collapse, geographical groups of men had been isolated from one another for a lengthy period. The natural mutation rate had been accelerated by radiation left over from a series of nuclear wars, and they had evolved into distinct races.

And the subspecies to which Heshke belonged – known in Titan racial science as True Man – didn't particularly resemble the *homo sapiens* that had existed, say, thirty thousand years ago, any more than the others did. It was simply the one that had come out on top.

'I wonder if Hwen Wu's scheme extends to rescuing the dev cultures, too,' he mused, dropping his futile attempt to make Ascar feel ashamed of himself. 'Did you know there's an organized underground on Earth, opposed to the Titans and trying to help the devs?'

Ascar grimaced. 'Yeah, I know of them. The Pan-humanic League. A bunch of nuts.'

'Well, I suppose the devs are pretty well beyond any kind of help now, anyway.' He put down the ice and wiped his brow with a towel. 'Tell me, Leard, what do you think of our hosts?'

'What do I think of them? Why, they're brilliant, of course!'

'I'm not sure I like them. There's something cold about them. Something too logical, too sophisticated. They're effete, over-cultured . . . without any real compassion.'

Ascar grunted. 'You sound like a Titan education tape.'

'Perhaps. But have you learned how their social system works? How they give up their children to be brought up as workers and technicians?' Heshke could remember the horror and revulsion he had felt when the system had first been explained to him. The two retorts were phased differently in time. The children of the Leisure Retort, taken from their parents at birth, were passed back twenty-five years in time. They grew up and usually, at the age of about twenty-five years, had children of their own . . . which were passed to the Leisure Retort. People gave up their babies and *on the same day* received a baby in return . . . their grandchild.

'I think it's fascinating,' Ascar said, a rare smile coming to his features. 'They play all kinds of tricks with time. They oscillate the Production Retort through phases, sending it on cycles – not just forward and backward but sideways in some way, in other dimensions . . . You know what this means? Here in the Leisure Retort you can order something that takes six months to make, and it's delivered five minutes later. Shiu Kung-Chien does it all the time. Beautiful!'

'Beautiful if you're Shiu Kung-Chien!' Heshke said angrily. 'What if you're the man who has to spend his life satisfying these people's whims?' It all made the Titans' plans for humanity – True Man, anyway – seem just and compassionate, he thought. At least the Titans believed in a kind of rough democracy. And they believed in culture – even for the workers.

'Oh, they do all right,' Ascar said vaguely. 'They're looked after, they're happy. And anyway we're not down there, so what are you worried about?'

'If you don't mind,' Heshke said wearily, defeated by the man's single-minded narrowness, 'I'd like to get some sleep. We're starting early in the morning.'

'Oh. Well, don't say I didn't warn you.' Ascar backed out of the room. He didn't bother to say goodbye.

11

Outside the big room's windows the murmur of traffic rose up from the busy street below.

By the general standard of Titan appointments the room – Limnich's own private office – was not luxurious, almost drab. The Planetary Leader was renowned for his modest life-style, his retiring habits. His office was not even situated in Bupolbloc, but in a two-hundred-year-old building outside the newly-built administrative sector of the city. Here he kept his collection of skulls, his library of racist lore, and his other collections and paraphernalia.

In the past few days the office had been the scene of an unaccustomed surge of activity, disturbing the contemplative silences of its dark, varnished wood and its soft-piled carpets. Limnich himself confessed to being shaken to the core; there was no time for a dignified convention at the great castle. Everything had to be done now, on the spot. His office had become the nerve centre of the planet as he reorganized the Titanium Legions for the unprecedented struggle ahead.

Many of the old generals had gone, either retired or shunted to administrative roles requiring less initiative. Limnich had replaced them with younger men who had fresh, brilliant minds and newly-minted fervour – men like Colonel Brask (until the onset of the emergency he had been Captain Brask) who had been associated with the time project from the beginning. These were the type who now worked at the centre of things, preparing a colossal Armageddon in time.

Brask was with him now. On a wall screen behind Limnich's desk he taped a time map that had been drawn up to show the advance of the alien time-system on their own. The map was a moving one, dramatically demonstrating the speed of approach and the estimated point of impact.

Limnich's bones felt chill as he looked with awe upon the advancing wall of time. 'So we have nearly two centuries?' he said.

'To total impact, yes,' Brask told him. 'But the effects will be felt far before then. Our knowledge at this stage is still incomplete, but we estimate that the interference effects will become noticeable in about fifty years. After a hundred years, we aren't sure what our operational status will be. Perhaps zero.'

'Thank God we discovered the truth in time!'

He turned from the screen towards Brask. In the room's grey light the younger man's oddly deformed eyelid looked almost grotesque. In a less talented man that eyelid would have excluded him from the Titanium Legions altogether, but the exhaustive genealogical investigation every applicant underwent had shown the defect to have no genetic origin, and Limnich had let it pass.

In spite of his own fanaticism in that area, he did sometimes exercise leniency if there was an advantage in it. There was actually an officer in the new Command Team – a Colonel Yedrasch – who was part Lorene. But he was a ferocious fighter for True Man, even more so, it seemed, because of his knowledge of his mixed nature, and his services to the race were of such a high order that Limnich had decided (and the World President agreed with him) that he couldn't be dispensed with. Thus, instead of liquidation, Yedrasch had merely undergone a vasectomy to ensure that he could not defile the future blood of True Man.

An oak-panelled door opened. 'Colonel Hutt is here, Leader,' Limnich's secretary told him.

Limnich nodded curtly. Titan-Colonel Hutt entered. Both men gave the hooked-arm salute, then Limnich sat down.

'About the question of public information, Leader . . .'

Limnich nodded again. 'I've made a decision. The average man's intelligence is too limited to be able to comprehend the whole truth all at once. The public announcements are to give a more restricted idea of the nature of time: they will speak of an attack from the future, where the alien interventionists have established their second attempt to settle the Earth.'

'In other words, the public is to understand the matter as we ourselves did until recently,' Brask added. 'Later, when they've been further educated, the full facts can be made clear.'

'I understand,' Titan-Colonel Hutt said.

'There's one other point,' Limnich resumed. 'The emergency, the greatest that has ever faced mankind, will entail a big political crisis. All political work must be intensified. Dissident groups must be totally nullified. To this end, I order you to apprise the Panhumanic League of *all* the facts at our disposal, through our secret contacts.'

'*All* the facts, Leader?' Hutt echoed in dismay. 'But why?'

'What better way could there be of pulling the ground from under their feet?' Limnich said, his face fish-cold and unsmiling. 'It's a certain bet that the larger part of the League will defect and come over to us, once they know the truth.'

A look of dawning realization came over the other's face. 'Correct, Leader. That is so.' He was reassured to see that the old fox had not lost his grip, that Limnich's sense of manoeuvre was as subtle as ever.

Limnich, for his part, fought to snatch his mind back from the edge of madness. His brain filled yet again with a dreadful, incomprehensible vision of two onrushing time-systems encountering one another. He hadn't even begun to think how this looked from the aspect of the Earth Mother, a deity in whom he believed without question. He didn't even want to think about it.

'Thank God we discovered the truth in time!' he repeated in a low voice. But had that done any good? Could *anything* save them?

The approach to the future-Earth aliens was necessarily less incautious than that planned for the Titans. The task before Wang Yat-Sen and Li Li-San, the two young philosophers selected for it by the Prime Minister, was a delicate one.

Firstly they had to convince the lemur-like creatures that they were *not* from the civilization that was threatening them. This was no easy matter, since the aliens were, naturally, insensitive to fine differences of physique. But already the previous expedition had decoded the aliens' language (in fact, several languages) from electromagnetic transmissions and had prepared language-course tapes. Consequently Wang Yat-Sen and Li Li-San were fairly competent in the hesitant, chittering tongue, though their pronunciation brought them barely within the bounds of intelligibility.

Eventually the aliens were, it seemed, persuaded, and the two young men were taken from the prison-hospital (actually a biological research station) where they had been kept with the other human prisoners (and what they had seen being done to those prisoners was most distasteful).

Now they sat in a conically shaped room of bare stone. The aliens seemed to go in for bare stone, as well as for conical shapes in building, and all the doors were triangular, too low for a man to go through without bending. The furnishings of the room were sparse, made of square-cut unpolished timber and board. The aliens' technological achievements were not matched by any interest in interior decoration.

But the two individuals who faced the young men across the rough plank table were among the highest authorities in their society. Wang Yat-Sen gazed at them calmly, fascinated as usual by their nervous sensitivity. Anything was enough to set their fragile bodies to quivering, and their fine nose-whiskers to twitching and vibrating.

'And why should you make us this offer?' chittered one. 'Why should you go to such lengths to help us? How are we to know that this is not some devious trick?'

'To take your points one at a time,' Li Li-San answered,

'our readiness to give assistance merely demonstrates the good regard of one intelligent species for another. Your second point: guarantees of good faith can be arranged. Our offer applies also to the other, human civilization. If you both agree, then you'll be co-operating with one another instead of fighting.'

'We will, if you wish, take your ambassadors to our ISS,' Wang Yat-Sen put in equably. 'Then they'll see for themselves.'

The lemur-creature ignored this last. 'You expect us to retreat from the enemy? To abandon our planet?' he said, his vowel-sounds indicating considerable passion. His limbs were trembling visibly, like those of a mortally wounded animal. 'It's *our* planet, ours since the beginning of time. We'll defend it to the last.'

The other lemur-creature joined in. 'Never do we retreat from an enemy. A few days ago they – your biological cousins – launched an attack upon two of our large cities, using weapons, which, judging by the intensity of the energy produced, relied upon the fusion of light atomic nuclei. Our cities were utterly destroyed and there is radioactive waste for distances all around. But we'll strike back! We'll strike back!'

Both men from Retort City, brought up to regard everything in a detached and clinical manner, were puzzled. 'But surely you realize that your emotional attitude towards your historical habitat is inappropriate in the current situation,' Wang Yat-Sen put forward. 'Your "enemy", as you put it, is merely reacting in the same manner, and to attacks you've made on him. Evacuation is the only hope for either of you.'

'We don't accept that it's the only hope,' chittered the lemur-leader shrilly. 'We know that enemy life-forms lie in our future, and that if they continue to exist, we'll perish. Therefore – we'll deal with it!'

'But how?' Li Li-San asked simply.

'We're developing viruses destructive to all life in the enemy *biota*,' the lemur said. 'We'll sow these viruses on a massive scale. By the time our time-system reaches the projected collision point, all trace of life in the enemy biosphere will be gone. There'll be nothing to obstruct the passage of our own time-wave.'

Glancing at one another, Wang Yat-Sen and Li Li-San saw from each other's expressions that they both concluded that their mission had failed. They stood up.

'Apparently your decisions are not guided by rationality and we take it that you reject our offer,' Wang Yat-Sen announced, still using the 'friendly' mode of speech. 'There is, then, nothing more to detain us. With your permission we'll call down our space lighter and return to our people.'

'Oh, no!' squeaked the lemur. 'You're not returning anywhere with information that can be used against us. You're of the same race as our enemy – so back to the bio-research unit with you!'

And so the two young men were transported back to the Biological Warfare Station, which they were never to leave.

As soon as he entered the cellar complex, Sobrie Oblomot knew that something was extraordinarily wrong.

This time the Council meeting was to have been in Sannan, Sobrie's native city. These ancient cellars were completely unknown to the authorities; they had been sealed over during a rebuilding programme years ago. The hidden entrances were few, and known only to trusted League agents.

A printing press was run down here and Sobrie was struck, first of all, by its silence: never before had he known it not to be clattering away. And yet the place was gripped by a sense of feverish excitement: the whitewashed brick walls almost visibly shone with it.

Groups of people stood around, talking with agitation. A small thin man wormed his way between them and rushed up to Sobrie.

'Oblomot! You're here!'

'What's going on?' Sobrie said with deference.

'If I were you,' the small man said in a low voice, 'I'd get out – now. And take your girlfriend with you. Because—'

But he was interrupted by the convener, who appeared suddenly at Sobrie's elbow. 'So you made it, Oblomot. You're late. We'd thought you might already have heard.'

'Heard what?'

'The news is all over the networks. Right across the globe. It looks like the end.'

To Sobrie's bewildered demands for enlightenment he responded merely by guiding him across the floor and through a low archway. A door opened, closed again once Sobrie was through.

The Panhumanic Council was sitting. Eyes turned to regard Sobrie sombrely. They weren't all there, he realized; about a third were missing.

With a start, he noticed that one of the faces was unfamiliar. It was the anonymous member, sitting for the first time without mask or voice modifier!

What could have brought about such a change in policy? Curiously he studied the face. It was striking: a strong, clear face with much character, fair-skinned, blue-eyed, flaxen-haired – it was such a perfect example of the Titan ideal that its owner just *had* to be a Titan. That was it: he was a high-ranking, famous Titan officer who also happened to be secretly a member of the Panhumanic League. Sobrie vaguely recalled seeing his face, now. He was one of the idolized heroes who appeared on the covers of glossy magazines, on vidcast pageants and the like.

'Sit down, Oblomot,' the Chairman said, his voice heavy with strain.

'Incredible!' was Sobrie's reaction. 'It's just unbelievable.'

'Unbelievable but true.'

'Can we be sure? Suppose it's just another Titan story? An invention?'

'It's true enough,' the once-anonymous member said. 'It comes from two sources. The Titans have intentionally passed the information to the League, through contacts they have. But I'm able to confirm it independently, through my position in the Legions. The consternation among ourselves is nothing compared with what's going on there, I assure you.'

Without the voice modifier the Titan's voice was strong and resonant, mature but somehow still youthful. 'I don't really understand all that scientific stuff you just read out,' Sobrie said to the Chairman. 'But is that literally true – that we'll all be annihilated? By an alien . . . time-wave . . . from the future?'

'Not only us, but all life on Earth. Unless we can find a way to stop it.'

'And where does that leave us – the League?'

'That's what we were discussing before you came in,' the Chairman told him after a heavy pause. 'It's no good denying that what we thought was Titan paranoia has, in the event, been vindicated. We *are* threatened by an alien power, albeit in a form so weird and overwhelming that the Titans could never have foreseen it. Our own objectives now seem futile, not to say insignificant . . .'

'The League must disband itself voluntarily and go over to the Titans,' a voice said. 'That will happen anyway, among the greater part of our membership.'

'Those of us who failed to attend this meeting doubtless have already taken that step,' the Chairman added.

Sobrie was shocked by this talk. To talk of joining forces with the hated Titans! To abandon the age-old goal of racial equality!

'But we *can't* do that!' he protested. 'We have a sacred mission!'

The Titan spoke. 'As I see it, there is very little choice. It's not a matter of saving threatened subspecies any more. It's a matter of the survival of mankind. I, who have lived with the Titans all my life, and have always hated them, now see that only they can save us. They're the only hope for humanity: from now on I'll be a loyal Titan officer.'

Sobrie's wasn't the only voice to express dismay at the way things were going. Two others broke in together, making angry denunciations of this betrayal of their ideals.

Sobrie added his own accusations. 'And what of the dev subspecies?' he flared. 'The Amhraks, the Urukuri and the others? Are they to be abandoned?'

'Regrettably, they must go by the board,' the un-masked Titan said evenly. 'They're too trivial to deserve our attention in a crisis of such proportions as this. It's humanity, not any particular subspecies, that's at stake.'

Voices rose in violent argument. And faces that had long grown hard in a life of continuous plotting began to show their determination, one way or the other.

Sobrie was not sure how, or when, shooting broke out. Guns seemed to appear in several hands at once. A bullet caught the Titan in the chest and he went down, slumping against the table, his handsome, clean-cut face sagging in extreme nervous shock. Shots exploded deafeningly. The Chairman, even as he squeezed the trigger, was hit in the shoulder and spun around with a snarl of pain.

Somewhat belatedly Sobrie produced his own gun, ducking below the level of the table, only to see that all the voices that had been added to his side of the argument had been silenced, their owners dead.

He ripped open his shirt, plunged his hand inside, and slowly rose.

Guns were trained on him. He took his hand from his shirt and held up the s-grenade he had taken from his body-pouch.

'Don't move, anyone,' he said in a strained voice, 'or we all get it.'

Step by step he backed to the door, their eyes watching him blankly. In seconds he had reached it, flung it open and then was racing through the cavernous cellars.

White faces, shocked by the sound of gunfire, stared

at him, their mouths black holes. He waved the gun and shoved people aside, strangely aware that no pursuit was, as yet, being organized. No more than twenty seconds passed before he had reached the nearest exit. He plunged into it, up the dank tunnel, pounding along it for yard after yard.

The tunnel ended in a concealed door which opened on to yet another cellar beneath a disused warehouse. Sobrie presently emerged in a side street in an outlying district of Sannan. He hurried from the spot to more populated streets, and stopped at the first vidbooth.

Layella's face came up on the screen. Her eyes widened at the sight of him.

'Hello. What is it?'

'Layella, get out of the apartment right away.'

Alarm showed on her features. 'What?'

'Get out of there *this minute*. Don't wait to take anything – just as much money as you can snatch up.' He thought for a moment. 'Meet me under the clock in Kotsin Square. Have you got that?'

Her face became pale, but calm. 'Yes.'

'Right.' He killed the screen, and a moment later was pacing the busy street, his mind racing, trying to figure the situation from all angles. They'd have to leave Sannan, and quickly. They could go – my God, where? Everything was in turmoil. Already the networks would be breaking open; there'd be almost nothing left.

He took a tubeway and came up some distance from Kotsin Square. Making a rough calculation of how long it would take Layella to get there, he walked slowly the rest of the way. When he arrived she was already waiting, looking nervous and fidgety, dressed in a drab brown coat.

'Where are we going?' she asked, looking at him with round, Amhrak eyes.

'We'll go to Jorb Gandatt,' he said. 'He'll help us.' Some of the League was bound to survive, he told himself. There were bound to be some diehards, like himself and Jorb, who wouldn't surrender. Enough would pull through so that some kind of organization remained.

He felt sure that Jorb was trustworthy and that he'd be able to help them. The Sannan circuit (his own circuit, he thought ruefully, the one he commanded) would be entirely blown, but Jorb didn't belong to it; he was one of Sobrie's contacts with the outside. He might be able to tell them where to go to be safe.

She took his arm as they crossed the square. At first he didn't notice that the entrance to Kotsin Square seemed a little crowded, or the grey van, without any insignia or designation, that was parked unobtrusively to one side of the square. But just before they entered the throng they were both taken roughly by the arms and propelled towards the vehicle.

The back of the van was open. Inside sat a pudgy little man who had been scanning the square through a set of periscopes. Sobrie realized, with a sudden jump of his heart, that they'd fallen into one of those Titan devices one heard about but never met: a roving racial street-check. And the pudgy man was that half-legendary figure, the dev expert: one who could tell a dev or a part-dev at a glance.

The dev expert looked Layella up and down as though she were something dirty. 'She's one all right,' he said in an acid, slightly nasal voice. 'I don't know how she's got away with it so long.'

Sobrie gave a strangled cry. Whether he'd have had the nerve to use his s-grenade, thus killing Layella too, he'd never know. Because two plain clothes Titans held him with arms outspread, while one reached under his shirt and yanked out the deadly device.

'Interesting,' murmured Limnich. 'And Leard Ascar is still out there, you say?'

'Yes, Leader,' said Heshke.

'Hmm. Of course, we've always known there was a possibility of human settlements existing out among the

stars – some of them perhaps dev. There are indications
of interstellar flight in the records of the Pundish Aeon –
but you know that, of course, Citizen Heshke.'

'Yes, Leader,' Heshke said again, slightly embarrassed.
Planetary Leader Limnich was, as Heshke had found
during meetings with him earlier in his career, obsessive
about anything bearing on the history of True Man.
His knowledge of archaeological detail came close to
challenging Heshke's own.

Heshke faced Limnich across the latter's massive desk,
and was spoken to respectfully by him. Hueh Su-Mueng
was also present, but was forced to sit in the corner,
flanked by two guards. Planetary Leader Limnich cast
him a disdainful glance every now and then, plainly
disliking to have the dev in his office.

'And what do *you* make of this plan of theirs, Heshke?
What's their ulterior motive?'

'I sincerely believe they have no ulterior motive,
Leader,' Heshke told him frankly. 'They evidently have
no designs on Earth, indeed no direct interest in our planet
at all. Strange though it may seem, they're prompted simply by the urge to help a neighbour in distress.'

'The fiendishly clever Chink,' Limnich muttered audi-
bly, nodding to himself as if with some inner satisfaction.

'Yes, I've heard the phrase before,' Heshke said stiffly.

Behind Limnich stood Colonel Brask, looking on the
scene much as Heshke recalled him doing on that day in
Titan-Major Brourne's office. The looks he gave Hueh,
however, displayed undisguised loathing.

'And how did you find it, living with . . . the Chinks?'
Brask asked him.

Heshke squirmed uncomfortably. 'They are . . . not
like us,' he admitted.

'Indeed not.'

'I was impressed, however, by how much they could
help us,' Heshke added.

Brask gave a smile of wintry sarcasm, and Limnich
replied: 'Whatever their intentions were, their scheme

has come unstuck this time. Surely you're aware, Citizen Heshke, that we'll never give up our efforts to hold Earth for True Man. The son doesn't desert his mother, even to save his own life – and no matter how dire the peril to them both. We're building up our power to defend our birthright. That defence will be total – desperate, perhaps – but overwhelming. Titan-Colonel Brask here, as it happens, is in charge of the formation of the Titanium Legions of Kronos, named after the ancient god of time, that will enable us – already are enabling us – to strike across the centuries. *He* can tell you that we're not beaten yet.'

'But you know the nature of the catastrophe that's coming!' Heshke exploded. 'It's a *natural* catastrophe, not due to any living enemy. How are you going to deal with that?'

'We already have a plan,' Brask told him loftily.

'And what's that? I'm fascinated!' Despite being in the presence of such charismatically high rank, Heshke couldn't keep the sarcasm out of his voice.

'Our aim is to effect the total annihilation of the enemy's biosphere. By means of a massive nuclear attack we'll eradicate all life, so that not a microbe remains. Their time-system is associated with the existence of life: consequently, by removing that time-wave, which will die with the death of alien life, we remove the impediment to our own existence.'

Heshke twisted around to look questioningly at Hueh Su-Mueng. But the Retort City technician merely shrugged. He turned back to Brask.

'If you're letting off thousands of fusion explosions—'

'Hundreds of thousands,' Brask interrupted tonelessly.

'—if you're doing that four centuries in the future, what happens when *our* time reaches that point? Aren't we going to be headed into all those explosions?'

Brask smiled faintly. 'That's one of the peculiar things about time. By the "time" we get there the effects will have died away – provided we *do* succeed in cancelling out the enemy time-front. If we don't, it won't matter anyway.'

348 *Collision with Chronos*

Noting Heshke's incomprehension, he added: 'I know it sounds odd, but that's how time works, apparently.'

Heshke looked again at Hueh, who nodded. 'He's quite right – *provided* the reversed time-system were to be destroyed.'

'Can you now doubt our determination?' Limnich said in his low, fruity voice. 'The coming struggle may be the acme of our glory. Let all who come against us know—' He clenched his fists spasmodically, and Heshke thought he actually saw him, as in fact Limnich had done many times, draw himself back from the edge of madness.

Are we an insane race? Heshke wondered darkly. Perhaps so. Perhaps it's good that all is lost. And, in those very thoughts, he thought he detected then the emergence of the death-wish that Blare Oblomot had once claimed pervaded Titan mentality.

'Thank you for seeing us, Planetary Leader,' he said humbly.

'Your adventure has been so extraordinary that I could do no less,' Limnich responded with a touch of graciousness. He rang a little gold bell that lay on his desk. 'Escort these two back to Bupolbloc,' he ordered to the extra guards who came in.

In the subterranean levels of Bupolbloc, as Heshke and Hueh were being taken to their adjacent cells, the archaeologist suddenly pulled up short. Coming along the corridor, also under escort, was someone who, after a momentary start of false recognition, he realized was a person he had met but once: Blare Oblomot's brother, Sobrie.

'Oblomot!' he exclaimed.

The other looked at him for a moment, and then smiled bleakly. Their guards made to goad both of them along, but Heshke turned angrily. 'I demand to be allowed to talk to this man! I'm not exactly a prisoner, you know!'

'True,' said one of the guards indifferently. 'Citizen Heshke is in custodial detention only. And he has the ear of the Planetary Leader.'

The guards eyed one another for a moment, and then one of then pushed open a door. 'In here.' And because they didn't want to split the escort, Hueh Su-Mueng was prodded inside too. The guards stood by the door, eyeing their wards, swinging their batons.

Heshke found it easy to ignore them. After some diffidence he explained how he had seen Blare die, but Sobrie merely nodded dismally: he already knew.

In a rush of words Sobrie told him everything that had happened: his involvement with the Panhumanic League, his part-Amhrak girl-friend, their arrest and how they'd been brought here to Bupolbloc in Pradna.

'They're trying to make a deal with me,' he finished bitterly. 'They want to mop up the Panhumanic League once and for all. If I put the finger on enough League members who haven't so far defected they'll let Layella live on the Amhrak reservation instead of . . . putting her down like a dog.'

'Could you do that?'

'I could, but . . . oh, God . . .'

Heshke gave a sad sigh. 'Well, at least they show a *trace* of civilized conduct,' he said gently. 'They could have used third degree.'

Sobrie looked at him, startled, and then laughed incredulously. 'You don't think they have scruples, do you? It's a matter of time, that's all! They're so busy now that the torture facilities at Bupolbloc Two are being overworked. They don't want to wait while I stand in line!'

One other item of deference Heshke had wrung from the Titans was that he and Hueh were in connected cells, so that they could talk to one another. They held a brief conversation after leaving Sobrie Oblomot.

'I feel sorry for them both,' Heshke said. 'They're in a hopeless position . . . the Titans will do just what they like with them. This is an evil world, Su-Mueng.'

'All worlds have their evils,' Su-Mueng observed.

'Perhaps. At any rate, I'm too old for the kind of role I've been expected to play lately. I've done what I can; now I just want to be left alone.' Heshke was lying on his pallet. He closed his eyes.

'This plan your friends have won't work,' Su-Mueng told him. 'They make a basic mistake: the time-wave isn't dependent on organic life, it's the other way around. Biological organization is a by-product of a time-system, not a cause of it.'

'So?'

'It will make no difference if they destroy an entire biosphere: the time-wave will come rolling on just the same.'

'Just so,' said Heshke faintly. 'What can I do about it?'

Moments later he was asleep.

Although it was late into the night, Limnich was still at his desk, poring over the genealogical charts of Titan officers who had come under suspicion. Racial vigilance within Earth's elite force was something in which he took a personal interest.

Outside, the murmur of traffic had lapsed into silence, broken only by the drone of an occasional car, and all was quiet. But suddenly Limnich jerked bolt upright and gasped with shock.

There, standing before him in the half-darkened office, was the dev Chink Heshke had brought back with him from space.

Limnich wouldn't have believed it possible for anyone to penetrate the building uninvited; the Chink seemed to have materialized out of thin air. He snatched up a pistol that always lay on a shelf under the lip of his desk, and pointed it at the intruder's stomach with trembling fingers.

'How in the Mother's name did you get in here?' he rasped.

'By being fiendishly clever,' Su-Mueng said with a smile, remembering Limnich's earlier remark.

In point of fact his entrance had been made without the least difficulty. For while the Titans had made a thorough search of his person, they had failed to find a number of gadgets which had been strapped to his body *in past time*. Phased one minute into the past, these had been quite undetectable. To make one available, Su-Mueng merely brought it forward into the present.

Chief among these gadgets was a compact personal time-displacer, like the larger, clumsier version he had used to escape from the Production Retort. He had phased *himself* one minute back in time, sprung the lock tumblers on the door of his cell, and simply walked out of Bupolbloc. He had made his way here to Limnich's office, walked unseen past guards and secretaries, and once he was in Limnich's presence phased himself back into normative time.

How to explain this to Limnich, to whom his sudden appearance must smack of magic? 'I have a device which renders me invisible,' he offered casually. 'Please don't be alarmed, Planetary Leader – I'm not here to do you harm. I have a proposal to make, which I hope will work to our mutual advantage.'

Limnich kept his gun trained on the dev, trying to control the revulsion that being in the presence of the creature caused him. His free hand strayed to the golden bell that would summon help. But then his sense of calculation overcame his natural feelings. He withdrew his hand and leaned back, looking up into the svelte young Chink's repugnantly inhuman face.

'Go on,' he purred.

'Your civilization is in deep trouble, Planetary Leader,' Su-Mueng said easily. 'Your planned hydrogen bomb attack on the future-Earth aliens may destroy an enemy, but that will be all. The basic problem will remain: hydrogen bombs *won't* wipe out a powerful time-stream.'

Limnich listened carefully to his words, and appeared to take them seriously.

'Indeed? Well, we'll have made progress, nevertheless. And we still have fifty years, perhaps a hundred years, in which to deal with the situation . . .' His words trailed off broodingly, and his eyes left Su-Mueng's face. He gazed down at his desk, apparently forgetting the gun in his hand.

'Let me tell you something of ISS Retort City,' Su-Mueng said. 'It has a social system which is inhuman, unjust and cruel. Do you know why I was chosen for this mission to Earth? Because I'm a renegade, an embarrassment to the masters of my city. They were glad of the chance to get rid of me – because I'll do *anything* to change things as they are there.'

Limnich gave an explosive grunt. 'They get everywhere!'

'Hah?' Su-Mueng inclined his head enquiringly.

'Subversives. Like worms in the woodwork. All societies are riddled with them. But how does this concern me? Be brief; I have much work to do.'

'Don't you realize,' Su-Mueng said softly, 'what an asset Retort City could be to you? Its industrial capacity is enormous: it could double the output of your whole planet. Besides this, you have much to gain from Retort technology. Our control over the forces of time is far in advance of your own.' He held up a smooth ovoid object that fitted into the palm of his hand. 'How do you think I was able to make myself invisible and enter your office unseen? I'll show you how to invade and occupy Retort City if, in return, you'll wipe out its social system and allow a more equitable one to replace it.'

Limnich finally put down his gun. 'How could we invade it?' he asked, his eyes bulging behind his round lenses. 'I understand it lies some light-years away.'

'Not only that, it's removed in time as well. But you have rocket-driven spaceships, do you not? They'll suffice. I'll show your technicians how to make space-time devices for them – I am,' he added incidentally, 'a fully trained engineer. With perhaps thirty or forty such ships, carrying a few thousand well-armed men, the city could be taken.'

The Planetary Leader became deeply thoughtful, considering this remarkable offer from all angles. A feeling of excitement grew in him as he realized the vast benefits that could accrue.

Hueh Su-Mueng's enormous treachery didn't surprise him in the least. The creature was a Chink, following his natural tendencies. Also, Rond Heshke's report on the dev city confirmed his claims.

'Very well, it's agreed,' he said abruptly. 'You'll have what you ask for – provided things go as you promise.'

A look of triumph came suddenly over the dev's face, quickly to be followed by his usual blandness.

'Now that matters have reached this stage, perhaps I might add one more condition?' he said. 'Rond Heshke, whom I've come to look upon as a good man, is saddened by the plight of two friends of his who are being held in Bupolbloc: Sobrie Oblomot and Layella Frauk. Instead of having them put to death, allow them to live on the reservation as he hopes for them.'

'What? *You* dare to make petty conditions?' Limnich glowered to find himself being dictated to by this subhuman. 'Do you think we depend on your goodwill? More of this and I'll simply *torture* co-operation out of you.' And the ugly look on his face showed that he meant what he said.

'Remember, we are not as you are,' Su-Mueng said coldly. 'Perhaps I can withstand torture. And have you not asked yourself why I'm doing all this? I alone of all my people seem to know the meaning of strong human relationships. That's why I feel for the man and the girl in Bupolbloc – they have such a relationship. Such a bond. There was a bond between my father and myself, and he was put to death for it. *That* is why I'm doing this – because I am a son to my father. *You* can understand that, can't you? Your people aren't strangers to these feelings.'

Limnich didn't answer immediately. But for the first time the hint of a smile, even of amicability, came to his features.

'Yes,' he said sardonically. 'I can understand that.'

'There's one other small problem,' Su-Mueng said with a frown, a few days later.

'And what's that?' Limnich leaned back, strangely at ease. In spite of the physical revulsion he still felt for the Chink (at first he'd been obliged to stifle an impulse to vomit), alongside with that revulsion he found that he derived a perverse pleasure from their dealings together. It was spicy, like having truck with the devil.

'The ship that brought us here is still in orbit around Earth. It would certainly spot our armada.'

'Can't we destroy it?'

'Possibly, but it's doubtful. And if we failed, it would return immediately to warn Retort City. By the time *we* got there, we'd find them prepared.'

'Then we need to get it out of the way. I suggest you contact the ship and tell it to return to base forthwith.'

'They wouldn't go without either myself or Rond Heshke. That would be against all protocol.' For once Su-Mueng was at a loss.

'So? Send Heshke,' said Limnich impatiently. He didn't like to be upset by such details.

'Apparently he doesn't want to go either.'

'Hmm.' Limnich pondered. 'Can *he* contact this ship?'

'He could if I gave him my communicator.'

'Good. Then I'll make him *want* to go. You asked for some friends of his to be sent to a dev reservation, didn't you? Well, they will be – and *he* can join them.'

'I don't understand.'

The Planetary Leader gave a humourless smile. 'The dev reservations are to be closed down within the next few weeks, their inmates liquidated. I'll see that he gets an advance warning. *That* should send him screaming for your orbiting spaceship.'

Su-Mueng was uneasy. 'I don't like using him as a pawn . . .'

'All men are pawns,' Limnich purred. 'When he leaves for the reservations, give him your communicator. Urge him to call the ship to take him off, so he can make a report to your city on his mission. But no hint of what we're really about, mind.' He eyed Su-Mueng speculatively. 'Maybe you Chinks aren't so clever after all.'

12

The sun was setting on a dusty yellowish landscape broken only by bare, bone-like trees and scattered houses of brick or mud. Rond Heshke, sitting on a verandah backed by a neat bungalow of red brick, looked upon the scene with an unexpected feeling of calm and peace.

Herrick, the Amhrak who owned the bungalow in which Heshke, Sobrie and Layella were staying came walking towards the building with easy strides, his body swinging characteristically, and Heshke found that even the sudden sight of a full-blooded dev didn't upset his contentment.

At first it had been a tremendous shock to him. He'd been angry and bewildered that he, a respectable citizen with a certificate of racial purity, could be summarily packed off to a dev reservation. His protests had been ignored and he'd gathered that it was because of his friendship with the Oblomot family. After all, Sobrie was being banished too, simply because of his association with Layella. Yes, it had been shocking, at first, to be thrown in with the Amhraks. Had not his experiences with the Chinks already prepared him to some degree, he was sure he might have gone insane.

But now . . . Herrick mounted the steps of the verandah. He was wholly, unstintingly Amhrak. He had the red skin, the compact, round head, the round eyes and the foreign,

big-lobed ears. His body, too, had all the disturbing oddness of proportion and of lank, too-easy movement. And it
didn't bother Heshke at all. It seemed entirely natural for
him to accept Herrick as a charming member of a charming
people – all the more so, perhaps, because they represented
a now dying culture.

'Hello, Rond,' Herrick said with a heavy Amhrak
accent. 'Is Sobrie in?'

Heshke nodded and Herrick swept inside without
the usual pleasantries. Heshke continued looking at
the receding sun, reflecting on how well the surviving
Amhraks had adapted to their circumstances. There were
three million of them on this reserve, which measured
about two hundred miles across (and yet they had once
populated two continents). Most of the land was as
Heshke saw it now, arid and useless for cultivation, but
the Amhraks had solved that by turning to hydroponics.
They had organized themselves into a comprehensive
little community, with several small-to-middling towns,
and had resurrected a modest amount of industry – all
small-scale, just enough for their needs. They were all
very much aware that their existence was contingent upon
the whim of their conquerors.

While Heshke had known that the Amhraks were
technically advanced, he'd always thought this to be
due to their copying the inventions of True Man, and
it had surprised him, while staying with Herrick, to
discover how inventive they were in their own right.
Herrick often reminisced about the Amhrak war, when
he'd been a young scientist working for the Amhrak's
last attempt at defence. He'd been involved, typically,
in a project that never reached fruition – a force screen
to ward off nuclear warheads.

'The reason why you Whites were able to win,' he'd told
Heshke (Whites being the Amhrak term for True Man),
'is that you have such a capacity for submitting to a central
authority, which makes you able to organize yourselves all
in one direction. Our social organization was too loose to be

able to stand up to you. Even at the end our energies were being dissipated in countless unco-ordinated projects.'

'I can't accept that explanation,' Heshke had objected. 'What about the Lorenes?'

'True, the Lorenes had this ability to an ever greater degree. But then, we helped you to defeat the Lorenes. You wouldn't have done it alone.'

And to that Heshke had no answer. It was strange, talking to someone whose picture of history didn't follow the Titan version of True Man versus the rest. In official histories past alliances with other subspecies were always played down, and it was never admitted that they could have been important for the outcome. True Man had saved himself unaided, so the text ran, from numerous horrible enemies.

Heshke had soon ceased to battle with contending concepts; it was a relief to be away from it all.

Sometimes he watched Herrick as the Amhrak tinkered, using whatever components he could get his hands on, with an old project of his that had been interrupted by the war: television without any transmitter or camera, only a receiver. Herrick had discovered that by means of a long-range interference technique light-waves could be converted, at a distance, into radio or UHF waves, and these could then be picked up at the control station. In other words it was possible to snatch pictures out of thin air from hundreds of miles away. Heshke would sit with Herrick for hours while he fiddled with his crackling apparatus, occasionally getting a fuzzy, briefly recognizable picture of a mountaintop or a stretch of ocean. There was little control over where the pictures came from, as this apparently depended on the Earth's magnetic field.

The sun slipped down the horizon. Heshke began to feel cold. He got up, stretched himself, and went inside.

Herrick and Sobrie were seated at a table, both looking grim and sober – Sobrie more so, Heshke thought. He looked up as the archaeologist came in.

'Bad news, I'm afraid, Rond.' He gestured to Herrick. 'We've just heard from Pradna.'

'You can still do that?'

Sobrie nodded. 'In the past few weeks we've been able to pick up with whatever remnants of the League survived the mass defection to the Titans. Slowly, they're putting themselves together again and thanks to that we still have contacts inside the administration.'

He paused. Heshke, in fact, had been impressed by how easily Sobrie had been able to make arrangements for them in Amhrak country. The Panhumanic League's networks apparently extended right into most of the dev reservations; Herrick himself was involved in it.

'Limnich has ordered all reservations to be terminated,' Sobrie said quietly. 'It's the end of the road for the Amhraks, for all of us.'

'We always knew it would happen sooner or later,' Herrick said without bitterness. 'All we can do is accept it.'

Heshke, too, had suspected that this might be coming on.

He reached into his pocket and took out the little communicator Su-Mueng had given him. That young man might have had some intimation of what was impending, too. How else to explain his embarrassed, evasive manner at their last meeting, when he'd urged Heshke to use the communicator and leave Earth?

Su-Mueng had obviously managed to worm his way into the Titans' good books somehow. He'd waved away Heshke's concern for his safety; he had an understanding with Limnich, he'd said vaguely; he was doing important work for him. What an improbable partnership, Heshke had told himself.

He placed the communicator on the table. 'You can get out of here,' he said to Sobrie. 'Go to that space city I told you about. They'll receive you; they're very hospitable.'

'Like a rat leaving a sinking ship? No, I don't think so. You should go, naturally, Rond. You've no cause to be here in the first place.'

'No, I'm staying behind,' Heshke said with a sigh. 'Not out of any sense of heroism, but because this insane world has given me too much of a spin as it is. Things have been much too hectic for me lately; I was growing more and more tired by the day. This reservation's the only place I've been able to rest, and I like it here.'

'Rond is right,' Herrick rumbled, 'if you have a way of escape you should take it, Sobrie. Not necessarily for your sake, but for Layella. It would be false heroism to sacrifice her, too, when she's entirely innocent.'

Yes, Layella . . . Sobrie pondered. 'Couldn't we take some Amhraks off, too?' he suggested shyly. 'A few . . . breeding pairs?'

Herrick shook his head, smiling with bittersweet amusement. 'Lonely survivors of a vanished race? No one would be found to fill the role. We've long been accustomed to the idea of species death.'

'I'll write out a report,' Heshke said, 'and you can be an envoy to Retort City for Su-Mueng and myself. They ought to be told what Limnich's answer is, anyway.'

'I wish you'd come too.'

'No, I'm finished with gadding about through space and time. Having to die doesn't worry me; I'm just going to relax and enjoy being alive until the Titans get here.'

The vast cavern complex echoed and thundered to the clatter and roar of machinery. Limnich, looking on the scene from the manager's gallery, nodded with satisfaction. So far his inspection tour of the thirteen main installations involved in Operation Century had proved the efficiency of his administration.

His eye swept over the progress reports, abstracting with skill the salient figures. 'I see that, starting from baseline, you're twelve per cent ahead of schedule,' he commented.

The manager, a rough-looking individual with a hard, lumpy face, was standing stiffly by his side. 'That's right, Planetary Leader,' he said, pride edging into his voice.

'I'll expect the same rate of progress, namely a twelve per cent increase over projected output – plus your current output – during the next identical period.'

'That represents an exponential increase in production, Leader. But if the materials and components arrive as ordered—'

'They will,' Limnich told him curtly. He'd found that demanding the near-impossible frequently produced miracles.

Followed by his entourage, he went with the manager the length of the gallery and passed through a tunnel to an adjoining series of caverns: one of the training grounds of the Legions of Kronos. They walked past row after row of sleek time-travelling war machines, each projecting from its launcher as if eager to depart for the future.

From ahead came hoarse shouts and stamping of feet as men were put through the drill designed by psychologists to bring the nervous system to a peak of alertness. Titan-Colonel Brask met Limnich at the entrance to the drill cavern, saluted, and then turned to bellow commands, forming the squads into open-order ranks and standing them to attention. Limnich took his time over the inspection, pausing at nearly every man to look him over, glancing at the special gadgets of the time-combat kits they wore. Meanwhile, from yet another cavern came a massive fuzzy roaring noise: the sound of scores of time travellers warming up.

Finally he pronounced himself satisfied. Brask escorted him to the third cavern where the crews stood by their machines in readiness for the demonstration. At a signal from Brask they filed aboard. Moments later the fuzzy racket intensified and the time travellers all vanished together, fading away to go hurtling in formation through non-time.

'Impressive,' said Limnich. 'Very impressive.'

'It will be even more impressive when they arrive in enemy time loaded to capacity with hydrogen bombs,' Brask said with incisive satisfaction.

Brask took the Planetary Leader to his office to discuss various details. While they were there the vidcom rang with a message for Limnich.

The yellow face of the dev Chink, Hueh Su-Mueng, came up on the screen. Only a faint habitual expression of distaste came to Brask's features, and none at all to Limnich's.

'It appears that your ploy has worked, Leader,' Su-Mueng said. 'My instruments tell me Retort City's ship sent down a lighter to the Amhrak reservation, and now has left orbit.'

'So soon?' mused Limnich. 'But my tip-off can't even have reached Heshke yet. There must be other information pipelines at work – either that or he couldn't stomach life on the reservation!' He smiled unpleasantly.

'I presume that nothing further need delay the expedition?'

'No, I'll issue the requisite orders.' The remaining work to be done should only take a week or two, he thought. The drive-units had already been constructed to the Chink's design, and now could be ferried into space to be fitted to the interplanetary spaceships that had been prepared to take them. The men, the weapons, the organization, were all ready.

It should be a grand adventure, Limnich told himself. He almost wished he could go along.

Herrick had brought in a tape that had appeared on the reconstituted network somehow.

'It shows the closing down of the Bugel reservation,' he said to Heshke, a little apologetically. 'You needn't watch it if you'd rather not.'

'Please go ahead,' Heshke told him, though with a tightening in his stomach.

Herrick put the tape on the playback. 'This didn't come through the usual channels,' he said. 'In fact it looks as if it might be a plant.'

'A plant?'

'Yes. The Titans might have wanted us to see it.'

The tape came to life, feeding the screen a long, roughly edited succession of sequences from the cameras of the official recordists, without any proper order or commentary. After a few minutes Heshke found himself wanting to close his eyes.

The landscape was not unlike the one outside his door: dusty and bare. As the Titans units advanced into it their half-tracks sent up clouds of dust which drifted in from the horizon.

The Bugels were a copper-skinned, pigmy-like people of a comparatively low cultural standing – little more than savages, in fact. Never very numerous, their reservation was a small one. They ran hither and thither before the implacable Titan vehicles, facing their end without dignity but with much excitement and terror.

The Titans herded the Bugels into compounds. They were given injections or else shot, and buried in lime pits.

Heshke imagined the same happening here – the clouds of dust as the exterminators rolled forward (during the wars, when operating behind the lines in dev-populated territory, they'd been known as SMD's – Special Measure Detachments), the compounds, the clerks checking off names against endless lists (though with the Bugels those lists covered only the noble families), the medics giving the injections and the doctors signing death certificates.

From the looks on their faces, the Titans plainly didn't relish their work. They regarded it as unpleasant, distressing – but necessary. It would have been worse if they'd been killing people; but these were only verminous animals.

Why on Earth had the Titans sent the tape into the Amhrak reservation, Heshke wondered? – if in fact they had, as Herrick suspected. To taunt? To strike fear? Perhaps it was an act of nastiness on the part of some hate-filled official.

Herrick was watching the tape placidly, smoking a tobacco roll, as if he were thinking of something else.

13

Shiu Kung-Chien and his able assistant Leard Ascar had nearly finished setting up the all-sense transmitter when the vidphone at the other end of the observatory tinkled. A cybernetic servitor rolled forward with the screen, on which the face of Prime Minister Hwen Wu looked out.

'Forgive the intrusion,' Hwen Wu apologized, 'but a matter of greatest urgency has arisen. Evidently our posting that young man Hueh Su-Mueng to Earth, so as to end his "awkward presence" here, so to speak, has misfired. He has returned with an invasion fleet.'

'I take it you refer to those lumpish vessels which have been hovering outside my observatory window for the past hour,' Shiu replied with a trace of exasperation. 'I had thought they were part of your own improvident plans. Fortunately they appear to rely on reaction motors for close manoeuvring and are no longer jamming our instruments.'

'They're entirely the work of Hueh Shao's son and his new friends,' Hwen Wu assured him. 'That family seems capable of endless mischief. The invaders have discharged four ship-loads of men through the dock, which they now control, and are rapidly discharging the rest. Haven't you heard the rumpus? They're proving quite destructive.'

'Yes, I've been aware of an undignified amount of noise and have several times sent out requests for it to be diminished,' Shiu said acidly. 'Why are you calling me about it?'

'Well, you're a cabinet minister,' Hwen Wu pointed out. 'I feel we should meet to discuss the situation. Hueh Su-Mueng has sent a message demanding our unconditional surrender.'

The Prime Minister's words were punctuated by a low, distant roar: the sound of an explosion.

'Very well,' Shiu consented resignedly. 'I'll come at once.'

He turned to Ascar as the servitor rolled away with the vidphone. 'This really is tiresome,' he complained. 'Are your countrymen accustomed to behaving like this?'

'I'm afraid so,' Ascar said laconically.

'Barbarians!' muttered Shiu.

'May I continue in your absence?' Ascar asked politely.

'Yes, of course . . . you understand everything?'

'Yes, thanks to an unexampled teacher.'

Shiu Kung-Chien departed. Ascar, impatient to get on with it, continued checking the work of the servitors, carefully scanning the streams of calligraphic ideograms that came up on the monitor.

It was damned good to get away from desk-work. He'd been hungering for action for some time.

Titan-Major Brourne stood in a large concourse, a sort of intricate plaza, watching the flood of men, materials and weapons that came surging in a disciplined operation through the docking ports. The flowers and shrubs, the miniature trees and tinted screens, had all been trampled down and cast aside to make way for the traffic, which was heading deeper into the space city. The immediate area was solidly secured, ringed by heavy machine guns and even light cannon, and hour by hour came reports of whole districts taken without any show of resistance.

At this rate the whole city would be in his hands in a day.

Already he'd made an excursion into the occupied areas and everything he saw confirmed his instincts. It was exactly as he would have expected: decadence, nothing but decadence. Decadent art, decadent science, decadent customs. The Chinks were effete, ultra-sophisticated, wallowing in sensual pleasure – the whole city was simply an orgy of effeminate prettiness. And the people didn't seem to know how to react to the invasion. They had none of the rude, healthy vigour that made True Man great.

Brourne strode to a small building near the ports where he had set up his field HQ. Hueh Su-Mueng sat looking over a complicated map he'd prepared of the city. As the reports came in he was marking more and more of it in blue, his code for 'taken'.

The plan of operations was largely his brainchild. His idea was to have the whole city under control before the masters of the Leisure Retort could gather their wits sufficiently to take any effective action. He was striking down towards the bottleneck joining the two retorts, so as to cut off any retreat in that direction or any orders for weapons that might be given to the workers. Once the Leisure Retort had been seized he'd been promised that he himself could take a small force of Titans into the Production Retort. He hoped for a good response from its inhabitants to his news.

'All in order?' Brourne rapped.

Su-Mueng nodded, looking up at the stubby, barrel-like man. 'We're keeping to our timetable remarkably well.'

'Too well,' Brourne rumbled sulkily. 'I like the opposition to put up a bit of a fight.'

Su-Mueng ignored the remark and continued studying the map, wondering where Hwen Wu and the rest of the cabinet were.

A Titan sergeant appeared at the door and saluted smartly. 'We've found a white man, sir.'

Brourne turned with interest, but the man who stood there flanked by two troopers was unknown to him. He was a tall, slim man, his eyes steady, wearing garments of an unfamiliar cut – basically Earth style, but probably tailored here in the space city, Brourne imagined.

'Who are you?' he barked.

The other paused before answering in a low tone. 'My name is Citizen Sobrie Oblomot.'

The Titan-Major glared at him, then decided on a less threatening posture. 'Well, it's certainly a change to find a white man in a place like this,' he said briskly. 'How did you come to be here?'

'A Chink ship brought me,' Oblomot told him. 'From the Amhrak reservation.'

'Amhrak? Are you an Amhrak?' Brourne was startled, almost indignant. 'Frankly I wouldn't have known it—'

'No, I'm not Amhrak. I was banished there for . . . political reasons.'

'Oh, I see.' Brourne grimaced. 'As a matter of fact, my men were expecting to find Rond Heshke, the archaeologist, when they brought you in. Presumably he was on the ship too?'

'No . . .' Oblomot said slowly. 'Rond stayed behind.'

Brourne looked disappointed.

Dismally Sobrie's eyes took in the scene in Brourne's HQ. It depressed him, having thought he'd escaped the Titans for good, to see them come pouring into Retort City as well. For a moment he'd had the crazy idea that they were taking over the universe.

His first thought had been for Layella. Even in Retort City costume she stood out a mile. But a group of women had taken care of her and hidden her somewhere. With luck the Titans wouldn't notice her for some time.

For some reason he hadn't tried to flee himself. Probably, he rationalized, he'd become infected with Rond Heshke's style of defeatism.

The young officer at the table turned around and spoke to the Titan-Major. It was, Sobrie realized with a start, Hueh Su-Mueng – wearing Titan uniform! The spectacle of a full-blooded Chink dressed out as a Titan-Lieutenant made Sobrie burst into laughter.

Brourne silenced him with a scowl and lumbered over to glance at the map. His troops had reached the centre of the city – of this half of the city, at any rate. Even if its rulers tried to organize some sort of defence it would do them no good now.

'Excellent, excellent,' he murmured. 'Well, there it is, then. The job's practically done.'

Su-Mueng rose to his feet and spoke respectfully. 'Now that matters have reached this stage, Major, may I request that I lead a force into the Lower Retort, to assess the situation there?'

The Titan laughed brutally. 'Sit tight, Chink, you're not going anywhere.'

Alarm showed on Su-Mueng's yellow features. 'I don't understand, Major. Planetary Leader Limnich made a firm promise—'

'We don't do deals with devs,' Brourne sneered. 'Sometimes they come in useful, like animals come in useful. You've done your job, and thanks very much.' He jerked his head to two huge guards at the back of the room, who promptly strode forward and stamped to attention on either side of Su-Mueng.

The boy's a simpleton, Sobrie thought. He really didn't know what sort of people he was mixing with. He probably doesn't understand, even now, what racism means.

And Su-Mueng did, indeed, look bewildered, like a child who's been cheated.

'This – this is outright treachery!' he spluttered breathlessly, swaying as though about to faint. 'When Limnich hears—'

'Limnich, Limnich!' Brourne jeered. He laughed again, loudly. 'After you left, Limnich had his office fumigated!'

'You need me to get co-operation in the Lower Retort—'

'The Lower Retort will get the same treatment this one is getting – and soon.' He would have moved into the Production Retort first, in fact, except that there was no dock there for the spaceships. Still, Brourne didn't anticipate any trouble. The masters are gutless, he thought. The slaves must be even worse.

'If you have any further role to play, it will be as an interpreter,' he told Su-Mueng. 'We'll probably need a few of those.'

He gestured to the guards. 'Take him into custody. This fellow Oblomot, too. I'll decide what to do with him later.'

Su-Mueng stood blankly for a moment. Then he did an astonishing thing. He took one step to the rear and both hands went smoothly up to both men's necks. The troopers jerked momentarily, then fell back, unconscious.

The lithe youth bounded forward to meet the party escorting Sobrie. His hands seemed scarcely to touch them, merely weaving in and out in a graceful arabesque. But the soldiers were caught up in that arabesque, tumbling in a flurry of limbs until they finished up dazed on the other side of the room.

The people of the Upper Retort practised the arts and all mental pleasures; those of the Lower Retort practised sport. Su-Mueng was using *Hoka*, the culmination of thousands of years' development of unarmed combat. Compared with the enthusiasts in the Production Retort Su-Mueng was but a beginner, but he could stun – or, though that was forbidden, kill – with but a light touch upon a nerve, and in his hands an untrained man's body was but an assemblage of self-destructive levers.

Brourne's gun was in his hand. Su-Mueng too drew his own Corgel automatic in one easy movement – the Titans, treating his honorary rank as one huge joke, had delighted in fitting him out with all accoutrements, including an 'honorary certificate of racial purity' – and bent forward in a supple stance, bringing his gun hand forward to shoot the Major carefully in the arm. Brourne swung away, cursing with pain.

Su-Mueng put a hand between Sobrie's shoulder blades and propelled him through the door. Sobrie, surrendering his will, ran with him across the plaza towards the stream of guns and vehicles that bounced across the occasionally uneven flooring.

Glancing behind him, Sobrie saw Brourne struggle to the door, leaning against the jamb. Su-Mueng threw up his hand imperiously, bringing to a halt a light truck.

The driver glanced curiously at him, but he already knew about this strange dev officer; it didn't seem odd to him that he should be hitching a ride, while Sobrie's presence went unremarked. Su-Mueng urged his companion into the covered rear, joined him, and banged on the driving cab for the Titan to continue.

The truck was half-filled with crated ammunition. They settled down tensely as the vehicle jolted forward. 'When we're out of the area we'll slip out and make our own way,' Su-Mueng said, speaking low.

Sobrie nodded. They rode for some minutes with no apparent sign of danger, and now that he had time free from action Su-Mueng let his dismay and resentment flood like a tide of sickness through his bloodstream.

'Anyone could have told you,' Sobrie admonished, noticing his distress. 'It was a pretty silly thing to do, tying yourself in with the Titans.'

'I thought I would give my father's death some meaning,' Su-Mueng answered. 'Never again would a man die for loving his son . . .'

He trailed off, realizing that Sobrie didn't know what he was talking about. His face creased in a pondering frown. 'Perhaps the Titans will go away again when they have what they want.'

'Not likely. They'll probably try to fly this city to the solar system and orbit it somewhere. It gives them a ready-made industrial system, complete with millions of trained slaves, and they'll make all the use they can of it, for a long time to come. Even if they decide to abandon it, they wouldn't leave anybody alive,' he ended. 'To their way of thinking you people are a blot on nature. I'm amazed you couldn't see it.'

'I knew they hold to some sort of biological creed, of course,' Su-Mueng admitted grudgingly, 'but I hadn't supposed it would make any difference. Ours was a practical arrangement purely, to our mutual advantage – as I thought. There was no conflict of interests.'

'Ah well, I suppose it would have gone the same way whatever race you belonged to,' Sobrie sighed. 'The Titans always seek only their own advantage – never anyone else's.'

Su-Mueng was silent for a while. 'It's all yet another indictment on Retort City's social methods,' he said then, grinding the words out. 'I was brought up in a closed system, unable to adapt myself to the mores of another world.'

'Your remarks, nevertheless, are acute,' said Sobrie with a wry smile. 'All you need is a chance. But where exactly are we supposed to be going?'

'Having brought disaster to my city, the least I can do is to try to rectify the situation. Perhaps something can be salvaged from all this yet.'

'I'd like to know how you're going to do that, young man.'

Su-Mueng brooded, and after a while peered out of the back of the truck.

'Here,' he commanded.

They dropped lightly from the truck, stumbled, and ran for the shelter of a grove of willow trees. The convoy passed by without pause.

Behind the grove was a colonnade flanked by walls slatted and louvred in rosewood. They set off down this and then Su-Mueng, hesitating frequently, led Sobrie on a long, circuitous tour of the Leisure Retort.

Sobrie, who wasn't yet very familiar with the retort, saw much that was new to him. The beauty of the place was offset, to some extent, by the ubiquitous black-and-gold Titan uniforms. Amazingly, no general order for their arrest seemed to have gone out and Su-Mueng was several times saluted smartly by patrolling troops.

An unreal air pervaded the city. The inhabitants, contrasting sharply in appearance with their newly arrived conquerors, displayed no apparent alarm. There was much laughing and joking as the sweating Titans set up their emplacements. If Sobrie hadn't already sampled the mental sophistication of these people, he would have thought them to be simple children who didn't know what was happening.

At last they entered what Sobrie took to be a nursery. Cribs lined the walls of a sunny room, nearly every crib bearing a baby. All, Sobrie guessed, were newborn.

He couldn't imagine why Su-Mueng should have

brought him to a maternity ward. A young woman came forward, inclining her head while Su-Mueng spoke to her rapidly in a low voice. She frowned, looked doubtful and incredulous by turns, and then the two of them went off somewhere together.

Sobrie was beginning to feel uneasy by the time Su-Mueng returned. 'They've agreed to it,' the young man said. 'It's kind of hard to get these people to admit there's an emergency afoot. I thought I was going to have to use force.'

'They've agreed to what?' Sobrie asked, following the other. They passed along a corridor, smelling pleasantly of perfumes, and came to a chamber that evidently served some function not clear to Sobrie. There were cradles, set on rails that vanished into the wall. A barely perceptible hum filled the air.

'We're going down into the Production Retort,' Su-Mueng informed him. Men entered the chamber, removed the cradles and replaced them with a platform on which were mounted a number of padded chairs.

One of them grinned cheerfully at Su-Mueng. 'A long time since this was last used,' he said.

At his direction Sobrie seated himself in one of the chairs beside Su-Mueng. The wall facing them rolled away, revealing a tunnel that dwindled into the distance.

Su-Mueng's expression was matter-of-fact. The platform moved into the tunnel, which was unlit and soon pitch-dark. They travelled smoothly, without noticeable acceleration – without, indeed, any noticeable breeze – but Sobrie became aware of an unusual feeling, as if he were being lifted and compressed at the same time, and the faint hum intensified. After perhaps two minutes a light showed ahead, brightening until they emerged into a chamber much like the one they'd left.

Su-Mueng leaped up from his chair, shouting excitedly at the receptionists, young women who seemed astonished at their arrival. Sobrie followed him as he dashed into an adjoining chamber. From nearby he heard the crying of very young babies.

There were no babies, however, in the room in which Sobrie found himself. There was a bank of instruments and controls arranged in a workmanlike way around a bucket seat and desk. In that seat was a controller – but dressed in a simple blue garb rather than the sumptuous finery Sobrie had come to expect in the Leisure Retort.

Energetically Su-Mueng pushed the controller aside and applied himself with great concentration to the controls. The displaced controller gawped from the floor, too staggered to rise.

The ever-present hum that lay just within the bounds of audibility died into silence. With satisfaction Su-Mueng drew his automatic and fired several times into the main switch, sealing the settings temporarily at least.

The two retorts were now totally separated in time: no time-gradient connected them. If the Titans were to come along the tunnel Sobrie and Su-Mueng had just travelled, or to enter by any other route, they would only arrive into its unpeopled future.

Su-Mueng turned to the controller he'd just treated so barbarically. 'Come with me,' he said. 'It's imperative that I speak with the retort managers!'

'We've captured the ruling clique, sir.'

'All right, let me see them.'

Brourne stared at the impassive, droopy-moustached, silky-bearded, satined and silked old men who came up on the screen. 'How do you know this is the ruling clique?' he demanded.

The youthful, enthusiastic Captain came back into view. 'They admit it, sir. We've found a kind of computer that knows a few Earth phrases.'

'Oh? How many?'

'Not enough for a useful interrogation, I'm afraid.'

'I see. Well, lock them up until later.'

'Yes, sir.' The Captain snapped off a salute and went off the line.

Brourne turned away, gingerly massaging his injured arm, which lay in a sling. What was the point of capturing anybody when he couldn't talk to them? He cursed again for having let Hueh Su-Mueng get away. At the time he'd thought nothing of it, hadn't even ordered any pursuit or search. Why bother? The Chink's first move had doubtless been to divest himself of his uniform, whereupon he might as well have been invisible. It was practically impossible to tell these Chinks apart.

There was another possibility, Brourne reminded himself. Leard Ascar was still in the city somewhere and sooner or later his men would find him. By all accounts Ascar was an intractable, unbalanced personality – in his preflight briefing Brourne had been advised that he was 'unreliable' – but presumably he knew the language, as Heshke had. He would have to do.

The vidcom burred again. Brourne returned to it.

'HQ. Major Brourne.'

A serious-faced tech officer gazed out at him. 'The sortie to the lower retort has sent back a report, sir.'

'Yes?'

'They say it's deserted. Crammed full of factories and workshops – but there's not a single human being there.'

'Deserted? You're sure they're not hiding out somewhere?'

'That's not how things look, and no one's been found yet.'

'So maybe that cur of a Chink was lying,' Brourne responded. 'The whole place could be automated – no workers at all.'

'Perhaps – but again, that's not how it looks. Right now there's not a wheel turning. And there are signs of decay, as though the whole complex had been abandoned about fifty years ago.'

Brourne became thoughtful. 'That doesn't figure,' he rumbled. 'It doesn't figure at all. Wasn't there supposed to be something about the two halves of the city not matching in time?'

'Our men simply went through a tunnel about a third of a mile long,' the tech said. 'But there are other ways in. There's a marshalling yard where the produce of the factories comes through. I'll investigate further.'

'Do that. And keep me informed.'

Right now, he thought, is where Leard Ascar would really come in handy.

Ascar was trembling with excitement.

During the past few weeks Shiu Kung-Chien had told him a great deal about the Oblique Entity that had once nearly annihilated Retort City – as much, indeed, as the elder scientist himself knew. Ascar had begged that he, too, be allowed to visit this strange intelligence via the all-sense sender, but Shiu had prevailed upon him to delay the experience. The all-sense transmissions, crude at the moment, needed refining.

And so Ascar had worked patiently under the old man's direction, studying and thinking deeply. The Oblique Entity, Shiu had intimated, had powers beyond the merely human. It wasn't a biological intelligence; it wasn't associated with any planet or celestial body; its nature, though it had a material structure, wasn't really intelligible to human beings.

During the last phase of their work to improve the transceiver the Titans had arrived and invaded the ISS. Shiu, imperturbable as ever (Ascar was impressed by the way any event, no matter how grave, failed to shake the placidity of the people here; they were, Shiu had told him once, dilettantes at everything, even living), had left Ascar to carry on, which he did while the noises of destruction as the Titans pulled down sections of the city to facilitate their easy movement grew nearer and nearer.

For the past half hour the sounds of conquest had died down. Presumably the Leisure Retort was now in the Titans' grip, which meant that they'd soon be battering

down his door. He was anxious to have made his trip
before they did that, because they would very likely de-
prive him of any further opportunity and he was impelled
by more than mere intellectual curiosity. Some time ago
he'd asked Shiu Kung-Chien how the Oblique Entity's
own knowledge of the physical universe compared with
their own.

Shiu Kung-Chien had hesitated. Compared with men,
he'd said, the Oblique Entity had knowledge that was like
that 'of one of your ancient gods'.

Ascar had some very definite questions to put to this
entity.

And so Ascar completed the countdown. Shiu had already completed a trial run with the new equipment; all
Ascar had to do now was to made the final checks.

The flickering ideograms froze at last; the apparatus
was poised in readiness. He rubbed his eyes. Although
he'd been trained in a matter of minutes to read the
specialized calligraphy Shiu used, he still found the ideograms hard to focus on at speed.

He glanced over the big, gleaming, block-like transformers of time energy that were dumped unceremon-
iously in the middle of the observatory, humming fuzzily.
They had, he supposed, taken a couple of years to
manufacture, yet they'd been delivered to Shiu within
an hour of his submitting the designs. Such was the
nature of the resources he could draw on: resources
he used so carelessly, and in so cavalier a fashion, that
Ascar was constantly amazed. He'd order new equipment
with absolutely no thought for the labour time involved,
drawing up version after version of some difficult design
and demanding an operating model of each so as to try out
his various (and sometimes offhand) ideas. His storeroom
was jammed with machinery, much of it never used, and
many items that arrived were sent back to be scrapped
after a few desultory experiments.

The Oblique Entity was already reciprocating on their
contact stream, expressing its willingness for the

exchange. The cybernetic servitor moved into position to operate the equipment. His heart thumping, Ascar stepped into the transparent sphere. The hatch closed behind him as he sat down in the central chair, and then he was in darkness.

The transceiver seized his senses and snatched them out of intelligible time, hurling them in a direction no compass could ever find.

At first there was only silence, and continued darkness. Then out of that darkness a voice said suddenly: 'I am here. You have arrived. What do you want?'

The voice, though loud, was smooth and confidential. It seemed to be spoken close to his ear – or rather, to both his ears. Behind the voice was a silence, but behind that silence Ascar fancied he could hear a whispering whistle, like the susurration that sometimes accompanied radio transmissions.

'I want to see you,' Ascar said into the darkness.

'How do you wish to see me?'

Ascar didn't understand the question for a moment; then he answered: 'I want to see you as you are.'

'Very well. Here is our physical reality.'

The change was brutally abrupt. Ascar suddenly found himself amid an uproar in a long gallery. He was kneeling, for the height of the gallery was only about four feet and gave approximately the same room on either side, though it stretched away ahead of him seemingly into infinity. Furthermore it was only one of a multiple of such structures arranged around him, and which he glimpsed through the iron frameworks separating them. And those frameworks contained—

He inspected the complex closely. As near as he could judge, the objects would best be described as machines. The galleries were, in fact, avenues for the siting of a continuous machine process which clattered, rotated and shuffled through indefinably intricate operations. Ascar was in the midst of a roaring, close-packed factory of vast extent, like some industrialized hell.

'Did you construct this?' he asked into thin air.

'No,' came the immediate answer, easily audible despite the deafening racket. 'This *is* us – a small part of me. All this came into existence spontaneously, as a result of the process of time. I/We is not biological.'

Ascar felt himself moving forward. The floor offered no perceptible resistance to his knees, but a hot wind played against his face. The endless galleries swept past blurrily as he gathered speed and went darting into a claustrophobic infinity.

Then, without warning, he came to a stop. The machine complex was behind him in the form of a towering serried wall; its array, he recognized, was reminiscent of the array of atoms in a metal.

He faced now a huge gulf from whose depths came tumultuous boiling, a giving forth of steam clouds and acid vapours which seared his skin. Its size was impossible to judge. Ascar moved along the edge of this infernal pit until he came to another of its boundaries: a second wall of solid-packed quasi-machinery. But this time there were no narrow galleries through the honeycomb; the whole mass was impenetrable, none of its interstices being large enough to admit his body.

He glanced overhead, attracted by a regular, gigantic noise. Slanting obliquely over the space above him was something like a moving belt, or a high-speed printing press. It roared on its way at a colossal speed, for all that it must have been a hundred miles long.

'Perhaps you would prefer to meet me in different surroundings,' the Oblique Entity said. Everything vanished, and was replaced.

Ascar was sitting in a moderately-sized room. The walls were of pale blue decorated with a white cornice. The light, coming from an unseen source, was very radiant, reminding him of sunlight. Before Ascar stood a table of polished walnut.

A door opened. In walked a young woman who sat down opposite him. Her skin was silver-blue. A slight smile was on her lips. Her eyes were bright blue, also, but they looked beyond Ascar, as if they weren't functional.

'Good day,' she said in a pleasant, full voice. 'Is this more agreeable?'

Ascar took a moment to recover himself. 'But this isn't you as you really are, is it?' he said then.

'No, that is true.'

Ascar was vaguely disappointed. 'Then it's just an illusion you're putting through the all-sense receiver. I didn't come all this way looking for illusions.'

'Incorrect: it is no illusion. I have constructed the environment as a physical reality, into which I then projected your senses. Even the woman is a real living woman.'

Now Ascar was startled. 'You can do that – in a moment?'

A pause. 'Not in a moment, exactly. To produce the woman took a hundred years. Duration is of no consequence when time can be turned in a circle.'

So that was it, Ascar thought. It was the Production Retort all over again, but on an even larger scale. Here, the beginning and the end of a lengthy process could be bent around to occupy successive moments. He mulled over another point.

'Sometimes you call yourself *I*, and sometimes *we*,' he observed. 'What are you, a single intelligence or a community?'

'I am neither individual nor plural,' the Oblique Entity replied. 'Neither *I* nor *we* is adequate to describe my nature.'

'Then just what *are* you?'

The girl inclined her head, her eyes seeking a point beyond the wall, and a slight, quizzical frown crossed her features.

'Perhaps these surroundings, even, are disconcerting?' she suggested. 'Let us try again.'

She rose, and pointed to a second door that opened itself behind Ascar. 'Please continue on down the corridor,' she invited. 'Another room has been prepared.'

After a last doubtful glance at the girl Ascar obeyed. At first the corridor was featureless, grey and doorless, stretching away to a bend, or dead-end, about two hundred yards ahead. But as he proceeded a peculiar illusion began to occur. Out of the corner of his eye he glimpsed arcaded openings beyond which fish-like shapes flitted among green stalks and through wavering groves. Yet when he turned his head to look directly at this phenomenon his eye met only a blank wall.

He began to get the odd feeling that the elusive fish-shapes flitted, not externally, but through the recesses of his own mind. After a few tens of yards, however, the illusion ceased. But at the same time the character of the corridor began to change subtly, to become less featureless and more familiar. Suddenly Ascar stopped. He had come to a door: a door with the number 22 stencilled on it.

He looked around him. Just ahead was a T-junction, where arrowed notices pointed out departments in either direction. He looked again at the door with the number 22, recognizing scratch marks and pimples in the paint.

This place was a corridor in the Sarn Establishment! Or a perfect replica thereof.

With thumping heart he opened the door. Within was a cosy, cabin-like room with a bunk, chairs, and a table strewn with abstracts and reports together with a large scratch-pad. The wall to his left was a bookcase holding a small library of specialized volumes.

It was his own room and refuge that he'd inhabited for five years.

Slowly he closed the door and sat down in his favourite chair, realizing as he did so that the Oblique Entity must have extracted all these details from his own memory.

Above the door was a small speaker that had been used in the Sarn Establishment for paging. The Oblique Entity spoke now through this grille.

'To answer your question,' it said in its former male voice, 'the type of consciousness I possess is neither an individual consciousness, nor is it a group consciousness or a community of individuals. In your language I could come closer to the facts simply by referring to ourselves as *here*, rather than *I* or *we*. Henceforth then I will give ourselves the personal pronoun *here*.'

Ascar pondered that, nodding. The Entity's ploy, he decided, was working. He *did* feel more relaxed to be sitting here in his own room. It would have been easy to forget altogether that this was not, in fact, the Sarn Establishment.

'Since you can evidently read my mind, you already know what I mean to ask you,' he said. 'Tell me, how much do you know of Earth?'

'Here know all about Earth,' the Oblique Entity replied.

'You mean you've read all about it in my mind?'

'No. Here knew about Earth already. By direct observation.'

'Then you know what's about to happen there?'

'Yes.'

'Then' said Ascar, giving his words emphasis and deliberation, 'is there any way – any way at all – that the stream of time can be turned aside or stopped? Any way that collision can be avoided?'

The Oblique Entity didn't answer immediately. Instead, a rich humming note issued from the speaker. All at once everything exploded around Ascar. He was floating in an inchoate void. Around him swam coloured shapes of every description, drifting in and out of his vision like sparks.

His body seemed to become elongated, like a streamer of smoke in a breeze; he was being stretched out to infinity. This process seemed to go on for a long, long time; and then, just as suddenly, he was back in his favourite chair in his comfortable room.

'There is nothing *you* can do,' the Oblique Entity said.

When Brourne's troops finally broke into the space-time observatory they found Leard Ascar still sitting in the transparent sphere of the all-sense transceiver.

After a matter of minutes they contrived to open the hatch. Ascar appeared not to see them. He sat muttering unintelligibly to himself, offering no resistance when they grabbed him by the arms and hauled him out.

'This must be Ascar,' the sergeant said. 'If you ask me these Chink gadgets have driven him out of his mind!'

'Maybe he's fallen foul of a Chink puzzle,' a trooper offered helpfully.

'Eh? What?' Ascar began to come round, peering at the trooper with narrowed eyes.

'Let's get him away from here,' the sergeant ordered. 'Major Brourne wants to see him right away.'

They steered Ascar out of the observatory. And then an unexpected sound caused them all at once to come to a stop and gaze at one another wonderingly. For some hours the city had been quiet, but now, from the distance, came the sudden, continuous eruption of heavy gunfire.

Heshke accepted a tobacco roll, inhaling the fragrant smoke with a sense of special pleasure.

It was, in the fullest sense, a farewell party. They all knew that the Titans would come rolling into the reservation tomorrow, or at the latest the day after. Herrick had called together a few of his friends, as he put it, to 'celebrate the end of the species'.

The atmosphere was relaxed and convivial. Heshke couldn't help but admire the calm way the Amhraks were accepting the inevitable. Perhaps, he thought, it was the inevitability that lent such dignity. If there had been any hope at all, that might have led to panic.

Much of the conversation was in Amhrak, at which Heshke was not as yet skilled. However, out of politeness, enough Verolian – the main language of white men that was used all over the Earth now – was spoken so that he felt by no means left out.

A lanky Amhrak girl chatted to him, sipping a glass of wine synthesized by a newly perfected process. 'You must find our village rather dull after Pradna,' she said, smiling.

'I wasn't actually in Pradna,' he told her. 'I spent most of my time in the field, working on alien ruins. Pradna is a pretty ghastly place anyway, to tell you the truth. I like it much better here . . . in spite of what's happening.'

As he spoke the last words he had the sinking feeling of having committed a *faux pas*. These people could have a taboo about speaking of . . . *that*, he thought timidly. But the girl merely laughed, quite without strain.

'It must be *really* awful in Pradna,' she joked, 'to prefer *that*.'

Herrick had opened the double doors of his workshop and was fiddling with his transmitterless television receiver. To hide his embarrassment Heshke joined him, and for some minutes Herrick phased through the magnetowaves, seeking coherent visuals and gaining more than the usual number.

'Conditions are remarkably conducive tonight,' Herrick commented with some surprise. 'The nodes are particularly strong. Here comes a good one.'

The view, as most of them were, was from the air. It showed the outskirts of a town of moderate size, judging by the layout of the buildings. The angle of the sun revealed the time to be mid-afternoon.

'Do you recognize it?' Herrick asked him.

Heshke shook his head. It could have been any of a thousand such towns.

Instead of dissipating after a few seconds, which was what normally happened, the picture lingered. Herrick managed to steady it further, until the quality was almost of commercial standard.

'At last I'm getting somewhere,' Herrick said sadly. 'It

seems a pity to – *what's that?'*

The frame of the picture itself remained steady and bright; but certain elements in it were fading. While the two men watched (Heshke was vaguely aware of other eyes peering over his shoulder through the double doors) all the buildings in the picture seemed to melt away, leaving a bare background. Not only that, but a grove of trees also vanished, together with a stretch of grass.

What remained was bare, arid soil.

'Some effect of the system?' Heshke suggested mildly.

'I don't see how,' Herrick muttered. 'There are television systems that *could* produce this effect – systems employing a memory bank to hold persistent elements in the picture, so that it's built up piece by piece – but I rely on a simple scanning procedure. Look, you can see the places where those buildings had stood. It's just as if the whole town had disappeared into thin air.'

'Then you must have been picking up two different images superimposed,' Heshke said. 'One faded out and you're left with the other.'

'Yes, that might explain it.' Herrick nodded reluctantly. 'That must be it. But as to how they came to blend so perfectly – and I thought I'd licked the tuning problem, too.'

Heshke wandered out of the room, leaving Herrick still absorbed in his apparatus.

He went on to the verandah and looked out over the desert. The night sky seemed to hold a strange, flickering light, as if lightning was playing somewhere beyond the horizon.

The attempted return to Brourne's HQ was hectic.

They'd gone about half a mile in the squad's armoured runabout – the Titans scorned to use Retort City's own public transport system – when they came upon one of the main arteries that had been cleared to give the city's new masters easy access. The highway was thundering with traffic, all of it heading towards the sound of bombs and gunfire that came from the city's bottleneck end.

'Towards the front,' muttered the sergeant.

The wild looks on the faces of the Titans who clung to the swaying gun carriages told them that the situation had more than a measure of desperation. No natives were in sight: presumably they were all huddling somewhere, terrified of Titan savagery when the going got tough. A Titan soldier, for example, would shoot anyone who happened to be standing in his way when a sense of urgency overtook him.

'What in the Mother's name is going on, sarge?' one of the troopers asked.

'Must be something big.' He ruminated. 'Maybe the Chinks were holding on to their defences.' He nudged the driver. 'Our job is to get this man to HQ. Get across the highway when there's a gap and go by way of the secondary route.'

The highway came in from the main supply dump, close to the dock. HQ was in a central part of the city. Eventually they crossed the busy viaduct and continued, past empty tiers, galleries and plazas.

'This place gives me the creeps,' someone grumbled. 'I'll be glad to get back to Pradna.'

Ahead of them was a machine gun post. Troopers yelled at them, brought them to a halt.

'You can't go up there,' a corporal told them, 'it's cut off.'

'Cut off by *who*?'

'The Chinks have an army,' the corporal said stolidly. 'Everything's in chaos.'

Suddenly the machine gun gave out a short stuttering burst. 'Here they come!' yelled the man firing it.

The sergeant reached into the runabout and brought out his burp gun. He could see them, too, now, emerging from the end of a tree-lined avenue. They wore rough, blue uniforms and wide-brimmed dome helmets.

He rapped out orders. The armoured runabout proceeded slowly up the avenue, its occupants firing from
its slits. He stayed with the machine gun crew, down on
one knee, peering over the barricade and fingering his burp
gun.

And then, without any warning, the Chinks were upon
them: all around them, as if they'd dropped from the non-
existent sky.

Titan-Major Brourne knew already that he'd committed a
tactical error when he moved his HQ from the cramped
accommodation at the dockside to his present palatial
quarters near the centre of the city.

At the time it had seemed reasonable. The city had been
taken. He needed an administrative centre, and the dock
just wouldn't do.

But now, up through the bottleneck from the Production
Retort which all his scouts had assured him was empty, had
come a huge army, well-prepared and well-disciplined.
Brourne still only had an inkling of where this army had
really come from, but in any case explanations, at this stage,
were very low down on his list of priorities.

When it first became clear that the threat was serious he'd
given thought to the route back to the dock, to a withdrawal
to the ships floating outside the city if necessary. With deep
chagrin he learned that the dock was one of the first points
to be seized by the enemy. His forces were still trying to
retake it.

Elsewhere the story was one of repeated disaster. The
invasion force was overwhelming, and none of the measures he'd taken to retain military control seemed effective. The Chinks were able to flit in and out of existence like shadows, by means of some device they possessed, apparently, and so were able to infiltrate all his
fixed defences. They carried only light arms and knives,
but more often than not fought using an unarmed combat technique that was as deadly as anything he'd come
across.

His ire rising, Brourne listened to the distressing tale of section after section of the city falling, of the enemy appearing simultaneously everywhere, that the battle reports told. He slammed down the key that opened the line to all district commanders. For some minutes now they'd been requesting instructions.

'Kill everything that moves!' he roared. 'Have you got that? Everything that moves!'

'Haven't I met you somewhere?' Leard Ascar asked, squinting quizzically at the white man wearing the uniform of the Lower Retort invaders.

'Sobrie Oblomot.' The other smiled. 'We met twice, a few days ago. For you it was a few days ago, that is; for me it was more than a year.'

'Oh yes, that's right,' Ascar muttered. 'You came in on the ship from Earth, in Rond Heshke's place. Forgive me, I've a poor memory for faces.' He waved a hand negligently. 'So the Titans haven't had it all their own way?'

Sobrie allowed himself a look of quiet triumph. 'They don't know what's hit them. You know the secret of the Lower Retort's success, of course – that it can always take as much time as it needs to work on something, even when results are required in minutes. We only spent a year in organizing our onslaught, but we could have taken twenty-five years if need be.'

'Yes, I thought there would be something like that,' Ascar said. 'I'm surprised the Titans let you pull off such a stunt.'

'They had no opportunity to stop us. Do you remember a young man by the name of Hueh Su-Mueng? The Titans brought him with them, back from Earth. They'd have done better to leave him behind: he switched off the time tunnel between the two retorts, denying the Titans access to it, in its normative time, at least. I expect they could have found their way into it with the new ships they have, but we were upon them before they fully realized what was going on. In Leisure Retort time, Su-Mueng and myself were back within an hour of leaving – with a fully-equipped and trained army!'

Ascar grunted. 'Somebody on Limnich's staff goofed. Not that it matters.' He stretched. He'd been separated from the Titan prisoners and put in more luxurious surroundings reserved, he guessed, for detainees of more exalted rank. Oblomot's visit, however, had been a surprise.

'I remember you now,' he said. 'You're some kind of revolutionary nut, aren't you? A dev-lover. Yes, that's right.'

'Say what you like. I'm not alone: Su-Mueng is a revolutionary too. Things are going to change around here.'

'If you're expecting the Production Retort workers to toe some kind of rebellion line, forget it,' Ascar told him. 'People know how to arrange society in this ISS. It's orderly.'

'Well, we'll see. Su-Mueng is an extraordinary person in some ways. It's really impressive the way he was able to get things organized in the Lower Retort. And we've saved Retort City!' Boastfulness crept into Sobrie's voice.

'They respond naturally to being organized down there,' Ascar retorted. 'It doesn't mean a damn thing.' He yawned. He felt tired. 'So you've saved Retort City, have you? Well, bend a knee to *me*, friend. You're looking at the man who's saved the planet Earth!'

'You . . .?' began Sobrie wonderingly, but he was interrupted by a call from outside the apartment.

Hueh Su-Mueng entered. He glanced disdainfully at Ascar, then turned to Sobrie.

'All goes well. The retort is ours, apart from a few pockets of resistance. Also, we've found out where the Earthmen were holding the Leisure Retort cabinet. They should be arriving here soon!'

'Good!' said Ascar vigorously. 'Since this little fiasco is finished, I take it my master Shiu Kung-Chien can now return to his observatory and attend to matters of greater import. And if you don't mind, I'd like to join him.'

'Oh yes, I recognize you,' Su-Mueng said. 'You're the man who preferred to devote himself to abstract things rather than try to help his own people. Go on your way, by all means. We have no use for you here.' There was a new hardness in the young man, Ascar noted. The past year had changed him.

'Wait!' Sobrie interjected. 'What was that you were saying just now – about Earth?'

Ascar put on a stubborn face and folded his arms. 'I want to see Shiu Kung-Chien.'

'I see what's in your mind,' Su-Mueng said after a moment. 'You're afraid that I'll execute all the cabinet ministers, including your beloved master. Don't worry, that's for the people to decide, not me. Perhaps he'll be put to work in a factory, to discover what it's like.'

He gave the word to Sobrie, who went out and returned a few minutes later with Shiu. The aged scientist murmured a perfunctory greeting as he entered the room, then spoke to Ascar.

'Was there time to complete the operation?' he asked.

'Just about,' said Ascar. 'I visited the Oblique Entity, anyway.'

'And did you learn anything encouraging?'

'It depends which way you look at it – but yes, you could say I did.'

He turned to Sobrie. 'You're an Earthman, I suppose, so I'll try to explain. You see, my efforts haven't been quite as devoid of practical motive as might be imagined. Several light-years from here there exists an . . . intelligence, an entity that has been known to Retort City for some time. It's called the Oblique Entity, because it exists obliquely in time. Our object – mine and Shiu's – has been to establish a good enough communication with this entity for an exchange of practical knowledge. Its understanding of the time process is much more profound than ours; consequently I was anxious to find out if it could help us, if there was any way available to science of controlling the onrush of time-systems so as to avert the impending collision on Earth.'

'I . . . think I see,' Sobrie said in a subdued tone. He felt slightly ashamed of having misjudged Ascar, whom hitherto he'd taken to be little more than a dropout.

Ascar looked at Shiu before continuing. 'To my surprise, sir, the Entity already knew about Earth. It makes a hobby, apparently, of watching planets where life exists. I was even more staggered to hear it admit that it has the power, if it chooses, to prevent the cataclysm there. It's able to exert an influence over the direction of time, even upon so massive a system as Earth's and even at so great a distance. Don't ask me how. But it did make it quite clear to me that this power is something human beings will never learn to control.'

'But that makes it like a god!' Sobrie exclaimed disbelievingly.

'Yes, like a god,' Ascar repeated, his lips curling slightly. That was exactly what he'd said at the time, and the Entity's reply still sounded in his ears: *I um as insignificant as you. The Supreme does not notice me, just as it does not notice you.*

'Is he speaking the truth?' Sobrie asked Shiu anxiously. 'Is that really what you've been doing in your observatory?'

Shiu's tone was cold and superior. 'That was indeed our project. I'd suspected long ago that the Oblique Entity has powers unknown to us.'

'*Deus ex machina,*' Sobrie muttered.

'Yes,' said Ascar tonelessly, 'a real *deus ex machina*. However, the Oblique Entity insists it's basically a spectator, a non-interventionist. When I asked it to use its powers on our behalf, it refused.'

A heavy silence fell on the room, and Su-Mueng stirred.

'My regrets for your planet,' he said stiffly. 'However, if you'll excuse me, Retort City will continue to exist and I have business to deal with.'

'That wasn't the end of the matter, sir,' Ascar said quickly to Shiu when the younger man had left the room, 'I argued with it further.'

His mind fled back to his recent experience, still fresh in his memory. At first his world-weary cynicism had come to the fore. He'd shrugged his shoulders and mentally written Earth off.

But then he'd found that he was unable to give up so easily. Something in him had pushed him on, made him press his case to this being beside which he felt like an ant. He didn't plead, exactly – no, plead wouldn't be the right word – but he'd come close to it.

The Oblique Entity had answered in a throbbing voice. 'There is considerable drama in this situation on Earth,' it had said. 'I am reluctant to interfere with that drama.'

For periods during their discourse the room in which Ascar sat had wavered and vanished, and he'd found himself drifting like a dust-mote through vast ratcheting machine-spaces, or through dark emptiness in which swam flimmering, half-seen shapes. This was not, he decided eventually, an attempt to frighten him or a show of anger on the Entity's part. It was simply that its thought processes occasionally distracted its attention from the job of transmitting sensory data to the receiver in Retort City, and Ascar was left picking up random images. Each time the Entity spoke, however, he was promptly deposited back in his simulated room.

Then, finally, the voice had changed. Ascar had heard the girl's voice again, coming through the speaker with a tinkly laugh.

'Enterprise such as yours deserves a reward,' she'd said. 'This is what I will do.'

And the Entity had shown him, not in words, but in a graphic, simple demonstration that had jolted right into his consciousness. It showed him time being split up into rivulets and streaming in all directions to bring deserts to life. And it showed him the main torrent from which those rivulets were taken, rushing headlong to where it would meet with an equal power and be convulsed into a horrendous vortex that would destroy it.

When Ascar explained this to Shiu the old man nodded, reflecting at length.

'Ingenious,' he said. 'And logical. The Oblique Entity clearly has a sense of justice.'

'I don't understand,' Sobrie Oblomot complained. 'I don't understand any of it.'

Shiu glanced at him and then wrapped his arms in his sleeves. 'It would be difficult for a layman,' he admitted in his slow, musing voice. 'Attend to the following description. Time moves forward, always in one direction. But there is more than just one direction in the real universe. Six dimensions can be defined, not just the three that the Absolute Present produces. So outside the stream of time that travels from the past into the future, there is yet more non-time, like a landscape through which the river of time flows. What this means in practical terms is that there are alternate Earths existing in the fifth dimension, side by side with the Earth you know. These Earths are uninhabited: they have no life, and no time. The river of time could be turned aside so as to flow into one of these alternate Earths, instead of directly onward. There would be no collision; an ideal solution to your problem.'

'And that, I take it, is not to be?' Sobrie asked, wrestling with these abstract ideas.

'Regretfully, no. The Entity is leaving the main stream of Earth's time untouched. It agrees only to split off rivulets from the main flow, sending each into a different Earth – there are a vast number to choose from, all more or less the same. The people involved in these rivulets will find themselves constituting a small island of life in an otherwise desert planet. But eventually that life will spread to cover the whole globe. In each case a new world will be born.' He nodded to himself, an unselfconscious picture of sagacity. 'It is, perhaps, a wiser solution than we would have chosen.'

'Each surviving dev reservation will be given a world of

its own,' Ascar explained to Sobrie. 'The Oblique Entity is giving every human subspecies its own future, free of interference from any other. A contingent of Titan civilization, even, is being given its own Earth to rule – an Earth where there will be no alien interventionists, no future-Earth aliens to destroy Titan ambitions. And the same holds for the future-Earth race: they also have various factions and nations, some of which will be saved.'

'And for the rest – annihilation?'

'Yes – almost.' A gleam, as of a vision, came into Ascar's eyes. 'The Armageddon, the great war through time, must take place, as must the collision in time. But even there, there will be survivors. Even now the Titans are drawing up blueprints for protective bunkers, buffered with intense artificial time fields to try to ward off the force of the collision. Some of these bunkers – a few – will probably survive, provided their equipment is rugged enough. So there will be a handful of Titans left alive after it's all over, to try to rebuild something on an Earth that will be unimaginably devastated.'

'This splitting up of time – when is it going to happen?'

'It already has happened,' Ascar said. 'It had happened before the Titans found me in Shiu's observatory.'

Sobrie wondered if his friends in the Amhrak reservation had noticed their changed circumstances yet. It was good, he thought to himself, to know that Amhrak civilization *would* continue.

Titan-Major Brourne flung the array of vidcoms off the table with one sweep of his arm. Nobody was reporting in now.

Brourne was alone in his office; he'd already sent his adjutant outside to help man the barricade. The time had come, he saw, for the last stand.

He strode from the office. As far as he knew his HQ was the only post not yet overrun, and an attack was expected any second.

A long gallery-like concourse stretched ahead of the building he'd chosen for his headquarters. It gave an excellent defensive position: a long avenue, bare of cover, up which an enemy must past. But that would avail little, he knew, against the tricks of these Chinks.

He'd barely reached the steel barricade set up against this avenue, and was giving a few words of encouragement to his men, when the attack started.

The Chinks were everywhere simultaneously. Several set to fighting them furiously at close quarters, while others appeared on his side of the barricade and some of his men were firing stolidly down the avenue. Once again Brourne observed the dreadful effects of *Hoka*, but fortunately the Chinks here were outnumbered. Then he directed his eyes down the avenue. There they were: blue-uniformed, broad-helmeted, flitting in and out of existence and advancing down the concourse like shadowy ghosts. He was facing an enemy one could only see half the time.

Suddenly Major Brourne gave a violent, almost joyous roar. He leaped forward to a gun emplacement, pushed the gunner aside, and lifted the heavy machine gun off its tripod. Normally two man were needed to carry it, but Brourne clambered over the barricade, the cartridge belt trailing behind him, and fired a long burst from the hip.

'No use squatting here, men!' he bellowed. 'Come on out and get 'em!'

He went lumbering down the concourse, firing intermittently from the big, clumsy weapon, into the crowd of flitting Chinks. This was the way to go, he told himself. To die like a man, fighting to the last breath against a sub-human horde.

He was still firing when a hand touched the back of his neck and he died.

The blue-garbed soldiers thronged the plaza before the balcony where Su-Mueng, Sobrie and Prime Minister Hwen Wu, with members of his cabinet, stood. Su-Mueng licked his lips nervously.

It had been his own idea: he would parade the cabinet of the Leisure Retort before his victorious soldiers. The venerable officials would lose face, would seem human and vulnerable. The workers would see for themselves the men who'd denied them their rights.

Hwen Wu, however, had been unexpectedly in favour of the confrontation. Indeed, he'd seemed not to understand Su-Mueng's intent, but had thanked him graciously for organizing the proceeding. He should have been more forthright with Hwen Wu, Su-Mueng thought.

Because, in rolling, sonorous tones, the Prime Minister was praising the workers of the Production Retort for their timely intervention.

'Your sense of civil duty is gladdening to the heart,' he said after a lengthy address, his aristocratic face impressively unreadable. 'And now that the foreign barbarian has been driven out, we can all return to our allotted places and restore the perfect harmony of an ordered society.'

He stepped back, folded his hands, smiled benignly upon Su-Mueng and upon the Production Retort managers who stood to one side, and retired to the rear of the balcony.

He's stolen the show, thought Sobrie. Poor Su-Mueng.

The managing director of the Production Retort came forward, inclined his head towards Hwen Wu, and then turned to speak a few polite words to the crowd, expressing his satisfaction at having served the city.

The workers gazed up at him with blank, curious faces. Everything was orderly and peaceful. With a shock Sobrie realized that they were going to return without argument to the Lower Retort, to their factories, their crude amusements.

The manager left the stage. Su-Mueng, Sobrie saw, was floundering. As a revolutionary, he was still a simpleton. He didn't have a clue as to how to effect social change: he thought it would happen of its own accord.

After hesitating Su-Mueng took a step forward, but

Sobrie overtook him and stepped into the centre of the crowd's attention.

What could he say that would begin the work of changing these people's minds? Of setting them on the course that would lead to equality between all men? Sobrie searched his mind, running through endless revolutionary texts until he came to the most ancient evocation of all: one that was legendary, almost mythical, having been handed down since long before recorded history.

He raised his clenched fist. 'Workers of the world, arise!' he began. 'You have nothing to lose but your chains . . .'

14

Their footsteps echoed loudly in the big underground cavern. Planetary Leader Limnich, surrounded by aides and guards, was met just outside the door to the office complex by a tall, self-composed Colonel Brask.

'You got my message?' Limnich said after they'd saluted. 'You understood its import?'

'I understood, Planetary Leader.' Brask opened the door, inviting Limnich inside.

The Planetary Leader signalled his entourage to wait, then went in alone. Thankfully he settled himself in a deep leather armchair, as though exhausted. 'You see why I had to contact you by code. Didn't want to trust vidphone transmission with this . . . these days secrecy is becoming imperative . . .'

He blinked, and then sniffed. He was feeling cold and shivery, but knew it was only his imagination, prompted by the knowledge that so many districts were down with the plague. The virological laboratories were working desperately to combat the flood of new diseases that were appearing, almost certainly alien-caused, but as soon as one antibody was found another virus seemed to arise.

'Have you had time to confirm what you put in your message, Leader?' Brask asked him.

Limnich nodded. 'It's true, all right. Whole regions have simply vanished off the map. Some new alien weapon, obviously, though the Mother knows what kind of device can annihilate people, buildings, and vegetation without leaving a trace. No radiation, nothing. Just bare soil.'

'But it's mostly dev reservations that have vanished? Isn't that a little odd?'

Limnich shrugged. 'Perhaps the aliens thought them convenient testing grounds. It isn't anything *we've* done, I can assure you of that. But you can see how serious the situation is. Is Measure C in hand?'

'Yes, Planetary Leader. The first wave will leave in a few minutes.'

He switched on a large vidscreen. Limnich saw fine, upright men in time-combat suits, just marching away from their preflight ceremonies. He looked at them closely, admiring their courage, their dedication.

There was no time, now, to wait until the Legions of Kronos were up to the strength Limnich had wanted for the final assault. There was no time to build up the measures that would have given the warriors of time a fighting chance of personal survival. These were suicide crews, men who would battle through against all odds to drop their hydrogen bombs, scores of bombs to each ship. Something like his old feeling of reassurance came over Limnich as he looked on their stern resolve. Hours before, he knew, each man had donated sperm for freezing and storage, so that he'd be honoured with the knowledge that his seed would continue to contribute to the blood of the race.

'Excuse me, Planetary Leader, but in accordance with the protocol we've set up, I must ask to be allowed to leave you now.'

Brask pressed a button. Another young officer came in – one more bright young man on which the Legions depended so much these days.

'Colonel Gole here will take over the project, as per your instructions, until the next wave is dispatched,' Brask said.

Limnich gave a perfunctory nod, and Brask left with a final salute to them both.

The Planetary Leader continued to watch the screen as Brask took his place down below with his men. He watched the continuing ceremony as they boarded their time travellers, Brask taking the command ship.

'Eventually we'll find a way to bring them back alive,' he said to Gole. 'Until then, this is good enough.'

'Yes, Planetary Leader.'

The squadrons all vanished together with a sound like a thunderclap. They went humming fuzzily into the future, gladly bearing their cargoes of death, death, and more death.

Author's note

The picture of time used as a background to this novel can be said to owe something to the discussions by J. W. Dunne, of *An Experiment with Time* fame, particularly from his book *The Serial Universe* where he sets forth the regression problem I describe in Chapter Nine.

The account of time I have chosen to derive from these arguments is, of course, a crude, fictionalized one, but it does manage to raise the question of whether the present moment is co-extensive throughout the universe, as Physicist Leard Ascar first believed, or whether it is a local process, as taught to him by the scientists of Retort City. I am inclined to imagine that the second version comes closer to the truth, though whether time is associated with biological systems, or with larger bodies such as galaxies, or with even larger structures such as, for instance, as much of the sidereal universe as would be observable from one point, is an open question.

B.J.B.